A.C. Arthur is a~ ~~~~~~~~~~~ ~~~~
Baltimore, Maryl~ ~~~~~~~~~~~~~~~~
grandson and an ~~~~~~~~~~~~~~~~~~
active imaginatio~ ~~~~~~~~~~~~~~~~
her to begin writing in high school and ~~~ ~~~~
stopped since.

Taryn Leigh Taylor likes dinosaurs, bridges and
space—both personal and of the final frontier variety.
She shamelessly indulges in clichés, most notably her
Starbucks addiction (grande six-pump whole milk no
water chai tea latte, aka: the usual), her shoe hoard
(*I can stop any time I... Ooh! These are pretty!*) and
her penchant for falling in lust with fictional men with
great abs. She also really loves books—which was
what sent her down the wild path of writing one in
the first place. Want to be virtual friends? Check out
tarynleightaylor.com, Facebook.com/tarynltaylor1 and
Twitter, @tarynltaylor.

If you liked
At Your Service and *Guilty Pleasure*
why not try

Hot Boss by Anne Marsh
Wild Wedding Hookup by Jamie K. Schmidt

Also by A.C. Arthur

A Private Affair

Also by Taryn Leigh Taylor

The Business of Pleasure

Forbidden Pleasure
Secret Pleasure
Wicked Pleasure

Discover more at millsandboon.co.uk

AT YOUR SERVICE

A.C. ARTHUR

GUILTY PLEASURE

TARYN LEIGH TAYLOR

MILLS & BOON

First Published in Great Britain 2020
by Mills & Boon, an imprint of HarperCollins*Publishers*
1 London Bridge Street, London, SE1 9GF

MIX
Paper from
responsible sources
FSC™ C007454

This book is produced from independently certified FSC™ paper
to ensure responsible forest management.
For more information visit www.harpercollins.co.uk/green.

Printed and bound in Spain
by CPI, Barcelona

AT YOUR SERVICE

A.C. ARTHUR

MILLS & BOON

To my law clerks: Vanessa, Manti, Gita, Beatrice and Ashley.

Thanks so much for your endless support.

CHAPTER ONE

LET'S DO THIS.

Whispering the mantra as she stepped out of the ladies' room, Nina smoothed her palms down the front of her navy-blue pencil skirt. With her portfolio tucked under one arm and her black leather purse hanging on the opposite shoulder, she walked easily in four-inch black pumps. Until she turned the corner and collided with something hard and delicious-smelling.

Her portfolio hit the ground as she threw her hands up and felt a strong grip on her upper arms.

"Whoa, there."

His voice was deep but smooth and made her feel like warm water was streaming down her body, easing to her core.

"Sorry," she mumbled with a shake of her head.

Nina pulled out of his grasp and went down on her knees to snap up the pages that had escaped from her folder. As if in rebellion, or just because they wanted her to look like a complete idiot, the papers had scattered across the dark-carpeted floor a distance away from where she was standing.

"Here, let me help," he was saying, but Nina didn't reply.

And she didn't look up, just continued to gather the wayward sheets, cursing herself and what had been a horrific start to this very important day. Clutching a handful of pages, she started to stand when her purse decided to slip from her shoulder. *Oh no, I'm not dropping anything else today.* She lifted her hands and caught the bag as Mr. Helpful came closer.

Anxious to just get this uncomfortable encounter over with and to make it to the meeting she was already in danger of being late for, Nina glanced up to meet his gaze. Warm root beer–brown eyes stared back at her while lips of medium thickness parted slightly as if he were ready to speak again. His words were halted when her hands took that moment to continue moving upward, brushing over this gorgeous guy's pants on the way.

No, not just his pants but his...

Nina's jaw dropped, heat immediately fusing her cheeks as her eyes widened and she yanked her hands back against her chest so hard she almost lost her breath.

"Are you all right?"

Hell no!

Nina was on her way to a meeting that would make or break her business and she was standing here touching a man she didn't know. A man who was the epitome of tall, bronzed, handsome and apparently very aroused.

"I'm fine," she managed to croak and then cleared her throat. Stuffing the papers under her arm, she reached for the black case he held. "Thank you."

"You're welcome. Can I help you get your belongings together?"

"No. Really. I have it. It's no problem," she said because the problem was obviously her. Or it could have been the train from York to Manhattan that was late because something had spilled on the tracks, or the gigantic rip in her stockings from when she'd slid across the torn seat of the taxi upon finally arriving at the Ronald Gold Fashions headquarters. Either way, this day was not getting better.

Nina stepped around the man, hoping he wouldn't say anything else to her. She walked as quickly as she could without running and appearing more like a crazy person. Not knowing exactly where she was going, she continued down the long hallway, turning the moment she saw an opening on the right and then moving just as fast in that direction.

Her phone buzzed and she stopped to dig into her purse to retrieve it.

"Hey, Angie," she answered after seeing her sister's name on the screen.

"Hey. I won't be able to run past Dad's tonight to check on him and Daisy's got a photo shoot so she doesn't think she'll get there until after eight."

Nina closed her eyes as her fingers tightened on the phone. She didn't scream the way she wanted to because everything that could go wrong today had already gone wrong. She inhaled deeply once more and let the breath out slowly before replying. "I'm in New York for a meeting, as I told everyone at dinner last night. I won't be back until tomorrow morning. So somebody's gonna have to go over there and make sure Dad takes his medications as directed and doesn't end up passed out on the floor."

It was, to Nina, as simple as that. But to her sisters what she'd just said wouldn't make any sense. Younger than her by four and six years, Angie and Daisy were so used to Nina taking care of everything—from their father to them when they were young girls—that the idea of doing some of the grown-up heavy lifting was too much for them to fathom. They'd much rather continue to dump it all on Nina's shoulders. Well, not today.

"I thought you were coming back tonight," Angie argued.

"No. I changed my mind. I don't get away from home often so I'm going to spend the evening in New York. I told you that also, in the reminder text I sent earlier when I was on my way to the train station." Nina lifted a hand to touch her hair, double-checking to make sure it was smooth and neat after her run-in with the hot guy.

"Well, that's not fair, Nina. Daisy and I are busy tonight and you're gonna be in New York living it up. You know Dad needs to be checked on daily."

Yes, she did know that, mainly because it was something she said on a routine basis to her sisters.

"It's one night, Angie. You and Daisy can figure something out for just one night." Her temples started that slow, persistent thumping that signaled a migraine, which wasn't good.

"Look, it is what it is. And I have to hang up because I need to get into this meeting. I'll call Dad to check on him as soon as the meeting is done, but you and Daisy are responsible for him tonight."

"But—"

"But nothing. Goodbye, Angie."

Nina pushed the button to disconnect the call. Technically she hadn't hung up on her, even though sometimes Angie and Daisy deserved just that. They were beyond old enough to handle a night without Nina giving detailed outlines of what they needed to do. And having just celebrated her thirtieth birthday last month, Nina deserved one night in New York, the fashion capital of the United States.

First, she needed to get to this meeting, make her presentation and grab this account. Everything was riding on this—having the money to get her father into an assisted-living facility and giving her app the boost it needed to compete in the big leagues of the fashion industry.

You can do this. It's what you've been working so hard for these last two years. You're going to get this account and everything else will fall into place. You've got this!

Nodding to herself, Nina dropped her phone back into her purse.

It took her another five minutes to walk all the way to the other side of the floor where there was a set of glass doors with the gold letters RGF on the front. Once she pulled the door open and stepped in-side, the rapid beat of her heart ceased. The heat that had still burned her cheeks subsided and she walked toward the reception desk, her shoulders squared, chin held high.

After introducing herself to the receptionist—a pretty woman with coal-black hair that fell down her back—Nina was directed down another hallway to the last door on the right. Nina entered the room with her ready-to-take-on-the-world attitude and super-star smile, only to have it falter the minute she locked gazes with the man sitting at the far end of the table.

The same man she'd bumped into only moments ago. The man whose hard dick she'd felt…inadver-tently, of course.

Damn.

Major sat back in the leather conference room chair with one hand on his thigh, the other rubbing the shaved skin of his jaw. He couldn't take his eyes off her throughout her presentation. Nor could he stop the erection that had sprung so quickly when they'd first met in the hallway and he'd watched her bend over in that tight skirt. Of course, that hadn't been their official meeting. No, that awkward moment had come the second she'd walked into the conference room where he was seated with his brothers and two of his tech department staffers.

Nina Fuller, owner and operator of the At Your Service fashion accessorizing app, was beautiful with toffee-brown-colored hair hanging past her shoulders and cinnamon-hued skin. Not only did her skirt fit the round curve of her ass and the stretch of her thighs just right, but the pale blue blouse she wore with it was tucked neatly into a high-waist skirt, the blouse's sheer material hanging alluringly over her breasts. Major's palms itched with the thought of cupping them and watching as they spilled over his fingers.

His dick jumped again and he eased his hand up higher on his thigh to give the pulsating shaft a gentle push. *Get it together!*

"What's the traffic like on this app?" RJ asked. "Is there so much that it could possibly become inundated and freeze? Customer complaints spread like wildfire online and an app crashing could be a PR catastrophe."

As the director of sales for the family business, Major's older brother RJ—Ronald Gold III—was always concerned about the customers and how much merchandise they were buying. RJ's comment solicited a nod from Maurice, Major's younger twin brother. But since this presentation was for a tech product, Major—the company's technical developer—was front and center on the decision making. That meant he should stop gawking at this woman like he was a horny teenager and get his head in the game.

His fingers involuntarily moved closer to cup his hardened dick. *Not that head!*

"What he means is…how are your configurations designed?" he asked. "Will the overflow in use cause the app's algorithms to go haywire?"

Technical speak was Major's thing and apparently so was getting turned on by a woman he barely knew.

Her gaze found his, and her tongue slipped out to lick her lips for just a second. Long enough for him to swallow. Hard.

She clicked the button on the small control device cushioned in the palm of her hand. The images on the screen across the room flipped back to one of the previous presentation slides where she'd outlined the beginning sketches of her app.

"Two years ago, when the first thoughts of At Your Service entered my mind, I planned exactly what I wanted it to do. Match accessories to outfits. Nothing more, nothing less. By staying focused on what the app absolutely needed to do to succeed, I was able to avoid many common pitfalls in new app development—overreaching ideas. With that said, during the first two years of the app's startup, I've fine-tuned and streamlined its function so that even with high volume it still functions as seamlessly as if there were only ten to twelve users."

Confident. Knowledgeable. Intriguing.

All things that were required for a good sales pitch. And things that aroused Major on a level he hadn't quite explored before.

Sure, he'd been dubbed the Fashion House Playboy three months ago by the press, but as the last thing on his busy schedule was to deal with the lies that oftentimes floated through the tabloids and on-line gossip sites, Major hadn't given the title or its implications the time of day. The executives in RGF's marketing department, on the other hand, had. It was now an actual agenda item to be dealt with when this meeting was over.

At the moment, however, he was staring into the lovely topaz-brown eyes of a woman who wanted RGF to integrate her app on its website. In essence, this was business. Not pleasure. He took another second to try to send that message to his aching dick.

"Your plans look detailed and well thought out. And you say this has been up and running for two years. How many clients do you currently have?"

"The first year was for planning, developing and trial runs," she said. "The second year was for getting all the licenses required and finding vendors to facilitate the app's main function. Three independent fashion designers have been satisfied with the application in the last five months. Letters of recommendation are included in the information packets I passed out. But my goal is expansion. This app in its current state is primarily designed to be a corporate plug-in. Eventually, as my brand gains visibility, I'll be expanding to target individual customers." She stood a few inches away from the projector screen, hands clasped in front of her, shoulders back.

A light layer of makeup covered a very pretty face, and hair that looked silky and shiny made his fingers itch to touch the long tresses.

"Amelia Jewelers is one of the vendors we work with for showings along the East Coast," RJ said, looking down at the papers Nina had referred to.

"Yes, they're reputable and reliable. I trust Amelia Cane's words implicitly." That came from Jenner Carlson, the lead tech developer in Major's department. "And the layout you've created is simple, yet efficient. All a customer has to do is upload the clothes they've purchased and accessory ideas are immediately assembled."

"Correct." Nina continued, "This is after they've set up their user profile, which collects pertinent information like body type, style preferences and budget. The customer will have a seventy-two-hour period to consider their selections before either being directed to purchase via third-party sites or to re-accessorize. A schedule of gentle reminders in that time frame keeps the app and the clothes just purchased prevalent in the customer's mind."

"But this app doesn't drive customers to the RGF site. We would essentially have to bring the customers to you, which makes this a winning opportunity for you and just an added benefit for us," RJ noted, leaning back in his chair, hands clasped in his lap. This was the not-so-impressed stance his brother took just before he was about to shoot down an idea.

"But what if there was a widget for the app on the RGF site telling the customer that we care about their overall look and not just the garment they purchase from us," Major said. "Then everyone benefits from the sale we've secured because we were savvy and compassionate enough to consider our customers' overall needs, bringing us even more customers who will like the idea of a sort of one-stop shop."

His comment was rewarded with a slow smile and

nod from Nina. An action that sealed the deal—his hard-on wasn't ceasing anytime soon.

The part of his brain that was determined to focus on work tried to press through. After all, he'd originally intended to shoot this idea down. He could admit it was partially a selfish act since some of the things Nina's app offered were in direct competition with what he wanted to feature through his own company—the company he'd be launching soon, which his family still didn't know about.

Discussion continued for a few moments more, ending when RJ mentioned he had another meeting to get to. "You're in that meeting, also, Major. So, Ms. Fuller, we'll be in touch."

Nina didn't falter even though Major recognized the dismal tone of rejection in RJ's voice.

"Thank you so much for your time, gentlemen," she said, clicking the button on the remote to clear the screen.

Major took his time tucking the packet she'd provided into his padfolio before closing and zipping it shut. He slipped his phone out of his pocket and quickly checked it for text messages.

"Ten minutes," RJ said. "Don't be late, we've got a tight schedule. Major? Are you listening?"

Lifting his gaze from his phone, Major found both his brothers staring at him. "Yes. I'll be there in ten minutes. Just have to rearrange my schedule a bit."

Landra, his assistant, had had to postpone the meeting with the agent and actresses Major was scheduled to meet with this afternoon so that he could attend yet another meeting with the marketing department to talk about the very reason he needed to hire an actress in the first place.

His brothers headed out of the conference room along with Jenner and Ken, leaving Major alone with Nina Fuller and that very tight skirt, which continued to make his mouth water.

CHAPTER TWO

HE WAS STARING at her and she liked it.

The warmth that had thankfully moved from her cheeks had spread down her neck and pooled in her breasts so that they now felt full. With every move she'd made during the presentation she'd felt his gaze on her and had reveled in it. Feeling attractive and wanted wasn't the norm for Nina and she'd forgotten how much she enjoyed it.

Now, she would enjoy him offering her a contract much more, but since she'd likely have to wait a couple days or possibly weeks for that answer, she was content with just feeling sexy beneath his intent gaze.

"Your bio says you're from York, Pennsylvania. Did you move to New York when you started this business?"

He'd shaved his beard, that's why she hadn't immediately recognized him in the hallway before the meeting. But she was certain she was never going to forget his voice. Not the way the rich, deep timbre eased over her skin like a massage, or the spurt of awareness it brought to every part of her body each time she heard it.

"No. I still live in York," she replied as she gathered the last of her documents and slid them into her portfolio.

Out of the corner of her eye she could see that he'd moved from the end of the table to stand closer to her, but she kept her gaze averted. Instead she zipped the case and picked her purse up from the chair then placed it on the table beside her portfolio. At that point there was nothing stopping her from looking at him and she sucked in a breath before turning to face him.

"But I can commute when necessary. However, one of the great things about this app is that it's a mobile function. Once my system has been integrated with RGF's, we'll be all set and I won't have to request any more meetings that will clog up your busy schedule."

He held his phone in one hand and the black-leather padfolio under his arm. She hadn't seen either of those things when she'd collided with him in the hallway. Then again, she hadn't been looking for them. Nor had she been planning to feel the guy up. Considering who he was in the company, she wondered if she should apologize for that now.

"I would gladly make time in my schedule for you," he said.

The easy tilt of his mouth into a smile came with a punch of desire that Nina was certain she'd never felt before. Not that she was a prude or inexperienced where men were concerned, it was just that none had ever affected her the way this one did.

But she wasn't going to let that distract her. "That's nice to hear. Do you have any other questions about the app?"

"I do, but unfortunately I have another meeting to get to. Are you heading back to York right away?"

"No. I'm actually going to stay and enjoy the city tonight. My train leaves tomorrow morning at eleven." She gave the specific time just in case he wanted to schedule a follow-up meeting sooner rather than later.

He was nodding slowly as he kept staring at her with those warm disrupting eyes. But she wasn't supposed to be looking at this man's eyes and thinking that way. She could, however, admire the fit of the black suit he wore and the purple tie that added a splash of color and highlighted his tawny-hued skin.

"That's great. I've gotta head out, but I definitely want to speak with you again. Do you have a business card with your contact information?"

That request came with him taking a step closer to her. Instinct told her to step back, to keep a safe, professional distance between them. But hell, she'd already somewhat fondled him earlier, what harm could it do to have him up close and personal again? Besides, she loved the way he smelled. That cologne had to be an expensive designer fragrance. Possibly even European. It was a heady, spicy scent mixed with something rugged and yet unique. It made her think of cold winter nights cuddled in front of a roaring fire.

But back to business. "Yes. All of my contact information is on the packet I passed out, but I do have cards."

She pulled her purse open and reached inside for the sky blue card case her father had given her last Christmas. She removed one embossed ivory-colored card, handed it to him and wasn't at all surprised when he touched more of her hand than was necessary to retrieve it. There was definitely some flirtation going on here in what should have been a simple business meeting. Maybe he thought she was easy considering what had happened in the hallway. But that had been an accident—surely he recognized that. And the question still remained: Why had he been aroused while walking down a hallway? Who had he been thinking of?

"I'll call you," he said in that delicious tone that this time had her thighs trembling.

How bad would it be if he tossed her on this table and she opened her legs to him in invitation?

Very, very bad.

"I'll answer," she replied before snapping her lips closed because maybe that sounded a bit too coy.

But there was no lie in the two words. If Major Gold called her phone, Nina was definitely going to answer on the first ring and there was absolutely no shame in that. After all, this was her career she was talking about.

"Good," he said with another nod.

His hand was still on hers. Nina knew the connection was lasting too long and she thought about letting it linger until it wore itself out or led to them climbing up on that conference table. But she had to be professional. If she were misreading his signals—even though she was certain she wasn't—she still needed to play this like the only thing either of them was considering was this business deal.

She eased her hand from his grasp. "I hope you make it to your meeting on time," she said, turning to pick up her things.

She was heading toward the door when he fell into step beside her. "I'll walk you to the elevator."

"Thanks, but I think I can find it." *This time.* She left that part out and continued walking, knowing that once again, he was staring at her ass.

This really was a totally different feeling for Nina. Back in York there'd been no suave and debonair businessman who could make her feel desired and wanted—on a business and a personal front. Not that she'd craved this type of attention; relationships weren't on her radar because they could abruptly leave a trail of pain that lingered. No, she was just fine focusing on work and her family. But, as strange as these new physical reactions were, they were exhilarating, too.

"How do you plan to enjoy the city?" he asked when they stood in front of a bank of elevators. "Catch a Broadway play? Visit the museums? Go shopping?"

"I actually don't have a plan, but all of your sug-

gestions sound fun. It's almost five now, so I don't
have much time, but once I get to the hotel I'll figure it out."

"Which hotel are you staying at?"

"The Hilton Midtown." She was giving him a ton
of information that at any other time may have been
considered unsafe. There was no explanation for why
she didn't think that was the case now.

"Not too far from here," he said with another nod.

What was he thinking?

He'd tucked her business card into his inside
jacket pocket and still stood abnormally close to her
for someone she'd just met.

The elevator dinged and the door opened. Nina
stepped into the car and leaned to the side to push
the lobby button. She gave him another smile before
saying, "Thanks again for your time. I hope to hear
from you soon about the project."

His response was a broader smile. "Oh, you'll
definitely be hearing from me very soon."

"You want to do what?"

Major ignored the shock lacing RJ's tone and
stared directly at Desta Henner, the marketing director who was working closely with Maurice, the
company's public relations manager, and his team.
Desta stared back at Major with expressive dark
brown eyes, arms crossed and resting on her desk.

"Let me get this straight. You're suggesting we
bring this woman, whom we haven't decided to do
other business with, into a meeting regarding a se-

cret marketing strategy and use her as your fake fi-ancée?" Desta raised a perfectly arched brow in what was known as her signature questioning glare.

Major had seen that look many times before in the five years Desta had worked for RGF. He pushed on regardless.

"She's perfect," he said, feeling those words take on a very different meaning inside his head than what he'd meant to convey to everyone seated in the room. He cleared his throat. "A fresh face. She's not a model, which was your idea. And neither is she an actress, my first idea. Instead, she's a woman from York, Pennsylvania, that no one in the fashion in-dustry has ever seen before. That makes her just like every other woman in the world, precisely who the Golden Bride Collection was created for. A career-focused woman earning a paycheck she hopes can cover the amount of her dream wedding gown."

"And she's never been seen with Major before," Maurice chimed in.

Major shot a quick look in his brother's direction but held back the "Thanks for your support."

Desta immediately glanced in Maurice's direc-tion, as well. "Pot calling the kettle…" she quipped with a half grin. "But I think I see where you're going with this. If we're going to have Major plan a fake wedding so we can generate buzz and promote the Golden Bride Collection, using a fresh face as his fake fiancée does make sense."

"What he's not saying is that she's created an app she wants us to sign a contract to work with," RJ said.

Major had thought about that on the elevator ride up to Desta's office. The immediate physical draw he'd felt toward Nina still puzzled him. As a thirty-three-year-old man with a sizable bank account and high visibility in the fashion industry, Major had been on his share of dates and had had a number of lovers. None of them had ever hit him like a bulldozer the second they'd bent over in a tight skirt. But what had really impressed him about the woman was the way she'd confidently stood in that conference room and made a slam dunk presentation just minutes after touching his hard dick.

Desta sat back in her chair, rubbing a finger over her chin. "You want to make a bargain with her that concerns her app and this marketing plan, don't you?"

Major slipped both hands into the front pockets of his slacks and smiled. "If she pretends to be my fiancée for six weeks, we'll use her app, exclusively, for six weeks."

RJ shook his head. "You're crazy. That woman's looking for a much longer connection to RGF than six weeks and she didn't look at all interested in anything else, let alone hanging around you for the next month and a half."

"I don't know, RJ," Desta said. She kept her gaze on Major, that smile she'd given Maurice just a few minutes ago now aimed at him. "He is the Fashion House Playboy."

"A completely bogus title that I wish we'd all stop referring to around here," he added, exasperation clear in his tone. The press had given him that name when they took the three dates he'd had in succession with three different models in the span of three nights as a sign that he was actually sleeping with each of those women.

If ever a label were unwarranted, it was that one.

"We took the Fashion House Playboy course the press has been on into consideration when talks about a campaign to heighten sales for Golden Bride began. Right now, a lot of fashion media is focused on you and who you'll date next, so we'll build on that momentum with the announcement of your engagement," Desta said.

Major folded his arms across his chest as he stood there staring at the people in the room. He spent more time with them than any woman, but nobody reported that to the tabloids.

"I wasn't the only option," he countered.

Desta shook her head. "To be fair, no, we considered RJ, but you know—" she nodded in RJ's direction "—he's RJ. He only talks about the company to the press and nobody's ever seen him on a date. I think he must sneak women into the basement of his brownstone."

"It's called being discreet. Nobody's entitled to the details of my private life but me. A very simple concept that people should learn to accept," RJ said in his very cordial but no-nonsense tone.

Desta shrugged his comment off. "And Maurice is with so many women all the time that making it believable that he's settling down was going to be an uphill battle."

"But it's more believable that ten seconds after I'm given the silly name of Fashion House Playboy, I'd mysteriously pop up married?" He'd entertained all these questions before and the outcome hadn't changed.

"Look," Desta said, lifting that brow. "You guys flat-out told me not to approach Riley with this plan even though she's dating a guy from RGF's rival fashion house. But I definitely understand you're her big brothers and you wanted to protect Riley from any more tabloid assaults. She's definitely had more than her share. But that just put the three of you on the hot seat, and Major, honey, as I said, your current media attention will work so well with this fake fiancée plan."

Actually, he'd acquiesced without putting up too much of a fight because now was not the time to ruffle feathers in his family. He already had a bombshell he was waiting to drop when he announced he was leaving the company. If agreeing to this marketing plan was going to keep things chill until he was ready to go public with his solo business venture, Brand Integrated Technologies, then so be it. He could endure for six weeks.

He nodded. "I'm fine with that. But this is the woman I want for the job of my fake fiancée." Each time he said those words he felt ridiculous.

"I just don't know about that," RJ said.

Desta stared at Major, considering everything he'd

said. Plans were already rolling around in her head. That's how she worked. Silent thinking and then, *poof!* great marketing idea, which is why she'd risen to the top of the department in such a short time.

"I say go for it," Maurice added. "If she says no, there's nobody better to convince her than Major with his brash good looks and unexpected heart."

The last was their family secret. Major was nothing like the press portrayed; his twin was the flamboyant lover of the Gold men. Major was the quiet computer geek.

"Do it," Desta said. "Get her to say yes by noon tomorrow and we can add your engagement announcement to the lineup at our annual Summer Sip 'n' Chat tomorrow evening," she told him. "Let me know when the agreement is made and I'll take care of everything else."

He resisted the urge to do a fist pump as he immediately turned and headed for the door. The sobering voice that resembled their father's stopped him.

"Get the agreement in writing. And this app better work to our advantage," RJ said.

Major looked over his shoulder at his older brother. "No worries, bro. I've got this."

CHAPTER THREE

MAJOR GOLD LOOKED worried that Nina's answer would be a resounding no. As he damn well should have been. What an arrogant thought to assume she'd fall over herself in a hurry to be his fake fiancée for six weeks in exchange for the biggest career break she'd ever imagined. Just who the hell did he think he was?

"Have a seat. I need to hear more details about this proposed arrangement," she said.

He'd showed up at her hotel room half an hour after she'd returned from seeing *Ain't Too Proud* on Broadway. She'd invited him in, anxious to hear what he had to say and if it involved a contract with RGF. She'd changed into black skinny jeans and a red camisole. The ballet flats she'd worn to the theater were still on her feet and the high ponytail she'd pulled her hair into was still intact. Now he was standing—well, he'd just hiked his slacks up a bit before taking a seat on the couch—looking even sexier than he had when she'd bumped into him at his building.

"I'm offering you a six-week contract to work exclusively with RGF. Think of it as sort of a test run for a possibly longer contract. Our marketing team will get started on a formal announcement to let our current customers know we're adding a new feature to their shopping experience. You'll be in touch with members of my tech team on linking At Your Service to our online store. After customers make a purchase, they'll be immediately routed to your app to open an account and get started with accessorizing their outfit. Win-win for both of us."

She didn't have to force herself to keep her gaze trained on him. Major Gold was a lovely man to look at. Six feet two and a half inches of lean muscle and gorgeous man. The light mustache accentuated the medium thickness of his lips. Dark low-cropped hair gave his tawny skin a bronze glow, while the Italian suit he wore fit every inch of his well-toned body to perfection. And he still smelled good at almost ten-thirty at night.

Nina cleared her throat. "First, regarding exclusivity. I already have contracts with two designers. They're small and in no way competition to RGF."

His hands looked strong, thick veins roped across the backs as they rested on his thighs. "We can probably work with that as long as you don't sign any other clients for the six-week term."

"Second. You also said something along the lines of me pretending to be your fiancée for six weeks. That's the part I'm not sold on, Mr. Gold—"

Actually, that was the part that confused the hell out of her.

"Major," he interrupted.

Fine. She could call him by his first name. He was sitting just a few inches away from her, in a hotel room. This was a pretty familiar setting, so first names made sense. Or at least she wanted all of this to make sense.

"Why do you need a fake fiancée, Major? And why do you think I'd fit that role?"

Because she didn't. Before her meeting, she'd done preliminary research on the family executives at Ronald Gold Fashions. She knew the father, Ron Gold, Jr., in addition to being CEO, was also the chief designer at RGF. She knew what his three sons did for the company, and that the youngest, and only girl in the family, was Riley, chief executive of market research and product development. She'd read about the matriarch, Marva Gold, who held a master's degree in education, served on RGF's board of directors and was currently developing several scholarship programs for underprivileged students across the US.

Nina's focus on the family had been solely on where they'd gone to college, what job they did, and how much the company made in just clothing sales last year. She hadn't bothered with any of the tabloid stories that had come up in the search; they didn't matter to RGF's bottom line. And she'd paid even less attention to the many pictures of each of the Gold children that filled the internet. It didn't matter how they looked—all Nina needed was for them to agree to work with her. It was that simple.

Yet now, Major was sitting too close and the task

of focusing on business was becoming much more difficult than it had ever been before.

"Look, I'll be totally honest with you. The reason I want you to do this is because of how you look."

Okay, he was going to be candid. Well, that was refreshing.

"And how do I look?"

"Great." He said the word as if she should have already known.

"I'm not the only great-looking woman in the world. Not even in New York. And you of all people surely know that. You can have any woman you want."

"I want you," he said. "I want someone who doesn't want me and isn't trying to fool me into getting what she really wants."

"I would like to work with RGF on a long-term basis, but if I can work with your company, for even six weeks, other larger fashion houses will take that as a gleaming recommendation. My business will take off. That's all I've ever wanted." Because she could be candid, too.

"Then say you'll be my fake fiancée for six weeks. Agree to take this assignment and I'll have contracts ready for you to sign first thing tomorrow morning."

He was serious. She'd been sitting there waiting for him to tell her this was all a joke and just go back to talking about her app, but that's not what was happening. This was real. His offer—every part of it was real.

"What do I have to do? As your fake fiancée, I mean?"

She sat back against the couch and crossed one leg over the other.

"Attend some functions with me, act as if you're planning a real wedding. Try on lots of gowns from the Golden Bride line, select bridesmaids gowns, and a host of other wedding stuff that our marketing department has planned."

"That's all. No kissing. No touching. No…nothing?" She needed to know all the terms, especially since she'd decided earlier that he had very kissable lips. Now, with him talking about fake engagements, kissing him had quickly popped into her mind again.

He paused and chuckled. Then he rubbed a hand over his mustache, down to his clean-shaved jaw, as he shook his head slowly.

"Ah, no, I don't think any of that's on the agenda."

"Then how will people believe we're really engaged? I'm guessing you want this to be believable. I mean, if not, then what's the point?"

A few seconds of him giving her a very heated glare only increased Nina's awareness of the sexual attraction buzzing between them since the first moment they'd met.

"The point of this arrangement is to boost sales for the new line. Our marketing department is convinced that seeing a Gold actually planning their wedding and selecting items from the bridal collection will encourage others to check it out for themselves," he said.

"And what happens at the end of the six-week period? After this wedding has been planned?"

He shrugged. "I'm told we'll have a huge and very public argument, followed by a press release the next morning announcing the unfortunate demise of the relationship. In this industry, negative publicity can sometimes work just as well as positive, as I'm sure you saw a few months ago when that ridiculous story about RGF stealing a design from King Designs surfaced. Marketing and sales are convinced that story, even after it was debunked, was partially responsible for the Golden Bride's phenomenal debut."

She was the one nodding now as the concept of "any publicity is good publicity" came to mind. "How very dramatic. Suits the Gold brand perfectly. So, like I said, you're banking on people buying this act, without kissing or touching. Do you not like to kiss and touch, Major?"

His gaze immediately moved to her lips. As if they were suddenly under pressure, she licked them slowly before clearing her throat. She should think of something else to say, to ease this awkward moment... Too late, he'd found her eyes again and now they were staring at each other, speaking that silent but knowing language of physical attraction.

"To the contrary, Nina. I like kissing and touching very much. I especially enjoyed the way you touched me earlier today."

She swallowed as the combination of his proximity, the silky tone of his voice and the blatant memory of her hand brushing over his magnificent erection shot to mind.

"Is that the type of touching you're referring to?"

"I'm not convinced we have to go that far," she said, because that was definitely going too far with a man she'd be entering into a business deal with. "But something along the lines of holding hands in public, perhaps a few chaste kisses...those might go a long way to creating the façade your company is banking on."

His hands had been resting on his thighs, but she could now see them moving to his knees, his fingers clenching slowly and releasing. If she dared to trace her gaze back just a little more she was certain that erection she'd felt earlier was making another appearance. Her breasts had begun to feel full and she barely resisted the urge to clamp her thighs together to keep the throbbing that had increased in her center at bay.

"I think—" he cleared his throat "—we'd just play it by ear in that regard. See what's needed and when. Go with the flow."

"Is that what the contract is going to say?" She prayed disappointment wasn't apparent in her tone.

"What would you like the contract to say? That we'll kiss five times in six weeks, hold hands ten times, hug twice?"

"If you think five kisses will be enough." Nina wasn't so sure anything would be enough where this man was concerned.

This time he licked his lips at her words. She did the same.

"Maybe we leave out a number. I wouldn't want us to be committed before we've considered how much we may like it."

"You think I'll like kissing you?" There was absolutely no doubt in her mind that she would.

"No," he replied. "I *know* I'm gonna like kissing you."

Nina couldn't stop thinking about kissing him and she had no idea why she'd even brought up holding hands or kissing in public. Especially since she wasn't a fan of PDA. Holding hands, touching, ogling, and yes, kissing, were reserved for behind closed doors. That's the way she'd been brought up and it was a rule she'd stuck to.

Your personal business is your personal business. Nobody else's.

Jacoby Fuller had said that more times than Nina or her sisters could count. But not for the same reasons that Nina had decided to adopt them. Her father didn't like public displays of affection because it reminded him of how much he still loved and missed his wife. Nina didn't like them because it reminded her of how quickly a happy couple could become a lonely man raising three daughters on his own.

Which was precisely why she didn't do relationships. The thought of investing her time, emotions and trust into one person who could potentially walk away without a care in the world, wasn't something she liked to entertain. But that wasn't what this was.

Major Gold had come to her with a business proposal, one she'd spent the bulk of last night contemplating. If this fake wedding was going to bring publicity—good and bad—to RGF, then what was she going to get out of it? Besides the six weeks to work with the company and the possibility of a longer contract, there was a measure of exposure here that Nina couldn't ignore. For every public appearance she made with Major, she was adding a face to her brand. The Nina Fuller behind At Your Service would be up close and personal with the industry she'd dreamed of working in all her life. And while she totally understood that any publicity was good publicity, she wanted as much of her exposure to this industry to be as positive as she could manage. Creating the most believable fake relationship possible was a must.

Her traveling outfit was jeans and a T-shirt with her school mascot—a mustang—on the front. She couldn't wear that to what technically was her second interview at RGF, where she knew she would be receiving and accepting a job offer. After a quick run to Macy's and the purchase of a gray pantsuit and white blouse, at exactly nine forty-five in the morning, she walked through the glass doors of RGF again.

Major was already seated at the same end of the conference room table as yesterday. Across from him was Maurice. Twins, not identical, but who favored each other enough that she hadn't needed Google to tell her they'd been born together. But the internet had informed her that Major was older and, while he wasn't as brash and indiscriminate as his younger brother, he was still quite popular with women. A fact that made no difference to her—this was a temporary assignment. One she'd spent some time plotting out.

She'd used RGF's online sales figures—retrieved from an article in a top financial magazine that had compared the fashion industry's growth from five years ago to the present—to approximate how many new accounts At Your Service would obtain and the percentage she would earn from each of her vendors once the app had successfully accessorized each customer. It would bring her more than enough to pay for her father to move into an assisted-living facility and remain there for at least two years. In that time, she would land more clients. King Designs, RGF's biggest rival, was next on her list to approach, and there were others. All of which would be impressed by her work with RGF and would pay her even more for the use of her app.

"Good morning, Ms. Fuller," Maurice was the first to speak when she entered the boardroom.

"Good morning. Please call me Nina," she said and watched as he stood and walked to her. When he extended his hand, Nina accepted it for a quick shake.

"Thank you for agreeing to meet with us again on such short notice," he said.

"It was no problem," she lied. She was going to miss her train and the ticket was nonrefundable.

"Yes. Thank you very much for coming back.

Now, let's get down to business. We don't have a lot of time before our first event."

The woman who talked while entering the room hadn't been in the meeting yesterday. She wasn't as tall as Nina's five-foot-eight height, but she was dressed just as sharply. Probably sharper since Nina was certain the woman's skirt and jacket were RGF originals from their Make the Woman professional-wear line. The outfit was a bold royal blue and she wore a pale yellow blouse beneath the fitted jacket and patent leather slingback pumps. The blond-frosted tips of her black hair fell in big curls to her shoulders as she gave Nina a quick look and then closed the door behind her.

"This is Desta Henner, our marketing director," Major said.

Nina looked from the focused woman to Major. He wore another black suit today—this one with a more casual jacket that zipped—and in place of a dress shirt and tie he was wearing a butter-colored pullover that molded against his muscled chest.

"Our legal department worked double-time to get these two contracts drawn up," Desta announced. "Have a seat, please, and we'll go over everything."

Maurice had returned to his seat and this time Major was the one to stand, pulling out the chair next to him.

Nina took the seat, dropping her purse into the empty chair to the other side. "Yes," she said in a voice she knew sounded as levelheaded and professional as Desta's. "Let's go over everything."

* * *

She'd signed both contracts.

A part of Major hadn't thought she would.

Nina Fuller was an entrepreneur. She'd graduated top of her class from the Harrisburg Area Community College in York, and had taken additional online classes to obtain her master's in computer technology and engineering. She'd used those degrees to build a sophisticated app that could be groundbreaking in the fashion industry. That is, if it didn't almost mimic some of Brand Integrated Technologies' functions, a fact that could potentially become a conflict of interest between them. Initially, he'd felt the urge to be honest with her about the possible overlap of their companies, but then he considered that by the time this fake engagement and her trial period at RGF were over, they could go their separate ways and their companies could exist as a form of healthy competition. At least, that's what he was telling himself.

Major had spent most of last night going through her app as a user, easily figuring out every step she'd taken from coding to debugging and creating the user interface. It was intricate, but Major had a master's degree in computer technology and engineering, as well. A degree he'd also used to help keep RGF three steps ahead of their competitors where technology was concerned.

"Well, that's done," he said when they were the only two remaining in the conference room.

"Yes, it is." She'd stored her copies of the contracts in her case and now stood a few feet away from him. "So, are we heading to the tech department to get started on the integration now?"

He couldn't help but notice that the suit she wore fit her nicely. The pants flawlessly molded the natural curve of her hips, accentuating thighs that were thicker than the models he was used to seeing. The jacket was an acceptable fit, the wrap blouse beneath hugging her full breasts tightly. But it wasn't an RGF ensemble.

"Ah, no, not just yet. My assistant, Landra, will be emailing you a copy of our itinerary for the upcoming weeks. There's a cocktail party scheduled for tonight at the Midtown Loft & Terrace. I believe you'll be assigned a stylist, but I'm not sure who that will be. Landra or possibly Desta will take care of that."

She nodded slowly.

Her hair was pulled back from her face again, this time held at the nape of her neck with a black band so that she looked almost demure. A look that was perfect for this campaign but didn't begin to touch the fiery passion he'd seen brimming in her eyes last night. Heat instantly began to stir through his veins as he thought about sitting on that couch with her in the hotel talking casually about how she'd felt him up only hours before. If he was half the Fashion House Playboy he was dubbed to be, there was no doubt Major would have spent the night in her bed, bringing them both the pleasure he knew they'd been thinking about.

"An itinerary. A stylist," she said and exhaled slowly. "I guess that's part of the agreement. Should

I just wait here or return to my hotel? How do we play this?"

Major stepped closer to her.

"I think we start by getting this out of the way."

His hands, which had itched to touch her all night and throughout this morning's meeting, rested on the tops of her arms as he pulled her against him. The motion was quick and her hands came up to slap against his biceps as she tilted her chin to meet his gaze.

"You asked about kissing last night?" His voice sounded unfamiliarly gruff.

She blinked, long, natural lashes brushing her skin before he was afforded the sight of her gold-flecked eyes once more. "You said it wasn't required."

"Not required," he whispered. "Desired. At least on my part. If you're not interested, say so now." Before he combusted from the desire that had boiled inside him all through the night.

"I'm interested."

The words were barely out of her mouth before his lips crashed down over hers, heat soaring through their connection, a force unlike anything Major could have ever imagined taking over every part of his body.

CHAPTER FOUR

NEVER BEEN KISSED.

The three words floated around in her mind as his tongue moved salaciously over hers. *Not like this, anyway.*

Major's hands had slipped from the tops of her arms to her waist until he was holding her tightly against him. It was a stern and commanding hold. A you're-not-going-anywhere type of hold that she actually enjoyed. So much so, that Nina laced her arms around his neck, pulling his head down farther so that she could sink deeper into the kiss. A kiss they probably shouldn't be sharing since there was no one to see them and hence wasn't moving their fake relationship forward.

But hell, she wasn't complaining.

When they finally broke contact, both breathing as if they'd just run a race, he rested his forehead against hers and Nina let her eyes remain closed for a few seconds more.

What the hell is going on? Twenty-four hours ago, she'd been preparing for a meeting she'd known could change her life. Never in her wildest dreams had she thought of how drastically things would change in such a short amount of time.

"Okay, that was…" He paused, searching for the words.

They popped into her mind effortlessly. *Explosive. Delicious. Addictive!*

"It was the kiss that sealed the deal" was what she actually said before pushing away from him and smoothing her hands down the front of her clothes.

He ran his hand across the back of his head while nodding. "Yeah, I guess we could say that."

As if on cue, her phone chimed and she moved much too quickly to retrieve it from her purse. "Itinerary!" she said, her pitch higher than normal as she held up her phone as if to explain what she meant.

Major cleared his throat. "Right. I'm going to head downstairs because I have a couple of things to take care of before tonight. There's a car waiting out front for you. The driver's name is Claude. He's great and he'll get you wherever you need to go in the city. He's at your disposal for the next six weeks. Landra will be sending you all of his contact information."

She'd been reading the first of a five-page document attached to the email sent by his assistant. Today was already jam-packed with things to do.

"Oh, okay. Um, I guess I'll be invoiced for all of this."

"All of this" meaning drivers, tips, clothes—their seemed to be a ton of fittings and makeup sessions scheduled and she'd only bought this one suit just a couple of hours ago. The only other thing in her hotel closet was the skirt suit she'd worn yesterday and her train-ride outfit. None of which would be acceptable for the events listed in the itinerary document.

"Everything you need will be taken care of and, if we miss something, just let me know."

She looked up at him, her gaze automatically going to his lips before she scolded herself and forced her eyes up to meet his.

"You're going to take care of all of my expenses?"

"Yes, for the next six weeks. That's part of the deal."

It made sense. The only reason she was staying in New York longer was this fake fiancée assignment. So why shouldn't he completely accommodate her? Making sense was totally different from being comfortable, and Nina wasn't comfortable with the thought of this guy she'd only met yesterday paying her way. Thinking back now, she recalled the contract vaguely mentioning expenses, but she'd been so focused on the language pertaining to her business functioning with RGF's that she hadn't considered the implications. No worries, it was all good, she'd get used to it, because again she had no other choice. There was no way she could afford to stay here and buy all the things she'd need before she began seeing any profit from doing business with RGF.

She took a deep breath and released it slowly, telling herself to let go of the trepidation and take this situation for what it was at the moment.

"Then I'll head out now. It seems I have a spa appointment and a fitting this afternoon."

For what seemed like endless moments, they both stood still, staring at each other.

"Thank you," he said when the silence stretched between them. "For doing this, I mean. I know it seems like an unusual arrangement."

"If the rhythm of the drumbeat changes, the dance step must adjust."

He frowned. "What?"

She shook her head as she grabbed her purse. "Sorry, it's just an old African proverb my father used to say."

"Your father is African?"

"Yes. His mother came to America when he was five years old. When she remarried, her husband adopted my father and so his last name was changed, but he was born in Sierra Leone."

"Interesting," he said, still staring at her.

"Yes. It's always interesting to know where you come from and it helps in determining where you're going."

And she had no idea why they were talking about this. He had work to do and she had a spa appointment to get to.

"Anyway, we'd better get started with this. Today's going to be a busy day."

He walked with her to the door. "You're right. I'll speak with my team this afternoon and arrange for you to meet with them tomorrow morning. If there's time on your schedule, Landra will coordinate everything. But I'd like to get you set up quickly. If this fake wedding works out, we should see an immediate bump in sales, especially since we're at the peak of wedding season."

"Then maybe we should have gotten engaged earlier this year," she said as they walked to the elevators in what felt like a moment of déjà vu. "We're already in the first week of May. If a woman's getting married this season, she likely already has her gown."

"Until she sees a Golden Bride original being tried on by a real-life bride who's also going to be a member of the Gold family," he said before leaning in to push the button to summon the elevator.

Except there was nothing "real" about this arrangement.

"So we're hoping for the impromptu bride. Or the indecisive one." She nodded as she thought about her vendors who specialized in bridal items.

"Or the one who's just been swept off her feet with a wildly romantic proposal and can't wait to be married. She plans a quick wedding but wants all the bells and whistles, starting with a couture gown." He talked while she stepped into the elevator car. Following her inside, he pushed the buttons for his floor and the lobby.

"Not couture, RGF already has their wealthy customers on lock," she said. "Think about the average woman who's looking for something fancy, unique, but economical. I'll do some research on the bridal line, see what budget-friendly gowns you have."

"But you don't need to select budget friendly. I told you I'll take care of everything for you," he insisted.

Was that a look of pity she saw flash quickly in his eyes? Lord, she hoped not.

"The rich won't care about the Fashion House Playboy being engaged," she pointed out. "It won't seem romantic and dazzling to them because they're already living their own dazzling lives. But the woman who picks up the fashion magazines in the supermarket and runs her fingers over the glossy pages full of designer gowns? She's the one who'll appreciate this whole charade and she's the one you should be targeting."

"You're a techie like me, how do you know all this stuff about marketing bridal gowns?"

"I'm that 'regular' woman. Wasn't that what Desta said in the meeting earlier? That's why you chose me and that's how I know what I'm talking about."

The elevator door opened on his floor, but Major didn't immediately move to get out.

"You should go, you have a lot of work to do today," she told him even though she sensed he wanted to stay.

She, on the other hand, needed some space. That kiss, her mentioning her father to him, and then the talk of weddings had her feeling a bit unsteady. Considering the old proverb, she'd just experienced a giant misstep in her dance routine and she needed to regroup.

"I'll see you later," he said finally as the door began to close and he extended his arm to stop it.

Nina nodded. "I'll be ready."

Every muscle in her body felt limp. In fact, when Nina flopped down onto her stomach on her hotel room couch, she felt as if she might melt into the upholstery. That guy at the spa had massaged every muscle in her body until they were like jelly. And she'd never felt better!

She'd need to hold on to this feeling when she made the call to her family to tell them she'd be here much longer than anticipated. Her text earlier today saying that she'd missed her train wasn't going to be enough. But she'd been putting that off, instead deciding to enjoy the luxurious offerings of the Tranquil Mornings Day Spa. From champagne to sparkling water, fruit to decadent chocolates, and a menu to order lunch or dinner, the place had accommodated all her needs—even the ones she hadn't realized she'd had.

Claude was waiting to take her to her dress fittings, but she'd wanted to stop and grab her laptop before heading out again. She was just about to push herself up from the couch, grab it and head back downstairs when someone knocked at the door. She moved across the room much faster than her very relaxed body wanted to.

"Hello," she said when she pulled the door open to see a woman standing there.

"Hello," the woman replied before stepping inside unannounced. "Bring the racks in and put them over there. Have makeup set up near the window so Natalia will have the best light. We have a couple hours until it's time to head to the venue, but I want to make sure everything is perfect, and we may have to go through a couple outfits first."

The woman—dressed in gray pants tapered at the bottom, bright yellow pumps and a white high-low blouse with the sleeves rolled up to her elbows—breezed into the room.

"Excuse me?" Nina asked, taking a step behind the three racks of clothes that had been wheeled into her hotel room. "I think there might be some mistake."

"There's no mistake."

Another woman spoke and Nina turned around to see her closing the door.

"Hi, I'm Riley Gold and you're Nina Fuller. It's a pleasure to meet you."

Yes, this was Riley Gold, the Ice Princess of RGF as the press had called her for years, until she'd started dating Chaz—Chadwick Warren. Her beauty far surpassed any of the pictures Nina had seen of her online.

As realization immediately set in, Nina accepted the outstretched hand and calmed down just a bit. "Hi. It's nice to meet you, Riley. I thought I was being driven to the fittings."

Riley nodded, her dark brown hair falling in deep waves over her shoulders. She wore a black, round-necked shift dress with gold stripes at the end of the three-quarter sleeves and across the hem, and cute strappy black sandals.

"I thought you'd be more comfortable here," Riley said. "As comfortable as you can get in this situation."

She was right about that. Nina's fingers clenched the strap of her laptop bag as she stood amid so much action not really knowing what to do. There were now seven people in her not-so-big hotel room. The stylist, whom she presumed was the woman giving all the instructions, four people moving clothing racks, shoe boxes, bags and hat boxes, a woman with super-long eyelashes, and a man wearing dark shades and dime-size diamond earrings in both ears. He was on his phone and carrying a huge clear bag with flat irons, combs, brushes and other hair paraphernalia inside. Nina and Riley made nine—enough for a softball team.

"Thanks for that," Nina said and set her laptop bag on the floor next to the nearest chair. "As much as I've always loved fashion, computers are my first love. Besides, the last twenty-four hours has been a bit of a whirlwind. I mean I haven't thought of what clothes I'd wear beyond the initial meeting."

Riley nodded again. "I can imagine. You look great in this suit, by the way, but I'm here to dress you up. I work with numbers and charts primarily, but clothes are my business and Lila over there, she *knows* clothes. She's one of the best stylists in New York and works with many of our high-end customers."

Looks by Lila, owned by Lila Cantone. Nina had heard of her, but she'd never imagined the woman was probably no more than five foot two without her heels and moved like an Energizer Bunny.

"Tonight, we want chic but grab-you-by-the-throat elegant. The annual Sip 'n' Chat is one of RGF's most notable functions where fashion critics, photographers, reps from modeling agencies and specially selected members of the press are going to get the surprise of the year with this engagement announcement." That was Lila giving her crew a pep talk. "She's being presented to the fashion world tonight. Let's make her dazzle so that every single woman that's still breathing will wish she were her."

Riley wrapped an arm around Nina's shoulders. "I know she seems scary, but I promise you this is the way to go. Major wanted the best and I assured him I would get it for you."

So he'd sent his sister to work with her. Nina didn't know how she felt about that. Did he not think she could pick out a suitable outfit on her own? So many questions whirled through her mind but she had no time to entertain any of them because Lila was heading straight for her.

"Okay, I was told size twelve or fourteen, so I brought both." Riley's arm had slipped from around Nina, leaving space for Lila to step in and touch her shoulders. "Turn," Lila directed Nina.

"I'm Nina, by the way. It's nice to be working with you, Lila," Nina said before moving because no matter how important this agreement was, there was absolutely no excuse for rudeness.

Lila blinked, wide gray eyes flanked by long lashes that looked natural. Her hair was shaved on one side and layered in perfectly glossy auburn strands with pink tips on the other.

"Hello, Nina. We'll see how nice you think this is when it's all over. I can be a real bitch."

Well then, honesty was going to be the name of all her dealings with RGF and the Golds. Nina smiled, because in her mind that was a good thing. Dishonesty, secrets and lies had played a big part in the demise of her parents' relationship and Nina had promised herself she'd steer clear of those things in business and in pleasure.

"Now, let's get started. You have nice curves, let's show them off, make some men as envious as all the women will be."

The comment was followed by Nina being whisked off into the bedroom to try on dresses.

The first was a black-and-blue, A-line, round-necked dress with a beaded waist.

"Hmm," Riley said. "Major's wearing a navy-blue suit, Excellence in Men line. Single button and a pale gray shirt. She should complement him, but they shouldn't be too matchy."

Nina glanced in the full-length mirror that had been brought in and propped against the wall in the living room. She looked like she was going to the prom and shook her head to express her dislike.

"I agree," Lila said, waving a hand to signal she needed to go and change into another dress.

Seven dresses and forty-five minutes later, Nina stepped in front of that mirror once more.

This one was an asymmetric panel of overlays with a one-shoulder fitted bodice and straight skirt of dark blue sequins. Her breasts looked amazing thanks to the strapless shaper Lila's assistant had brought into the room while Nina was changing. Thankfully, no undergarment lines showed and when she turned to glimpse the dress from the back, she smiled at the admirable, definitive curve of her ass.

The dress was gorgeous and more expensive than anything she'd ever worn before. She knew because there was no price attached. The only tag on these clothes was RGF Style or RGold Original, which equated to expensive because those were the signature lines at the fashion house. RGolden Label was their couture line and all other lines simply had the RGF logo attached somewhere on the inside of the garment.

The material of the dress was impossibly soft and hung decadently over her usually too-curvy butt and hips. Her body looked great in this dress, even with the slight pouch of a belly that on bloated days could push her into the next pant size.

Garen, the hair stylist came over and pulled Nina's hair up, leaving out a few tendrils.

Lila stood behind her to one side and Riley was on the other.

"I think this is it," Nina said as she continued to look at the shimmering material.

"With these shoes and the pounded-metal cuff. Cheree!" Lila yelled to one of her assistants and set a pair of silver, five-inch-heel slingbacks next to Nina's feet.

One by one, Nina slipped her feet into the shoes and waited while Anya, another assistant, buckled the straps.

Cheree placed the pounded-metal bracelet on her right wrist.

"Classy and retro. Not only will folk in the industry not have a clue who you are, they're gonna fall over themselves trying to label your style. We're gonna use this moment to set the stage for a whirlwind of different looks that will put you at the top of the fashion game." Lila was obviously excited as she nodded her head, hair swaying over one shoulder.

For a moment Nina didn't know who she was. This wasn't why she'd come to New York. But it was beginning to be a hell of a lot of fun!

CHAPTER FIVE

"WHAT ARE YOU laughing at?"

Major frowned as Maurice chuckled.

"You and this crazy situation you've gotten your-self into," his brother responded.

"First, I didn't get myself into this situation, it just happened."

Maurice frowned now, his full brows tilting downward, which added a more ominous look to the thick beard he sported.

"You're the one who suggested this tech woman become your fake fiancée."

"Yeah, but I'm not the one who came up with the whole fake fiancée idea in the first place. Oh no, that was Desta's brilliance, which you happily cosigned." Major walked around the king-size four-poster in his room, trying his best to ignore the suit, shirt and tie that had been laid out neatly on one side of the mattress.

Maurice had left the office and followed him to his penthouse. For what reason, Major didn't know. But considering what his brother was doing at this moment—lounging with one leg draped over the arm of a leather recliner across the room, staring at him and making irritating comments—he would assume his presence was meant to antagonize him to no end. If that were the case, he was doing a damn good job.

"We needed a plan, something that would grab the customer's attention and keep it riveted on the Golden Bride line."

Major shook his head as he yanked his shirt out of his pants before pulling it over his head and off. "And I look like the one to do that?"

"Your reputation—" Maurice started, but Major quickly cut him off.

"I'm not the one with a reputation, man. You know that's all you. You're the one who flaunts every affair you have. Hell, you pose for pictures for all those photographers and tabloid workers. You give them so much ammunition."

"I wasn't named the Fashion House Playboy. A snub, I might add, I'm still considering being salty about." Maurice gave a fake pout.

Major tossed his shirt into the hamper a few feet away and sat heavily on the bed—his back to the clothes. "Those dates were a coincidence. And, actually, one was a favor to Mom and Dad. I couldn't say anything about it because it would have embarrassed poor Hannah Lincoln, whose parents didn't want her to go out in public alone because her jet-setting, race-car-driving boyfriend had just dumped her."

Major's head fell back and he groaned. He loved his mother above all else in this world, but if she ever called his cell phone and started the conversation with, "Hi, my favorite son," again, he was hanging up on her. She'd made that sugary-sweet request for him to take Hannah out so she wouldn't appear depressed and lonely over the breakup and he'd agreed.

Hannah had spent the entire evening talking about her ex and how she was being super strong and not crying over her ex, and how her ex was the love of her life, but how glad she was to be rid of her ex. It was a long and insufferable evening that had capped off the three-day stint earning him the ever so wonderful title in the fashion industry. The tabloids loved to take any snippet of information and run with it. That was their job, and while Major could totally respect someone being dedicated to a job, he didn't have to like being caught up in it.

"But you still selected the woman to be your fake fiancée," his twin pointed out.

"That, right there—" Major turned to see that his brother had grabbed a beer out of his refrigerator on his way to the room and was now twisting the top off so he could take a long swallow. After a shake of his head, he continued. "That's the best part of this stupid stunt. At least she's someone I have something in common with and won't die of boredom or irritation from when I'm alone with her."

"So you like her?"

Major blinked and then shook his head. "That's not what I said. But yeah, I like that we're both IT techies and that she's smart and courageous enough to start her own business." Thoughts of how their companies overlapped popped into his mind and Major instantly pushed them back.

"Like you did," Maurice said.

Major leaned over and untied his Tom Ford leather sneakers, but he sat up before taking them off. "Yeah, like I did."

Maurice was the only person in his family who knew about Brand Integrated. Being fraternal twins came with a certain amount of closeness that didn't resonate with his other two siblings. And while he and Maurice weren't constantly on the phone or, notwithstanding this present moment, sitting in each other's bedroom talking the night away, he and Maurice told each other pretty much everything.

So when Major had started to feel a little itchy working solely for RGF, Maurice was the first to notice. And when Major confided in his brother about the idea for his new business venture, Maurice had stood firmly in his corner. As a matter of fact, Maurice hadn't agreed with Major keeping his business a secret from the family. He believed that Major should be proud of himself and bold enough to step away from the Gold fashion house, especially considering none of the other siblings had been able to do that.

"You've signed the lease in the building, started hiring staff, and have your first marketing plan ready to roll out on day one. I'd say you're set to do this," Maurice said before taking another drink.

"Yeah, I am," Major said. "But first, I've gotta get this fake wedding on a roll. After that, I'm out."

"Not out," Maurice said. "You'll always be a Gold,

no matter what building you walk into for work each day."

"Dad's probably not going to feel that way. You know how he is about loyalty. That was the crux of the whole family feud that almost threatened Riley's happiness." He sighed heavily, reliving how his sister's plunge into love a couple months ago had only made his decision to move on to other things in his career another sticky family issue to cope with. "But I'm through thinking about that. It's what I'm doing, so they can either accept it or disown me."

"You know Mom's never gonna let him disown you. She didn't let him disown Riley."

Major stood and took the sneakers into his closet. "That was never going to happen, I don't care who she slept with. Dad would have seriously considered shooting Chaz and Tobias before he'd ever thought about firing Riley."

Even though the news of his sister's affair with Chaz, whose uncle Tobias King was head of King Designs, had spread like wildfire through the industry, bringing old assumptions about the Gold/King feud back to the surface. While Major secretly hoped his engagement façade would help take the residual bad press from Riley's saga away, part of him knew that the subsequent announcement of his leaving RGF to run Brand Integrated Technologies would fuel its own fire.

"And look at them now," Maurice said. "Riley and Chaz are inseparable. When he's not at her place, she's at his. He's at Sunday dinner with the family and she's seen out at parties with him and Tobias. They're really in love, whatever the hell that is."

Oh yeah, in addition to being the twin who actually loved going on dates with different women and getting attention for it, Maurice was the one who hated, loathed and despised the word *love*. Major didn't let the word get that deep under his skin, although he didn't imagine himself feeling it any time soon. His new company, as well as continuing to help with RGF's technology development, were his priorities right now. The one time he'd ventured to believe he might be feeling something like love, Stacia Hudgins had given him a hard-and-fast lesson—love wasn't worth a damn.

"I gotta get home. If we don't get ready, Riley, Chaz and the rest of the family are going to be at the cocktail party before us," Maurice said.

Major stood and was about to walk toward the bathroom when he looked back at the clothes on the bed. "I still can't believe Riley picked out clothes for me."

Maurice eased his tall frame from the chair, tilted his head back to swallow the remaining dregs of beer from the bottle and then shook his head. "You know Riley's in control of everything that concerns the Golden Bride line. Whether or not you gave her permission to be involved with your fake fiancée, she was going to do it. And she's damn sure gonna make certain she controls everything you do and say regarding this engagement."

Major groaned. "That's what I'm afraid of."

* * *

No, what Major Gold was actually afraid of, an hour and a half later when he stood near the bar at the Midtown Loft & Terrace and glanced toward the door, was swallowing his tongue or otherwise making a fool of himself as Nina Fuller walked in.

She smiled when she met his gaze and began walking toward him. Major stuffed his hands into the front pockets of his pants, forcing them to remain still and not move toward the center to soothe the growing ache that was happening there.

Nina looked stunning in blue, the dark hue playing expertly against the lightness of her complexion. Her hair was pulled up, loose pieces hanging at each ear just brushing the skin of her neck. He'd bet every dollar in all four of his bank accounts the skin right there was soft to the touch and sweet to the taste. Silver earrings sparkled at her ears and matched the chunky bracelet on her wrist. His gaze lifted from that wrist up her arm to where her bare shoulder was showcased. A shoulder he wanted to rub his fingers over and drop featherlight kisses against. Her shoes were silver but her legs were really the clincher, grabbing his full attention. They looked long and luscious, coated with some type of glistening oil.

She walked like a temptress across the mahogany floor, her hips swaying from side to side, healthy breasts held high to tempt him and most likely every other guy with good vision in this room. He swallowed hard and tried not to think of the word *hard*. Not that it was going to help; his dick was well on its way to another stunning erection at just seeing this woman. He wished for a drink but didn't want to turn away from her to request one from the bartender.

"You look fantastic," he said the moment she was close enough to hear because he had to get those words out of his head.

"Thanks. I tried on so many dresses today, I'm glad to be standing in just one at this moment."

"This is definitely the best dress. Ever," he confessed and swallowed again.

She tilted her head, her smile wavering slightly. "Are you okay?"

For a few seconds he clamped his lips shut. He wasn't totally sure he could resist asking her to find some private place for them to hang out tonight.

"I'm good," he said and gave himself a good mental kick. It'd been a long time since he'd been a horny teenager chasing after models at fashion shows. Most of them had been around his age, even though they'd hit the runways in outfits that made them appear much older.

"Well, I'm not. I mean I'm a little nervous. I've never been to a Sip 'n' Chat before."

She was looking around as she spoke and Major finally managed to pull his gaze from her long enough to do the same.

"We rely on the media, but we can't always control what goes into print. The Sip 'n' Chat is our way of having an informal press conference where we release only the information we want the media to have, at the exact moment we want them to have it."

She nodded. "Smart."

"Yeah, just like me." He winked.

"You? I thought we were talking about your team who came up with this very smart idea." She smiled and he enjoyed the light that came into her eyes. A jolt of awareness hit him as he realized she really was different from the other women he'd met.

"I'm talking about how smart I was to have finally agreed to meeting with you when I did. Otherwise, I wouldn't be standing here with you." He'd stepped closer to her as he said those words. Another step or two and he would be on top of her, which wasn't a bad idea—except he wasn't down for an audience.

"Hi! You made it! That dress looks fabulous on you. Doesn't it, Major?" Riley asked when she approached, Chaz right beside her.

Why she was asking him the obvious, Major had no idea, but he gladly answered. "It does."

"Thanks," Nina said, holding a silver clutch in front of her as she nodded at Riley and Chaz. "I hope it photos well. I came up on the elevator with three reporters and two photographers."

"Nina, this is Chaz Warren, my boyfriend." Riley smiled as she glanced at Chaz and he returned the look before extending his hand to Nina.

"Hello, Nina. It's nice to meet you. Riley's told me all about you, your company and, ah, this marketing plan."

Major wasn't sure how he felt about that. While his first instinct was to be happy for Riley—who seemed more relaxed and content with Chaz than he'd ever recalled—there was still a small part of him that was on guard. Telling Chaz about their marketing strategies when he was still working—even if only on a part-time basis—with his uncle, didn't seem like the best idea. But tonight, Major had other things to worry about.

"King Designs is doing great this season. I've been keeping up with your shows and sales," Nina said.

"Ah, yeah. Wow, you're keeping tabs on us," Chaz replied. "Not sure if I should be worried or impressed by that. But, um, our line is doing really well after the relaunch and we're hoping for the same success with a couple other lines."

"That's good to know. And yes, in my line of business, I try to keep my eye on the top companies in the industry," she told him.

Okay, add another thing to the list of things for Major to ponder. Was Nina really going to stand there and pitch her company to their biggest competitor?

"It's almost time for the announcement," Desta said when she joined them.

Thankful for the interruption, Major slipped his arm around Nina's waist and gently led her in the direction Desta was now speed-walking.

"We're going to begin with pictures. The family has already started, but you two are up next. Reporters are chomping at the bit trying to figure out what's going on." Desta talked as she walked and

Major followed, enjoying the feel of his hand resting at the small of Nina's back.

The venue was crowded with people, most of whom he knew from the industry, some of whom he'd never seen before in his life. He supposed he should feel some measure of nervousness or possibly anxiety, but all he felt was anticipation.

"There are so many people here," Nina said when they made their way to the other side of the terrace.

It was a gorgeous night for a terrace party, not too humid and the sky full of stars.

Major came around behind her, his hand still at her waist as they moved through a group of people, one of whom did a double take when she saw him. It wasn't someone he knew, but he could tell the buzz around tonight's announcement was growing because the woman's gaze had immediately shifted from him to Nina with an inquisitive quirk of her brow.

"Are they normally like this?" Nina asked.

"Like what?"

"So hungry for whatever is going to happen next. Surely they've been to this event before, so they know what you're going to be talking about—your fashion house. But their anticipation is almost palpable."

That question came when they were just a few steps from an arch covered in white flowers made to look purple by the up-lighting positioned on the floor.

"Everyone here was sent a private invitation that

spoke of a big announcement," he said. "Are you all right? Is it too much for you?"

He wanted to say he'd take her out of here if it was, but he knew Desta would probably have a cardiac episode if he even thought about doing that. Even though RGF still held its title as the US's top fashion house, keeping a comfortable lead over their competitors was their marketing director's priority.

"No. I'm fine," she said. "Just wondering how this is all going to play out."

Major stood beside Nina, waiting for Desta's signal to step forward for pictures. He'd reluctantly moved his hand from her waist when his fingers had begun to tingle with the desire to either slide to the generous curve of her ass or up to the bare skin of her shoulder. Both, he was certain, were inappropriate movements on so many levels.

"As soon as the announcement is made, we can leave. Maurice and his team can field all the questions. All we have to do is stand here and smile for the cameras," he said.

She looked surprised at that comment. "You're not making the announcement?"

"No. My father's going to handle that. Is that a problem?"

There was a slight hesitation then a small shrug of her shoulders. "If this were real, I'd think you'd be so excited about getting married to the woman you love that you'd be bursting with the need to announce it to the world," she said, but then held up a hand and shook her head. "Don't get me wrong, I'm no expert. It just seems like the sort of thing they'd do in one of those romance movies."

Romance movies that she was obviously watching and paying close attention to.

"I don't know that this was planned for romance," he said. "It's just a hoax, remember."

He really needed her to remember that. Nothing personal or real was going to come of this six-week plan. That's not what he was in the market for and he was banking on them being so focused on their business goals that there'd be no risk of losing sight of the goal.

She nodded her agreement and in the next moment they were being moved to stand under the arch and positioned for one pose after another.

The photographer hired specifically to commemorate the event had been given a list of names and pictures Desta wanted. The guy, who was dressed in all black, directed Major to stand behind Nina and put his hands around her waist. It was the dreaded prom picture pose. He was inclined to frown once he realized it, but as her body settled back against his, Major felt something else entirely.

In addition to the warmth spreading throughout his body at her proximity to him, there was a rush of something akin to joy, excitement or—no, it was more intense, possibly ownership. As he looked toward the photographer, ready for the guy to snap the picture, Major was acutely aware of the men in the room staring his way. Surely they weren't looking at him, so they had to be staring at Nina, whom he already knew looked phenomenal in the blue dress.

He tried valiantly to keep from frowning as he realized he was the one forgetting this was all a hoax and that Nina wasn't his to feel jealous, protective or anything else about.

"Now, you stand still and, Ms. Fuller, you turn around." The photographer had moved on to another instruction that Nina dutifully followed.

She turned until she was facing him.

"Put your hands on his shoulders and turn your head to me," the guy said.

Again, she obeyed.

Now her front was pressed into his and Major's hands immediately went around her waist once more. Without instruction.

He could smell the floral scent of her shampoo and felt the curve of her breasts even through the material of his jacket and shirt. His fingers tightened at her waist before sliding down slightly until he could feel the curve of her ass. This time when the flash of the camera erupted, Major was clenching his teeth. He was holding so still he thought his bones might crack from inactivity. But that was preferable to giving in to the heat spreading through his veins like wildfire and pressing her closer to him.

Several pictures were taken in that pose and he was about to complain or pull away—anything to stop the assault his arousal had taken on his body when she looked up at him.

"You don't like holding poses for pictures, do you?" she asked with a smile.

"Not really," he replied while staring down into eyes that appeared to have more yellow highlights than he'd noticed before. "But I enjoy holding you."

She blinked as if trying to figure out if she should smile at his words or feel something deeper, something more potent than he'd assumed either of them would feel. When she remained silent, he lifted a hand to brush the backs of his fingers lightly over the line of her jaw. She continued to smile and surprised him by leaning her head into his touch. It was a quick and impromptu movement, one that had his breath catching seconds before more pictures were snapped.

With the warm air around them and the sound of violins, harps—or whatever instruments the quartet at the other end of the room was playing—echoing toward the sky, he was locked in her gaze, wrapped in this blissful attraction. She must have felt it, too, because she suddenly looked puzzled. He wanted to say something reassuring, to convince them both that they were simply beginning their series of acting assignments for the next six weeks, but Riley's voice interrupted the music and stopped his thoughts.

"Ladies and gentlemen, thank you so much for joining us tonight. While we have a few upcoming things happening within the fashion house that we'll also be talking about tonight, we don't want to keep you in suspense any longer about the big reveal. As always, the patriarch of our family, my father, Mr. Ron Gold, will start the announcements."

Major had taken Nina's hand without thought, moving them until they stood to the side with Riley. The white podium where his sister had introduced their father was alight with the same purple accent as the flowered arch, lounge chairs and high-boy tables throughout the space. On the other side of the podium stood Maurice and RJ, watching as his father stepped up to the microphone.

A tall, distinguished-looking man with a bald head and stern facial features, Ron Gold was the epitome of fashion dressed in an original RGF chocolate-brown suit, crisp white shirt and canary yellow silk tie.

"I'll echo my daughter's gratitude for your attendance tonight. We know you're normally ready for a few industry announcements at this event, but this year we have something a little more special," he began. "As you know, we've had a very successful launch into this year's Fashion Weeks with the unveiling of our Golden Bride Collection in February. Well, tonight the Gold family is pleased to announce that not only are we celebrating a phenomenal episode in bridal fashion, we're also overjoyed with the engagement of our son Major to the lovely Ms. Nina Fuller."

At first there were gasps followed by the low buzz of murmurs before multiple camera flashes lit up the room. Applause began with a quick burst and Nina's fingers trembled in his. Major gave her hand a little squeeze and then lifted it to his lips to kiss. Another impromptu action that sent the crowd into more clapping and more picture-snapping.

Normally, this would be the point where Major would turn away, leaving the beast of pictures and questions behind. If it wasn't after an RGF show, where Ron liked for each of his children to make comments to demonstrate they were all personally and professionally vested in the presentations, then Major didn't deal with the tabloids or the press. Yet tonight, he stood a little straighter and squared his shoulders. For the first time, he didn't mind having pictures taken with this woman beside him. Perhaps because this time he—meaning the marketing team—was orchestrating the response of every reporter and photographer in this space.

It was a surreal moment, one he'd never thought he'd experience. The announcement of his wedding. He reminded himself it was fake and shook off the feeling of excitement that had started to blossom in the pit of his stomach. Instead, he turned to look at Nina, who was smiling—no, she was beaming as she looked from one camera to another, the tilt of her head and easy movement of her body as if she'd practiced for this moment all her life. She appeared so natural, her hand so comfortable in his. That odd stirring he'd had when they first stood under the arch moved through him again and this time he knew it wasn't solely arousal. Desire was a definite between them and very easy to acknowledge and understand. This other thing, not so much.

When she returned her gaze to Major's, he immediately felt at ease. So, when the first question came directly to him from a reporter, he didn't think twice before responding.

"This is all so exciting and fast, Major. Where and when did you and Ms. Fuller meet?"

"We met earlier this year and I wasn't aware there was a time clock ticking on love." He had no idea where that response had come from, but it seemed like a good answer. And, if he wasn't mistaken, it made Nina's smile a little brighter.

Another reporter took advantage of the fact that Major was actually answering questions, even though it hadn't been announced that he would.

"So how did he sweep you off your feet, Ms. Fuller?"

She didn't look at him to gauge his response, she simply continued to smile and began a story that sounded very real.

"It was Valentine's Day and neither of us had a date. We ended up at the same bar, *not* crying in our drinks." Nina chuckled and so did the reporter. "Next thing I know, we're having dinner on a rooftop like this one, talking about all the people who put too much emphasis on Valentine's Day. After that we were together every weekend, either here in the city or in Pennsylvania where I'm from. So if you count quiet walks in Central Park and sitting in rocking chairs on my dad's back porch as being swept off my feet, then yeah, that's just what he did."

"Aww, that's so sweet," the woman reporter said.

"So you're the Fashion House Romantic instead

of the Fashion House Playboy. That's not as good a headline," the guy said, chuckling when the woman elbowed him.

"These lovebirds have lots of planning to do," Ron interrupted. "And we're going to keep you up to date with those plans. But for now, we have more announcements."

Thankful for the reprieve, Major offered the press another smile, before leaning in to whisper in Nina's ear, "Our part's done. Let's get out of here."

Her quick nod and the instant look of relief that washed over her face also reminded him the smile and natural movements he'd just glimpsed were part of the sham. She didn't want to be there any more than he did.

If Cinderella hadn't run away from the ball at the stroke of midnight, she may have walked into a room with Prince Charming following closely behind, feeling the quick jolt of excitement, anticipation and lust.

Nina was feeling every one of those things and then some as she slid the card over the panel on the door and walked into her hotel room. Just twenty-four hours ago she'd entered this same room, but she hadn't been wearing a designer dress that sparkled with what she'd now identified as success, nor had there been a great-looking guy standing just a few feet behind her.

"Would you like a drink?" It sounded cliché but polite nonetheless.

"Sure. I'll pour," he said as they moved into the

living area of the suite. Just a few feet away stood a large round table with two chairs on either side. It sat in front of the only window with a view of one of the New York streets. Buildings, people and lots of cars were below even at almost eleven at night.

"I'll be back in a sec." She made her way into the bedroom when she heard her phone ringing inside her purse.

"Hey," she answered as she sat on the bed.

"Where are you? I've been texting and calling you all night," Angie said. "Dad's worried sick and ready to call the police to file a missing person report, and Daisy wants to get in the car to drive up there to bring you home."

Nina sighed. She hadn't called them back after telling them this morning that she'd missed her train. So much had happened in those twelve hours that she hadn't completely forgotten about her family, but she had put them on the back burner for a change.

"Sorry. I meant to call you sooner to explain what's going on."

"Okay. Well, explain now."

Right. Explain how the deal she'd finally been able to land had somehow morphed into a six-week assignment that could either make or break her experience in the fashion industry. She glanced over at the window, to the night sky in the big city, still in awe of where she was and how she'd come to be there.

"They offered me a project for six weeks. It's kind of like a trial run for the business with a few other duties." There, that didn't sound so crazy.

"What do you mean 'other duties'? Are they going to use your app or not? And why'd you have to stay longer just to get the job? Dad's been asking for you and I can't spend another night here. I've got the night shift for the next five days at the hotel."

Angie worked at a casino hotel and often had the night shift, which meant Nina had the night shift with their father because Daisy was the most unreliable of the Fuller sisters.

"You and Daisy will have to work out a schedule. I'm going to be here for the next six weeks as part of this deal I've accepted."

"What are you talking about? It's just an app. Either they're using it or they're not—and if they are, it's not necessary for you to stay there during some trial period."

"It's necessary if I'm also pretending to be the guy's fiancée to help their company boost sales," she blurted.

After only a couple seconds' hesitation, Angie all but yelled through the phone, "What? Are you serious? You're like some escort?"

"I am not an escort," she snapped. She wasn't aware of escorts wearing designer gowns and getting a personal driver. Although she could be mistaken, considering she'd never made it her business to know what escorts did or didn't do, or have or didn't have.

"Look, this is the biggest opportunity of my life and I'm taking it. So for the next six weeks, I'll be Major Gold's fake fiancée and his company will be featuring my app on all of its web sites."

Angie was silent for a moment. "And what happens after that? He offers to put you up in an apartment and you continue to be at his beck and call?"

Nina rolled her eyes even though Angie wasn't there to see how exasperating her comments were. "This isn't *Pretty Woman*," she said, referring to one of the Fuller sisters' favorite movies. "It's a job that I plan to do to put my business in a better position in this industry."

"This is insane and Dad's not gonna like it."

"He'll like it when it provides a way for me to take care of him on a long-term basis," she quipped. "Look, I gotta go. Just figure out a new schedule with you and Daisy and keep me posted. I'll be home as soon as this is over."

Angie wasn't happy when she hung up and Nina wasn't nearly as giddy as she'd been when she'd first walked into the room. In fact, as she disconnected the call and let her hands drop into her lap, she wondered briefly if Cinderella's coach had just turned into a pumpkin.

Ten minutes later, she walked back into the living area. Major had removed his jacket and tie, and was sitting on the couch, surfing TV channels.

"Everything okay?" he asked when she took a seat beside him.

She nodded. "It's fine. My sister called, so I had to give her an update on the change in plans."

"Do you live with your sister?"

"Ah, no. I have two sisters and we each have our own apartments, but we take care of my dad, so we're in constant contact with each other about schedules and such."

"Is your father sick?"

The immediate hint of concern in his tone initially surprised her, but that was because Angie's comments about escorts were still rambling in her mind.

"COPD. He was diagnosed years ago, but it's getting worse." To the point where he was almost debilitated, although Jacoby would never admit that.

Major's expression turned thoughtful, his brow furrowing a bit. "I'm sorry to hear that."

She shook her head, wanting to think of something else and feeling slightly guilty for admitting that fact.

"Thanks. Actually, that brings up something I was thinking on the ride over here."

He muted the television and dropped the remote on the cushion between them. "What's that?"

"If we want this charade to be believable, we should get to know each other better. We managed to do pretty good tonight, but what if I'm asked some personal questions about you? How will I know what to say?"

He frowned, thick brows slanted over brown eyes. The top button of his shirt was undone and Nina could see not only the tawny hue of his skin but also the slight ridge of his Adam's apple. She licked her lips quickly as a flash of thought—her tongue gliding over that ridge—soared through her mind.

"I don't give interviews unless it's right after a show. You aren't required to give interviews, either.

Take pictures, attend parties or whatever events are on the itinerary, and that's it."

Like arm candy. She'd often looked through fashion magazines or watched shows where dashing industry big shots had gorgeous women on their arms. Those women never spoke, just smiled for the camera and looked beautiful.

"That's not going to work," she said. Late last night and well into the early morning hours, she'd decided that if this was going to be her first big introduction to the industry, she wanted it to look good. Playing the part of his fiancée as convincingly as possible would lessen the chance that someone might find out it was fake, and thus damage her credibility. "We need to be convincing."

For a few quiet seconds Major just stared at her. In those moments, she breathed in the scent of his cologne, loving the spicy edge to the fragrance. She let her gaze linger over the breadth of his shoulders and the way his pale gray dress shirt molded his biceps and chest. His hands were resting on his thighs, a gold watch on his wrist, a chunky gold ring on his third right-hand finger.

"Are you saying you want to kiss me again?"

Noooo, that wasn't what she was saying, but now that he'd mentioned it...

"I'm saying that we should take this time to get our story straight. We improvised how we met and the whirlwind love affair, but I'm betting word will spread fast that you actually talked to the press without being at a show and that's going to give every other reporter even more guts to ask both of us questions."

"Questions like when was our first kiss?" he asked with a lift of a brow.

"You're obsessed with kissing."

"I didn't used to be," he said with a shake of his head. "But I can admit that I've been thinking a lot about kissing you again."

She swallowed and wondered if Prince Charming had thought about kissing Cinderella. *Most definitely!* Hadn't he gone through an entire village using a shoe to try to find her? That wasn't just so he could ask her name and make sure she was wearing both shoes...

"The kiss was very nice, but I'm referring more to how we'll make our appearances seem believable."

He sat straighter, seeming to shake off whatever was preoccupying him. "You may have a point. So let me ask you this, how did you like feeling my hands on you tonight?"

Oh, she hadn't thought of that. He had kept an arm around her for most of the time they'd been at the cocktail party and it had felt...good. Before the announcement, it had also drawn lots of attention from the women in the room. For a few moments, her mind had wondered if Major had been romantically linked to any of them before. She'd told herself then that it was a silly thought and reminded herself again at this moment. Worrying about Major running off and leaving her for whatever reason or doing something else to break their trust wasn't something she had to worry about, because none of this was real.

"I liked it," she admitted.

"Good, because there were lots of pictures being taken. I fully expect to see us on the front page of one or two tabloids in the morning."

Even after her personal admonishment, she couldn't help thinking back to how his hand had stayed fixed at the small of her back, her side flush against his. There were also the tight embraces while they'd posed for pictures, the embraces that had left her feeling warm all over. The physical attraction between them was off the charts and there was no use trying to deny that.

"That's, uh, good, right?" She sounded hopeful, even though she prayed he couldn't hear that.

"In this instance, yes. You want to know what else was good?"

"What?"

"Feeling your body against mine. Do you think we should practice more of that to be more convincing to the public?"

CHAPTER SIX

"Yes."

It was a simple word. She could have begged off and talked more, sticking to them rattling off facts about each other, but she didn't want to. Tonight she'd worn a gorgeous dress and attended a lavish rooftop party in New York City, something she'd dreamed of happening once her position in the industry was solidified.

Well, if this were really her dream then Nina was going to make it the best damn dream ever!

"What I mean is, if we were really engaged, what would we be doing right now?"

He eased closer to her, his eyes going just a bit darker as he kept them focused on her. "Do you really want the answer to that question?"

"I do." Because she suspected his answer was similar to hers.

Nina couldn't even remember the last date she'd been on, which meant that the last time she'd had sex was even further back than she'd first imagined. It had been too long and here was Major, looking handsome and smelling like a slice of heaven. They were pretending they were involved in a relationship, why not pretend a little more?

"Well, if we were really engaged, I'd probably be ready to get you out of that dress."

She'd crossed one leg over the other when she'd sat a few minutes ago and now she was thankful because she could press her thighs together tighter this way. The timbre of his voice combined with the idea of his hands moving over her body to remove the dress was deliciously enticing.

"Then, once you were naked, I'd bend you over this couch so that I could taste you."

She didn't reply, thinking if she remained silent, he'd keep talking and the warmth of desire spreading through her veins like wildfire would continue. Her tongue wasn't as obedient and it snaked out to move over her bottom lip. His gaze immediately dropped, following the action.

"Do you know how you taste, Nina? You're licking your lips like you recall. Tell me, are you as sweet as I believe you are?"

He was inside her mind. It was an eerie feeling to believe that he could see into her deepest thoughts. Share her memories of when she was alone in the bedroom of her small apartment in York, using her favorite vibrator to find her pleasure. And afterward, when a deep urging inside had her lifting that vibrator to her lips so that she could taste herself.

"Sweet and spicy, like a delicious drink that leaves you feeling just a little light-headed and a lot addicted," she said with the same confidence she'd felt when she'd presented her app to him.

Now he was licking his lips. She recalled those lips pressing into hers and wanted to feel them again.

"I'll bet you're slick and warm right now."

"And I'll bet you're growing just as hard as you were the first time I met you."

He'd been very hard, like her hand was brushing over steel, warm and enticing steel. The memory had her clenching her thighs together again, but this time the pulsating continued to the point of throbbing.

"If we were really engaged, I'd fuck you on this couch. In that bed. Over that table. Against that wall."

His voice was gruff as he moved close enough that the side of his body touched hers. Initial contact sent sparks soaring through her, to the point she thought she might just combust with the friction.

"If we were really engaged, we'd have been unable to keep our hands off each other while we were riding in the car." Because, yeah, she'd wanted to reach out and touch him then, but she'd refrained. Now, she wasn't so sure they were going to keep playing by those same rules.

Seconds later she had her answer when Major reached out a hand to cup her jaw. He leaned in closer, his gaze once again on her mouth.

"This is the beginning," he whispered, his breath warm as it fanned over her face. "If you don't tell me right now that this is not what you want, that you're only down for the façade we put on in public, I'm going to continue."

Her hand came up from her lap to press against his toned chest where his heart thumped persistently beneath.

"I won't object if you continue." In fact, she might be at the point of begging.

He closed the distance between them, taking her mouth in what she knew was going to be a heated and hungry kiss.

It was delicious, the way her tongue instantly moved to meet his, the way his tangled with hers in a hot duel that felt at once familiar and decadent. He tilted her face as he leaned in closer, deepening the kiss. She moaned and wrapped an arm around his neck. The hand on his chest flattened against his taut pectoral.

"As beautiful as it is, I want this dress off." The words were a ragged whisper as he briefly pulled his lips from hers. His teeth scraped along her jawline as she tilted her head back to give him better access.

In seconds his tongue was stroking up and down the line of her neck while his words tumbled through her mind. Was he asking permission to take her dress off? Had she already answered him?

She couldn't think beyond the heated path of moisture moving along her neck and the feel of his hands on her shoulders, going down her arms until they brushed the sides of her breasts. She sucked in a breath and released it on a ragged moan.

The zipper to the dress was on her right side. She

could reach it, but she'd have to move her hands from where they'd flattened on his chest and the back of his head. She didn't want to, but the urge to be naked beneath him was quickly taking charge.

"Now…" he grumbled, lifting her right arm to join the other one locked around his neck.

Whatever he'd said before that one word led to his fingers nimbly easing her zipper down, until the dress felt loose against her chest. He eased away from her and stood, his breath coming in heavy pants that matched hers. Taking her hands, he pulled her to her feet and removed the dress.

For what seemed like much longer than a few seconds, he simply stared at her body. She'd decided against wearing the uncomfortable shaper Lila and her crew had provided earlier. Now she wore only the black strapless bra and matching thin wisp of lace that constituted panties, which had come from the small suitcase the crew had also left in her room. In those seconds, a quick spurt of insecurity shot through her. Did he like what he saw? Was her stomach too round? Were any stretch marks visible?

Swallowing and squaring her shoulders, she said, "Your turn," and reached for the buttons on his shirt.

He kept his gaze locked on her fingers as she worked along his torso and then to each wrist until she could push his shirt off. She wasted no time lifting the undershirt up and over his head, wanting to touch his warm skin as quickly as possible. Just a shade darker than his complexion, her fingers looked as if they belonged splayed over his muscled chest.

She slid her hands across smooth skin, letting the tip of her pointer finger linger on the tight nub of his nipple before moving down to the cut of his abs. When her hands went lower and brushed his belt buckle, he grabbed each wrist.

"Turn around." The words were gruff and a bit more forceful than anything else he'd ever said to her, sending a rush of pleasure through her body.

She stepped out of the dress and turned until she was facing the couch, her backside vulnerable to his perusal.

"What is this?"

His fingers touched her waist, raising one of six rows of waist beads she wore.

She'd almost forgotten she was wearing them. It was something she'd worn since she was a teenager, changing the colors to match whatever mood she was in at the time. She always wore them as a sign of femininity and also as a way of keeping an eye on her weight.

"African waist beads," she told him and left off the complete history and function of the beads because his hands were moving around her waist, lifting the beads and caressing the skin beneath.

"I've never seen anything so sexy before in my life," he whispered.

Sensuality was another effect of the beads, so while she'd had a moment of insecurity over the appearance of her body to him, it had quickly been replaced by her own assurance that she was a sensual and desirable woman. Hearing his confirmation that he was feeling the same way was only a boost to the confidence she already possessed.

When his exploration of the beads was over, his hands moved down farther, until his fingers were slipping beneath the lace panties. He pushed them past her hips and down her legs, keeping an arm around her waist to steady her as she stepped free of them. His hand cupped her juncture and he pulled her hard against his body.

"Soft, wet, hot." He leaned his face down and whispered into the crook of her neck. "Just how I knew you'd feel."

His fingers separated her folds, easing between to feel the moisture of her arousal.

"So good." He groaned. "So damn good."

He wasn't lying. His fingers, moving so intimately between her legs, felt better than anything she could have ever imagined. When he thrust a finger inside her, she hissed, coming up on the tips of her toes as pleasure shot through her like fireworks.

Her head fell back against his shoulder and she cupped her breasts.

"Let me see 'em," he mumbled as his teeth nipped her neck.

She pushed the bra down and her breasts were bared. Squeezing them in her hands, she kept her eyes closed while knowing that he was looking down at her ministrations. This position felt wickedly erotic, with him behind her, his finger thrusting inside her, his mouth at her neck and his gaze zeroing in on her breasts. She kneaded them harder, being sure to play with her nipples. He groaned, his dick getting harder as it pressed against the slit of her ass.

"I can't do this," he said, stepping back from her.

For a second Nina felt confused and incomplete, thinking this interlude might be over before it had really begun.

He pulled his hands from her and, just when she was going to turn and ask what was going on, she heard his belt buckle as he undid it and then dragged down the zipper of his pants. Okay, well, that answered her question. He wasn't done with her yet, and she was glad. Twisting her arms around her back, she unhooked her bra. She had no idea where he'd gotten it from, but the next thing she heard was the tear of the condom packet. Barely a minute later, he bent her over the couch, her hands planted on the soft cushions as he spread her legs.

"It's not going to be slow, but it'll be good. Damn, I can't wait, it's gonna be so good."

"I'm ready for good," she said and nodded her agreement before sinking her teeth into her bottom lip as desire and anticipation gripped her throat.

He didn't lie. He thrust into her in one fast, deep stroke that almost sent her soaring over the couch. But she'd planted her feet on the floor and clenched the cushion in her fingers. She did gasp as her body stretched and acclimated to his presence.

"My fiancée," he said as he pulled out slightly and thrust back in. "You're my fiancée."

He pumped fast, in and out, until she was breathless, full and so wet her essence dripped down to her inner thighs.

"Fiancé," she whispered. "You're my fiancé."

They were trying to convince each other and themselves. Taking the charade they'd agreed upon to a level neither of them had anticipated.

"Mine," he groaned.

"Mine!" she screamed when his hand came around to toy with her clit as he continued to pump into her.

Hard and fast and damn delicious, that's what this was. Fake engagements, contracts for app usage, bumping into him in the hallway, showing him her waist beads—none of it mattered. Not in these seconds, because there was only this. Only the pleasure that was soaring through her.

When her legs were through shaking, he eased out of her, maneuvering them until this time he sat and she straddled his lap. He ran his fingers over the beads again as she settled onto his length.

"These are driving me crazy. Do you wear them all the time?"

She sighed at the sensation of him filling her once more and circled her hips until his balls pressed against her wet lips. "Mmm-hmm," she replied.

"All day. Every day." He talked while he pumped and she gripped her breasts, kneading them as pleasure built inside her once more.

"Let them go," he told her. "I want to see them bounce."

She did as he requested and clamped her hands

onto his shoulders, bracing herself as his thrusts increased. She matched his movements, riding him until the sound of their joining echoed in the air. He leaned in until the movement of her breasts could slap against his cheeks.

"So good," he mumbled. "So damn good."

"Yes!" she yelled when she knew another release was imminent. "Yes!"

"Yes, so…damn…good." He held her close, his face buried so thoroughly between her breasts she wondered if he could breathe. She came at the exact moment her thighs trembled around him once more.

She wasn't his.

This was an arrangement; one designed for their mutual benefit. And since it was a business agreement, there should have been boundaries. Lines that they would not cross. Things they would not do that could interfere with the goals they'd each set.

An hour after leaving her hotel, Major rested his elbows on the desk in his home office and dropped his head with a heavy sigh. He'd messed up big-time.

But he could fix it before his slip endangered the arrangement. The last thing he wanted was for Nina to think he was taking advantage of their business deal, using it as an opportunity to have sex with her. So, he sat straighter in the chair and put his fingers on the keyboard. Nina's email address was already typed and now he added the subject line: GUIDELINES.

He shook his head and pressed the backspace button. Then he typed again: RULES.

No, that wasn't going to work, so he deleted that, too.

In all his years, he'd never had to type an email like this. He'd also never left a woman almost immediately after having sex with her.

"I'll see you in the office at ten," he'd said after coming out of the bathroom.

She'd been sitting on the couch. While he'd been in the bathroom, she must have gone into the bedroom to grab her robe because it was belted tightly at her waist as she sat with her hands in her lap.

"Right," she'd replied. "I received the email adding that to the itinerary."

"Good. Okay. Well then, good night." The words had come in a clipped tone and he'd walked out of her hotel room, closing the door soundly behind him.

Now he was at his desk, preparing to tell her that what had happened would never happen again. Via email. It struck him then that this might be a tad immature, or perhaps even unnecessary. What if she was having the same never-again conversation with herself right at this moment? What if…he'd really messed up. It never occurred to him that sex with her would be so…so fantastic and intense and, damn, he'd messed up bad. Yeah, he was definitely sending her an email because in person this might turn into a discussion and the boundaries he needed to set for his own sanity weren't up for negotiation.

FOLLOW-UP.

He stared at the letters for a moment before deleting them, too.

This was ridiculous. Was he really going to tell this grown and exceptionally attractive woman that they couldn't touch each other again? Because that's what it was going to take. He'd decided on the ride back to his penthouse that touching her—in any capacity—was only going to make him want her more. There were plenty of couples who didn't engage in PDA, so that wasn't out of the ordinary.

But he and Nina weren't a real couple. They never would be after Stacia's conniving ways. Major had learned his lesson about being a Gold and trying to have a real relationship.

With that thought, Riley and Chaz immediately sprang to mind. His sister and her boyfriend were always touching—holding hands, Chaz touching her arm, Riley leaning in to him as he said something. All acts that, as Riley's big brother, made Major uncomfortable to see. But his parents were no different. How many times had he seen his father squeeze his mother's ass while growing up? He closed his eyes tightly and groaned. The answer was too many for his comfort. But Ron Gold loved his wife Marva without reservation. They were a partnership in love and in business and still going strong after thirty-seven years of marriage.

ADDENDUM.

Major typed the letters and this time didn't stop typing until a five-item list and two paragraphs were complete.

He hit Send and closed his computer before he could think better of the action. Sex with Nina had been great—if he were inclined to be specific, it was jolting, surprising, tantalizing—but it wasn't part of the plan. The plan that Major had worked on for far too long to be curtailed by a beautiful woman wearing colorful and sexy-as-hell waist beads that he knew would forever stay on his mind.

CHAPTER SEVEN

"I RECEIVED YOUR EMAIL." was the first thing Nina said
when she walked into Major's office the next morning.

He was sitting behind his desk and had looked up
the moment he heard her voice.

"Landra told me to come right in since you were
expecting me." She set her bag on the floor next
to one of the guest chairs across from his desk but
didn't take a seat.

Before getting started with business, she had to
say what she'd rehearsed since reading his message
at two this morning.

"What happened last night was consensual, just
in case you may be thinking you used your Fashion
House Playboy vibes to seduce me. You didn't. I do
what I want when I want."

That came out much better than the dozen or so
times she'd said it to the bathroom mirror.

"I'm aware of that," he replied as he put down the
pen he was holding and stared at her. "I just thought
it would be a good idea to outline some rules."

"Rules to outline a charade." She nodded. "Okay,

I can get with that." She didn't really have a choice. She wasn't walking away from this deal and she'd had him once, that would suffice. "I've noted each of the rules you've set—from the 'no kissing' all the way down to the 'no standing too close to each other in private'—and replied to the questions about my basic likes and dislikes."

"I saw them."

But he hadn't responded. So they were going for the cordial coolness. She could do that, too.

"Good. Now if we're questioned on the basics of our family, where we came from, schools we went to and future goals, we've got that covered." By habit, she smoothed the gunmetal-gray pencil skirt down before sitting, even though it was so tight it wasn't moving anywhere without some assistance on her part. This was definitely one of her size-fourteen days.

"They won't ask us questions like that. All they're really concerned about is the wedding date and who'll be designing your gown."

And yet his email had asked questions like "What's your favorite movie?" and "Do you read while sitting on your father's back porch?"

"Well, I'd think that would be obvious," she said and tried her best not to think of how handsome he looked sitting behind his cherrywood desk in that mammoth burgundy office chair.

He was just a guy and there was no need for her to act any differently because she'd thought about this guy all night long.

"The others on my team will be here in a few moments. After I make the introductions, they'll take you to an office we had set up for you and get you started on the integration."

"But you're going to stay here," she said slowly. "You have other work to do. More important work."

He ran a hand over his chin and sat back in his chair. For endless moments he didn't speak, only stared at her as if he were memorizing everything about her. It made her wonder if he was possibly reconsidering this distance he'd decided to put between them, but then he cleared his throat and shook his head.

"I run an entire department as well as a few outside projects. I can't be at every meeting."

Nor did she need him at every meeting with her. She was being silly when she was supposed to be presenting a strong and unshakable front. That had to stop now.

"Great. I'm ready to get started. There's nothing on our agenda for tonight, so I'll make some plans to take in another play or possibly do some shopping to pick up something nice for my dad." And he didn't need to know all of that.

"Sounds good," he told her and went back to staring at whatever papers were on his desk.

Well, that hadn't been awkward at all. Except, yeah, it had.

Obviously, Major wasn't as good as she was about being calm, cool and collected. When Ken and Jenner, who'd been in her first meeting, came into the room, she stood and shook their hands. Major made more formal introductions and they ushered her out of his office. He didn't say another word to her and she didn't bother to look back at him or say anything else to him, either. If this was how they were to conduct their working relationship, so be it. She hadn't signed up for anything more, anyway.

Three days later, Nina sat in the backseat of the town car looking out the window while Claude drove through traffic. This afternoon her style was sexy bohemian. At least, that's what Lila had told her three hours ago when she'd entered Nina's hotel room as if she were a runway model.

"You're going to look subtly sexy in this, honey!"

Nina had smiled at the woman's exaggeration as she spoke. She was getting used to how the woman talked and worked. And since this was the first runway show she'd ever attended in person, Nina figured she'd trust the stylist's directive. Riley had also told Nina she could decline to wear anything Lila suggested if she truly didn't like it or felt uncomfortable, but Nina was finding it pretty easy to trust the woman's judgment.

And true to form, Lila had been correct. The light material fell over her body like a soft breath, the muted-color stripes complementing her complexion. The plunging halter neckline was super sexy. She wondered how Major would react to seeing her in the dress.

Number three on his list of things they weren't going to do anymore was "touch each other sexually." And he hadn't, not since the night they'd had the hard, fast and totally titillating sex in her hotel room.

Of course, not touching had been much easier since they'd only been together one other time following the meeting in his office the day after their sexcapade.

Yesterday's lunch had been at Sarabeth's Central Park South, a restaurant where Desta knew they would retain maximum visibility. And she'd been right; they'd been stared at the entire time they were eating by other guests at the restaurant and even some of the staff. Nina was certain that a few people snuck pictures on their cell phones. But there'd been no touching. In fact, Major seemed to have gone out of his way to be as reserved as he possibly could—a fact that was slowly starting to bug her.

Not for the obvious reasons. She wasn't falling for him and didn't need him to reciprocate feelings that weren't there. But they did need to appear comfortable with each other for their charade to be believable.

Nina brushed those ideas from her mind as the car came to a stop in front of what looked like an industrial building. The itinerary stated she would be attending an intimate showing of RGF's couture gowns with Major.

"I'll walk you inside," Claude said when he opened the door for her.

Nina stepped out onto a quiet sidewalk in the Financial District, which was in stark contrast to the streets around her hotel or the RGF building. Claude closed the car door and walked with her a few feet until he could open a huge steel door for her to enter.

Inside, the place looked very different. Golden lights hung in large circles from an exposed-beam ceiling, creating soft light that mingled with the natural light pouring in from a wall of paned windows. Bleached hardwood floors stretched throughout and up the wide staircase.

"I'll call when I'm ready," she told Claude after she'd looked around, but he was already shaking his head.

"No need. Mr. Gold informed me that he would take care of your transportation for the remainder of the evening."

Oh he did, did he? Well she wondered what that meant.

But it was too late to think too hard on that because Maurice came up to her, devilishly handsome smile already in place.

"Hey, Nina. How are you?"

"I'm great. How's everything going here? Is there anything I can do to help?"

His thick brows furrowed, an action she'd seen Major do on a few occasions. It was amazing how much alike the two of them were without being identical. There was, of course, a resemblance—but there were differences, as well. While Major seemed to always be in control of his thoughts and actions, Maurice gave off a more relaxed demeanor. His ready smile, and that twinkle in his eyes she knew women were most likely dying for, identified him as the more extroverted twin.

"Not at all. We've got a great event staff and they're

taking care of everything. How've your first few days been at the fashion house?"

"So far, so good," she replied. "The integration went better than expected and we've already started to see sales."

"Cool. That sounds like a good sign."

"It is. And this place is great, so I know the show will be terrific. I'm really excited to be here." And that wasn't a part of the charade.

"The production team has put a lot of planning into it, so I'm sure you're right and it'll be terrific. But we're about to start and I was told to escort you to your seat."

He extended his arm to her and she accepted it, telling herself there was no need to ask who'd sent him. It was Major, who was obviously still trying to keep his distance.

The room they entered was full of photographers standing with cameras in hand, and she was willing to bet there were several reporters, bloggers and fashion journalist seated in the chairs positioned in rows around a glossy white runway.

The show started seconds after she sat, and she crossed her legs, trying to ignore the empty seat beside her. Maurice had walked behind a black curtain and, when Nina looked around, she didn't notice anyone else. But there were many eyes on her, so instead of looking the way she felt—confused and teetering on angry—she smiled and pushed one heavy curl of hair behind her ear. Anything was better than the obvious—that Major wasn't with her.

The music was hip-hop, the models were amazing and the gowns exquisite. When the show was over, Nina stood, clapping just as loudly as anyone else in the room. Until Major stepped up beside her.

"Glad you're enjoying yourself," he said when he leaned in to whisper in her ear.

"Glad you could finally join me," she replied without turning to look at him.

Maurice and two other men stepped through the black curtain with smiles and partial bows as the crowd continued to applaud in appreciation of the twelve gowns they'd just been treated to. Cameras were busy clicking throughout the space.

"We're going to go out this side door before the crowd begins to disperse. The room is set up for a press conference, but Maurice and the designers from today's collection are prepared to deal with it. We're just here to be seen."

He spoke to her like he would to any other employee and Nina tried her best to accept his cool demeanor as the new norm.

"Fine. Shall we go now?"

This time she did look at him, but she ignored the way the beige jacket hung enticingly on his broad shoulders. The white shirt that molded to his chest and the matching beige slacks completed what should have been a bland outfit choice but instead, on him, was just another symbol of how attractive this man really was. He nodded at her and she stepped in front of him, walking toward the only exit she saw and praying he was following closely behind her. Otherwise it might appear that she was angry and walking away from him, something that would most likely set tongues to wagging.

"It should only take twenty minutes, then we have reservations for dinner. After that we'll be done for the night."

"I read the itinerary, Major. I know what we have to do tonight."

He snapped his lips shut tightly and when she thought he might give a different retort, the first of the reporters filed into the room. Maurice came up behind them and Major clapped one hand on his brother's shoulder while shaking the other.

"Another slam dunk," he said.

"You bet your ass!" Maurice replied. "Cordell and Expo are phenomenal designers. This limited Spring in the City line is going to do great, especially once it hits the overseas market."

As if to magnify his words, Cordell Spriggs and Expo—one name only—the designers who had walked the runway and taken their bows with Maurice, came up to join them.

"Congratulations," Nina said, looking at each of them. "The dresses were fabulous."

"Thanks," Cordell said. "You should wear one to something. Maybe as your second outfit at the reception. We can make some changes, cater it specifically to you and your theme. Have you selected a theme for the wedding yet?"

Her mouth opened then shut, and then she simply

shrugged. "Not just yet. But your gowns have definitely given me some ideas."

"It's time to get the press conference started," Major interjected. "We don't want to mess up our timeline."

"He's right," Maurice added after a questioning look between Major and Nina.

Maurice stepped up to the podium, an act that quieted the crowd already assembled in the room.

"Thank you for coming this afternoon. Now, as promised, for the next fifteen minutes, we're going to take a few questions."

A woman in the front row raised her hand and immediately stood.

"I have a question for the new addition to the Gold family, Nina Fuller," she said pointedly. "What's it like working with your fiancé? You've joined the Gold family on two levels—business and pleasure. How did you and Major manage to keep not only your engagement but also your new business partnership a secret for so long?"

Silence filled the room as all eyes rested on her. For a few seconds, Nina wondered if she should speak and, if so, what she would say. Maurice came to the rescue.

"Let me clarify, Cordell, Expo and myself will accept questions about today's show."

"Then why are they here?" the reporter persisted with a nod of her head at Nina and Major. "Are they just showpieces for the company?"

She was brash and persistent, wearing a black

jumpsuit and red mules on her feet. The way she was staring at Nina said she knew something that nobody else knew. Or that she was making an assumption that maybe others were too afraid to make.

"If the Fashion House Playboy is actually getting married, why can't we talk to him or his fiancée about it? Why wasn't the business collaboration announced the other night at the Sip 'n' Chat? Oh, and the most important question, where's her engagement ring?"

It took every ounce of control Nina possessed to not look down at her left hand or the finger she knew was missing an engagement ring. Dammit! Why hadn't she thought of that in her quest to make this fake plan seem as real as possible?

A better question: Why should they have to talk about anything they didn't want to, or that wasn't directly related to this show? But then, that's how this marketing plan was supposed to work—to spark interest and keep the buzz going around the Golds and their new bridal collection. It was her debut in the industry and its very public lifestyle, so if she didn't like invasive questions about an engagement ring she probably should've been wearing, well then, she'd just have to get over it.

"I'm not in the habit of answering questions about my personal life," Nina said to the shock of everyone in the room, except maybe the reporter.

Nina moved until she was behind the podium, multiple microphones banked on the edge to point directly at her.

"But I recognize your need to intrude, especially since we made such a bold and exciting announcement just a few days ago."

"Exactly," the reporter replied with a look of measured satisfaction. "Shall I repeat my question?"

Nina held her gaze and smiled. "That's not necessary. Major and I believe in keeping our personal relationship to ourselves. So while we've announced our engagement, and you'll probably be hearing a lot more about the upcoming wedding plans, everything else between us, including the ring, will stay that way. Regardless of how many surprise questions are tossed at us. And on the business front, the At Your Service app is designed to work alongside fashion houses to offer customers a complete experience. There was an announcement on the home pages of RGF's domestic and international websites a few days ago, which is how I presume you found out, so that hardly qualifies as a secret."

The woman's smirk faltered a bit at Nina's words and, out of the corner of her eye, Nina could see Maurice grinning. She didn't bother to try to see Major's reaction. He probably wasn't having any.

"So you've been dating for four months and now you're getting married. How nice. When's the big day? Have you picked out a dress? Will Riley be one of your bridesmaids? I must admit I thought if there were going to be a wedding in the Gold family, it would be Riley. But then again, she is dating the company's biggest competitor, so making that union legal would probably be a stretch."

This woman is a piece of work. Correction, she's an ass.

"So glad you mentioned Riley. She's been such a great sister-in-law-to-be these past few days. You're correct in assuming she'll be in the wedding, along with my sisters, and we'll all be wearing dresses from the Golden Bride Collection. I'm very excited about selecting the perfect gowns. Are there any more questions about the wedding plans, or should I turn this over to the talented men who made to-day's show possible?"

Another reporter thankfully spoke up, directing a question to Expo and the phenomenal—his word, not hers—turquoise gown they'd just seen in the show's finale.

As Nina stepped away from the podium, Major reached for her hand. She hesitated just a second, looking up at him in question. His facial expression was still grim and he didn't offer any explanation, but she placed her hand in his and stood beside him for the remainder of the press conference. If he'd thought them not touching for the past few days was in any way going to dull their attraction to each other, he was wrong.

Warmth instantly spread through her body at his touch and her fingers clung to his as they walked. He didn't say a word until they were in the backseat of the car, and that was when he pulled her so close her lips parted on instinct in preparation for his kiss.

CHAPTER EIGHT

"I'M NOT GOING to kiss you, not again." The words hurt his throat as they came out in a scratchy growl.

His chest was heaving as anger poured through him. How dare that annoying Morgana McCloud question Nina the way she did? Major should have known this would happen. There were some reporters and bloggers who hated that he never gave them the comments or interviews they requested. Morgana hated that he'd never accommodated her and that he'd never accepted any of the advances she'd made toward him. If he were the loneliest man on earth, he wouldn't have sought the company of such a woman. He'd known a woman like her before and had sworn to never again get sucked into their clutches.

Now the news about At Your Service was out and that had him wondering once again about the division of Brand Integrated that involved accessorizing for fashion house designs that was very similar to Nina's. When Brand Integrated made its appearance in the fashion world, there was no doubt that very fact would be mentioned. But their charade would be over by then.

"I…um, I didn't ask you to kiss me," she said and then licked her lips.

But she didn't pull away from him. They were in the backseat of the limo he'd reserved for tonight. He released the grasp on her arm and extended one hand to press the button that would close the privacy barrier between them and the front seat.

"It's what got me in trouble the first time. The kiss." He shook his head because he knew he sounded irrational, but that was exactly how he was feeling. It was how he'd been feeling for the past few days, the longer he'd stayed away from her. "Kissing is too intimate. I'm not going to do it again," he stated, trying to calm his tone because her eyes had grown a little wider.

"I'm not going to ask you to kiss me, or to do anything with me, Major." She looked down to where his other hand still gripped her arm and then back up to him in question.

He pulled back as if he'd been burned, cursing at the mere sight of his fingers pressing into her arm. "I'm sorry," he said and sat back against the seat. "I don't know what's going on."

And that was the truth. He didn't know what was happening to him because whatever it was had never happened before. So he'd slept with her, big deal. He'd slept with other women before, and he and Nina were pretending to be a couple, so it should've been fair game. Everything that had happened between them up to this point had been consensual, so why had he needed to write that list creating rules to separate them? And if he'd thought that list was the best plan for them to move forward without any threat of entanglements later, then why had he spent these past few days feeling like crap and needing desperately to be alone with her, to see her, to touch her?

Nina cleared her throat. She sat back and smoothed the skirt of her dress, letting her hands rest in her lap. "Look, maybe you don't have to take this seriously, but I do. Everything we do from the night of the Sip 'n' Chat to the day we have our fake argument is part of my first impression to the fashion industry.

"My work so far has been on a much smaller scale, but this is my opportunity to show the industry who I am and what my business can do for them. We're supposed to be an engaged couple. But I've gotta tell you, we need to do better. That reporter in there was intentional in her questions. There's doubt about this relationship. For whatever reason, she doesn't believe us and if one person doesn't, then others may be wondering, as well."

She was right. Appearances were everything, especially in this industry. Wasn't that why Desta and Riley had come up with this idea in the first place? It's why they knew including a Gold in the campaign would ensure its success. And now, this woman who had no stake in his family company was essentially telling him he wasn't pulling his weight.

"What do you think we should do?" If she said get naked in the back of this limo right now, he'd do it. Damn him, he would.

"First, you've gotta relax and you've gotta act like a man in love."

His head snapped to hers and he saw that she was staring at him. She looked spectacular today. He'd noticed the moment he'd peeked through the curtain and seen her walking in on Maurice's arm. A spurt of jealousy had pierced his chest before he'd cursed and pushed it away. But he hadn't been able to look away from her, not for minutes after she'd taken her seat.

The dress wasn't formfitting but flowing breezily down past her ankles. The halter top cupped her breasts the same way his hands had before. And the muted colors complemented everything from her skin tone to her eye color, to the soft, barrel curls that fell past her shoulders.

"I'm not going to give the press the innermost details of my life, they're not entitled to that." No one was.

"But you'll agree to a stunt that has the prime purpose of playing to the public? Look, whatever we say to them is a lie. It's all a lie." She shrugged as if it were that simple. "We're not engaged. We're not a happily-in-love couple and we never will be. This is a means to an end for both of us."

He wouldn't kiss her. Major had sworn he wouldn't kiss her again. But the touching rule? That was out the window. So he closed the slight distance between them on the seat and he reached for her. She came willingly, sitting across his lap.

"This…" he said quietly. "The tug you feel between us? The one that starts deep in your gut and

reaches out, wanting to cling to something, someone… We cannot deny this. You can't deny it."

She shook her head. "No. I can't. I'm not. But I'm
also not going to play this game with you. I'm okay
with taking our façade into the bedroom. I can separate work from personal. But I'm not going to be at
your call. Either we stick by your rules implicitly for
the duration of this agreement or we don't. There's
no in between and there's no up and down."

Basically, she was telling him to get it together.
As she had every right to since he was being a jerk
with this hands-off, hands-on situation.

He was impressed. He'd thought watching her
masterfully handle Morgana in that press conference
was awe-inspiring, but holding her on his lap while
she fundamentally just ripped him a new one was
damn commendable. He cupped her face in his hands
and leaned in. Her lips parted and he almost… Major
tilted his head and kissed her neck, suckling slightly,
creating a path to the skin between her breasts, which
was the softest he'd ever touched.

When her arms came around his shoulders and
she arched into him, he sighed with relief and with
resolution. He was going to play this game by her
rules, but first, he was going to have her again.

He continued running his tongue and lips over her
skin, moving his hands so that one was at the nape
of her neck, pulling her hair gently to tilt her head
back. The line of her neck was bare to him and Major
stared down as if he were a vampire, hungry for the
taste of her. He licked a straight path from between

her breasts up to her chin and back down again. She hissed and arched further in his arms. He loved kissing her. It was a fact he could not deny.

To push that thought out of his mind, he eased a hand beneath the halter top of her dress, cupping her bare breasts and sucking in a breath at how good it felt.

"Why do I want you so much?"

Had he said that aloud? He'd been thinking it so much, he no longer knew whether or not it was in his head or if he finally was ready to hear an answer.

"Take what you want," she whispered, bringing her hand up to cover his, moving it so they were both squeezing her breast. "Take what we both want."

Permission. She'd given it before and she was giving it again. Another woman may have walked away from him and this arrangement because of the ridiculous way he'd been acting these past few days. Stacia had walked away from him for less. Any other woman certainly wouldn't have come to his rescue at the press conference, after he'd asked for answers to his questions in that juvenile email he'd sent her. And she damn sure wouldn't be in his arms right now, asking him to give her what she needed.

What he *desperately* needed.

He pulled his hand away, running it down her torso and to her legs where he could pull the material of the dress up. Her legs were bare, and she opened them the moment he touched her skin.

"I'm gonna give you what you need, baby."

"Please," she whispered. "Please give it to me."

It took almost no effort to push the thin silk material of her panties to the side and slip his fingers along the warm folds of her pussy.

She moaned, the arm wrapped around his shoulders tightening against him.

"Yes, baby. You're so hot and ready for me. Ready for this pleasure."

He was, too. His jaw clenched with the need to sink himself so deep inside her that he could no longer think of his past mistakes with women, the present situation he found himself in, or the future that seemed to rest on this beautiful woman in his arms.

She gyrated against his fingers even before he could press them inside her.

"You're ready and you're hot."

"You're talking too much and not doing enough," she said, grabbing his hand with her free one and pressing it into her juncture.

He needed no further encouragement but eased two fingers deep into her, loving the feel of her inner muscles tightening against his intrusion. It was like a cave, a hot cavern of deliciousness that only he could taste, only he could have at this moment. It took him seconds to twist her around until she was lying flat on the seat. He dragged the panties down her legs, dropped them to the floor and propped her legs up onto his shoulders before dipping his head low. His mouth was on her in seconds, tongue stroking over the plump folds of her pussy, lapping up the thick nectar that tasted sweet sliding down the back of his throat.

She yelled out at the contact and he continued, reveling in the sound of her taking the pleasure he offered and the feel of her soft inner thighs rubbing against his face. He suckled her clit, taking the tight bud into his mouth and holding it there until she squirmed beneath him. When her hands went to the back of his head, pushing him further, he groaned and whispered, "Greedy little goddess."

But he gave her what she wanted, thrusting his tongue inside her and moving it with the same urgency he would have moved his dick if he were pounding into her.

"Yessssss."

He would never get tired of that hissing sound in her voice. Never get tired of the scent or taste of her. The taste that was melting all over his mouth at this moment. She moved with his motions, undulating her hips as she held him to her, giving as good as she was getting.

He worked his mouth over her until he thought his chest would explode with desire. Pulling back slightly, he sank his fingers into her again before dragging them out and letting one slide back to her rear. This time she sucked in a breath and held completely still. He rubbed his finger over the tight sphincter, using her juices to ease only the tip of his finger into her.

"Major, I don't... I can't," she whimpered.

He knew the feeling. He couldn't think, either, not past the need and the hunger. His mouth was on her again, tongue easing deep into her just as his finger

moved slowly into her other opening. She shivered
beneath him, and yelled out until he was certain anyone on the street would hear her. And with that cry
came her release, pouring like liquid heaven into
his mouth. Major swallowed and he held on tight to
the sensation moving through his body along with
her essence.

He'd never felt anything like this before and he
knew he never would again.

If somebody had told Nina that she'd have a backseat sexcapade in a black limousine, she would have
called them a bald-faced liar. Yet, here she sat, closer
to the window this time than she had before, staring out at the New York skyline while they drove to
her hotel. They'd decided to skip the restaurant and
Major was on his phone arranging for dinner to be
brought to them there.

She had an elbow propped up on the door, her
cheek leaning against a closed fist while thoughts of
what they'd done in the back of this limo ran through
her mind. Her inner thighs still tingled, and thoughts
about whether or not she was doing the right thing
ran rampant while her hormones continued to take
charge.

There simply was no more right thing to do other
than what she was doing. For too long she'd sacrificed everything for someone else, namely her family. Her father hadn't been the same after her mother
had left seventeen years ago. And while only twelve
at the time, Nina had known that it would be up to

her to help Jacoby in any way she could. And so she had. It had never occurred to her to do anything else. It had also never occurred to her that at almost thirty years old, she'd still be dedicating so much of her time to her father and her sisters. But not for the next five weeks. This time was for her, while all that she was doing would ultimately help her family, these days in this city, with this man, doing this job, were for her. And she planned to make the best of every minute.

Even if that meant spending every minute irrevocably aroused by a man she'd never imagined being with.

"The food will be there shortly after we arrive."

His voice jolted her out of her thoughts, and she sighed before looking over at him with a wan smile. "Thanks. I didn't really feel like being out in public again."

"That makes two of us," he said with a nod. "It's been a pretty long day."

"I bet. How long does it normally take to get ready for a show?" She'd been learning more about the inner workings of the industry while working with RGF. The business aspect of the design house seemed to be a smooth-running machine, but it definitely took the skill and expertise of every one of its three-hundred-plus employees. Before this week, it had been easy to believe her app's target was just the Gold family because they called all the shots and had made what was one of the world's most influential and successful Black-owned-and-operated fashion houses what it was today. But this past week she'd definitely learned differently.

"I don't personally do much with the planning of the shows. I make sure all the technology they need to facilitate them is up to par."

"A man of my heart," she said and then clapped her lips shut. It was probably best not to talk about her heart where he was concerned. This wasn't that type of party and she didn't want it to be. Watching her father nurse a broken heart was enough to swear her off any type of emotional connection with a man.

"The programs you've put in place at the fashion house are innovative and seem to be helping to keep things running smoothly," she continued, trying to stay focused.

He stuffed his phone into his pocket and looked over at her. "Technology is the way of the future. And nobody else in my family has the patience for it, so that became my contribution to the company."

Nina felt the same way.

Her sisters worked and sometimes—when berated and guilted to no end—contributed to the expenses associated with taking care of their father when his savings and insurance didn't meet the need. Her love of computers and desire to create had landed her a few contractual jobs that pulled them out of a financial bind a time or two, but she wanted something more stable, something that would allow them to live more comfortably without having to go through the guilt and arguments with her sisters.

"Everyone in your family seems to have found their niche," she said.

"Yeah. I think so."

"Did your parents always expect you'd go into the family business?" She figured if she talked more about his family, she'd feel less depressed about her own.

"Ah, yeah, I think so. I mean we didn't grow up with sketch pads in our hands or fashion magazines instead of literature for reading time. But we learned how much the company meant to our father and my grandfather at a very early age. We all went to college and selected a major with the notion that we'd bring that knowledge back to RGF. It was like an unspoken expectation."

"And none of you strayed. That's amazing and commendable. There's something to be said about family loyalty." Jacoby had taught her and her sisters that when they were young. While Nina knew it was her father's not-so-subtle jab at her mother's leaving, she could also see the overall value in the lesson.

Major didn't reply, but it didn't matter, they were already pulling up in front of her hotel.

Minutes later they were walking into her room.

"I'm just gonna go freshen up a bit. I'll be right back." She headed to the bedroom, did a quick washup and changed into leggings and a bright yellow shirt that hung past her hips, its black-sequined letters spelling "QUEEN" across her chest.

An hour later Major had removed his jacket and

they'd finished the most delicious stuffed cheese-burgers, fresh-cut fries and chocolate milkshakes she'd ever tasted. When he'd suggested they order from the burger place instead of some fancy restaurant, she'd almost hugged him. Now, full from the good food and amiable conversation, she sat back against the cushions and sighed.

"I'm sorry for being such a jerk these past few days." He was sitting with his head resting on the back of the couch, just like her, both with hands folded over now full stomachs.

"It wasn't how I intended to start this agreement between us," he continued.

"Me, either," she admitted. "I mean I really hadn't thought our pretending would lead to actual sex, but I wasn't totally bothered by it."

"I wasn't, either." He paused for a second. "At least, not while it was happening."

"What bothered you about it afterward?" Why she wanted to know, she had no clue. If Major Gold, the reputed Fashion House Playboy had some hang-ups about sex in real life, that was none of her concern.

"I didn't want to seem like I was taking advantage of the situation or mislead you in any way."

"Oh." She hadn't expected that answer. Truthfully, she didn't know what to expect from Major from one minute to the next, but this solemn, compassionate admission definitely wasn't it.

"Despite what the press says, I never want any woman I'm with to have misconceptions about what our relationship is or what it isn't. Even though our connection is more rooted in business, I feel obligated by the same standard."

"That's understandable. But so is being physically attracted to someone."

"I agree."

"So how did you manage to get this reputation that follows you around like a lost puppy, if you're so careful about how the women you date perceive your relationship?"

"When people don't have enough information, they make things up."

"And you don't care to give them more information," she said, thinking back to the way he'd refused to speak at the press conference.

"They're not entitled to know every aspect of my life. Nobody is unless I want it to be so. Just because my family is notable and our business is in the spotlight, doesn't mean I have to personally be there, as well."

She was quiet while she digested those words. Being in the spotlight had never been a problem for her, but she wondered if there was something to the thought that her family wasn't entitled to every aspect of her life, either.

"But you did date three different women in three days. That's gotta mean something." She chuckled lightly after the statement because the pang in her chest as she'd thought about her relationship with her family was far more uncomfortable than ever before.

"One was a distribution rep that was in town from London and was having problems with her laptop. Another was a family friend and a favor to my mother. The other was a real date that I'd scheduled weeks before and didn't feel comfortable backing out of at the last minute. Does that sound like the life of a playboy?"

It didn't. It actually sounded kind of lonely, because at no point had he said he "wanted" to be on a date with any of those women. At least Nina made the choice when and who she dated and, for the most part, she was active in that date. Major sounded as if he were just along for the ride.

"Well, you've got yourself a fiancée now, Major Gold." She reached out and grabbed his hand, lifting their arms up over their heads in a combined fist pump.

He laughed. It was the first time she'd heard the sound and she immediately liked it. She liked it a lot.

"Yeah, I guess I do. And she's a pretty terrific fiancée if I must say so."

"Oh, yes," she said when she'd lowered their hands. "Definitely say so. Frequently."

They both laughed then, and in that moment Nina realized she'd never felt as at ease with another man before. They weren't thinking about having sex— or at least she wasn't—and they weren't discussing work. They were just talking, just being, and she just liked it. A lot.

CHAPTER NINE

THE DUPLEX ON the Upper East Side was bigger than two of her apartments back in York. The stripped-wood flooring and private rooftop terrace were amazing. Nina loved it and she'd told Major so when he'd brought her yesterday to stay here for the remaining month of their agreement.

Today was the first bridal dress fitting. Last week, she and Riley had gone to lunch and afterward sat in Riley's office for the duration of the afternoon going through sketches of wedding gowns, fabric swatches and color wheels. By the time they were finished, six sketches had been selected for Nina, there were three color-scheme finalists and she'd discovered that when it was her turn, Riley didn't want a big wedding.

"Something small, maybe on an island, with just our family and closest friends. That's the perfect wedding for me," Riley had said.

Nina had noted the light in her eyes when she'd spoken about her wedding ideas. A spark that Nina presumed was from being in love and actually believing that a wedding was on the horizon at some point. Nina didn't have that type of imagination.

But she was ready for today. Sitting at the table next to the biggest set of windows with the best northern view of the city, she monitored the activity on her app in correlation to the sales directly from RGF. All the numbers were up. This trial run was going well so far. She clapped her hands together and reached for her mug, frowning when she sipped very cold coffee.

Minutes later she walked out of the gorgeous gray-and-white kitchen with a bottled water and a banana when she heard the doorbell ring.

Somebody was early.

Nina went to the door and smiled when she saw Riley looking fashionably chic in dark jeans, a tan blouse and heels that were way too high for a Saturday afternoon. After greeting Riley and stepping to the side so she could come in, Nina looked down at her weekend attire: gray sweatpants with a matching sweatshirt that was a couple sizes too big, so she looked like a sack of potatoes.

"Sorry I'm so early. I was just eager to get this started and Chaz is out of town until Wednesday. This place is great," she said as she walked straight through the living room/dining room and into the kitchen.

Nina followed.

"Yes, it is. I know Major wanted to make sure we were in a nice place for the fitting and photo shoot, but this might be a little above and beyond." She'd been thinking that ever since last night when Claude had carried her bags from the hotel to the car and driven her over here.

Riley leaned on the island. The eight-foot-long, gray-and-white-marble waterfall island had a stainless steel sink in its center and five clear-backed stools along one side. Nina slid onto one and set her water bottle on the marble top before peeling back the layers of her banana.

"You think he rented this apartment just for the photo shoot?" Riley asked.

"Of course he did. Why else would he rent it?" She took a bite of the fruit and chewed it slowly.

Riley watched her and slipped a grape from the fruit bowl into her mouth.

"I suggested we do the fitting at the office, where we normally have our sample showings. There's a runway there and space to do anything else we wanted."

"That would've been a good option, too," Nina said and seconds later realized the point Riley was trying to make.

"The office is only ten minutes from here and, just like the rest of us, Major spends most of his time there. So this apartment was kinda extra effort."

Nina chewed on another piece of her banana, knowing the woman watched and waited for her next comment to refute the assumption that there was a personal reason Major had gotten this place specifically for her.

"Well, your brother is smart, I can tell you that.

The light in this place is amazing. Pictures are going to come out great. How soon do you think they'll show up in a newspaper or tabloid?" Nina took her last bite of the banana before throwing the peel in the garbage.

Riley was still moving with deliberate slowness, putting one grape at a time into her mouth while watching Nina as if she thought some different words were about to spout out of her mouth. If Major's sister thought she was about to tell her that they were lovers, she was mistaken. While Nina enjoyed Riley's company and had secretly wished her own sisters were as mature and business-minded, there was no way she was telling Riley that there were aspects of this fake engagement that she and Major had decided to make come true.

"We only hire the most reputable photographers in the industry and they've each signed a privacy agreement. We'll get first look and final approval of any pictures to be published and have already sold them to *Infinity* magazine. It's not a fashion-only magazine, but it's Black-owned and respectable. My father is good friends with the owners, Reginald and Bruce Donovan. They're doing a complete spread on the engagement."

It made sense that they would contact a reputable magazine for a story about this engagement. Calling that magazine respectable, however, flew rudely in the face of the fact that the Golds knew this engagement was a sham. So they were asking this great Black-owned magazine to lie. Nina twisted the top off her water and took a gulp to get the bad taste of that idea out of her mouth.

"I know what you're thinking," Riley said. "And remember the argument and breakup that's planned for the end of this campaign. Nobody will know that it wasn't ever real to start with."

"Morgana McCloud doesn't think it's real." Nina couldn't believe she was still thinking about that reporter after Major had explained the woman's fixation with him.

Morgana had written two stories since the one after that show that featured her, Major, the engagement and the mention of the At Your Service/RGF business venture. In each she'd placed a lot of emphasis on where Nina had come from and how she was apparently "marrying up." The words stung because Nina knew she wasn't getting married at all. The only consolation was that other tabloids had run with Morgana's lead but were actually highlighting the innovative idea that the two businesses connect. Still, Nina couldn't shake the feeling that Morgana was specifically feeling some type of way about her.

"She's fishing and has no source that will tell her any different," Riley stated.

It had been suggested that Nina bring her sisters to the fitting since Morgana had mentioned her quote about who was going to be in the bridal party, but Nina had been vehemently against that. She wished she'd thought about what she was saying when she'd said it, but there was no way she would bring Daisy and Angie into this farce. As much as she wanted this to seem believable, she hadn't considered that it would put her family in the spotlight. Now, with Morgana hot on her trail, she wasn't sure how long she'd be able to stop that from happening.

The doorbell rang again and Nina quickly slid off the stool to go answer it. She usually liked talking to Riley but she couldn't shake the feeling that their conversation was about to shift in a direction Nina didn't want to go. When she opened the door this time she fully expected to see Lila and her crew, but instead Marva Gold smiled at her.

"Mrs. Gold. Ah, hello. I wasn't expecting you to attend the fitting." And now she was a little more uncomfortable, not just because of the conversation with Riley, but because there were two Gold women in the room with her.

"Hello, Nina. When Riley told me about today's events, I thought it only right that I be here. Do you mind?"

The woman was Black royalty with her tawny-brown complexion and thick silver-streaked hair that was curled and pulled back from her face with a thin black band. She wore a white pantsuit with a pale pink blouse beneath it. Diamond studs dotted her ears and a thin bracelet cuffed her left arm. On her left ring finger was a massive diamond. Nina instantly balled her hands into fists, hoping nobody would see that she still wasn't wearing an engagement ring. Major hadn't mentioned it since Morgana's comment about it—or the lack of it—at the fashion show, and there was no way Nina was asking him to get her a ring. Her pride just wouldn't allow it, not even to make this fake engagement look good.

"No, of course not, I don't mind at all. Come on in," she said and stepped out of the way to let the woman in. She was about to close the door but heard someone clearing their throat.

Nina pulled the door open again and Lila came in with the crew, clothing racks, bags, boxes and her normal flair. By the time Nina closed the door this time she was breathing a sigh of relief that a buffer— or rather a whole group of buffers—had arrived. This should definitely take the pressure off.

It didn't.

Two hours later and the fitting was in full swing. Three photographers from *Infinity* had arrived. Anya and Cheree were pulling the gowns and matching them with shoes and veils while Riley and her mother sat on the couch giving their opinions as Nina walked out into the living room. Garen would quickly give her hair a new look each time she tried on a gown, talking her to death while he worked. And Lila was announcing each gown as if she were the emcee of her own fashion show.

"Now this long-sleeved nude gown includes a pleated tulle overlay and a dusting of shimmering gold Chantilly lace," Lila stated the moment Nina entered the living room.

The photographers immediately moved in, each capturing a picture from a different angle.

"I'm not sure about this one," Nina said as she

moved closer. "It might be a little too nude. My father would have a conniption if he saw this."

Growing up, her father had been extremely strict about his daughters' clothes—how much showed through sheer or tight-fitted items. Although Nina believed she possessed her own style and appreciated clothes that made her feel sexy, some of Jacoby's teachings had stayed with her into adulthood.

"I can understand that," Marva added. She'd risen from the couch and was now standing next to Nina, lifting the tulle out so that it flared even more from her waist down.

"But this is a classic look. It's formfitting but gives the illusion of being natural," Riley added when she joined her mother, standing on the opposite side of Nina.

"And it's so sexy. There's just a hint of innocence in that it covers her completely, but that punch of desire as it hugs her natural curves," Lila added.

"I agree," Marva said. "I love how each of the gowns complements a diverse body type. That's one thing this line does very well."

Riley, who wasn't nearly as curvy as Nina, stood back, one arm across her chest, a hand to her chin while she continued to survey Nina. "Definitely something we were aiming for," she said. "But I can see what she's saying. If I wore this, Dad would have solid opinions about the almost sheerness."

Marva chuckled. "You're right about that. Fathers can be very particular about their girls."

"Too particular," Riley quipped.

"You can say that again," Nina added.

"Okay, let's try another one," Lila prompted.

The photographers had snapped photos of the two Gold women standing with her, adjusting and commenting on the gown. In her mind, Nina could visualize how it would look in print. Normal. Sentimental. A slice of time a woman and her family would remember for the rest of their lives. A pang of unexpected sadness hit her.

They went to the next dress and the next, repeating the process until deciding on a gown that evening. While Nina's personal favorite had been a wine-colored tulle over an ivory fitted bodice and A-line skirt, they'd collectively chosen the classic white trumpet dress with bias-cut organza tiers and rosettes that Garen called romantic.

"I'm exhausted," Nina said when she returned to the living room once again, this time back in her comfortable sweats as she dropped down onto the cushioned chair across from the couch.

"We should grab some dinner," Riley suggested.

"Oh no, I have to get back home," Marva said. "Your father and I have an engagement this evening."

Riley nodded. "That's right, the Rutherford Gala is tonight."

"Yes. You and your brothers should be there, as well. You know your father likes to present a united front at these gatherings," Marva said as she reached for her purse.

"The Rutherfords are old friends of yours and

Dad's. They have nothing to do with us or the company, so we figured we could skip."

"Yes." Marva nodded. "The four of you like to team up whenever possible."

The words weren't spoken with any sting, just a mother's love for her children.

Riley stood with her mother and hugged her. "But we still love you lots," she said with a huge smile just before kissing Marva's cheek.

The sadness that had punched Nina in the gut earlier this afternoon now draped her body like a horrific plague. Lynn Fuller had left her family seventeen years ago, so why did it feel like it was only yesterday?

Nina was just standing when Marva came over and pulled her in for a hug.

"You look tired and we've monopolized your entire day. We'll get out of your hair now so you can get some rest."

Nina had been thinking of doing that and probably squeezing some work in while she ate something quick, like a chicken salad sandwich, in bed. Now, however, a hot bath and burying herself beneath the covers for the next few hours seemed like a better plan.

"Thank you," Nina said without mentioning how good that brief hug felt.

"We're going to have a girls' night soon before we get too crazy with planning and appearances." This time it was Riley who stepped up to pull Nina into a hug.

How did these women know exactly what she needed right now?

"But you'll join us tomorrow for Sunday dinner," Marva said and turned to walk toward the door.

"Oh yes. That's a good idea, Mom." Riley had picked up her purse and was now walking behind her mother.

Nina followed them, not sure what was happening. She'd been here for two weeks and hadn't attended any private family gatherings. "Ah, tomorrow? Dinner?"

"Yes," Riley said, looking over her shoulder at her. "Sunday dinner is a Gold family tradition. It takes place at six every Sunday evening, unless we're all out of town. Then it's usually a phone call from wherever we are in the world."

"Because, above all else, family is first," Marva said.

Nina looked at her and could almost hear her father quoting another African proverb. Jacoby did that often, especially after Lynn had left them. It was as if he'd thought by pouring the teachings of the importance of family from his ancestors into their heads, they would never make the same mistakes.

"Nina, are you okay? You seem so different now. Would you like me to order you something to eat before I go?" Riley asked after her mother had opened the door and they'd walked through.

Nina stayed in the apartment, placing her hand on the doorknob to steady herself. "No. Thanks, really, for being so kind to me, but I'm okay. I have some stuff in the refrigerator and I'm going to have a bath and just chill for the evening." Or wallow in how much she'd missed by not having a mother-daughter relationship to lean on, or even a sister relationship that didn't feel like everyone was leaning on *her* all the time.

Marva stepped close, cupping Nina's cheek. "All will seem better in the morning," she said before kissing Nina's forehead. "I'll see you tomorrow."

Riley smiled at Nina. "Yes, tomorrow. But call me tonight if you just want to chat."

"I will," she said with a nod, really believing that she would reach out to Riley if she could no longer bear the silence or her thoughts tonight.

Nina was lying in bed two hours later, watching some old movie on the television, when her cell phone rang. She glanced over at the phone and saw her father's name on the screen. It was as if Jacoby had somehow known she needed her family tonight.

Nina smiled as she answered. "Hi, Dad. How are you?" She sat up, the pillows behind her back.

"Not too good since I found out my daughter's been lying to me."

Oh no, what had Daisy or Angie done now?

"Who's been lying to you and about what?"

"You and you know what."

Okay, she had to refrain from replying with a "what" because her father wouldn't like that. Instead she rephrased her question.

"I don't understand what you're saying, Dad. What's going on?"

"How's it possible that my oldest child is getting married and I didn't know about it? Just who is giving you away and to what type of man? I don't understand these young folks that don't respect any kind of tradition. He couldn't come ask me for your hand in marriage? Or maybe you didn't want him to."

CHAPTER TEN

"IT'S NOT WHAT you think, Dad," she replied after the silence had stretched too long and she knew her father was getting antsy for a response.

"Well now, I think I can still read pretty well. Daisy brought me my papers when she went to the market for me the other day. And I sat out on the back porch like I always do and read them. Damn near choked on my coffee when I saw those pictures of you and some guy named Major Gold announcing your engagement. What kind of name is that for a man, anyway? And now you're in that big city planning some fancy wedding when you know I've always told you girls that you should have a traditional African wedding. It's what your grandparents always wanted."

Damn, he was bringing up the African wedding.

After going on permanent disability leave from the hospital where he'd worked in the maintenance department seven years ago, Jacoby had developed a routine of fixing a pot of fresh-ground coffee every morning. He'd pour that coffee into the old, stained, white carafe with the faded flowers on the front and take it to the back porch with him. There he'd sit from eight to ten, listening to the birds and smelling the fresh morning air—at least that's how he explained it.

She should be pissed at Daisy for taking him the paper with her picture on it, but then again, at least her sister was doing her part to help take care of him.

"It's my job," she said and then wanted to snatch the words back.

"You're working as some man's fiancée?"

That sounded awful.

"His family's company is the one I came here to meet with. They've agreed to give me a six-week trial period." She paused and took a deep breath. "In exchange for this opportunity, I agreed to be the guy's fake fiancée. It's to help with a sales campaign they're running. That's all, Dad. It's not real."

And that somehow didn't make it sound better. She was sure her father would feel the same way, which was precisely why she hadn't told him these details.

"Why would you agree to such foolishness? Running around with some man you're not in love with, trying to fool the world into believing you're something that you're not."

"I need this deal to work, Dad." It was as simple as she could explain her reason for being there.

"Why? You were doing just fine here starting your business. You can't always put the cart before the horse, Nina. Growing a business takes time. I don't know why my girls always want everything with such urgency. Never want to take the time to see how things will turn out, just like…" His words trailed off and Nina tried not to feel the bite of the comparison he'd almost made between her and her mother.

"I'm not doing this just for me. I want you to be able to move into that facility we looked at a few months ago."

He was quiet for too long and she braced herself for an explosion of temper. Although it didn't happen frequently, Jacoby could yell and argue just like his daughters.

"If I wanted to go into that facility, I could. I've got some money saved up. You don't need to worry about me. I want you to be happy. That's all I've ever wanted was for all of my girls to be happy."

And by "all" of his girls, Nina knew he was including her mother. Lynn hadn't been happy with the man she'd married and the three children she'd given birth to. But that wasn't their fault. Nina only wished her father would finally come to that conclusion. She also wished that everything her mother had done didn't affect everything she was doing now. Nina needed to believe that if she wanted a relationship for herself it could flourish. But the demise of her parents' marriage had a much bigger impact on her than she'd ever believed before she'd met Major.

"Your savings isn't enough, Dad. There are ongoing expenses and we have the portions of your medical bills that the insurance doesn't cover. I'm just trying to do what's necessary for my family. If relatives help each other, what evil can hurt them? You taught me that." Tossing old proverbs back at her father might not be the best idea, but it was all she had. She wasn't going to let him talk her out of what she'd started.

"I don't want to be a burden," he said quietly. "And I definitely don't want you degrading yourself in any way to help me."

"I'm not. I promise. Major is a good guy and this is a wonderful opportunity for my business to get the exposure it needs."

"If he's such a good guy, why can't he find himself a real wife?"

Nina didn't have an answer for that. In fact, hours after the conversation with her father while she lay in the dark bedroom, she let herself think about Major finding his real wife and how she would ultimately feel knowing it wasn't her.

Maybe if she were a different type of woman, one who hadn't been showed so early in life the devastation that failed love could bring. Perhaps then she could allow herself the dream of falling in love with a man like Major and him falling in love with her. But that barrier she'd had no choice but to build around her heart just wouldn't allow her to trust those types of thoughts. It wouldn't allow her to hope for something that just couldn't be.

"I wasn't expecting to see you here," Major said when Nina was escorted into the den at his parents' house on Sunday evening.

He hadn't been avoiding her this time. Something had come up at Brand Integrated that had taken him all weekend to deal with. But he'd wanted to see her.

Major had also been dealing with the engagement ring. Among all the other plans, that detail had somehow fallen to the wayside. It had taken six days for the ring Major wanted for Nina to be ready and it had been delivered to his apartment yesterday morning. He'd refused to address why he felt a jewelry designer was required for a fake engagement, but he wanted the ring on Nina's finger before their next public appearance.

Now, she was here, in the house he'd grown up in, looking around the room, one hand to her chest before she settled her gaze on him. "Sorry, still trying to catch my breath from that magnificent foyer I just walked through. That staircase is breathtaking, and I've never seen anything like the brown-and-gold marble floor." She gave her head a little shake and then cleared her throat, dropping her arm to her side. "But yeah, your mother invited me to dinner while we were at the fitting yesterday," she said, waving to Maurice and RJ who were sitting in chairs behind him.

"She was at the fitting?" Was that on the itinerary?

"Yes, Mom was at the fitting. Everything doesn't have to be on the itinerary, Major. It's all right to be impulsive sometimes," Riley said as she entered the room. The smile on his sister's face solidified the feeling of dread in the pit of Major's stomach. "We had a wonderful afternoon. The gowns were all so beautiful on Nina. We had a terrible time deciding on the final one."

RJ stood and went to the bar in the far corner of the room to fix himself a drink. "Why? It's not like there's really going to be a wedding."

The room went silent for a few seconds and Riley chimed in again.

"The name of the game is to get customers to buy into the whole process, which is why we have *Infinity* doing the six-page spread for June. The dress is the center of any wedding, so it made sense that we start there. Next week there will be coverage of our venue hunt and talking to artists about the reception." Riley, wearing a long, pleated green skirt and casual T-shirt, sat on the coal-colored couch, leaning back on its huge fluffy pillows.

RJ shook his head as he dropped ice cubes into his glass. "For all this effort, I sure hope this fake wedding campaign works to our advantage."

"Oh come on, RJ. Man, you were just talking about the bump in orders in the casual wear sections," Maurice said.

"I saw that, too," Nina added, excitement clear in her voice. "Since the media has decided that, in addition to the wedding, they want to do stories on who I am and our business partnership, I took a chance and ran a digital ad on some of the fashion blogs and did numerous posts on my Instagram page, tagging fashion groups and other influencers."

Major noted how lovely she looked in a long

animal-print skirt. He wondered if she and Riley had conferred on their attire for tonight. Her plain tan T-shirt was also on the casual side, as well as the three-quarter dark denim jacket she wore over it. For a few seconds he wondered about the beads riding low on her hips beneath the clothes she wore.

"That was a great idea," Maurice continued. "Customer service reported some mentions in their feedback box when we met with them Friday morning."

"That's in the area of the app. I'm talking about this engagement sham," RJ continued before taking a swallow of the vodka he'd just poured.

Marva wouldn't like that he was drinking before dinner, but Ron would defend his oldest son, claiming if a man worked hard he had every right to drink hard whenever he wanted to. As long as the work was done and above reproach—that was always the unspoken part of anything their father said to defend them. He could condone just about anything if RGF came first. A fact that had Major's jaw tightening.

Nina moved around him to take a seat in one of three brightly colored and mildly disgusting salon chairs his mother had added to this space a couple years ago. He realized he hadn't offered her a seat and had basically left her hanging in a room full of siblings. To compensate, he moved over to the chair as soon as she sat. "Can I get you something to drink while we wait for dinner?"

"That would be great. I'll have a—"

"Cranberry juice with lime," he said before she

could get the words out, and the room went silent once more.

She smiled up at him and, in that moment, it didn't matter what his siblings were doing or saying behind him. Major smiled in return and went to the bar thinking of the ring in a black-velvet bag in his pocket. Before learning she'd been invited tonight, his plan had been to take it to her after dinner. Now he was thinking there didn't need to be any special moment or perfect words said; he should just give it to her. That idea was tabled when RJ moved to the side while Major reached for a glass.

"Ain't that cute, you know what she likes to drink," RJ jokingly whispered until Major elbowed him and continued.

He did know what she liked to drink and that she only liked extra cheese and onions on her pizza. When he kissed her neck and palmed her breasts, she melted in his arms. And on the two occasions he'd spent the night at her hotel over these past two weeks, he noticed she liked to sleep on the right side of the bed. But none of that meant anything—it couldn't.

"It's a drink, don't get it twisted," he replied, keeping his voice low, as well.

"I think I should be saying the same to you."

Major frowned. "What's that supposed to mean?"

"Where've you been spending the bulk of your evenings? At your place or at her hotel? And before you answer, think about why you really got that apartment for her. After that, think about how this is going to end when the six weeks are up."

"Dinner is served," Kemp, the Golds' longtime butler, announced just in time for Major to slip away from his brother and the assumptions he was making.

"You were very quiet during dinner," Nina said later as they walked along one of the many stone pathways outside the main house.

He'd needed some air after sitting at the table listening to the talk about work and wedding plans. Major wasn't usually the quiet one of the family—laid-back, but not quiet. Riley had taken that torch and held it for years. Now that she was in love, that seemed to have changed.

"I know, sorry. I've got a lot on my mind."

"About the fake engagement? Because, really, I think that's going well."

She was right. The charade was going well. Desta's last email to him asking that they keep up whatever they were doing had confirmed that. What had they been doing? In the last few weeks they'd been dating. That was the simplest way of putting it. Dinner out, even more dinners in, watching movies, laughing, touching, sleeping together—all the things a dating couple would do. All things that had tabloids abuzz with wedding speculation, which always included comments about Nina's wedding gown. He was pretty sure they were doing a great job as far as the campaign was considered.

"It's not that," he said, stuffing his hands into his pockets as he walked.

It was a warm evening, not humid as it had been

earlier. A summer thunderstorm had rolled through while they'd been inside having dinner, cooling the air down slightly.

"But whatever it is, you don't want to talk about it." She didn't pose that as a question, just a simple statement she let hang in the air like bait.

After another few steps, Major gave up the pretense. He didn't know what it was about her, but whenever they were together he was always changing his mind about something, doing more than he'd anticipated, adjusting. It wasn't something he did often, there wasn't usually a need. He knew what he wanted and he did whatever it took to get it. Simple. But not this time—at least not when she was around.

"It's business, but not RGF business," he said, feeling a bit uneasy about what was on his mind.

"Okay."

That one word didn't seem like enough and, after a few seconds, he realized he wanted Nina to ask the question so that it wouldn't seem like he was giving her the information. To the contrary, she seemed content to give him space to decide when and if he wanted to tell her more.

"I'm starting my own company. It's called Brand Integrated Technologies." And it might be your biggest competitor. For some reason, he couldn't bring himself to say that part.

"Good for you," she said when they took the curve that would lead to the garage or down farther to his mother's gardens. "Starting a business can be a mixed bag—exciting and daunting."

"You're right about that." He managed a light chuckle. "Launch day is a few weeks away, so we're just ironing out some final things. But the last couple days, there've been some wrinkles."

She nodded, her hair, which she'd left alone so that it lay straight down her back, swished a little with the movement.

"That's always the case. And it probably won't get better after launch. I know I was troubleshooting almost 24/7 in my first couple of weeks. But what got me through was knowing that it was all mine—my concept, my execution, everything. That motivated me to keep going and to get it right."

Looking over at her, he saw the light in her eyes as she talked about her business. He'd seen it before and realized it was always there when they talked about work.

"My dream," he said and only briefly wondered why he'd found it so easy to admit that to her. "I've wanted to do something like this for a long time and now that it's happening, I just want it to be perfect."

"Perfection is a myth." There was an edge to her tone, but when she glanced over at him and caught him watching her, she smiled. "It's designed to pull every bit of action and reaction from you until you're either spinning in circles in search of more, or falling flat on your face from exhaustion. Completion is a more attainable goal."

He thought about that for a second and eventually decided there might be some truth to her words. "Brand Integrated is a consulting and design firm.

We'll assess the technological needs of a fashion house and design unique software to facilitate their growth. Kind of what I've been doing at RGF, but on a larger scale."

"That sounds amazing, Major. And there's definitely a need. The shield program you've developed to seamlessly combine all aspects of RGF is phenomenal."

So far so good. He gave her a tentative smile.

"Thanks. At Brand Integrated, all of that would be expanded. We have plans for more personalized technological development such as fabric generators, accessory hubs, data extrapolators and more. The idea is to get into a company and create a skeleton that will support the entire body of its work."

"Yes! I can see that. There's certainly a demand for that type of technological support, especially in the fashion industry. This way it lets designers focus on just the clothes. Are you targeting smaller houses? Because I feel like they're the ones who could really benefit from programs like this. It would position them to be competitors."

"Exactly," he admitted. How was it that she got him so completely and so quickly?

A light drizzle of rain started to fall and Major led them toward the garage.

"So, anyway, the past couple days have been filled with little problems. I feel like it's some type of conspiracy designed to make me think of turning back."

"You getting cold feet, Major?" She chuckled. "I wouldn't have expected that of you."

Her tone was light but the fact that she had any type of expectations of him on a level outside of their fake engagement was a little surprising. And a lot intriguing.

They approached the garage. There was an automated keypad on the wall beside the door and he pressed the code. When the locks disengaged, he pulled the door open and held it so that she could walk past, giving off a hint of her perfume as she did—warm, floral, charming.

"So wait—you said accessory hubs. You have plans for programs that will accessorize? Sort of like my app?"

Major had just pulled the door closed behind him and was about to reach for the light switch when she asked that question.

"Ah, yeah, that's in the portfolio. I mean, we wouldn't contract with any vendors, we're solely technology focused. But a simulator that takes the designer from sketch to prototype to runway, complete with suggested accessories, is on the menu."

He found the switch for the lights and the fluorescent bulbs across the large, open ceiling came on, bringing thirty vintage cars and motorcycles into view.

"Oh," she said and looked around. "Well, I guess a little healthy competition is good."

Of course he'd known about this similarity since the day she'd pitched At Your Service; what he hadn't wanted to consider was whether or not it would mean anything at the end of these six weeks.

Logically, she could go her own way with her company and continue doing business. He could do the same and they'd just be two people working in the industry, same as RGF's competition with any other fashion house. But this was different—the deal he'd made with her, having Sunday dinner with her at his parents' house, a seventy-five-thousand-dollar ring in his pocket, talking and walking with her on a quiet summer's night… He couldn't help but admit things were totally different now.

She walked farther into the space. "These are amazing. Whose are they?"

The place was set up almost like a runway with vehicles parked along the two sides of the structure, leaving a wide walkway in the center to be used for perusal.

"My Dad and RJ have always been into vintage cars. Another thing they have in common."

"But you don't like them?"

"I didn't say that. They're nice, but just not my thing. I'm more impressed by the room of control boards and digital infrastructure at my place."

"I'm sure that's impressive, but since I haven't been invited to your place yet, I'll just have to enjoy these cars." She walked toward a sage-green Jaguar, running her hand over the shining hood. "My dad would get such a kick out of this. He loves cars."

"I do, too. They get you from place to place."

She looked over her shoulder at him. "Ha."

He chuckled.

It was so easy being with her, much easier than

he'd ever thought it would be with another woman. Stacia was the only other woman he'd ever brought to his parents' home and the whole time she'd been there that night, all she'd wanted to do was talk about the fashion house. Major's technology ideas or anything about their future together had seemed to be off-limits.

"This one reminds me of *Grease*. You know, the movie with Danny Zuko and the T-Birds? Every time I see an old Thunderbird, I think about it."

He was grateful for her question, disliking the turn his thoughts had taken. "No, I don't know the movie, but I do know this car. It's probably from the fifties or sixties as my Dad is fixated with that time frame. This one used to be my grandfather's, I believe."

They'd stopped by the red convertible and she walked down to the driver's side, leaning over to look at the steering wheel and the white-leather interior.

"Ever made out in one of these?"

The question was so off topic from what they'd been discussing. It was also more than a little arousing.

"If you mean any car, uh, yeah. A couple weeks ago with this really hot chick who came to one of our shows and took over the press conference." The memory of that day would forever be etched in his mind. How beautiful and amazing she'd looked while taking Morgana down a notch and then how sweet she'd tasted as he'd feasted on her in the back of the limo.

She blushed, heat fussing her high cheekbones to add a sexy flash of color to her face. A more enticing sight he'd never seen.

"I meant a T-Bird," she told him as she shook her head and looked away. "In the movie they go to this drive-in and all these cars are lined up. Only a handful of people are watching the screen, the rest are necking in the back of the car."

Her hand caressed the soft leather of the seat and then moved to the side of the door. Major watched that hand, growing hard at the thought of it running over him that way.

"Let's do it," he said.

Her head popped up from where she'd been looking at the sideview mirror. "Do what?"

"Do *it*." He nodded toward the backseat of the T-Bird. "In here."

She followed his gaze, a smile spreading across her face. "*It*? Now? Here?"

His dick was hard and the hint of intrigue in her tone was encouraging.

"Hell yeah. Right now. Right here."

He stood at the passenger side of the car and, for a few seconds, their gazes held, his heart beating just a little faster as he waited for her response.

She pursed her lips—sweet, suckable lips—and shrugged. "Let's do it!"

CHAPTER ELEVEN

"SO ARE WE going for seduction here, or just hard-core reach-for-the-orgasm as quickly as possible?"

Her question only made him harder—if that was even possible. Major already felt as if he were going to explode from the force of the arousal or go into some type of coma from the most painful erection ever. They'd both opened the doors of the car and climbed inside. He dug out his wallet and found a condom, dropping it onto the seat between them as she watched. Then he reached for her, clasping his hand at the back of her head and pulling her close. She licked her lips and he parted his, moving in closer, prepared to answer her question.

"I need to be inside you right now," he whispered, the words rough.

"Say no more." She pushed him back on the seat and undid his belt and the snap of his jeans.

He reached for the jacket, pushing it off her shoulders and down her arms. She paused so that he could pull it off and it fell to the floor. The zipper to his jeans made a loud sound as she eased it down, her fingers brushing over his thick erection just like the first day they'd met. Without wasting a second, she reached through the slit of his boxers and wrapped her hands around his dick, pulling his full length out.

The groan that rumbled in his chest and ripped through his throat was savage. Her hands were too warm around him, rubbing along his skin and sending rivulets of pleasure throughout his body.

"You said you want to be inside me." Her voice was a throaty whisper as she lowered her body to fit between his spread legs.

She wasn't going to… He would never make it if she did. When her head was bent over his groin, Major let his head fall back, his eyes closing slowly. She was going to and he was definitely going to explode.

The moment her mouth closed over the head of his dick, his hips jutted forward, his hands falling first to the seat where his fingers dug into the upholstery. As her tongue circled his tip, he moved his hands, burying them in her hair.

"I'm gonna take you all the way inside," she whispered, her breath warm and teasing over him.

He simply nodded in agreement, rubbing his fingers along her scalp before wrapping her hair around his hand in preparation. There was an explosion— not the one he'd been predicting—but another one, as sparks burst behind his closed lids. She had one hand on his balls, massaging them until they tingled. The other hand was wrapped around the base of his dick as she held him upright and lowered her mouth down his length.

Gasping for air—that's the sensation he first felt. It was immediately followed by an insatiable thirst for more. He applied light pressure to the back of her head, his body aching to be fully ensconced in her. The tip of his dick touched the back of her throat and air burst from his lungs, coming through his mouth in a ragged moan.

He cursed and his fingers tightened in her hair, somewhere in the back of his mind, cautioning against hurting her. She lifted her head, dragging her tongue along the underside of his erection, causing it to jerk and release pre-cum that she immediately licked away.

"I didn't imagine." The words were rough and tumbled free of his thoughts. He hadn't imagined being inside her this way. Thrusting in and out of her pussy was one level; it was erotic and good as hell. But this, being drenched in the heat of her mouth, touched by the stroke of her tongue, it was more and it was intense, pulling him in a direction he'd never thought he'd go.

She eased her head down again, until she was actively sucking him, applying pressure so that he felt as if she might actually drain his release from him the second he came. But before she could do that, she pulled her mouth away.

"I need more," she said through panting breaths. "Now."

Without wasting another second, Major reached

for the condom. She took it from him, ripped the packet open and sheathed him. Major pushed her skirt up around her waist, feeling those colorful beads moments before he ripped the flimsy strings of the thong she wore straight from her hips.

"You keep destroying my underwear," she said as she climbed on top to straddle him.

He cupped her ass cheeks, kneading them as she positioned herself over him and then, when she'd aimed his tip at her center, he pressed her down until she was completely impaled. "I'll buy you more," he groaned, and she moaned as she settled over him.

The only other sound throughout the garage was that of their skin slapping together. He groaned as he dropped his face into her cleavage and she screamed as she cupped the back of his head and bounced on top of him. Minutes later her thighs tightened around his waist and his fingers gripped her ass harder.

"Yessssss," she moaned.

"Yes!" He followed her lead, gasping as his release pulsated and poured into the condom.

For endless moments they just sat there, both struggling to catch a breath. She leaned forward with her hands on his chest, her head resting on his shoulder. Major turned his face to hers, letting his chin rest against her forehead as thoughts flailed around in his mind.

What was he doing? Why was this happening? And when had it happened—when had this arrangement started to feel like so much more?

He'd opened up to her about his business, something he hadn't done with anyone else besides his twin, and he wanted her to feel free to do the same with him. To tell her his secrets and know that they were safe with him, to come to him when she was feeling conflicted, worried, even happy. This was a new feeling, an eerie and confusing one, and he didn't know what to do with it.

His hand slid from where he'd been rubbing it up and down her back, until he could reach his pants and fumble to get his hand into the front pocket. The black-velvet bag almost slipped from his fingers to fall on the leather-covered seat, but he held on to it, bringing it up to his other hand. Her eyes were still closed, lips slightly parted as her panting began to slow.

With the fingers of one hand, Major pulled the strings of the pouch apart and reached inside to pull out the ring. He dropped the bag to the seat and grasped for her left hand.

"What…not yet—" she started to say and then stopped as she pulled back to look at what he was doing.

Major slid the ring slowly onto her third finger and frowned as he watched her hand shake. When the ring was on and she didn't speak, just stared down at it, he did the same, watching the sparkle of the four-carat, emerald-cut diamond set in platinum with tapered baguette side stones. That was the complete description the jeweler had given him, but all Major saw as he looked down at her slender fingers and manicured nails was a memory.

His gaze moved up to her face. When he saw that she was still staring down at the ring, he lifted a hand to touch his finger to her chin and tilted her head up. There was a bit of confusion in her eyes, but a lot of light, like a shield had been raised. Warmth spread in the center of his chest and one side of his mouth lifted in a smile.

"You can't be engaged without a ring," he said while his throat felt tight and his hand still shook a little while holding hers.

She smiled, a slow and dazzling smile that reached into his chest and squeezed so tight he struggled to breathe.

"And this is one beautiful ring," she said, her voice hitching on the last words.

"I would say for a beautiful woman, but that seems so cliché and there's nothing cliché about you, Nina. Not one single thing." This was the part where he should kiss her. And damn he wanted to. He wanted to wrap his arms around her and drown in her kiss, feel the warmth of her surrounding him until all his cares and worries disappeared and there was just her.

She looked like she wanted to say something or to do something. Their gazes held but hesitancy hung between them like a blockade.

"I think I like doing it in the backseat of a T-Bird," she said playfully, then eased her left hand away from his and lifted it into the air to wiggle her fingers. "You get great gifts!"

Major chuckled, part of him appreciating the way

she'd broken that uncomfortable tension between them, another part wishing the moment would have ended differently.

"I like doing it in the backseat of a T-Bird with you."

Two hours later Nina was at Major's penthouse, stepping out of his shower. If her legs weren't so sore from their second backseat sexcapade and her mind wasn't filled with new questions about the huge diamond on her finger and the foreign emotions sifting through her soul, she might have been overwhelmed by being here in Major's private space.

"Here, let me help," he said when he stepped out behind her.

She'd already grabbed a towel from the shelf near the dual vanity but had been holding it in her hands while she struggled to get a hold on what was happening. And letting the water drip from her naked body pool onto the heated gray-slate floor.

Major reached for another towel and wrapped it around her, turning her to face him when he was done.

"I suppose you'll want me to dry you off in return." It was easier to joke than to put words to what she was really feeling.

"Of course. That's how this works," he said and proceeded to move the towel over her body. He eased the soft, fluffy material along her arms, over and under her breasts and down her stomach.

"These beads are going to be the death of me,"

he said while rubbing the towel past her hips, down and between her thighs.

"I've got some aunts back in Sierra Leone who could probably use their skills to add death as a result of looking at the beads. Or, most likely, loss of a limb, impotence or something along those lines."

He hissed and pulled back, looking up at her from where he'd knelt down with a horrified expression. "That's not funny."

She chuckled. She couldn't help it. He was adorable when he was scared. "Yeah, it is."

He shook his head and eased the towel between her legs, lifting one off the floor to rub down to her feet, then up again. He did the same with the other and before he stood, eased the towel between her legs taking special care to dry her there.

"Your turn," she said when those stirrings of desire started to buzz.

How could she be so turned on by him, so frequently and so soon? The tryst in his father's vintage car was different from the limo on so many levels she didn't know where to begin. Perhaps at the part where she was certain his family would despise her if they knew she'd just disrespected their dinner invitation in such a way.

The moment he stood to his full six-two-and-a-half inches stark naked in front of her, she knew that what she was feeling had nothing to do with what his family thought of her and everything to do with him. Drops of water still rolled over his tawny-hued skin and he stared down at her with dark brown eyes that held more warmth than any she'd ever seen.

She raised the towel and rubbed his chest then moved down each of his arms before returning to his torso, all while that diamond on her left hand sparkled like a bright reminder of what this could never be.

"I don't think this was in either of our job descriptions," she said, her voice hollow to her own ears. They weren't supposed to be doing any of this and yet they were doing it, and she suspected they were doing it as well as any real couple.

He caught her hands just as she was about to drag the towel past his waist. "That's because there's really no accurate way to describe you."

And what exactly was that supposed to mean?

Maybe he was just as confused as she was about what was happening between them, or what she thought might be happening. She'd never felt this way before and wasn't sure if she was ready to take it from lust to love, but knew for certain it was more than what their fake scenario called for.

"Yes, that's me." She dabbed the towel over his hips. "The indescribable fake fiancée." Reminding herself that keeping things light between them was for the best, she bent down to dry his thighs—strong and fit—then his calves and his feet, which were a lot prettier than she'd imagined. Coming up again, she rubbed the towel over what could arguably be one of the best parts of him. To say this part of Major felt the same way about her might have been an understatement if it hadn't begun to stiffen at her ministrations.

He took her by the shoulders and pulled her up to stand in front of him. "Come on, Fake Fiancée. Let's get ready for bed."

She hadn't realized she'd frowned until he asked, "Whoa, what's that look for? You don't want to sleep with me in my bed? Should we have gone back to your apartment instead?"

"Oh no, that's not it." In fact, she'd been flattered when he'd announced during the drive from his parents' house that they would be coming to his place. She'd refused to ask why he hadn't brought her here before, chalking it up to their little charade instead of any other personal reason he might not want her there.

He looked at her strangely, a brow lifting in question. "Then what is it?"

"I'm hungry," she said, because it was true and because she wasn't sure what she was feeling for him at this moment. Or what he was really feeling for her.

"I mean no offense to your mother's dinner. It was a wonderful spread, but I'm used to a little more than soup, salad and the smallest portions of beef rib tips and asparagus that I've ever seen."

That's right, insult his mother instead of telling him she was afraid she was really falling for him.

When he threw back his head and laughed, Nina relaxed. Laughter was definitely better than his ordering her to get dressed and get out.

"I planned to wait until you were asleep before

sneaking into the kitchen to grab something else to eat."

It was her turn to laugh. "Why didn't you say something? I thought that's the way your family was used to eating, so I didn't want to comment."

"My mother doesn't cook, so dinners are always catered. The only time we get loads of food is on Thanksgiving and Christmas. My father says that's the best time of the year."

He continued to laugh while they finished with the towels and dropped them into the hamper by the door.

"You go on into the bedroom and find something to sleep in. I mean, I'm good with you staying just the way you are, but I'm guessing you'd like to be dressed to eat."

They were still naked. Yet they'd been standing there talking as if they showered and talked in the nude every day.

"Oh, are you going to order something?"

"No. I'm going to cook us something."

"You cook?"

She knew she was frowning this time because she couldn't believe that Major was good in the kitchen.

As it turned out, twenty minutes later, when they were sitting on stools in his kitchen, he could bake a homemade pizza that tasted just as good as any pizzeria she'd ever been to, if not better.

"What's on this?" she asked as she took another bite.

"Alfredo sauce, ricotta and mozzarella cheeses, plenty of black pepper and oregano."

"It's delicious," she said over the mouthful, and wasn't lying. "Where'd you learn how to cook if your mother hires caterers?"

"In college. I didn't like going out much, so I figured it was best to not starve for four years."

"Why didn't you like to go out?"

He hesitated, took another bite of his pizza, chewed and then used a napkin to wipe his mouth.

Nina hadn't realized she was waiting for his response until he looked at her and shook his head.

"It's not such a big deal now since I've learned how to deal with it. But it was because of a girl."

Never in a million years would she have guessed he'd say that. "What? A girl had you holed up in your dorm for four years?"

"Not exactly. It was during my sophomore year. I thought it was love. Stacia Hudgins poured it on real thick, was talking marriage, kids, the whole package. Come to find out she and her parents had it all set up. They knew who I was, who my family was, and they wanted in. A fake pregnancy scare, lots of tears and then a threat of scandal, and it was over by the time I came home for the summer. That's when I knew relationships weren't for me."

Nina chewed another bite all the while thinking she'd like to have been at school with Stacia Hudgins so she could serve the girl a good dose of "get a life." Or, as Nina and her sisters would have called it, "whoop ass."

"Yeah, I'm not into the 'happy-ever-after' thing, either." She was almost positive that was still true.

"But not because of any guy in particular. My culprit was my mother. She left when I was twelve. Had enough of the family life and decided there was something better away from the home she'd built. Left my dad with three girls and a broken heart that he's still nursing. Probably why he's gotten so sick, but I guess that's not medically possible."

"Broken heart" had likely never been listed on anybody's death certificate.

"Your father has COPD, right?"

She nodded. "Yes. It wasn't so bad at first, but seven years ago he had to stop working and go on disability because it had gotten to the severe point. He's weak most of the time, has intermittent swelling in his legs and ankles, and gets confused easily. The confusion isn't a symptom of COPD, I think it's more from loneliness. Anyway, my sisters and I have been taking care of him up to this point, but the doctor suggested he might need more assistance to make sure he's taking his medications and to help him do some of the daily getting around."

It had been a hard conversation to have as a family, but they'd had it. Her father didn't want to be a burden to his children, insisting he could take care of his own arrangements when the time came.

"That's a tough situation," Major said. "Do you have a facility in mind?"

"We've visited a few and there's one that he favors." She drank from the glass of wine he'd poured for her. "This boost in business from partnering with

RGF will be just what I need to get him into the care home."

She took another bite of pizza because she'd had enough of talking about herself.

"Maybe I could help. I can make some calls, maybe find a place for your father here in New York." When she only stared at him, he cleared his throat and continued, "I mean, that way you'll be close to two of the biggest fashion houses in the States, stylists, models and plenty of other industry people that could talk up your app and provide endorsements."

"But I live in York. That's where my family and everything I know is." That was the truth, but there was suddenly something sad about the way it sounded.

"Right," he said with a curt nod and a quick smile. "If you're done, we should clean this up and get to bed."

"Right. I can take care of the mess since you cooked."

"Nonsense, we'll do it together."

Like a couple did things together. Nina didn't say that but went along with his suggestion until the kitchen was clean and they headed off to bed...to Major's bed where she would lie all night wondering if he was the man to make her think twice about happy-ever-after.

CHAPTER TWELVE

THE WINE-COLORED tulle was even more beautiful as it swayed around them on the dance floor. With Major's arms wrapped securely around her waist, Nina's arms remained locked at his neck as they danced. The screens positioned around the banquet room, having earlier displayed a lovely video of their childhood years all the way up to their engagement party, now showed them dancing. Even the people at the back of the four-hundred-seat room could see them close-up.

A slow song played, one that was a favorite of theirs. But she couldn't hear the lyrics. She just swayed to the rhythm and stared up into his face, remembering the exact moment that she'd agreed to become Mrs. Major Gold.

They danced until the scene changed and she was once again walking through the doors of the RGF building, with a determined smile on her face as she approached the now familiar pretty receptionist with the coal-black hair.

"Good morning, Mrs. Gold. Are you here to see your husband?"

The question startled her and Nina looked down to see the huge emerald-cut diamond on her ring finger.

"Uh, no. I'm actually here to work. I need to check in with a few vendors and make sure that products are being shipped on time." She continued to talk even though the woman was frowning at her. "There were a couple complaints on the website and I need to get things ironed out."

"I don't understand. Maybe you want to report some issues with the company site to your husband?"

"No. I want to take care of the issues—they're with my company, At Your Service."

The woman was shaking her head, her silky hair moving from side to side. "You're welcome to go see your husband. But I've never heard of At Your Service..."

Nina's eyes opened wide into a room filled with slashes of moonlight coming through the partially closed blinds. She pressed a hand to her chest, her heart beating wildly. A few blinks later and she swallowed hard, her gaze falling on the nightstand beside the bed where a clock flashed bright white numbers: 3:54. Beside the clock was her phone, plugged into its charger. She'd put it there just before joining Major in the shower.

She was at Major's penthouse... He'd fixed her pizza...

A sigh of relief rushed from her as she realized it had only been a dream. The wedding, going to RGF...it was all a dream. A strange and alarming dream that now had her sitting up in the bed.

The sheet slid to her waist and she rubbed her hands over her face. That dream was strange and it left her feeling even stranger. Full of emotion and empty at the same time. But it wasn't real, nothing about being with Major was real, even this moment.

She glanced over her shoulder to see him sleeping. One arm was thrown above his head while the other lay across his bare stomach. The sheet was riding dangerously close to revealing what she already knew was a delicious part of him.

He seemed real.

Leaning back and propping herself up on one elbow, she stared down at him. He had thick eyebrows that she wished she had. Hers were thin and most times she penciled them in. His nose was straight, wide and proportional with his face, his squared jaw and average ears. Her gaze fell on his lips and her own parted. They were usually warm when they met hers. And soft. Did men like being told they had soft lips?

She was leaning over before she thought better of the action. But when her lips hovered just seconds away from his, Major's eyes opened, and she froze.

His response was to move the arm that had been resting over his abs, snake it around her waist and pull her on top of him. She licked his bottom lip as his hands splayed over her ass. Then her tongue stroked his top lip. Their gazes held.

He parted his lips slightly, just enough so that his tongue inched out, and she pounced, sucking it deep into her mouth. He groaned and pressed her bare mound into his thickening erection. Only the thin sheet separated them, but she sucked on his tongue like it was his dick, and desire pierced through her, falling with clever accuracy in her center. She spread her legs so that she was now straddling him, rubbing her pussy over the sheet. He thrust his hips up to meet hers, his hands moving upward to bury themselves in her hair.

He pulled her back then, her mouth reluctantly releasing him. For endless moments, they just stared at each other.

She didn't know what he was thinking. The only thing running through her mind right now was that this felt real. From the throbbing in her center to the tightening in her chest, as she continued to stare down at him, it felt very real.

"I don't know what this is," he said, his voice cracking slightly.

"Neither do I," she admitted. "But I don't want it to stop."

It was an admission she hadn't planned to make. That made sense because she hadn't planned for him.

In response, he pulled her head down and took her mouth in a kiss that was as achingly slow and sweet as it was deliciously tempting and erotic.

He rolled her over and kicked the sheets aside before reaching over her to the nightstand and pulling open the top drawer. He tossed the condom to her and she caught it, ripping the paper and retrieving the latex. Coming up on his knees, he whispered in a hungry voice, "Put it on."

She sat up, rubbing her hand along his thick length as her mouth watered. She couldn't resist dipping her head and taking him in deep.

"Dammit," he cursed loudly. "You're killing me."

And he had awakened an insatiable need in her.

With deep suction, she slid her mouth from his base to his tip before easing down once more. This had never been a favorite of hers during sex. It was more intimate than she'd ever wanted to be with anyone else, but she loved the taste of him. Loved the feel of him in her mouth, pressing at the back of her throat, sliding over her tongue and easing past her lips.

"Put it on. Now!"

She let him slip from her mouth with a popping sound and inched the condom on until he was covered. He pushed her back onto the pillows before leaning his head down to drag his tongue along the first row of beads at her waist.

"Yesssss." She let her hands fall to his head. He captured the beads between his teeth and lifted his head slightly to watch her as she looked down at him.

With a quick yank he ripped the beads free. At any other time, with someone different, this may have upset her. Tonight, coupled with the roller coaster of emotions she'd been feeling about him, the touch of the beads that empowered her sensuality rolling over her skin mixed with the passion swirling between them and the anticipation of more, caused her to come with a fierceness that left her breathless and trembling. Before she could recuperate, he'd moved up the length of her and was inside her, thrusting wildly.

The rush of sensations swirled through Nina like a tornado, twisting and hitting every part of her, even the part she'd never wanted to be touched. When he leaned forward, flattening his hands on either side of her to brace himself, her hands pressed against his chest. Her mouth opened as if she were going to say something. Tell him to stop because she felt overwhelmed with sensation and emotion? Or beg him to continue because it all felt so damn good?

It felt real. Too real.

She raised her legs and wrapped them around him, locking them in place.

"You," he whispered before dropping his head to take her mouth. She slid her arms from his chest to cup his face and hold him to her, dragging her tongue over his, tilting her head to take the kiss deeper.

You. The one word echoed in her mind. *You.* Him. It was him. This warm feeling spreading throughout her chest was all because of *him.*

On a ragged moan, he pulled his mouth from hers as he moved in and out of her at a slower pace. The change was fast and intense, pleasure now building with his strokes in a slow, methodical rhythm that had her biting her bottom lip and dropping her arms to the bed and gripping the sheets. He eased over her again, this time scooping his arms beneath her to hold her firmly to him. His lips were right next to her ear as he thrust into her repeatedly. She wrapped her arms around him, holding him just as tightly as he was holding her, as if they were each afraid to let go.

"I want you, Nina." He whispered those words over and over again.

She closed her eyes tight, savoring every syllable. "I want you, too." It was a quiet admission, but an admission nonetheless. And it was real—his comment, her response, it was all real.

They came together in a storm of moans and sighs, bodies trembling and pressing together as if being any other way was not an option.

By Wednesday afternoon the following week Major was in a pretty foul mood.

In a month, Brand Integrated would go public and he still hadn't told the rest of his family that he was significantly cutting his time at RGF and branching out on his own. The fake fiancée proposal would also be over. Desta had just sent an updated itinerary for the last activities he and Nina would complete together.

He sat back in his desk chair, moving his feet so the chair would spin slowly while he stared out the wall of windows in his office. With his hands clasped and resting on his lap, his mind whirled with the most pressing issues in his life at the moment. The fact that there should only be one pressing issue didn't escape his notice.

But Nina Fuller was intertwined in his every thought in a way that he hadn't anticipated. She'd been at his place, in his bed, since attending her first Gold family dinner. At night they fell asleep, cuddled in his bed, and in the morning, they awoke and moved around his bedroom and bathroom like a couple getting ready for work.

Each day had become a repeat of wake up, sex somewhere between the bedroom and bathroom, traveling to work together, then home again in the evening.

Home.

That's what it'd felt like for the past week and a half, until now, it seemed permanent.

He spun the chair until he was once again facing his desk and could see the dual monitors with the business plan for Brand Integrated on one and the services offered by At Your Service on the other. Nina had pointed out what he'd already known and what had been floating in the back of his mind since before their first meeting.

The accessory hub Brand Integrated would offer was very similar to what her app provided. The only difference—and the one thing Major had repeatedly reminded himself of—was that his company did not retain vendors, nor did it plan to sell anything directly to the consumer. Their product—software and consultation services—was exclusively designed to benefit fashion houses.

But the similarity was still there, and it had been nagging at him for days. Their businesses were poised to clash big-time. His brow furrowed with the thought and he let out a little huff as he once again searched for a viable solution. There had to be one. There had to be a way for his business to coexist with hers without compromise or confusion, and he needed to find it before their planned breakup.

Or it could be the reason for the breakup. That thought came with a sharp sting to the center of his chest as he stopped moving in the chair and his frown deepened. Desta still hadn't outlined what the final argument would be. The end of their engagement was coming quickly and he had no idea what it would be like. So what if it was the realization that their businesses would clash? Did that make sense? Was it believable? He sighed at the irony. It was the one thing that had come of their time together that was actually the truth.

A knock at the door jolted him out of his thoughts just as that pain in his chest started to spread.

"Hey, what's up? Got a minute?" RJ opened the door without consent and walked in talking. He hiked up his slacks and took a seat in one of the chairs across from Major's desk. "I need you to do something for me. You and Nina."

His brother had his full attention the moment he mentioned her name.

"What?"

"Riley wants to meet with Dad and me in an hour at a proposed location for this expansion idea she's got," RJ said.

Deciding it was probably best for the moment to wrap his mind around something else, Major sat forward, resting his elbows on his desk. "Yeah, she copied me and Maurice on an email she sent earlier this week outlining her proposal. Her research and data pan out. An RGF-exclusive storefront in the city is a good idea. Lots of other fashion houses have one, especially overseas."

"Look, I'm not totally opposed to the idea. So, Riley doesn't need you to be her cheerleader," RJ said with a sigh.

"That may be the one thing our sister has never needed. She's always been capable of being her own biggest supporter, which is probably why she was able to fall in love with the family enemy and not bat an eye when we approached her about it." Why his thoughts always returned to Riley and her relationship with Chaz, Major didn't know. Perhaps he admired the fact that she'd found love, even though he didn't believe in the concept himself.

"Ugh, that's the last thing I want to talk about."

Major chuckled, more so to keep his mind from drifting from the word *love* to the woman who would soon be meeting him in his office to go home. Or, rather, to his apartment.

"Fine, then what do you want, man? You come barging into my office at the end of the day like it's some big emergency."

"It is." RJ leaned forward, resting his elbows on his knees. "I was supposed to go to this trade show tonight to check out some new vendors for the Paris and Milan Fashion Weeks coming up, but now I can't go, so I'd like you and Nina to go instead."

"Isn't that the production department's responsibility? And did you say you want Nina to go?"

"Riley's not the only one thinking about taking RGF to the next level. I've had some thoughts about expanding in the area of accessories. We already have purses and luggage. Why not create a full line, accessorize our customers from head to toe? So, yeah, I've been looking into Nina's business a little more and watching the numbers from our temporary collaboration closely. If anybody should be checking out new vendors and giving her thoughts on specific items for the company, I think it should be her."

"Wait, you weren't even certain making this temporary arrangement with Nina was a good idea. What changed your mind?"

"You're right. I wasn't sure about her in the beginning because she was some woman from Pennsylvania who we'd never heard of until you agreed to meet with her and she presented this new app that would tap into our existing and new customer base. She had no experience with large fashion houses. So, yes, I was skeptical." RJ took a breath and shook his head. "And I definitely didn't think she was a good pick for this marketing plan. Hell, I wasn't even certain this marketing plan was a good idea on its own."

That was something Major could agree with. The moment Desta and Riley had come to him with the idea, he'd been doubtful and had wanted to beg off, to push it onto Maurice who would have loved spending a few weeks in the company of some random woman. But then he'd thought about the fact that he was planning to jump ship on RGF and figured the least he could do was submit to his family, and this company, one more time. His father would appreciate that in the end.

"But I've seen her at the office every day, working diligently, and I've heard of how she's been handling the press," RJ continued. "Then, after seeing the two of you together at Mom and Dad's house, I changed my mind."

RJ Gold never changed his mind. Ever. He was a decisive man with a proven track record in everything from commanding the sales force at RGF to building his own unique brand as the next head of the company. He was a debonair young businessman and unapologetic bachelor.

"It's her job, and that was just dinner." Major didn't believe these words so he only half expected his brother to believe them.

RJ laughed. "Yeah, keep telling yourself that. Look, here's the info and your passes. You, Nina and I will grab some lunch tomorrow and we can talk about her thoughts."

Major accepted the envelope RJ had stood to hand him. "She doesn't work here. I mean, she has her own company, and her own goals. Do you really think we should have her making decisions on behalf of the company?"

"You're going to be with her," RJ said. "And something tells me she's gonna be around long after this fake scheme you've got going. So get yourself together, stop brooding, put your game face on. Do all that, grab your woman and get to that show."

RJ walked out the same way he'd come in: quick, unannounced, without taking any questions, comments or concerns.

"She's not my woman," Major mumbled into the quiet office as he sat back in his chair once more.

Was she?

CHAPTER THIRTEEN

"Look at this picture! He's with another woman and this was just last week," Daisy said, her lips pursed, head tilted as she stared at Nina through the computer screen.

Nina had been on this Skype call with her sisters for approximately six minutes and already her temples throbbed with an incoming migraine.

"This woman looks like a model. There was a fashion show that day and I was there," Nina said as she glanced at the tabloid Angie so helpfully held close to the camera for her to see.

She remembered the beige outfit Major had worn that day and the model. Of course, the girl, wearing a very short skirt and a gold-lamé blouse that barely covered her tits with its plunging neckline, had draped her slim body over Major's shoulder as if she were somehow physically attached to him.

"You were there but he was taking pictures with her? I thought you were supposed to be his arm candy for six weeks." Angie, the matter-of-fact sister, dropped the paper and stared pointedly through the screen.

How rude would it be if she slammed the laptop closed and went on about her business?

"That's pretty rude of him. But then again, he is the Fashion House Playboy," Daisy quipped.

"Is there a point to this conversation?" Nina asked because she did have other things to do. And none of those things included thinking about Major leaving her for another woman. Even though he'd have to actually be with her to leave her. And he wasn't… Or, rather, they weren't really together.

"Aren't you bothered by this?" Angie asked.

"Why should I be? This was a business arrangement and it's almost over." In seventeen days.

"What were you doing while he was feeling up on this model?" Daisy asked.

"I was probably with his brother, Maurice, or seated in the audience where the reporters could see me—or rather, Major's fiancée. Look, if you two don't have anything better to do, I do have work to take care of."

"Work? That looks like a new dress you're wearing. And by the looks of the pictures you're showing up in with him, it seems like you're living one big shopping spree," Angie said.

"And going to lavish restaurants and Broadway shows. I read somewhere that you even met Michelle Obama at one of her appearances in the city. You're having the best time there and it's not fair!" Daisy whined.

"First, I got both of you a signed book from Michelle Obama when I met her. And I am working.

The app is doing great numbers for me and for RGF. I'm certain they're going to extend a formal contract for me to keep working with them at the end of the six weeks." She huffed. "Besides all of that, the press I'm getting personally as a result of this business deal will have my name firmly set within the industry. And from there I'll be able to move on to other companies. But I'll be home soon and then we can get Dad moved into the assisted-living facility and all of our lives will get a little easier."

That had been the plan from the start. So why did saying it aloud now make her feel unsettled?

"Are you really coming back here after the six weeks are up?" Angie asked.

"Of course I am. Why would you ask me that?"

Daisy rolled her eyes. "Because you look like you're having the time of your life."

Angie elbowed her sister. "Because you look like you might be taking this business a little more personally than you planned."

"Knock, knock." Nina looked up from the screen to see Major standing in the doorway. "Hey, we've got a change of plans for this evening. You ready to go?"

"Yeah. I'm done here, so we can go now," she replied and then looked back to the screen. "I'll call you tomorrow." She hurriedly disconnected the chat and closed her laptop.

"You okay? Did I interrupt something?" he asked as he entered the office.

She shook her head, trying to clear it of her sisters' accusations and the picture of him and that model that still floated there.

"No. Nothing. Just my sisters calling with an update."

"Oh yeah, how's your dad doing?"

"He's good." She stood and grabbed her purse, adding, "He has a doctor's appointment in the morning and Angie's going to take him, so I'll check in with her tomorrow afternoon to see how that goes."

"I had my assistant get a list of all the facilities in York and two of them are owned by people my dad's done business with at some point. I wanted to run it by you first, but if you approve, I could reach out to them and see if we can get your dad in sooner and without any big payments on your behalf."

She put her purse strap on her shoulder, slipped her laptop into her bag and stepped around the desk. Coming to a stop in front of him, she looked up in surprise. "What? You would get my dad into a facility for me?"

"Yeah, I want to help you in any way I can. You want your father to be well taken care of and you said you didn't plan to move to New York, so I found some places in York."

He was talking as if he'd just told her he'd selected something off the menu for them to eat. His tone was nonchalant as he stood with one hand in his pocket. He reached out the other hand to tuck some strands of hair that had escaped her messy bun back behind her ear.

"Thanks," she managed to finally say. "I mean… really. You didn't have to do that, but thank you."

"Don't thank me," he said. "I wanted to do it."

"But why? You didn't have to take time out of your busy schedule or ask Landra to do that. It's not your responsibility. But, again, I really appreciate you doing it." She smiled at him then because she wasn't sure what else to do. Part of her wanted to throw her arms around him and hug him tight, but she wasn't going to do that. Since her admission that night after the family dinner that she wanted him, and the subsequent nights she'd spent in his arms, she'd been trying to rein in her emotions where he was concerned.

"This is why," he said, tracing a finger along her cheek and down below her lips. "Because I like seeing you smile. And when you talk about taking care of your dad, you always frown with the stress of it."

And now she thought she might break with the force of her growing feelings for this man.

"What's the change in plans?" she asked when the silence stretched between them.

He dropped his hand and pulled an envelope from the inside pocket of his suit jacket. "Accessory trade show at the Javits Center. RJ needs us to go and check it out. He specifically wants your input on new vendors."

RJ. The one who hadn't been sure of her after their first meeting in the conference room.

"Sure. I'd love to provide input. Let's go." Now this, she could do. Work. Focus on her company and her most prominent client so far. The rest—her sisters, the way that picture had made her feel and the subsequent reaction of Major's soft touch and sweet words—she could deal with later.

The convention center was full of booths with vendors displaying everything from earrings to nose piercings, belts to custom-designed hats and patterned socks.

"This is going to be great," Nina said, pulling her phone out of her purse. "I want to take some pictures. You said Major wanted to get my thoughts on items for the upcoming shows overseas? Do you know if he's looking for anything specific?"

From the moment he'd mentioned this show, her spirits seemed to have lifted. When Major had walked into her office earlier, he'd been afraid something had happened to her father because she'd looked so distressed. He'd been glad to share his news about assisting in her facility search, even though it was in York and not here in the city...with him.

"He's actually looking for two things—items for the upcoming shows and your thoughts on specific pieces."

"Why specific pieces? Does he need a gift for someone? Does RJ have a girlfriend?"

He chuckled as they moved further into the exhibit hall. "Not hardly. The very last thing RJ's interested in is a girlfriend or any other type of commitment other than the company."

"Is that true of all the Gold men? Because Maurice makes it known he loves his player status and isn't looking to stop anytime soon. And you..."

Her words drifted off, but he filled in the blanks.

"I've been focused on Brand Integrated and making my personal mark on the fashion industry."

"Everyone has a reason," she said with a shrug. "I have mine."

She didn't want to be abandoned again. A completely understandable reason, but one that made him much sadder than he thought anything ever could.

"Anyway, no, RJ's other reason for this outing is based on this preliminary idea he has about adding a full accessory line to RGF."

"Oh." She took a few steps farther before stopping at an earring vendor. She picked up a set of gold hoops that were almost as big as her hand. There were flecks of sapphire around each hoop and she held them up, staring, he presumed, at the color in the light.

"A full accessory line will eliminate the need for an app like mine." She put the earrings down and continued walking.

"It's not my idea," he said because he felt the need to defend himself against the suddenly bland tone of her voice.

She waved a hand and crossed in front of him to get to another table. This one had more earrings, but these were made with feathers. He watched, entranced by her fingers as they moved lightly over a deep burgundy feather earring.

"It's a smart idea," she said, moving to investigate another pair of earrings. These were of peacock feathers and she picked them up, holding them to her ear while she stepped over to a large oval mirror sitting on a glass case. "If RGF is making their own accessories, they'd be cutting out the middleman and making a bigger profit, all while catering to their customers in a one-stop fashion shop."

"Which was exactly what your app offered," he said. He was standing behind her, so she could see him staring at her through the mirror. When he shook his head, she nodded her agreement and put the earrings back on the table.

"Everybody wants the complete effect. RJ's thinking of gaining a competitive edge. There are plenty of other designers that have already ventured into accessories. And there are some accessory designers who're trying to dip their feet into the high fashion arena." She shrugged. "That's business."

"Are we business?" He had no idea where that question had come from.

No, that was wrong and he knew it. The idea came from the myriad emotions playing throughout his mind since the night at his parents' house.

She turned to him and smiled. That genuine one he looked forward to seeing every second of the day.

"We—" She corrected herself. "What we're doing is probably one of the most innovative ideas I've ever come across. Riley says the uptick in searches on the Golden Bride website is in direct correlation to our engagement announcement and each time a picture of us is printed in a tabloid, they get even more hits.

Orders are trickling in." She paused when a woman bumped into her and then continued, "There's even one from an R&B singer. She already had a dress but when two of the designers appeared on one of those stylist reality shows and mentioned they were working on my gown, she had to have an original design for her wedding that's coming up in four weeks."

"And you said people who already had their gowns wouldn't buy another one," he replied with a smirk.

"Yeah, I did say that. I was wrong."

And so was he. This was no longer just business between them. Thinking back to their first meeting, he wondered if there ever had been.

They walked for a few more minutes, passing other stalls. She stayed a bit ahead of him and he took that time to watch her walk, not in a way that aroused him, but more in a way that amazed him. She'd come all the way to this city just to meet with him and pitch her business, and had ended up staying as part of a business deal and to begin an affair that neither of them had been prepared for.

"Do you design and manufacture these?"

He snapped out of his reverie when he saw Nina had stopped and was holding up a leather handbag. She was talking to a tall man with gold, wire-framed glasses perched on his nose, his hair styled in locks.

The man walked over to the end of the table. "Yes," he replied in a heavily accented voice. "The bags, necklaces and earrings. I design and make them all. Do you like this tote?"

Nina continued to glide her hand over the dark purple bag.

"This is great craftsmanship," she said.

"It is called the Mawu, named after the African goddess of creativity," he told her.

Major stood at the other end of the table, watching the exchange, curious as to what she was thinking.

"Yes, I'm aware of who she is. The leather is supple, sustainable."

He nodded. "From the Karoo region of South Africa."

She seemed pleased to hear that and left the bag to pick up a necklace from another section of the table.

"And this is an African talisman," she said.

"Yes, you are familiar. It is the Springbok Horn and it is believed to bring good luck to those who wear it."

"It's simple and beautiful, whimsical and magical," she whispered.

"We'll take it," Major said, reaching into his back pocket for his wallet as he stepped up to the display table.

"Oh no," she said, shaking her head. "I didn't mean for you to buy it. I was just admiring it."

Major passed his credit card to the man and waited while it was being swiped. "It's pretty. You like it. You should have it." He ended with a shrug because he wanted everything with her to be that simple.

She didn't argue. Instead she handed it to him and turned around, lifting her hair from her neck. Major stepped closer to her, reaching around so that he could fit the necklace at her neck and clasp it. His fingers lingered at her nape, gliding along the soft skin as he inhaled the fresh floral scent she always carried. He stepped back, prepared to leave the table.

"Do you have a business card?" she asked and thanked the man when he handed her one.

"What are you thinking?" Major asked when they stepped away.

"How do you know I'm thinking something?"

"You get all crinkly right here when you've got an idea or something on your mind." He pressed a finger to the center of her forehead and she immediately relaxed until the crinkle was gone.

She smiled. "I do not."

He laughed. "Liar."

It wasn't until two hours later, when they were in the backseat of the car, that she decided to tell him what she was thinking. Even though she wore a seatbelt, she turned sideways, lifting one leg to rest on the seat.

"What would be really great to see is a complete line of African-inspired accessories from an African American fashion house. Let's uplift and display our heritage. RGF did a collection a few years back where they worked with a Nigerian designer. Maybe it's time for a new collection, find some new, talented African designers, and this time stretch it beyond the clothes to include accessories. This could be the kickoff to the accessory division and you could probably create an entire show based around these collections."

Major didn't miss the excitement in her voice as she talked. He could see where she was going with this.

"It has appeal," he said. "A lot of appeal."

"Right! Unique pieces like this one could be included," she said, reaching up to feel the necklace he'd bought her. "Maybe something inspired by your mother's grace and beauty and your father's strength and leadership."

"And your tenacity," he said before unhooking his seatbelt and sliding across the seat until he was touching her. One hand went to her leg that was on the seat while the other reached around to cup her face. "Your beauty and your independence. Your intelligence and compassion."

"No," she said softly, blinking quickly. "This would be about your family, the Golds, and everything they've built. It would be a direct reflection of all that your family has come to mean in the fashion industry."

"A reflection of love, loyalty, family—all things that are important to you."

She was shaking her head again and he didn't want to hear her denial because he knew better now. He could see it so clearly. Everything she really wanted in this world and all she would deny herself so that her family could have it instead. Before she could speak, Major leaned in to touch his lips to hers. The kiss was soft, slow, lingering, and before long she was moaning and leaning in to him.

"It's my turn to thank you," he said when he was finally able to pull his mouth from hers.

She looked as dazed and off balance as he felt at this moment. "Thank me for what?"

"For coming into my life and opening a door I thought I'd bolted shut."

She was about to say something else but the car came to a stop. Minutes later they were climbing out and walking through the lobby to the elevators that would take them to his penthouse.

They walked in silence and, for the second time tonight, he wondered what she was thinking. Had what he just said been too much? Were they never going to talk about how this arrangement had changed both their lives?

It wasn't until after they'd prepared dinner together, eaten and then moved to the couch in his living room, that he broached the subject again.

"We have a little over two weeks before the public breakup is scheduled." He'd thought about this during the meal and wanted to see how she was feeling about it first. Then he'd drift into the muddy waters of feelings.

She tucked her legs under her and draped an arm over the back of the couch, tilting her head as she looked at him. "I was thinking about that earlier today. We could always say I caught you cheating. I saw a picture of you with another woman in a tabloid and decided this is not the life for me."

"Wow, that's all it would take? A picture and you'd walk out on me?"

He'd exaggerated his reaction on purpose but the insinuation that he'd cheat on her prickled.

She shrugged. "I mean, it plays right into your title, so at the end of the engagement you'd just go back to being the Fashion House Playboy again. We both walk away unscathed."

That wasn't likely. He was already feeling the effects of being with her and doubted that would get better when she was no longer in this city with him.

"What if it's just a picture? And you're overreacting?"

"But what if it's not? What if settling down with one woman isn't going to work for you?" She seemed so adamant about this, a little more than he liked. "I mean... Look, you've been scorned before, so I wouldn't blame you. We've already gone over my trust issues, so if anybody understands, you know I do."

But he didn't want her to understand and, for the life of him, Major didn't know how to best get that point across to her without possibly scaring both of them to death with some mushy declaration of love.

Was he in love with her?

"Look, it's been a really long day. Can we talk about this tomorrow?" She uncurled her legs and stood. The nightshirt she wore was like a football jersey but it was hot-pink with double zeroes on the front and "Sexy" written on the back.

"Yeah, sure. We've got time."

She nodded. "Right, seventeen days."

So she was counting, too. Major stood and pulled

her to him, wrapping his arms around her. She hesitated but eventually gave in to the hug. He didn't know how long they stood there like that, his face buried in her neck, hers buried in his, their arms holding on tight because the time to let go was getting close.

Too close and he had to do something about it.

After she'd gone to bed, he went into his office to think about how he could keep Nina in his life. Because suddenly the thought of her not being there was more important than anything else, including his new business.

CHAPTER FOURTEEN

"COME IN!" MAJOR called and straightened his tie seconds before the door to his office at RGF opened.

"Hey, what's up man?" Maurice said as he walked in.

Major frowned.

"What'd I do? I just got here."

"I was expecting someone else," Major said, shaking his head.

The huge grin that immediately spread across Maurice's face was annoying.

"Oh. Let me guess. Nina?" he asked because Maurice obviously couldn't resist being in a position to pick on the older twin for a change.

"Yes, Nina. I sent her a text asking her to come down, so she should be on her way. What do you want?"

"Just checking on you. Is everything ready for the big launch? I'm ready to start passing out Brand Integrated cards."

"Not quite," he said. "And before you start, it has nothing to do with Dad. In fact, I'm going to talk to him tonight. I should have done this a long time ago, but better late than never."

Major had been thinking along those lines all night long. By the time he'd gone to bed, Nina had been asleep, and he'd eased into the bed so he wouldn't disturb her. But she'd awakened anyway and had rolled over to where he'd been waiting with open arms. They slept cuddled together all night. Or rather, she'd slept and he'd rested his chin on top of her head, going over the plan he'd made and praying it would work.

"Good. And, yeah, you should have done it a long time ago. Anyway, I also wanted to give you a heads-up that Mom wants to talk to you."

"About what?" Major asked, not looking at his brother but reading the latest email Ruben, his lawyer, had sent him. They'd been going back and forth all day.

"Don't know. She wasn't specific when she questioned me about why you weren't answering your phone and sent me to find you."

Major had asked Landra to hold his calls today and he hadn't paid much attention to his cell if he glanced at the screen and it wasn't Nina or Ruben. "I've been working on something important and time sensitive," he replied.

"Okay, well you can tell Mom that when she finally catches up with you. But I'll get out of your hair right now and let you handle whatever it is that's got you so focused."

He looked up to see that Maurice was standing but

wasn't walking out of the office. Instead his brother was looking at him closely, as if he could see through the words Major wasn't offering. It was moments like these that he hated being a twin.

Major sat back in his chair and rubbed a hand over his chin.

"I did something I swore I'd never do."

Maurice crossed his arms over his chest. "And that is?"

"I want her to stay so I needed to figure out a way to make that happen," he told him.

There was no clear reaction from Maurice, which was usually the case. Only those who knew him very well could tell what he was thinking or feeling; that's how good he was at keeping his poker face. To let Maurice tell it, that's the way it had to be in the world they lived in. After his college years, Major agreed with the characterization to an extent.

"So is she staying?" Maurice asked after a few seconds of silence.

"Not sure yet," Major admitted with a shake of his head. He swiped his hands down his pant legs because he was worried about the answer to that question. "Gonna tell her when she gets here."

"What if she doesn't want to stay? Or if she doesn't want to stay to be with you? How're you gonna handle that?"

"Like we handle everything else—we move on to the next thing," he said, praying that wouldn't be the outcome.

"I got a feeling she isn't like anything else you've ever dealt with before."

"How do you know?"

Maurice shook his head then turned to start for the door. "I know you better than you know yourself, bro. And that probably goes the same for you with me. I knew you'd fallen for her that first day in Desta's office."

And that's exactly when it had happened—that day she'd bumped into him. That had been the start of it all.

"If you were her, would you stay here and continue to build your business?" he asked when Maurice was at the door. "If it was a great business opportunity and helped you achieve all your goals, but you'd be leaving your hometown and your family… would you stay?"

"If it were just about business, yeah, I'd stay."

That was cryptic even for Maurice and Major was left staring at the empty doorway because his twin was gone before Major could ask him to explain.

She still wasn't here yet and he'd texted her fifteen minutes ago. Major stood and paced his office second-guessing himself and hating that feeling. He never second-guessed, always knew the right thing to do for himself. But now there was someone else. And what if she didn't want to stay?

There wasn't time to explore the issue for the billionth time because his cell phone rang. He leaned over to grab the phone and saw that it was Ruben.

"Yeah?"

"Okay, I'm working on these new contracts and there are a few places that have to remain blank until you get me more information," Ruben said.

"Fine. Can you just email them over to me now? I need them like ten minutes ago." His tone was testy, and he didn't want to admit it was because he was so nervous.

"Are you sure this is what you want to do? I mean, it seems sort of sudden and Brand Integrated has been your project for a while."

Major pinched the bridge of his nose and let his head fall back. He'd thought about this all last night and had decided it was the best solution.

Next to her family, Nina's business was everything to her. So, if he could make it that she had access to the best technology and equipment while continuing to build on the platform she'd created, she'd definitely think twice before turning down the opportunity. She was too good a businessperson to not at least give it sincere consideration. For Major, the decision was about making it easier for them to be together as a real couple. And because he didn't know if she'd readily accept that, this business plan was his best option.

"Yeah, I'm sure," he said to Ruben. "Bringing Nina into Brand Integrated takes care of the problem of our businesses overlapping each other. She can just oversee the accessory hub division, combining that with her app, and we'll still be able to offer fashion houses the same benefits. In fact, bringing At Your Service under the Brand Integrated umbrella will benefit her, too, because she'll get immediate recognition instead of having to build her name."

"What are you doing?"

Major spun around at the sound of her voice. She was standing in the doorway, looking every bit as good as she had when she'd walked out of his penthouse an hour before him this morning.

"Hey," he said to her and then, "Ruben, I'll call you back. Send the papers over now."

He disconnected the call, slipping the phone into his pocket just as Nina stepped all the way into the office.

"If the papers you're referring to involve At Your Service coming under the Brand Integrated umbrella, you won't need them because I'm not selling my company to you," she said, her voice even, cool and very angry.

"Just hear me out," Major started after he circled around her to close the door to his office.

But Nina was already shaking her head. "I know what I heard, Major. And I'm telling you now it's not going to happen."

"It can be a great thing," he said.

She whirled around and he was right there just inches away from her.

"For who? And how long have you been thinking about this?" Her heart was thumping in her chest, her fingers clenching and releasing at her sides.

"Not long—but just let me explain. There's so much more I want to say." He ran a hand across the back of his neck and sighed heavily. "This isn't how I wanted to start off. Let's take a seat."

"No," she said, yanking her arm away when he reached for her hand. "I don't want to sit."

She'd rather be standing when he tried to stab her in her back. Just as her mother had done to her husband and children. The comparison came quick, slicing through her with white-hot pain.

"How could you even suggest something like this?" Because, dammit, she'd started trusting him. She'd started to feel things for him even when she knew she shouldn't. But she wasn't going to fall apart in front of him. She wasn't going to let the ridiculous fantasy she'd begun to weave in her head make her look like a fool in front of him. Not the way her father had cried over her mother's leaving.

Instead she squared her shoulders and lifted her chin before asking, "What gave you the impression that I'd ever want to come under the umbrella of your business to gain recognition?"

"Nina, that's not what I said. You only heard part of the conversation. What I'm proposing is much bigger. It means so much more than just you gaining recognition for your little app."

"My 'little app'?" She backed away because on top of the pain freely flowing now, fury bubbled in her stomach and her entire body began to shake. "Is that how you see my company? Haven't you seen the bump in sales RGF has gotten since we linked my 'little app' to your website?"

Sales in three of their key casual clothing lines

had jumped forty-three percent since the partnership began. RJ had even sent her an email this morning requesting they get together to discuss how they could make the arrangement permanent. She'd spent the bulk of the afternoon preparing a report on drafting terms for a formal permanent agreement. On top of that, RJ had asked her to be prepared to share her thoughts about the trade show with him. She'd outlined her complete idea for the African-inspired accessory line for RGF and how they could link its launch to At Your Service.

But Major wanted to take her company and make it part of his. He wanted to take every ounce of trust and genuine rapport they'd built in these past weeks and treat it as if it were nothing, as if they were nothing.

"I didn't mean to say it that way. I know your app is doing well. That's part of the reason I thought of this. Could you just calm down for a second and let me explain everything?" He'd dropped his arms to his sides, giving up on trying to touch her.

That was a good thing because she wasn't sure how well that was going to go if he tried again.

"How dare you?" she began, trying like hell to keep her anger under control. She needed to move or she was certain she would explode. She'd trusted him. Dammit, she'd promised herself to never trust anyone, not on this level. People broke your heart, always.

"Was this your plan all along? Was the whole trial period and fake engagement all a part of some diabolical takeover of the company I've worked so hard to build because it was similar to your own?" The words stung her throat, hurt and some other emotion swirling to form a sour mix deep in her chest.

"Nina," he said, his tone stronger than he'd ever used on her before. So strong it stopped her in her tracks where she now stood close to the window. "I'm in love with you."

Her hands began to shake. A sign of weakness. She was breaking, just like her mother's departure had broken her father. Jacoby's drinking and smoking had increased in the months after Lynn left. Twelve-year-old Nina recalled the extra packs of cigarettes she saw in his bedroom trash can and the bottles of vodka that appeared throughout the house.

"Don't." She whispered the word as if it were her last breath. "Don't say that to me."

"I need to say it." He took a step toward her and she shook her head to warn him away. He stopped, sighed and then started again. "I don't want you to go. Last night we were talking about the fake breakup and you had a plan for how it would go, but I was hastily thinking of a plan to make you stay."

"You can't make me do anything, Major."

He closed his eyes, the eyes she'd been staring into every night for the past few weeks. Eyes she thought she'd come to know and to lo— Now, she was shaking her head.

"I know I can't. But I was hoping, I thought we were feeling the same thing."

"When did I ever give you the impression that

I'd be willing to sell my business to be part of your world?" She wasn't part of his world. Angie and Daisy had tried to tell her that yesterday. All these weeks she'd not only been part of a fake engagement, she'd been living a fake life. A life she'd never imagined for herself because it wasn't who she was or who she wanted to be.

"This isn't just about business, Nina. It's so much more than that, and I dare you to stand there and truthfully tell me it's different."

She couldn't and he knew it. Damn him, he knew how she felt about him. Just as Lynn had known how much Jacoby had loved her and yet she'd still walked out.

"My business is not for sale. *I* am not for sale!"

"Is that what you think this is?" he asked her quietly. "You think I'm so desperate for a fiancée that I'd try to buy your love in a mutually beneficial business deal?"

"You obtained a fake fiancée in a mutually beneficial business deal," she snapped back.

His brow furrowed and, for the first time, she thought he looked as angry as she felt. Good, he could be angry. She didn't care. He wasn't going to run over her and take what he wanted just because he was one of the fabulous Golds! His money and prestige in the fashion industry wasn't enough to take the life she'd worked so hard for away from her without a fight.

She was just about to say that and tell him exactly what he could do with his business deal and any other collaboration between her and RGF, when her phone rang. It was tucked into the back pocket of the pants she wore because she'd left her purse in her office.

"Please," Major said solemnly. "Can we just sit down and talk about this like levelheaded adults? I could be wrong—this may not work. We should just talk it over and see how we can fix this."

Her cell rang again and she yanked it out of her pocket, staring down at the screen. It was Angie. Nina turned her back to him and answered the phone.

"What is it?"

"It's Dad," Angie replied. "He fell. It's bad, Nina. You've gotta come now."

Her heart dropped and the room seemed to spin around her. Nina held tight to the phone as if that could ground her and keep her from falling. She took a deep breath and released it as slowly and as evenly as she could. "Okay. I'll be right there."

Disconnecting the call, she turned back to see Major staring at her. He looked so good in his gray suit pants and white dress shirt. The tie was a deep purple; she'd seen it hanging in his closet on the tie rack full of over one hundred others in different colors and patterns. He looked stricken, but maybe that was just because she was feeling that way. Maybe he'd looked so good and appealed to her so quickly because a part of her had wanted to see him that way. Perhaps everything she'd wanted to see and believe about this man and the situation he'd offered her was just a fantasy, a dream she hadn't known she wanted to live, even if temporarily.

None of that mattered now.

"I have to go."

"Nina—" he started to say.

"No!" Now it was time for her tone to be strong, for her to take the control her father had lost the day her mother walked out on them. "I'm leaving now, Major, and you need to let me go."

"Please, just… Okay, let me take you wherever you need to go. If it's back to your apartment, I'm okay with that, just don't walk out of here without… I don't know, Nina, just don't."

He couldn't get his words out and she thought that was strange. Major always knew what to say. Well, that was fine. She knew what needed to be said.

"I have to go and Claude will drive me." She didn't wait for another response as she started for the door. This time when he reached for her, Nina didn't pull away, she couldn't find the strength to do so.

He touched her elbow lightly at first and then let his fingers trail to her wrist and finally lace with hers. "I messed this up," he said quietly. "Let me fix it."

She looked over her shoulder at him.

"There's nothing for you to fix because I never planned to let you break me." She let her hand slip from his grasp and walked out of the office.

CHAPTER FIFTEEN

MAJOR HAD NO idea what time it was or how long he'd sat in the dark on the couch in his living room glaring at the city skyline. He'd stood in his office for endless minutes staring at the open door that Nina had walked through before cursing fluently and grabbing his jacket and phone and leaving, too. He'd thought he'd find her at his place, gathering her clothes, but she'd been there and gone. The engagement ring he'd given her left in the center of the coffee table. So he'd just dropped down onto the couch where, coincidentally, twelve hours before they'd sat talking about their impending breakup.

He leaned forward, letting his elbows rest on his knees and feeling his head drop down. Where was she? How was she feeling? What could he say or do to make this better? Or, at the very least, to make the burning pain that had spread throughout his chest and settled there like an impending storm go away.

The doorbell rang and he ignored it. Whoever was on the other side wasn't going to make this better.

Because no matter who it was, it wouldn't be Nina. He was certain of that.

She wasn't coming back, not to him, and definitely not to RGF. RJ was going to be pissed about the latter but Major didn't care. Once upon a time, business—his family's and the one he'd built for himself—had been all he'd cared about. But that was before the marketing plan. Before Nina.

The bell rang again and this time it was followed by a familiar voice.

"Major Frederick Gold, if you don't open this door, I'm going to take it off its hinges."

He lifted his head at the sound of his mother's voice.

When he was seven years old, he and Maurice had spread peanut butter over the floors in one of Riley's dollhouses. When Riley had seen it, she'd been hysterical for hours. Maurice had laughed it off and taken his punishment in the nonchalant way he always did. But Major had been devastated by the pain in Riley's cries as well as the fury and disappointment in his mother's voice. He'd locked himself in his bedroom to get away from it all and Marva had stood outside the door, knocking for a few moments before repeating the same threat she'd just stated.

Major stood and walked to the door. Moments later he found not just his mother but Riley, too, standing on the other side.

"Silly boy," Marva said as she entered, stroking him on the cheek.

Riley shook her head as she walked past him.

He closed the door and prepared himself for the barrage from the only two women he'd ever thought he'd love.

Riley sat in one of the side chairs, placing her purse on the end table. Marva sat, too, and patted the cushion beside her as a signal for Major to take a seat.

"Are you done sulking?" she asked once he settled beside her.

"I'm a grown man, Mom. I don't sulk," he said.

"Ha!"

That came from Riley and Major chose to ignore it.

"What did you do to mess things up with her?" Marva asked.

He didn't even bother to question how she knew. Somehow his mother always knew everything, and he suspected Landra may have overheard the last portion of his argument with Nina. His assistant didn't miss much that went on in the office.

"She overheard me talking to Ruben about combining our businesses so that she wouldn't have to work to get recognition in the industry."

"Dumb ass," Riley quipped.

Major glared at his sister.

"Well, you have to admit that wasn't very smart," Marva said.

He sighed. "In retrospect, I can see that. But at the time—"

"You thought you were doing her a favor," Marva finished for him.

"You thought you were saving her," Riley added. "Men are so dense sometimes."

He should have left them in the hallway.

"If you wanted her to stay with you, Major, why didn't you just ask her?"

"I didn't know how."

"Oh, it's simple. 'Nina, I love you. Please don't go.' Seven measly little words," Riley said.

Times like these Major hated having a sister, especially one as smart as Riley.

"Again, at the time, I didn't think to start it off that way. But I did tell her I loved her. She didn't seem to care," he admitted, feeling a renewed wave of pain soar through his chest.

"It's hard to believe someone loves you when they try to take what you've worked hard for. Isn't that what you thought your father would do if he found out about you wanting to leave RGF to start your own business?"

Major straightened and stared at his mother.

"Your father and I've known for some time that you were itching to move beyond RGF," she replied in answer to his unspoken question. "You and Maurice always thought you were keeping your little twin secrets, but you forget Ruben's mother and office manager is a longtime friend of mine."

He sighed again because he hadn't forgotten that, but he *had* instead relied on confidentiality from his attorney's office. While that professional courtesy should've stretched to Ruben's staff, Marva didn't play when it came to her children and if Ruben's mother had let anything slip about Brand Integrated, Marva would've pried the full story out of her.

"Look, I'm not here to talk about your business. You know I love and believe in you, whatever you do and wherever you do it," Riley said. "But Nina's a good woman and I'm really pissed off that you pushed her out of your life. Out of our lives."

It was hard for any of them to have real friends, unless they'd been there since childhood like Ruben had been for Major. But for Riley, with all that she'd been through with her past scandals involving idiotic men, it was doubly hard for her to form bonds with people other than family. She'd obviously bonded with Nina.

"I didn't want her to go, Riley. I tried to get her to stay."

"Well, now it's time to try to get her back," Marva said as if that were as simple as making a phone call.

"I don't know how," he said, dragging his hands down his face. "She's got so much on her plate right now. I don't want to be another issue in her life. If this isn't what she wants, I have no right trying to force it on her."

"Did she say it wasn't what she wanted?" Riley asked. "I don't think having you in her life is add-ing a responsibility. To the contrary, I think the time she was here may have been the most relaxed she's been in years."

Just last night she'd been in her element at the trade show. The moment she'd found those African pieces, she'd lit up like a Christmas tree, all bright and giddy with her idea. And it was a brilliant idea, one that had sparked the plan he'd eventually come up with.

Major stood and walked over to the window. He folded his arms across his chest and stared into the night, wishing it were as simple as reaching out into the big city and touching her.

"There are probably trains leaving for York as early as seven tomorrow morning," he said more to himself than to his mom and sister. "Or I could just drive. Be there first thing in the morning, ready to grovel if need be. Anything, just so long as I get the chance to apologize to her and to tell her how much I love her."

He didn't wait for a response from anyone, just went into his bedroom and started to pack.

Jacoby yelled out in agony as he sat up in his bed.

"I told you to wait and let me help you," Nina said, coming around to the side of the bed and slipping her arm under his to help bear his weight so he could stand. "And you need to use the crutches, like the doctor told you."

"Well, I want to go sit out on the back porch. That pain pill had me sleeping so long this morning, I missed my normal coffee time."

That was true, but Nina had appreciated those three hours of solitude. It had been the first time she'd been able to sit with her thoughts since she'd raced home yesterday morning.

"I got some iced tea in the refrigerator. I want a glass and some cookies while I sit outside," Jacoby said.

"Okay, I'll get you settled outside and then I'll get your tea and cookies," she told him.

"Where're your sisters? Did they run out the moment you got here? Those two stay busy."

Nina sighed and concentrated on easing her father to the crutches so that she could get his weight properly distributed and keep them both upright. His fall down the last four stairs in the basement had left him with a broken left ankle and a gash on his head that had to be sutured. He was now sporting a white patch of gauze over his right eye to match the white cast on his ankle.

She settled him on her right side and worked her way around him with the other crutch, tucking it under his left arm.

"There, now take it slow. I'll get your snack and sit on the porch with you and go through my emails."

Since she was certain her deal with RGF was over.

Jacoby huffed and mumbled some more as she stayed a few steps behind him to offer support should he need it. Her father was a proud man; a stubborn and opinionated man who loved his girls more than he loved life at this moment.

"I want the Oreo cookies, not those dry butter ones Daisy keeps buying," he said when they finally made it into the kitchen.

The master bedroom of the ranch-style house was closer to the kitchen than the other two rooms, so their trek had been short. Nina immediately went to the cabinet to grab a glass and filled it with the crushed ice her father preferred from the ice machine on the refrigerator.

"The butter cookies have less sugar," she told him even though she knew he couldn't care less.

"Yeah, well all the baked goods and snacks could cause elevated cholesterol or diabetes. Everything does something bad and something good. So with the time I have left, I'm doing whatever makes me feel good. I want eight cookies. Count 'em and put them in a napkin for me."

He was already heading for the back door, which Nina had left open when she'd gone out onto the porch to sit while he slept. After this morning, she now knew why her father liked to sit on that porch so much. It was quiet, peaceful, revealing. She'd come to terms with a few things about herself and her life while sitting in one of the twin rocking chairs just staring out toward the sky.

With the glass in one hand, his eight cookies folded into a napkin in the other, and her laptop tucked under her arm, she walked out onto the porch just as her dad was trying to settle himself into a chair. She hurried over to him, placing the glass, cookies and laptop on the small wooden table between the rocking chairs that looked as if they were on their last legs.

"Here, let me help you," she said and eased the crutches from one arm and then the next.

Standing in front of him, she put both her arms under his and then bent her knees as he reclined into the chair.

Jacoby huffed when he was finally seated. "Your sisters should have stayed here to help," he grumbled.

She ignored him because she was glad Angie and Daisy had left. They'd been a nagging, arguing pain in her ass from the time she'd arrived yesterday, until the moment she'd told them to go late last night. They weren't being helpful, just judgmental and annoying, traits they'd spent most of their lives perfecting.

"It's okay, Dad. We're fine," she told him, sitting in the chair next to him before grabbing her laptop from the table.

"Not okay," he said when he reached for his cookies.

She could hear him crunching on the first one as she booted up her laptop and waited to log in to her inbox.

"You should be in New York working," Jacoby said after a few moments.

"You weren't happy that I'd stayed in New York, remember?"

"No, I wasn't happy if you were in New York pimping yourself out to some rich dude," he snapped. "But you said that's not what you were doing."

"It's not," she replied, clicking on an email from RJ Gold, wondering if this was his message telling her she'd breached her contract with them by leaving town.

"And that guy you were in New York with? He was helping you with your business?"

She was only half listening to her father now, but

she replied, "Yeah, his family's company was taking a chance on my app."

If you're reading this right now, I'm on my way to you and it's too late for you to stop me.

That's what the first line of the email read and her heartbeat had immediately picked up its pace.

I hope you'll hear me out this time and once you do, whatever you want, whatever you tell me to do, I will.

RJ hadn't written this email. Her eyes shot up to the subject line of the message again as she read the oldest Gold brother's name and email address.

"He sounds like a good guy. You should hear him out."

Her head snapped up at her father's words and she looked over at him and then past him.

Major walked around from the side of the house and her laptop almost slipped off her lap. He wore dark blue jeans and a crisp, white polo shirt. His hair looked freshly cut and his shape-up was sharp, his thin mustache trimmed. Her pulse rate quickened as her mind whirled with questions.

"Hello, Mr. Fuller. It's nice to meet you in person, sir."

She watched as Major walked up onto the porch and immediately went to her father, extending a hand for Jacoby to shake. Her father, the surly old grouch that he'd become, accepted that hand and looked up at Major.

"You mess this up again and I'll beat you with my crutches."

Major nodded. "I understand, sir."

"What's going on? You two know each other?" She put her laptop on the table because she couldn't afford to pay for another one and if one more surprise popped off, she was sure to drop this one.

Her father answered. "Got a call from this gentleman early this morning while you were sitting out here rocking in my chair like you thought you could find the answers to your problems."

"I thought you were asleep," she said.

"Not with my chair squeaking the way it does when it's being rocked too fast. And then that cell phone you and your sisters insist I keep close to me started ringing."

She looked to Major then. "You called my father?"

Before he could answer, Jacoby spoke. "You got something for me, young man?"

"Ah, yeah. I have it right here." Major reached around to his back pocket and pulled out some folded papers. "All you need to do is read over the lease and sign it. I can take it back to the facility today and you can move in as early as tomorrow."

Nina stood. "Move? What facility? Will somebody please tell me what's going on?" Her hands were trembling and her heart was about to pump right out of her chest.

Jacoby took the papers Major handed him and

then waved his free hand. "Go on, take her in the house and say your piece before she flips out. She never did like not knowing or controlling everything. Gets that from me, I suppose."

Major stepped closer to her. "Can we go inside and talk for a minute?"

She didn't know what to say and still couldn't believe he was there. "I guess that's what we're supposed to do at this point."

Before Major or her father could say another word, Nina walked into the house. She passed through the kitchen and stopped in the center of the living room, turning to see Major as he followed her inside.

"What are you doing? You got my father into that facility you were talking about, without consulting me?"

"I consulted your father," he said with a nod. "And before you go off telling me I had no right to do that, I wasn't going to. When I called your father this morning, it was strictly to ask him if he would mind me coming by to see you. He brought up the facility, asking if I knew of any places in New York that he could afford on his budget."

"No," she said, her voice cracking slightly. "That's impossible. His budget isn't enough to hardly cover the expenses in this house. And his home...our home...is here in York."

"I wish it could be in New York with me," he said quietly.

"Major—"

"Wait," he said, holding up a hand. "Just give me

five minutes. Let me just get this out the right way this time and then you can react. You can tell me to kick rocks and leave you alone forever, if that's what you want. But please, just listen."

She folded her arms over her chest because the warmth that was now swelling there alarmed her. This wasn't supposed to be happening. Early this morning she'd sat on that porch resigning herself to having fallen in love when that hadn't been her plan and to making the best of the help she'd gleaned working with his family's company for the short time she'd been blessed to do so. She hadn't thought of contacting Major again or going back to New York to see him. She would deal with whatever legal repercussions were brought on by her breaching the contract, but her new plan was to move on.

"I love you," he said when she nodded for him to continue.

"I didn't plan on falling in love and neither did you. We planned to do what was best for our businesses. And to be totally honest with you, Nina, I believe in my heart that you and I partnering together in a consulting and development firm that will cater to a full scale of technological needs to the fashion industry is the best career move for us."

She opened her mouth to speak and Major stepped closer, touching a finger softly to her lips.

"I'm not here to save you, your father or your business. Because you don't need to be saved. You're a brilliant, beautiful woman with a bright future ahead of you whether or not you take me up on this offer.

But I don't know how to move forward without you, Nina. You walked into that building all those weeks ago and the moment you bumped into me, *you* saved *me*."

He slid his finger away.

"You saved me from the lonely life I'd resigned myself to because I refused to trust again. You agreed to do what was a crazy job from the start and, every step of the way, all you were concerned with was doing your very best to make that crazy job work, for my family's company as well as for your own. I can't thank you enough for your help and I couldn't let you go without admitting to you that I need you. I want you, for real this time."

Tears welled in her eyes but she refused to let them fall.

"You knew all I wanted was to take care of my father." Her voice was shaky and she wanted to stop. She wanted to turn away from him and go somewhere alone to break down under the pressure of emotions that had steadily built with each word he'd spoken.

"You've taken care of your family for so long. You thought it was your job, but it wasn't. Your father asked me to find him a place in New York because he feels that's the only way you'll follow your dreams. I did it because I love you and I want your dreams to be my dreams. I want us to do this business thing and the family thing together."

The first tear rolled down her cheek and she cursed the warm, wet feel of it.

Major used his thumb to brush that tear away.

"You weren't planning to buy my business," she said slowly. "You wanted us to be partners all along?"

He nodded. "I would never take anything away from you. I believe what you've built can enhance what I've started. And my father and RJ loved your ideas about the accessory line for RGF. I told them about it when I was hijacking RJ's email account to schedule that message you received."

She chuckled and shook her head. "I knew RJ hadn't written that."

"No, but he had a good time saying he told me so while I typed it. My dad appreciated my groveling to you a bit more than I expected, as well."

He used both hands to cup her face now, tilting her head up to his. "I'm dying to kiss you."

"Kisses aren't part of the negotiations this time, Major."

He froze at her words.

"I want more," she said, coming up on the tips of her toes to touch her lips to his briefly. "I want a real engagement party where you'll officially slip my ring back onto my finger, and a huge wedding and when we launch *our* business, I want it to be called the Gold Service."

His smile spread slowly and warm tendrils wrapped around her heart. "I think that can be arranged," he replied.

* * * * *

GUILTY
PLEASURE

TARYN LEIGH TAYLOR

MILLS & BOON

Thanks for helping me with my homework, Crystal.

And for Jo. We made it. Thank you for everything.

CHAPTER ONE

SOMEONE WAS GOING to pay.

Wes Brennan just had to figure out who.

Accepting the lumpy manila envelope the guard slid under the Plexiglas barrier, Wes ripped into it and dumped the contents on the stainless steel counter.

He grabbed his watch first, fastening the platinum band around his left wrist. His blue silk Brioni tie was unceremoniously shoved into his pants pocket, along with his keys. After a quick inspection of his billfold—one hundred dollars and all his plastic—it, too, was tucked away, this time in the breast pocket of his suit jacket. If he'd known he was going to end up in jail, he would have stopped at an ATM first. A hundred bucks probably wouldn't even cover his cab ride home if traffic was bad, and in LA, traffic was always bad.

Wes picked up the last item on the counter. He barely recognized his bearded reflection in the black screen of his phone. Well, what was left of his phone, anyway. He'd watched an FBI agent strip it of its SIM card, which was still evidence in his active and ongoing case, the day they'd put him in cuffs. He pressed the power button a few times, but to no avail. Clearly no one had thought to turn his phone off after whatever the hell they'd seen fit to do to it during his incarceration. With a sigh, he slid it into the same pocket as his wallet.

The mandated hiatus from the digital world was probably for the best, he decided. *Cybersecurity expert rips off his clients.* Yeah, he could see the press getting some mileage out of that. He'd take the reprieve while he could get it.

Then he tossed the empty envelope in the designated bin and walked out of prison.

Ten days he'd been held like a mongrel at the pound, focused on this moment—liberation—but when he stepped beyond the squeaky metal door and back into the world, what he felt was not so much relief as wariness. A haunting certainty that the dog catcher loomed around the next corner, or the one after that. He wasn't out of this nightmare yet. Not by a long shot.

It didn't help that California's famous sunshine was nowhere to be seen, swallowed by dank, gray clouds that reflected his mood. The air was foul with smog. Wes took a deep breath anyway, inhaling the tainted scent of freedom.

He wanted to incinerate the suit he'd been arrested in with a blowtorch.

He wanted to scald any remnants of the experience from his skin with a blistering shower.

But most of all, he wanted vengeance. With every cell of his being.

Odd, then, that he was so easily and thoroughly distracted when he caught sight of the woman who was waiting for him at the end of the sidewalk.

She'd been wearing a red dress the first time he'd seen her, at an overstuffed party, in a frat house that reeked of booze and pot and hormones. Her dress now was the same color, but streamlined and structured, tailored to perfection to skim the long, sleek lines of her body. Back then it had been short and flowy, fluttering around her thighs in a way that made his fingers ache to inch it higher.

Gone, too, were the wild brown curls of her youth, replaced by an angled bob that showed off sharp cheekbones and made the generous curve of her mouth look even softer and more inviting in contrast. Her lips were painted the same red as her dress.

Vivienne Grant.

The *last* person he wanted to witness his personal and professional nadir, and yet, an oddly fitting choice.

After all, what was hell without your very own devil incarnate?

"Hello, lover."

Her voice still grabbed him by the balls. Throaty. Sexy. Poisonous.

Wes's chuckle held no mirth as he stopped in front of her. "And to think I thought things couldn't get worse."

The slow curve of her mouth was mesmerizing.

"I knew you'd be surprised." Vivienne's eyes glittered, hard and sharp.

Beautiful. She'd always been so fucking beautiful.

"Did Whitfield send you?" Just saying his former client's name made anger surge in Wes's veins, and he had to actively relax his fists. For the last two months, he'd poured all of Soteria Security's time and resources into figuring out how someone had bested their top-of-the-line security system and hacked Max Whitfield's tech empire. As thanks, Max and his business nemesis, Cybercore CEO Liam Kearney, had joined their considerable forces and accused Wes of the crime before siccing the FBI on him. Not that he and Whitfield had ever had the fuzziest feelings for one another, but he'd deluded himself into believing there was respect there.

Now, all bets were off.

"Hardly. He's still very upset with you."

Wes hiked his pant leg high enough to reveal his state-of-the-art, tamper-proof ankle monitor. "You can tell him the feeling's mutual."

"I can't actually. I quit last week. Max is no longer my concern."

The announcement surprised him, though he masked it. Lead counsel at Whitfield Industries was the sort of power gig Wes had assumed would need to be pried out of her cold, dead, lawyerly hands. Vivienne's career had always been priority number one. Six years ago, he'd been stupid enough to test that theory, and his hubris had resulted in an incisive verbal flaying, a glorious breakup fuck and her walking right out of their place and onto a plane bound for Yale.

The resulting years of radio silence had come to a crashing halt a year ago, when she'd returned to LA to accept a position as Max Whitfield's legal consigliere.

The current state of their relationship consisted of little more than the coldest of professional acknowledgments and an undercurrent of venom whenever they sporadically ended up in the same meeting.

Of course, now that neither of them worked for Whitfield in any capacity, the thin layer of civility that had coated their professional interactions for the last twelve months was no longer required.

"Then to what do I owe the distinct lack of pleasure?"

Icy amusement arched Vivienne's brow. "I was in the neighborhood."

Dread settled cold and flat in his gut at her ill-timed appearance in his world, but he kept his expression bland. "Terminal Island seems a little outside your usual radius. Are you in the market for clients? Or dates?"

There was no reason it should bother him that her laugh sounded rusty.

"Invectives, Wesley? And to think I was expecting a thank-you for using my kick-ass lawyer skills to get you out on bail."

Not good. Not fucking good at all. "You're not my lawyer."

She wasn't his anything. Not anymore.

"Well, I believe you were made aware that Denisof Price Goldberg is no longer interested in representing you going forward."

Ha. The bastards couldn't disassociate fast enough. DPG had dumped his ass almost the moment he'd been arrested, citing conflict of interest with their ongoing role as counsel to Soteria Security.

Proof that his company, the one he'd built with brains and sweat and sacrifice, was disassociating. It was what he and his partner, Jesse Hastings, had agreed to when they'd been making contingency plans, something they'd written into the contract when they'd incorporated. Just one of many business-first precautions—a *what-if* that was never supposed to happen.

Wes gave a terse nod. "I was."

That, he'd been expecting. What he *hadn't* been expecting was the hesitancy by several other large law firms—all directly or indirectly affiliated with some of Soteria Security's biggest clients—to also balk at the idea of representing him.

Blackballed. Whitfield and Kearney wielded their clout with devastating precision, he'd give them that.

"I wasn't, however, made aware that I had new representation."

Something flashed across her face that he might have labeled remorse if he hadn't known that Vivienne was incapable of it.

The odd look was replaced with haughty disdain as she straightened to her full height. In her heels, she was only about two inches shorter than his six-three. "So how did you think you got released today? Magic legal fairies?"

"I figured my assistant had finally hired someone." Wes aimed for an offhand shrug. "We had a very promising meeting scheduled with one of LA's most elite attorneys. You might have seen his picture on some of the bus stop benches downtown."

He was only half joking. Because every cell in his body was screaming at him to back away from the woman in front of him, his freedom be damned.

The two of them had imploded in spectacular fashion last time they'd been in each other's orbit. It had fucked him up for longer than he cared to admit. And if he was going to clear his name, if he was going to get his company back, he couldn't afford even the slightest distraction.

"So you're saying you'd rather hire some hack ambulance chaser who will be thoroughly outmatched by the elite law team representing your former company than be represented by me?"

"Yes." That was *exactly* what he was saying.

She blanched, and against his will, Wes found himself trying to soften the blow. "You're a corporate lawyer, not criminal defense."

So fucking weak, and she knew it, too.

Determination manifested itself in the set of her chin. "I can do this, Wes."

The use of his name threw him off. Slipped beneath his defenses. Crawled under his skin.

His blue eyes cut to her dark ones. "As a rule, I

don't like to mix current business and former pleasure. Things tend to get messy."

Vivienne pressed the remote starter in her hand, and the glossy Vanquish S Coupe behind her purred to life. It was a gorgeous car. Sleek and sexy, just like its owner.

Tendrils of unease fisted around his spine as she pulled the door open for him.

"Doesn't matter if you like it, Brennan. I'm all you've got."

And *that* was exactly what he was afraid of.

Wes looked good.

Vivienne sent a covert glance at her passenger as they zipped over the suspension bridge that led to the 110 and back into LA proper.

In fact, he looked better than good, considering.

She had to strangle a macabre laugh. *Considering.* A bland euphemism for being arrested, having your assets seized and losing your cybersecurity business and your reputation in one fell swoop.

She'd worried that he'd look different, that prison might have irreparably changed him. It was the one thing he'd vowed would never happen—ending up in jail, like his deadbeat father. But now it had.

And yet, as far as she could see, the only outward evidence of his ordeal was ten days' worth of facial hair and a slightly wrinkled suit that fit him to perfection—an ode to both the breadth of his shoulders and the skill of his tailor.

Wes had come face-to-face with his greatest fear and emerged sexily disheveled.

An unwelcome heat prickled across her skin, some kind of carnal nostalgia, and she shifted against the black leather bucket seat like it was a lightning rod that could dissipate the sudden charge of attraction inside the Aston Martin.

She was desperate to pop the bubble of awareness that had so easily consumed her, but her haste made her careless and the conversational pin she chose was a mistake.

"How is...everyone?"

Bland pleasantries with anyone else, but between them, the question felt shockingly personal.

Wes's shoulders stiffened. He obviously hadn't expected her to go there either.

The fact that Vivienne found she cared about the answer—after so many years of purposefully not thinking about his mother, his sister, *him*—stung more than she'd expected. Like she'd accidentally ripped a scab off her heart.

"What are you doing?"

She didn't know. She'd returned from her annual three-day pilgrimage to the Phoenix Inn, a little B&B in Connecticut, to the news that her boss had put Wesley in the FBI crosshairs. She'd quit her dream job and spent the last week pouring everything she had into getting him out of jail. She'd called in every favor, pushed her legal acumen to the brink, wheedled, cajoled, outsmarted and insomnia-ed in anticipation of this moment. And now that it was here, now that he was free...*ish*...she had no answer to his question, no explanation that wouldn't reveal more than she wanted to give. He was a weakness she couldn't afford. He always had been.

"It's called small talk. It's a form of politeness that acquaintances use to fill the silence."

Wes's sudden grin dominated her peripheral vision and tightened Vivienne's hands on the steering wheel. She remembered a time it wasn't quite so mocking.

A time when a flash of it was all it took for her to surrender her panties in the unisex bathroom at Señor Taco's a mere two hours and three tequilas after her roommate had dragged her across campus to the lamest of frat parties. Then they'd headed back to her dorm room for orgasms two, three and four, and woken up the next morning wrapped around each other and well on their mutual way to orgasm number five.

Wes hadn't been wearing a suit then. Just a white T-shirt that seemed to glow against the tan he'd acquired doing manual labor in the California sun, a pair of faded jeans that were soft from washing, the worn fabric hugging thighs thick with muscle, and *that smile*. The one that gave her the kind of XXX butterflies that skipped her abdomen altogether and headed straight for her—

"Oh, is that what we are? *Acquaintances?*" He sneered the word.

Viv forced air into her lungs and kept her glance dismissive. "Would you prefer something more colorful?" After a quick shoulder check, she maneuvered the sports car into the far left lane. "Former paramours? Scorned exes?" Her voice broke, and she had to clear her throat to finish her list. "Star-crossed lovers?"

Wes blew out an audible breath, tinged with defeat. "Acquaintances it is," he conceded. "You going to tell me where we're going?"

The moment of truth.

"My place."

For the first time since he'd gotten in the car, she was in his sights. She could feel the burn of his stare on her profile. "I don't think so."

Vivienne's spine hardened with resolve. She wasn't that idealistic, lovestruck girl anymore, and he was no longer the object of her affection. No amount of reminiscing—sentimental or erotic—was going to change that fact. She was a lawyer. He needed a lawyer. And that was that.

"As a computer wizard and a flight risk, there were a couple of provisos I had to agree to in order to get you out on bail."

He resettled his big frame against the passenger seat, a whisper of fabric on leather, but the flex of his fist against his muscled thigh belied his calm exterior. "No tech. No internet. No travel beyond the range of my ankle monitor. I got the speech, Vivienne. Stop stalling"

The sound of her full name on his lips was a bullet to the heart. Taciturn and austere, with no flicker of the heat that used to burn strong and insatiable between them.

Tangible proof the past was gone.

And the present was a cold, hard bitch.

Just like me, she reminded herself, buoying her resolve.

"In addition to those stipulations, you've also been remanded into my care until the trial."

"Fuck that."

There was no particular emphasis in his words, but that didn't make his shock less palpable. It was a living thing in the confines of the luxury car. The air around them crackled with the restless energy of it.

"Should I turn around then? I can call ahead to make sure your cell is ready by the time we arrive."

She felt him bristle at the constraints of his current situation, as though his essence was pacing the car like a caged lion, testing the bars for weaknesses. It didn't take him long to realize there was no escape. Wes had always been a staunch realist.

The charged silence of his acceptance oozed over her skin, thick and uncomfortable, unbroken aside from the soft rush of the air-conditioning and the muttered curse that crossed his lips.

She refused to label the loosening in her chest, because it felt a little too much like relief for her own peace of mind. She arched an eyebrow in his direction. "Good to know my company still ranks higher than incarceration."

"Just barely," he mumbled, and with that unflattering summation, he purposefully and studiously ignored her for the rest of the trip which, thanks to the notorious LA traffic, took three times as long as it should have.

Not that it mattered. His opinion didn't concern her, and he'd proven a long time ago that he wasn't susceptible to anything as basic as human emotion, so the state of his *feelings* was irrelevant. Vivienne was going to set things right, and his cooperation was neither essential nor desired. She would do what needed to be done, and once she had, she could finally lance this painful, recurring boil that sprang up every time their lives intersected.

Besides, Vivienne reasoned, flipping on the signal light, his silence was no more than she deserved.

She was, after all, the reason he'd gone to jail in the first place.

CHAPTER TWO

WES HAD SPENT a lot of years convinced that prison was his worst nightmare.

He'd had only a vague notion of what it meant to be locked up back then, but he was intimately familiar with how it affected those you left behind. He'd watched his mother wait for his father, first with dreamy idealism, then with stalwart resolution, and finally with glassy, narcotic-numbed indifference. At six years of age, Wes had promised himself he'd never end up like his dad, never do that to his own family.

His scoff was silent and self-directed. He'd managed to keep only half that bargain, and on a technicality, no less. Because he didn't have a family of his own. Ironic, then, that his punishment was to be a court-enforced game of playing house with Vivienne Grant.

Maybe jail hadn't been so bad after all.

The erroneous thought hit him just as Vivienne glided the luxury automobile into its designated spot in the underground parking garage of her high-rise condominium.

The building was posh. Top-of-the-line. The kind of place he'd been determined to be able to afford for her one day. Their relationship had been long dead by the time he'd reached that goal.

She'd changed a lot since then, a lifetime ago, but not this. Not her easy familiarity with the best the world had to offer.

There were some physical differences, of course, but nothing that couldn't easily be attributed to the passage of time.

A sleek, straight haircut, a rigidly professional wardrobe, and the daring glint in her eyes had mellowed and morphed into confident determination.

But the shift from the girl he'd loved to the woman he resented wasn't in her surroundings, or her appearance, so much as a tectonic shift in her *essence*. As though some part of the Vivienne he'd known had not made it through the carnage.

She was still a force to be reckoned with, but there was nothing scattershot about her anymore. She was laser focused. Precise. A corporate warrior who'd abandoned the volatile bow and flaming arrow of her youth in favor of the cold, exact steel of a scalpel. And her new weapon of choice suited her well. So well that Wes wondered if his memories of her, wild and reckless and overwhelming, were mistaken. The woman getting out of the car seemed impenetrable to him, an avatar.

Wes closed the door on his useless musings and followed her through the parking garage toward the elevator, the staccato beat of her heels bouncing in the cavernous structure lined with expensive cars. He watched as Vivienne swiped a small fob in front of the receiver before dropping her keys into her purse. The brass door slid open to reveal the elevator car, paneled in dark, carved wood that had been polished to a gleaming shine. An intricate brass handrail bordered the interior, glinting in the diffused light of the crystal chandelier.

Since he was closer, Wes lifted his hand to press the button before realizing that he didn't know where she lived.

Vivienne slanted him a glance that felt significant, before she reached past him and pressed the button numbered 37 with a perfectly manicured finger. Scarlet.

The spicy, sultry fragrance of her signature scent hit him in the gut. Made especially for her at the same little French *parfumerie* that her mother used to frequent. He wasn't sure if he liked the fact that the stranger beside him still smelled like Viv.

Wes took a self-preserving step backward. "I promised you the day we met that I'd never use my tech skills to find out anything about you," he reminded her.

He knew it was the wrong thing to say the second it came out of his mouth, even before her spine stiffened and accusation flooded her eyes. Despite his best intentions, all he'd managed to do was conjure the ghost of another vow he'd made to her, one that he'd reneged on.

Promise me, Wes, that no matter what, I'll always

be more important to you than work. That we'll always put each other first.

Stupid, childish notions that had been selfishly asked and callously disregarded.

But obviously not forgotten.

"How very chivalrous of you, Wesley." His name on her lips dripped with scorn.

She wasn't so bad with invectives herself.

Any other time, he'd be glad the building was too distinguished to subject them to Muzak, but not today. Not when the silence between them was thick with tension. With history.

Hell, he'd have given his left nut for a little soft jazz right now, and he *hated* soft jazz.

This wasn't going to work. Them. Together.

Not if the past was going to haunt them like this. And how could it not?

You've been remanded into my care until the trial.

What the hell had she been thinking accepting that deal? And what the hell was he doing, going along with it, like the proverbial lamb?

When they passed the twentieth floor, Wes pulled the shell of his phone out of his suit jacket.

He popped it open and removed two thin plastic rods that could pass as part of the casing in any reputable scan.

As they approached the twenty-fifth floor, he screwed them together and stepped up to the elevator controls, inserting the tool into the small hole at the bottom of the brass panel. With a quick push, the latch released. From there, he popped open the plate and set to work.

Wes could sense the moment that her interest piqued, could tell that she was leaning to the side in an attempt to see around him. Even pissed at him, Vivienne's curiosity had always gotten the better of her. He shifted his shoulders to block her view—and the security camera's—so neither could see what he was doing. Wes disabled the coax cable for the camera first, then bypassed the alarm. They'd just passed the thirtieth floor.

"What the hell are you doing?"

"I'm pretty sure that's my line," he countered, his fingers on the wires as he watched the floor count tick upward. Then he unplugged the twisted-pair cable—blue and white—just as the thirty-sixth floor lit up, and the elevator juddered to an early halt. The chandelier swayed above them, tinkling in the silence as he shoved the pieces of his phone back into his pocket and turned to face his quarry.

"Why'd you get me out?"

She owed him that answer, and they weren't going anywhere until he got it.

"This couldn't have waited until we got to my apartment?"

No way was he giving her full home-court advantage. Hell, he never should have gotten into her vehicle in the first place. In his desperation to get as far from FCI Terminal Island as possible, he'd failed to play this obscene scenario out to its obviously doomed conclusion.

Sloppy.

And if there was one thing he prided himself on, it was not being sloppy.

"I'm more comfortable in small spaces these days."

If Wes didn't know better, he'd have thought she flinched at the bleakness of the jibe, but before he could be sure, her expression deadened. She shook her head. Disappointed in him.

Well, welcome to the fucking club. He'd let someone get the drop on him, and he'd ended up in handcuffs for that oversight. Now he was out for himself, and the rules no longer applied.

"I'm so glad you enjoyed your time in the slammer, because if you keep this up, you'll be going straight back." She lifted her fingers to her temple, as though a sudden headache had struck.

"My God, Wes. You've been out for less than an hour, and you've already hacked an elevator!" Viv's helpless laugh held a note of desperation as she gestured at the missing control panel. "And here I thought maybe, just maybe, you'd care that you're the target of a federal investigation. That for once in your damn life, you wouldn't flout the rules just to prove that you could."

That's what she thought this was about? A jab at authority?

"I'm sorry. Am I not being rescued right? I'd hate to deviate from your script. I know how much you hate it when your plans go slightly awry."

"What I hate is your single-minded devotion to

making sure everything ends up awry, whether it's my plan or not!" Her brown eyes were sharp with accusation. "Do you have any idea how serious this is? Max Whitfield is a very powerful man. Never mind that Liam Kearney has joined forces with him to end you. They think you screwed them both over. This is personal to them. They can ensure your whole life falls apart. Do you get that?"

"My whole life has already fallen apart!" The words snapped in the tight confines of the elevator car with a heat he couldn't contain. Fury sparked in his blood, lightning in search of a conduit.

He wasn't afraid of Whitfield and Kearney. He didn't give a shit about the FBI. His life's work was about to be taken from him, the company he'd built out of nothing and sacrificed everything— *everyone*—for. And he'd be damned if he'd stand by and watch it all go to hell.

"And how is being in jail for the rest of your natural life going to help that?"

"I'm not going to sit around and let this happen!" And if she didn't understand that about him, then she'd never really known him. The realization that maybe she hadn't lent a dangerous edge to his voice. "If I don't fight this, I will have *nothing* left. Do you understand that? Nothing to show for all the years I poured into building Soteria Security from the ground up." He didn't want to look at her in that moment, but he couldn't look away. "I gave up *everything*."

The word was layered in the bitterness that always

coated the resurrected memories of her, of *them*, he'd worked so hard to bury.

"Oh please. As if anything in your life has ever meant more to you than work."

His body vibrated with the fight, and he stepped closer, exploiting his height advantage.

"I'm not asking for your permission, Vivienne, and you'd do best to stay out of my way. Someone fucked me over, and I *will* make them pay."

He was riled up now, chest heaving, every breath fueling the fire, the anger, inside him. But Vivienne didn't heed the warning. Instead, she fed the flame.

In the span of a heartbeat, Wes's shoulders hit the elevator wall, and before his brain had fully registered that she was clutching a fistful of his shirt, her purse hit the ground and she surged onto her toes, crushing her mouth to his in a bruising, rage-fueled kiss.

Yes. The word blazed through his blood. Through his body.

Wes dragged her close as he reversed their positions, shoving her back against the carved wood. He opened his mouth over hers, angling for more, more of her tongue in his mouth, more of the heat coursing through his veins, more of the way she consumed him.

He'd been expecting fight.

Prepared for flight.

And then she'd gone and blown his mind by choosing fuck.

Her hands were frantic, shoving at his jacket, and

he let go of her to help pull it down his arms, fighting free of the confines.

She broke the kiss as she yanked his shirt out of his pants, and Wes tried to catch his breath, to slow the roar of his blood and the heaving of his lungs, but he was too far gone. Too far in. He needed it. Needed this.

Her hands worked the buttons on his shirt and he shoved his fingers in her hair, anchoring his palms on either side of her face so he could taste her again.

High voltage.

Lit gasoline.

It had been too long since he'd touched her.

He craved this, the slide of her tongue against his, the rake of her nails down his bare chest.

The confines of the elevator filled with the harbingers of sex: the rasp of their breathing, the clank of his belt, the rush of his blood in his ears, the scrape of his zipper.

Fuck yes.

Her fingers galvanized him, and his cock pulsed in time with the thick beat of his heart.

She made a sound in the back of her throat, a needy hitch that he recognized, and just like that, they were *them* again. It erased the distance, the fights, the years between them, and he hated her for the power she held over him. But he couldn't resist it, either.

He'd never been able to resist her.

With a growl, he pulled his mouth from hers and spun her to face the wall. Her hands came up to press against the wood and she turned her head. Despite the desire pounding through his veins, he was transfixed for a moment by her profile, her long lashes at half-mast, the quick tug of her teeth against her full bottom lip. He did his best not to ruin the gold zipper that ran the length of her spine as he yanked it out of his way with less finesse than he'd have liked, but he was desperate for her skin, for the constellation of beauty marks high on her shoulder blade, just to the right of her bra strap, that he used to idly connect into a star pattern, sometimes with his finger, sometimes the tip of his tongue, back when they used to kiss and talk and fuck the night away.

He shoved the material out of the way to reveal them, tracing them with his thumb before dipping his head and blazing the same trail with his mouth. Vivienne shivered under the hot swipe of his tongue before turning to face him, her delicate shoulder blades pressed against the dark wood, and just like that, she was pulling her top down, revealing her black mesh bra with strategically placed seaming, and he was pulling her skirt up, baring creamy thighs and matching panties. The red dress bunched around her waist as they met in the middle.

There was relief bound up in the heat that slammed through his body. She'd always had a thing for delicate, sexy underthings, the kind that could send a man to his knees. Not everything about her had changed.

Wes grasped her by the back of her thighs and hoisted her up until she was balanced on the brass railing. She wrapped her legs around his waist, high heels digging into his ass, urging him closer. His hips lurched forward, and she bit his lip as their bodies made contact, skin to skin.

Everything got mixed up then. Past. Present. Anger. Desire. Right. Wrong.

And Wes was powerless to do anything but feel it all as he tugged her delicate panties out of his way and slid deep into the slick heat between her legs.

It was heaven. The kind that would invariably end with a long, slow descent into hell, but in that moment, in Viv's arms, he didn't care. He just gave in to the burn.

God, it had been forever since she'd had sex like this. The hard punch of lust. The bittersweet edge of desperation. Just the right amount of rough.

Wes had always had a knack for just the right amount of rough.

She'd gotten wet in an instant, the second their mouths had met. Proof that, despite her best efforts to erase the past, her body remembered him—the spiraling ache, the dark, hot friction of them together.

Why it surprised her, she couldn't say. Chemistry had never been their problem. Not back when they'd dated, and not now when she hated him and craved him in equal measure.

She didn't care that she was kind of his lawyer.

She didn't care that she still bore the scars from their breakup.

She just wanted this, the wild that he brought out in her.

The heady pleasure of having Wes hot and hard between her thighs overwhelmed her senses. She breathed him in, tracing the ridges of muscle that lined his shoulders and flexed in his back as they moved together. The rock of his hips made her whole body come alive, pulsing with need.

Vivienne let her head fall back as his mouth traced the sensitive skin of her neck, shocking her with his tongue, surprising her with his teeth, soothing her with his lips.

Heat, wicked and delicious, twisted inside her, peaking her nipples. Every part of her ached to be closer to his big body and she tightened her legs so she could grind against him with each thrust, needing more. More pressure. More everything.

"Harder." The plea fell from her lips, and the answering shift of his muscles as he drove into her with more force blurred the edges of thought until all she could do was feel him. Feel the power they'd unleashed between them.

He'd always done this, pushed her so high, so fast, it made her head spin. She was dizzy with lust and it was so good. So damn good. Then he lifted his head and seized her mouth, and the sharp throb and catch of her inner muscles caught her off guard.

No.

Her imminent pleasure was edged with panic as Viv dragged her right hand down from where it had accidentally ended up tangled in his hair, and shoved it between them to touch herself, working her clit to ensure that later, when she remembered this devastating lapse in judgment, her climax couldn't be traced back to his kiss, but to her own fingers.

Because she wouldn't give him everything. She couldn't. Not again.

And yet, as pleasure swamped her, consumed her, it was his name she cried out, drowning in the intensity. Wes dropped his forehead to her shoulder and gave in to the same pulsing drive that had caught her in its maelstrom. He swore as his hips jerked with his own release. The low, guttural curse imprinted on her brain.

Somewhere at the edge of her consciousness, she knew everything was different between them now, but with her eyes closed his body felt the same, and Vivienne let herself stay there a moment, clinging to memories, as she dragged air into her lungs and settled back into her body.

He lifted his head as her feet touched the floor, and the scrape of his beard against her jaw vanquished the haze of nostalgia and catapulted her back to the present.

Because the Wes in her head didn't have facial hair.

The Wes in her head didn't exist anymore.

Viv loosened the arm she'd anchored around his broad shoulders, and his fingers dug into her waist for a moment before his touch disappeared altogether.

He pushed a hand through his disheveled hair and set to work on the buttons of his shirt as Vivienne slipped her arms through the sleeves of her dress and pulled the top into place, readjusted the skirt so it covered her thighs.

Less than an hour alone with him, and *this* had happened. It was a tale as old as time—an addict and her fix. Six years of personal growth down the tubes, and all she had to show for it was an orgasm.

The soul-melting kind that erased time and space, leaving her wobbly kneed and desperate for more.

God. She needed to get her clothes back on before she begged him to do it again.

"Could you...?"

She turned her back to him, glancing over her shoulder in question. He finished tucking his shirt in before giving her a brusque nod, stepping forward to tug her zipper back up.

Vivienne made a swipe to move her long hair over her shoulder and out of his way, momentarily forgetting she was currently rocking her sleek, angled bob.

The past version of her, the one with long hair, didn't exist anymore either, she reminded herself, ignoring the rasp of her zipper and a thousand memories of other times his big, capable hands had skimmed the curve of her spine...before moving on to more interesting places.

Wes stepped away from her, bending to pick his suit jacket up off the floor. She faced him as he pulled it on.

He frowned, reaching out to tip her chin up and to the left.

"I didn't hurt you, did I?"

Vivienne shook her head, dislodging his finger and tucking her hair behind her left ear. It wasn't completely a lie. She was fine, except for the lurch of her heart when he touched her, but that was entirely of her own doing. Romantic residue that she should have put out of its misery long ago.

Wes's eyes shuttered in the space of a blink. "I should have used a condom."

His words were a jarring crash back to reality.

It was silly to be upset by them, to have wished, for just a brief, foolish second that he'd say something dreamy and quixotic instead.

Vivienne straightened the seams of her dress and notched her chin up, brushing off the bleak reminder that they weren't lovers anymore. Just people who'd given in to baser passions. Strangers. To counteract that weakness, her tone was brusque and business-like. "Is there anything I should know?"

His head snapped up at that, brows drawn together, and his eyes turned to blue flame...not lust anymore. Anger. "You think I would've—" He cut himself off, shook his head. "No." The word reset his expression to neutral, like he'd flipped a switch. "I'm clean."

"Same. And I'm protected," she added, hating that she'd lost control. Despite her IUD, it bothered her that she hadn't learned her lesson all those years ago. Despised that he still held the power to override her better judgment. That she still liked it when he did.

He gave a curt nod.

She ran her hands over her stomach, smoothing imaginary wrinkles from her dress, hating the sympathy clench of her abdominal muscles over the tragic consequences of the last time one of their fights had devolved into a bout of vertical-surface rage sex.

The doomed pregnancy that had heralded the end of them. And Wes didn't even know.

Guilt gnawed at the lining of her stomach, acidic and vile, as it always did when she remembered her own cowardice.

She should have told him. Should have told him before there'd been nothing to tell.

Wes's gaze remained steady on hers as he fixed his collar. It felt for a moment like he could see into her soul, read her darkest secrets and most painful memories. She dropped her eyes, in case he could, and busied herself with retrieving her handbag from the floor. But when she stood up, she could still feel the weight of his stare.

"What?" She wished the question had sounded defensive at least. Not so…searching.

Wes dropped his hand to his side, shook his head like he was clearing the lingering cobwebs of a dream. "Nothing. You just…you kiss different now."

She wanted to ask how. To tell him that he did, too.

To understand exactly why he'd met her mouth with an edge of desperation that she'd been compelled to match and what it meant that kissing him still made her weak in the knees.

Her fingernails dug into her palm around the leather handle of her purse, just enough pain to bring her back to reality. "That's a pretty nuanced take on a hate fuck in an elevator."

"Yeah. I guess I've grown as a person since we were together."

The wry answer brought her head up, but Wes had already moved to the control panel so Vivienne couldn't gauge his expression. Within seconds, everything was back in place, and the elevator had resumed its course. The bell dinged as the car drew to a smooth stop on the thirty-seventh floor.

CHAPTER THREE

HAD SHE ALWAYS lived this damn far from the elevator?

The tastefully bland hallway felt never-ending with Wes following along behind her. Especially when they both smelled like sex. Amazing, animalistic sex. It was almost enough to make her forget that they'd broken up years ago. Or that she'd just picked him up from his unjust stint in prison.

Almost, but not quite.

Her pace slowed as they approached the last door on the left, just as it always did since that day, a little over two months ago, when she'd walked down this hallway, blissfully unaware that her life was about to change. That her security panel had been overridden, and a nondescript envelope was waiting for her on the other side of the door her mysterious visitor had left slightly ajar.

She'd had a brand-new door installed the next day, complete with a dead bolt and a chain lock, as well as a state-of-the-art security camera in the foyer, in case anyone managed to bypass her upgrades. Too little, too late, of course. Her life had already been irreparably thrown off course when she'd curiously ripped into the manila packet.

No, not then.

A moment after that, when she'd decided to follow the neatly typed instructions that accompanied a thumb drive with the Whitfield Industries logo emblazoned on the side of it and a copy of the medical records detailing the lifesaving surgery she'd underwent in the dangerous wake of her ectopic pregnancy that would be made available to *interested parties* if she failed to comply.

The realization that she was being blackmailed turned quickly to panic in an instant, and she'd doubled down on the same decision she'd made years earlier, when she was a scared, pregnant twenty-two-year-old bound for law school. Installing the program on one of Whitfield Industries' computers had seemed so much easier than letting Wes back in her life in any capacity.

And now she had to deal with the consequences of her cowardice—forced proximity with the man she'd been trying so hard to avoid—ironic though they might be.

Vivienne stopped in front of her condo and glanced over her shoulder at her court-appointed houseguest.

Whatever he saw on her face made Wes haul up short. He lifted his hands in surrender, hanging back to give her more space, unaware that inside, she was crying out for the comfort of his arms around her, for just a moment where she could set down her burden and rely on his strength to hold her up.

But that was solace she didn't deserve.

Viv let the misinterpretation stand, accepting the extra distance between them as her due as she stepped up to her access keypad.

She automatically angled her torso to block the numbers from his view—a move he'd taught her—but she realized the pointlessness of it a moment later. After all, he'd built his fortune on testing for weaknesses.

"What did I tell you about using your mom's birthday as your passcode?"

Her shoulders drew tight at the rebuke. "That I might as well not lock the door at all." There was a liberal amount of snark in her voice as she parroted back part of the lecture he'd given her when they'd first started dating.

Which pissed him off, just as she'd intended. "It's a—"

"—top ten guess," she finished, shoving her key in the lock with way more force than was necessary.

"Top five if the thief did the barest amount of research on me," she added, just to goad him. "I remember, okay?" Then the heat left her voice and the dead bolt disengaged with a twist of her wrist. "I just miss her."

The words stole all his righteousness, and she heard him sigh. "Habit," he said, by way of non-apology.

She stole another glance over her shoulder, watching him drag a hand down his beard.

"It's none of my business."

"No. It's not." Vivienne pushed the door out of her way, dropping her keys into her purse so they wouldn't give away the tremor in her hand. This had all seemed so simple when she'd embarked on her plan to get him out of jail. Now that he was here, there was nothing simple about it. "Are you coming in?"

He started, as though he hadn't realized he still hadn't crossed the threshold, as though maybe he was having second thoughts about doing so. Which was fair enough. Because when he finally stepped into the foyer, closing the door behind them, it felt like the whole world had shifted.

Wes was here.

He reset the dead bolt with a thunk.

Slid the chain into place with a rattle.

Ominous sounds that sealed their fate inside these four walls. It hadn't turned out well for them the last time they'd cohabitated. And as she'd proven moments ago, being alone in confined spaces with this particular man had never resulted in her most brilliant decision making.

"You'll have to sleep on the couch." The words fell out of her mouth like a challenge, blunt and abrupt. "I turned the spare room into an office."

Wes just nodded.

His subdued acceptance made her feel churlish,

and she did her best to sound conciliatory. "Make yourself at home. I'm just going to freshen up."

"Sure. Yeah." Wes's gaze had migrated up to the pinhole in the crown molding, where she'd had the camera installed post-envelope. Figured that's where his attention would go. Work had always been the first thing on his mind.

"Motion sensor, or constant feed?"

"Both. Motion alerts come straight to my phone."

When his blue eyes met hers, she could feel his silent approval at that particular security upgrade, and the fact that it warmed her, even now, set off a different kind of alarm in her brain.

How in the hell, after everything they'd been through, could she still care what he thought of her choices?

It took everything she had not to run from the room at the realization.

She counted her steps to keep the strike of her heels against the hardwood floor even, though she granted herself the concession of using the main bathroom, because it was closer than her en suite, and because she was afraid her knees might give out with the effort of appearing unconcerned if she had to fake it for even a second longer.

She slammed the door shut behind her in her haste for privacy. Once it was locked, Vivienne blew out a breath and set her purse on the counter.

Get your shit together, she lectured herself.

Leaning forward, she met her own eyes in the

mirror. Her pupils were large, her hair was mussed, and her lipstick was smeared.

She looked like she'd just been ravaged in an elevator.

She lifted her hand, restoring order and precision to the sharp angle of her bob.

It was just sex with the ex, she assured herself.

No big deal.

Digging into her purse, Vivienne pulled out her small makeup case and extracted a travel pack of makeup wipes and her signature red lipstick, laying them with precision on the marble countertop, as though she was about to scrub for surgery, rather than tackle the faint crimson stain that had migrated outside her lip line.

Tugging one of the disposable cloths free, Viv set about restoring the cool, controlled facade she was known for.

She'd curated a very precise version of herself in the years since they'd been *Wes and Viv*, but today was the first time she'd considered how much he'd changed, too. With his expensive suit and his fancy watch.

All the trappings of his success, so different from the boy she'd known, and yet…

He still had this way of sucking up all the oxygen in the room, dominating her thoughts without even trying. Hell, the aftereffects of him were still fizzing in her blood. Not that she was surprised. That body of his had always affected her like a narcotic.

Even the first time she'd laid eyes on him.

God, he was beautiful. So intense that she couldn't look away.

A tiger in a room full of hyenas. Or more accurately, a man in a room full of drunken frat boys. She'd be surprised later that night, over tacos and tequila, to learn that he was a mere two months more experienced with being twenty than she was, but in that moment, he'd seemed so mature and so above the frat party that Jesse Hastings had all but begged her and her roommate to attend. And the way he'd filled out his white T-shirt and worn jeans hadn't hurt, either.

She'd never believed in instant lust before that night. She'd seen plenty of hot guys who hadn't affected her beyond the clinical acknowledgment of their good-lookingness.

She'd never been desperate to taste any of them.

Mesmerized, she watched him survey his surroundings as he lifted the red plastic cup full of foamy keg beer to his mouth. Frat party booze was cheap and utilitarian, the path of least resistance to drunkenness. Even in the awful lighting—a bunch of neon beer signs and some bargain-basement, light-up disco ball provided by the delusional frat brother with visions of DJ stardom in his future who had cranked up the bass to teeth-jarring levels—she was entranced by his throat, the bob of his Adam's apple as he swallowed, and the way his tongue darted out to catch the remnants of the foam that had dotted his upper lip.

Something warm throbbed to life between her thighs.

Then, as though he sensed her single-minded fascination with him, he turned his head, and their eyes met with a jolt of instant attraction that, a split second earlier, she'd thought only existed in the dirty-sexy romance novels she favored when she could afford to take a study break.

Viv dropped her gaze immediately, heat washing over her skin at being caught staring like some perverted stalker. As much as she wanted to blame the burn on embarrassment, it wasn't *just* that. Beneath the fabric of her short, flirty red dress, her nipples had drawn tight so quickly that it hurt. In the best possible way.

Composing herself, she ventured a peek at him, relieved to find the full weight of his attention remained on her. Whatever the undeniable force that had sprung up between them, he wasn't immune to it either.

Something dark and hot slid through her as he started toward her. He walked with the loose-hipped ease of someone who was comfortable in his skin, and the crowd seemed to part for him as he drew closer. Vivienne couldn't help but notice that there was none of the boastful swagger of a college jock in his approach. Just quiet, determined confidence.

Bam! Lust-struck.

She was thoroughly seduced before he even reached her.

"Seven out of ten." Viv raised her voice to be heard over the thudding bass.

He quirked a brow at the assessment.

"Your approach could use some work. Most guys would have brought me a drink to break the ice."

"Are you here with one?" he asked. His voice was deep and sexy.

"One what?"

He leaned closer under the guise of being heard over the music, and his breath on her jaw was like the lick of a flame. "One of those guys who would have brought you a drink?"

Touché. She dipped her head, hiding her smile. "Maybe I'm keeping my options open." Vivienne looked up at him through her lashes, pouring it on thick. "Or maybe I was waiting for you."

He, on the other hand, didn't even try to hide his lopsided grin, and the flash of white teeth hit her veins like nitroglycerin. "I find that hard to believe."

She shrugged in a way she hoped was mysterious. "Daddy issues. He never put me at the center of his world, so now I sit in the shadows, waiting for someone to notice me." Viv shook her head melodramatically so that he'd assume it was a lie. "It's all very tragic," she assured him.

"Somehow I doubt that you wait around for much."

"Oh yeah?" She reached for his beer, which he relinquished with a smirk, his eyes fixated on her mouth as she took a long sip of the slightly too-warm brew. When it was her turn to lick the foam from her lips, she milked it for all it was worth, reveling in the role of the daring seductress in the short red dress. "Why's that?"

"Because you strike me as the kind of woman who doesn't let anything stand in her way." He tipped his chin to the beer she'd commandeered. "You take what you want."

Oh, and she intended to.

"So?" he asked, taking the cup back from her. Her belly fluttered as he lifted it to his mouth, sipping from the exact same spot that she had. "Do I pass?"

The smile that curved her lips was genuine. He'd run her gauntlet with style and wit. It was exceedingly rare to encounter such advanced verbal chess moves at a frat party, let alone from someone with muscles like his.

"That was a very good answer. I haven't heard that one before." She lowered her voice just enough that he had to lean in to hear her. "Most guys just ask me what I want to drink."

"Maybe that's because you've been wasting your time with slick college douchebags who regurgitate what their textbooks tell them to think." He cast a cursory glance over the drunken crowd. She'd forgotten they weren't the only two people in the world. "Not a truly original thought among them."

Vivienne reminded herself that it was ludicrous to fall a little bit in love with someone whose name you didn't know. Then she gave him a pretty moue. "That's not a very nice way to talk about my friends."

He stepped closer. "Tell me they don't bore you."

"If I confess they do, will you whisk me away to somewhere that will delight and amaze?"

He reached up and set the half-empty beer on the trophy shelf a couple feet above her right shoulder. "I guess that depends."

"On what?"

"On how much you value the artistic merit of tacos."

It might have been the most sublime pickup line she'd ever heard.

"A fellow taco-lover, huh? With so much in common, you'd think we would have crossed paths before now. How come I've never seen you around?"

"Because I'm not a student here."

Interesting. This big, beautiful man was just full of surprises.

"Then what are you doing crashing frat parties and luring co-eds off campus with the promise of delicious Mexican cuisine?"

"Jesse Hastings invited me."

Vivienne grinned. Jesse Hastings was your typical narcissistic son of a senator, nice enough if you got past his penchant for schmoozing and name-dropping. The thought of Jesse hanging out with this guy was like imagining a chihuahua hanging out with a Doberman.

"And how do you know Jesse?"

"I landscaped his family's estate."

Well, that certainly explained the muscles.

"And he's my business partner."

Vivienne's eyebrows shot up at the announcement. She hadn't seen that one coming.

"I didn't know Jesse knew how to handle a lawn mower."

"He doesn't. But I know how to bypass a lot of high-tech systems to siphon internet access from a senator's mansion, and Jesse assures me that he has the kind of contacts who can fund talents like mine, if I choose to use them for good."

Vivienne would be lying if she said she wasn't a little turned on by his white-collar, bad-boy tendencies. It was just the right amount of disreputable.

"And do your talents extend beyond hacking into senators' mansions?"

His slow grin made her knees weak. "I consider myself a man of many talents."

And Vivienne was suddenly desperate to experience all of them.

"I'll let you take me for tacos on one condition. You have to promise that you'll never use your computer skills to find out anything about me."

"Well, if I'm not allowed to hack your phone, how am I going to impress you with insider knowledge of all your favorite things?"

"Guess you'll have to find out what I like the old-fashioned way."

His gaze darkened in a way that unleashed a rush of heat in her abdomen.

God, flirting was fun. She sent him her best look of prim admonishment. "I meant with small talk."

He leaned close again, and the world faded away. "No, you didn't."

Perfect. He was absolutely perfect.

She extended her hand and sealed her fate. "I'm Vivienne."

"Wes."

If she hadn't known she was a goner already, she would have the second their palms met, and first contact jolted through her like she'd picked up a downed power line. A mere two hours of small talk later, replete with tacos and tipsy on cheap tequila and lust, they'd consummated their inability to keep their hands off each other in the bathroom at Señor Taco's, before they'd kissed and groped their way back to her dorm room and had their way with each other until the sun rose.

A rather quixotic beginning for where they'd ended up, mired in the technicalities and intricacies of the law.

Vivienne tipped her chin up, examining the whisker burn that had marked up the underside of her jaw.

I didn't hurt you, did I?

She ran her finger along the patch of reddened skin.

They'd hurt each other.

But things didn't have to play out the same way they had. They were older now. Presumably wiser. And this was strictly business.

She'd do well to remember it.

With a reinforcing breath, Vivienne threw the

makeup wipe into the trash bin and straightened the seams of her dress.

It was probably best they'd gotten this out of their systems, she decided, squaring her shoulders as she reached for the tube of lipstick.

She wouldn't let it happen again.

CHAPTER FOUR

YOU KISS DIFFERENT NOW.

Jesus Christ.

Wes barely held back an eye roll at his idiocy.

Hell, she'd all but run from him the second she got inside, leaving him to wander around her place as though he gave a shit about home decor.

As though he didn't still have lust coiling in his belly. As though his fingers didn't itch to pull her close. *Jesus.* He was so wound up you'd think they hadn't just screwed each other senseless. He wanted her all over him. Naked. Panting. Begging him for more. Or hell, he'd do the begging…

Wes raked a hand through his hair and did his best to focus on something less dangerous than his rekindled lust for Vivienne Grant.

Predictably, his mind turned to work. Or at least what he would have considered work before he'd become a disgraced cybersecurity specialist with nothing to his name.

The cameras in the hallway were almost undetectable, which impressed him, but the coverage pattern left a lot to be desired.

So far, he'd rate the building's security as *decent*. Which wasn't nearly good enough considering the caliber of vehicles in the parking garage. The elevator had been laughably easy to override, and the security panels on the doors they passed wouldn't take much more effort to crack. A skilled burglar could clean up.

He'd shore up a few things while he was here. And change her goddamn password.

Christ. Dead mothers' birthdays could get you into houses, safes, bank accounts…especially if the mark had lost hers young, like Vivienne had.

Not that he was that surprised by the reversion. Viv had always been sentimental—to the point of packrat-itis.

That was probably why he still hadn't made it past the foyer.

"Make yourself at home," she'd said, but the words struck a dissonant chord in his brain.

They'd shared a tiny apartment while she was finishing her undergrad at UCLA and he was still busting his ass landscaping, trying to get Soteria Security off the ground. Back then, when being with her had been his version of "home," Vivienne had stuffed their space with nostalgia—framed photos of friends, mementos from trips, the blanket her mother had knit.

This place was sterile. Barren.

It had less personality than some hotel rooms he'd been in.

Wes ventured farther into the condo, reminding himself that she wasn't his concern anymore. She hadn't been for a long time now.

But the truth of that didn't stop him from taking in her home through the lens of their past. To his left was a professional chef's wet dream—way too much kitchen for a woman who used to pride herself on how many take-out places' numbers she knew by heart. Straight ahead sat a spacious living room/dining room combo with a killer view of the city. Vivienne had always been a sucker for a view.

Dark wood floors, light taupe walls, an uninviting, high-backed cream couch. Nothing in the bold hues she used to favor.

Hell, even the meticulously hung abstract paintings that dotted the walls were drab. Which, he assured himself, was the only reason his gaze snagged on the single punch of pigment in the bland suite—a vase of wilted tiger lilies centered on the fancy dining room table.

It certainly wasn't because he'd given her some before their first official date—Viv insisted that the night they'd met at that stupid frat party, which they'd bailed on to get drunk at a divey little Mexican joint before consummating their lust in the unisex bathroom and then groping their way back to her dorm room so they could love each other until the sun came up, didn't really count as a date.

Either way, it still ranked as one of the best nights of his life.

So when he'd shown up the next night to take her to a movie, armed with a bouquet of orange blooms, it had been a joke, a callback to her taco-and-margarita-fueled rant about flowers being a cop-out gift. "The pinnacle of generic present giving," she'd called them. "Little more than socially accept-able thoughtlessness."

He'd been hooked on her right from the start.

The way she'd stared down her nose at them when she'd opened the door.

"Flowers?"

"The perfect flowers, yes." He held them out to her, but she made no move to accept them.

"You're pretty, but you don't listen so good, huh?"

"Oh, I listen just fine. And what I heard is that the wrong guys have been giving you flowers."

The unimpressed arch of her eyebrow stoked his competitive streak. "Because *you're* the right guy to give me flowers?"

"No." Wes stepped closer. "I'm just the guy who's giving you the *right* flowers."

Something subtle shifted in her eyes at the dis-tinction. She finally accepted them. "And how come these made you think of me?"

Wes held up a finger. "Because they're beautiful."

She didn't bother to temper her eye roll. "And the same color as cheese, apparently."

Undeterred, he held up a second finger. "Because they're named after a sleek, dangerous predator."

She was adorable when she scoffed. "So I'm a tiger, and that makes you what? My helpless sex antelope?"

Smart and smart-mouthed. The desire to kiss her was overwhelming, but he couldn't afford the distraction. Not when she was so close to being charmed.

"And last but not least—" Wes raised a third finger "—they're ballsy as hell."

Heedless of her present, she crossed her arms, and the cellophane crinkled as it got trapped under her elbow. "Oh, this I can't wait to hear."

"These flowers are cat-killers. Notoriously toxic for felines and yet they're named after one. That's some hard-core badassery, right there."

She uncrossed her arms and looked at the flowers, as though reassessing. "That's the story you're going with? That I remind you of a sleek, dangerous, pet-murdering predator?"

Wes placed a hand on either side of her door frame and leaned forward, waiting until she lifted her gaze from the bouquet to him. "A *beautiful*, sleek, dangerous, pet-murdering predator." He took a step closer. "Don't forget beautiful."

Something sparked in her chocolate-colored eyes, the heat of it turning them melty and inviting, and his blood picked up. "Is it weird that I'm kind of turned on by that description?"

God, this woman. Wes hoped his shrug looked casual, even as his knuckles whitened against the jamb, his restraint as thin as a razor's edge. "I mean, I dared to hope."

"Also, I have a very strong urge to donate a large sum of money to a local cat shelter."

"We could stop on the way to the movie," he suggested, his voice low and rough with anticipation born of the way she was sizing him up. Like a tigress.

"Definitely. We should definitely do that. But I have to take care of something first."

Heat arced between them, and Wes dropped his hands to his sides. It took everything in him not to reach for her. "I'm pretty tall. You want help reaching a vase?"

Her answering smile was slow and naughty. "Not exactly." She fisted a hand in his T-shirt and tugged him through the doorway. "C'mere, sex antelope. I feel an ambush coming on."

They never had made it to that movie.

And they'd celebrated every birthday, every anniversary, every *just because* with tiger lilies and sex for the next two years.

Until it had all shattered under them…

The sound of Vivienne's heels against the hardwood yanked him out of his reverie in time to see her striding toward him in pristine condition.

Her hair had been smoothed, erasing any hint that he'd had his hands in it, and the whisker burn he'd left on her jaw seemed less red, thanks to her stellar makeup skills, he assumed, taking in her precisely applied lipstick, no longer smeared from his mouth. In seven and a half minutes, she'd managed to erase the past.

He'd do well to follow her lead, he realized, as she stopped in front of him.

Instead, Wes gave in to the perverse urge to reach out and stroke a finger down the cold glass of the vase that contained the six drooping lilies, their orange petals limp and curling as they wilted in the murky, fetid water. Not unlike their relationship.

"Is this symbolism for my benefit?"

Something stark flashed across Vivienne's face. "It's been a long time since 'your benefit' played any role in my life decisions."

Wes tried not to let it bother him when she slid the bouquet out of his reach. He shoved his hands into his pockets, but he ignored the warning to drop the subject. "And yet my presence here would suggest the opposite."

Silence crowded the space between them, so thick that Vivienne had to punch through it. Unlike him, she'd never liked the quiet.

"Are you hungry? I think there's some leftover takeout in the fridge."

A slow, mocking smile tilted the corner of his mouth at the dodge, but he followed her as she retreated into the high-end galley kitchen. "So this is how it's going to be now?"

She lifted her brows, feigning ignorance over her shoulder, but he didn't buy it for a second. Vivienne was way too smart to play dumb.

"That might work on strangers, but I know you better than anyone."

She froze with her hand on the refrigerator door,

and a wry smile twisted her lips. "And you don't know me at all. Not anymore."

The stark truth of that settled around them, like ash. It was all kind of poetic, Wes decided. That they'd end up here, as fun house–mirror versions of themselves. Older and wiser but shoved back into the same constraints—her with some grand plan; him with nothing to his name. The first time they'd been alone together in years had ended up just like the last time they'd been alone together.

When she'd given him the *your-business-or-me* ultimatum and called him "a money-obsessed workaholic," and he'd chosen his business over her and told her she was "so goddamn selfish," and then they'd banged each other's brains out up against the wall of their cozy apartment one last time. Before he'd walked out of her life. Before she'd hopped a plane out of his.

It had been a long time since he'd let himself think about their spectacular crash and burn, but today, he couldn't stop thinking about it.

He realized, in that moment, with his body still buzzing from the contact high, what a colossal mistake elevator sex had been. Instead of getting her out of his system, it made him want things he'd thought he'd exorcised ages ago.

"Don't do that." Vivienne let her hand drop from the stainless steel handle and stepped away from the fridge. "Don't reassess how we ended up here. This isn't one of your security systems. You can't work backward through the problem and figure out where it all went wrong. You can't reset this. We were hot for each other, and it flamed out."

Her shrug was insultingly dispassionate. "The experiment failed. It's time to accept it and move on. We didn't even last long enough to get to the part where we got bored with each other."

"Is that what you think? That if we were this far in, I wouldn't want you anymore?"

Something raw and painful crossed her face. "Please. By now we'd be scheduling sex. Every second Friday, like clockwork. I'd have to break out the sexy panties."

Lies. If nothing else, the elevator had proven that. "All your panties are sexy," he offered, trying to diffuse the uncomfortable tension vibrating between them like an out-of-tune guitar string.

"Life gets in the way." Her voice was soft. "We're nothing if not proof of that."

The philosophical detachment stoked his anger, and his words held more heat than he'd intended. "So that's it, then? We just pretend like what happened didn't happen?"

Something almost wistful flitted across her features, but she tamped it down. "We're not pretending it didn't happen, Wes." When she met his eyes, hers were stone-cold. "We're just not pretending that it meant anything."

Back to the status quo. Cool politeness. Respectable distance.

He had to remind himself that was how he wanted it.

"Now," she tucked her hair behind both her ears, "am I your lawyer, or not?"

The challenge was quintessentially Viv. And despite the excuses he'd flung at her in the prison parking lot, he knew there was only one answer for a smart man in immense legal peril. "You are."

Her nod was almost…relieved? "Then if you'll excuse me, I have a lot of work to do on your case. There's bedding in the linen closet beside the bathroom if you want to make up the couch."

And with that, she turned and disappeared around the corner, leaving Wes with the distinct impression that, despite the square footage, there was no space in her house for anyone else.

CHAPTER FIVE

AND PURSUANT TO these charges, legalese, legalese, blah, blah, blah.

With a silent scream of frustration, Vivienne braced her elbows on her desk and dropped her head into her hands. Her legendary ability to plow through piles of legal documents had abandoned her, as though her tireless obsession with Wes's case had fallen victim to her less welcome preoccupation with the man himself.

He took up space. In her house. In her mind. And because he didn't fit there anymore, it was distractingly noticeable. She'd been at this for hours, trying to figure out how to get the charges dropped, but she couldn't focus. Couldn't forget that there was only a wall between her and the defendant.

Well, a wall and six years of growing in opposite directions.

With a sigh, she glanced at the clock in the lower right corner of her screen. It was just past midnight.

Shutting everything down, she undocked her laptop and stuffed it into its padded case. Wes's release was contingent on her not giving him access to any electronics, although the precaution of hiding her computer felt like too little too late, considering that he'd already bypassed an elevator...not to mention her newest lingerie.

Vivienne squeezed her thighs together at the inconvenient flutter low in her belly and shoved the dirtier bent of her thoughts aside. Great sex might have been enough to sustain a relationship when she was twenty-two, but it wasn't enough for her now. And there was too much history between them to entertain the notion of the strictly carnal, no-emotions-allowed fling that her hormones were currently begging her to consider. Best to forget their lapse in judgment altogether.

Reaching beneath her desk, Viv fished her Louboutins out from under her desk, where she'd kicked them off earlier, and got to her feet.

She wasn't proud of the tentative way she opened the door. The exhale of relief when the living room was dark and silent.

Wanting her visitor to get some sleep was just being a good hostess, she assured herself. It certainly had nothing to do with avoiding any further run-ins with her big, sexy houseguest.

And she repeated that lie to herself over and over as she crept silently down the hallway, with her laptop under one arm and her shoes in the other hand.

Only after she'd pushed her bedroom door closed behind her with the softest *click* she could manage, did she allow herself a full breath. It had been a hell of a day.

Vivienne padded across the plush beige carpeting and into her walk-in closet. She placed the nude pumps back into their designated spot—third from the left on the rack allocated for work-appropriate shoes with heels three inches or higher—before crossing to a rainbow collection of handbags. Although she was alone, guilt lent a furtiveness to her actions as she reached up to pull her blush Chanel 2.55 handbag down from the shelf so she could hide her laptop behind it. The chain caught on something, and a black shoebox came crashing down, spilling its contents beside her feet.

She froze, heart pummeling her ribs as she tried to listen for Wes over the sound of her racing pulse. After a long, tense moment of silence that assured her that the noise hadn't disturbed him, she lowered herself to the floor.

And came face-to-face with her and Wes's past. Various sundries littered the carpet, including a pressed tiger lily from their official first date, a Señor Taco's matchbook from their unofficial first date, a bunch of silly photos of them and their friends that she'd removed from frames years ago, and the reason she was mired in this court-mandated Greek tragedy in the first place—a hospital bracelet with her name on it.

Ghosts of a future that wasn't to be.

Vivienne stuffed the offending mementos into the box and put it back on the shelf, next to her laptop. She didn't need to linger over them to know that she'd made a lot of mistakes in her life. But getting Wes's bogus charges dropped would make everything okay. Even the score between them. Her lie had gotten him into this mess. Her skill would get him out. And then she could cram all these unwanted feelings back in that damn shoebox with the rest of the things she couldn't bring herself to let go of and get back to her normal life.

With a nod, she shoved her designer handbag up on the shelf, blocking the memories and her computer from view.

Vivienne reached behind her, tugging on her zipper as she walked back into her room. She stopped in front of the ornate cheval mirror in the corner and stepped out of her dress. But even as she tossed it over the nearby antique chair, her gaze remained fixed on the mirror.

Her body looked different to her, tonight. Softer somehow. In addition to the whisker burn along her jaw, Wes had left his mark on her right breast. She lifted her hand and ran the pad of her finger across it, wondering if she'd left traces of herself on him, too.

It had always been like that between them— incendiary—even that first night.

She'd had sex only with her high school boyfriend before Wes—and while Rob had been sweet and kind and she had no regrets, they'd mostly fumbled around in the dark, equal parts nerves and hormones. Too young, she thought in retrospect, and not equipped to deal with the emotional ramifications of what they'd done. But Wes...

Vivienne let her finger drift along the curve of her cleavage.

Wes had been a different level all together. While she hadn't fully felt like a woman that night, he'd seemed all man to her. Their frantic fuck in the taqueria bathroom had been hot and sexy and panty-meltingly good, but it was later, back at her dorm room, when they'd had the time and space to worship each other's bodies that crept back into her fantasies every now and again.

She hadn't been ready for the sight of him, the rush of warmth between her legs that had come from watching him take off his clothes.

Goose bumps broke out across her décolletage as Vivienne removed her bra, and her breasts tingled at the memory.

She'd been mesmerized by his body, his shoulders thick with muscle, his hands, roughened by work and tanned by the sun, veins prominent along the backs of them, and up his forearms. He used to landscape back then, to help take care of his mom and his little sister and to fund his dreams of world domination, and the hours of manual labor showed in all the best ways. His abs were a masterpiece, and while his chest was smooth, there was a trail of hair that drew her eyes downward from his navel toward the bulge of his erection.

Vivienne let her hand wander down past her own navel, watching the flush of her skin in the mirror as her fingers trekked lower. She licked her lips as she breached the gathered waistband.

He'd touched her like he knew what he was doing, like he wasn't in a hurry, like she was safe with him...but not too safe.

That edge of danger was like catnip. Addictive. She'd tried to make it into a cliché in the intervening years, tell herself it was nothing more than dating a guy from the wrong side of the tracks. The thrill came from the fact that her father wouldn't approve...or at least he wouldn't have if Harold Grant had cared enough to notice anything going on in her life. If he'd cared about something besides his eponymous law firm. If he'd looked up from work for even a second to see how much she'd needed him, needed someone to help her through the loss of her mother.

But it had been a long time since she'd given a damn what her father thought.

Then again, she'd thought it had been a long time since she'd given a damn about Wes, too, and look how that had turned out.

That try as she might, she couldn't banish Wes from her body, let alone her brain. Which, she thought wryly, might have something to do with the fact that she was touching herself to a mental highlight reel of their greatest orgasms.

The elastic snapped against her abdomen as she yanked her hand free.

She needed a goddamn drink.

Viv stalked over to her dresser and grabbed an

oversize T-shirt from the drawer, tugging it over her head as she headed for the door.

She wasn't some starry-eyed, hormone-infused college junior anymore, she reminded herself as she headed for the kitchen, doing her best to wrestle her weird sexual obsession with Wes into submission through sheer force of will. They'd lived separate lives. They'd grown into different people. They had nothing in common anymore, no ties to one another.

"Is that my shirt?"

Vivienne started at the sound of his voice, swearing as her hand flew to the base of her throat and she whirled to face the couch. "God! You scared the shit out of me."

"Sorry."

But he didn't look sorry, propped indolently on her designer couch, his back against the armrest, his beautiful chest bare, and the blanket pulled up just high enough to make her wonder if he still slept in the nude.

In the interest of distraction, she focused on his original question and glanced down at herself.

Wes's shirt. One she'd stolen from him a lifetime ago.

Considering the name of the landscaping company was emblazoned across the front of it, she figured plausible deniability had left the building.

Hoping the blush prickling up her neck wasn't visible in the dimness of night, she lifted her chin to an angle that was all bravado. "As for this being your shirt, I guess that depends."

"On what?"

"On whether you subscribe to the idea that possession is nine-tenths of the law."

Wes's deep chuckle raced along her skin as he threw back the blanket and planted his feet on the plank flooring.

Boxer briefs.

White.

And tight.

He'd always had the sexiest thighs.

Viv cleared her throat. "Sorry I woke you up."

"You didn't." He dragged a hand through his hair, leaving it sexily disheveled. And right then, in the intimacy of the shadows, the living room lit faintly by whatever moonlight managed to join the light pollution of Los Angeles at night, it was easy to slip back to a time when midnight conversations with Wes, her in his T-shirt, him in his boxers, had been normal.

And all she had to do to maintain the illusion was ignore the electronic monitoring device blinking on his left ankle.

He stood up, stretching, and Vivienne took a step backward in self-preservation.

"This couch sucks."

Glad for the distraction, Vivienne frowned, taking more offense than his words warranted. "It cost ten grand."

"Well, none of that cash was funneled into adding cushioning to the cushions, I'll tell you that much."

She stared at the mod-style cream monstrosity, realizing for the first time that she didn't really like it. Funny that she'd never noticed before. "Is it that bad?"

"Back in the day, you dragged me across the entire city, made me sit on fifty-seven couches before you would commit to one, and now you're trying to tell me you've never sat on this overpriced torture device once?"

"A designer picked it out." She glanced around the pristine, muted apartment, suddenly aware of how blank it was. "When I'm not at Whitfield, I'm sleeping. And if I can't sleep, I'm in my home office. Working."

That was her life since she'd come back to LA. And if she were being honest, she liked it that way. Being busy with work was much safer than being alone with her thoughts.

"So what are you doing out here now?" Wes's voice sounded deeper in the dark, and the question stymied her for longer than it should have.

"Alcohol," she blurted, remembering herself. "I need alcohol. Do you want a beer?"

He cocked an eyebrow. "I just got out of prison."

"Whiskey it is."

His mouth twisted with bleak humor, and her heart did the same as he followed her into the kitchen.

CHAPTER SIX

SHE MIGHT NOT be much of a cook, but he was damned impressed with her bartending skills. Wes leaned a hip against the counter and watched her. Within minutes, she was handing him a crystal tumbler of top-shelf whiskey, complete with a spherical ball of ice.

"Fancy." He lifted the glass in a wordless toast, and she clinked hers against it before they indulged.

The smooth burn was exactly what he needed.

"Your taste in alcohol has definitely improved over the years."

"Hey. Señor Taco's cheap tequila Tuesdays will always hold a special place in my heart," she countered.

The reference to the night they'd met charged the air, stealing the jaunty smile from her lips. She hadn't taken off her makeup yet, so they were the same deep red they'd been in the elevator. Except now they'd taste like whiskey and sex, instead of just the latter.

Wes drowned that dangerous thought with another swallow of premium liquor. He should walk it back. Hit the eject button. But as she stood there, in his shirt, her pale thighs dappled with shadows, he said what he was thinking instead. "Mine, too. Señor Taco's changed my life."

Their gazes held in the darkness of the kitchen, and for a second, she looked like the fearless, passionate girl he'd known, before she'd smoothed it all out into precise angles and lines.

She opened her mouth, probably to make some excuse and retreat, so Wes kept talking, unwilling to let her disappear quite yet. "Jesse dragged me to that party at his frat house. He wanted me to see this girl he had a crush on."

She relaxed a little at the promise of gossip, even though this particular secret was in the rearview mirror. "How did I not know that?" Vivienne took a sip of her drink, and he used the moment to admire the graceful line of her throat as she swallowed. "Did he make a move?"

"Nah. She bailed on the party to get tipsy on cheap tequila with some blue-collar lawn jockey before he had the chance."

Dawning understanding tightened her fingers around her glass. "I never thought... I didn't know he... Jesse and I were just friends."

Wes nodded, twisting his wrist so the ice sphere rolled around in his glass. "I figured that out when you left with me. And I wouldn't have gone into business with him if I didn't believe he was cool with it. Can't build a solid company with someone you don't trust..." He set his drink on the counter. "Or someone you want to beat the shit out of."

The not-quite confession sharpened her gaze, and for a split second, something flared in her eyes. Like she understood that that night, the night they'd met, he would have dumped Jesse—all his money, all his business connections—in an instant for her. Would have shoveled decorative rocks and schlepped Bermudagrass sod for the rest of his life, if that's what it took for a shot with her.

Then she blinked and it was gone, like the failed strike of a match.

Considering that, in the end, he'd chosen Soteria Security over her, it was a fair reaction.

"It's getting late."

She brought the glass to her mouth. Finished it in one go. The tumbler seemed loud when it met the counter, even though she set it down carefully.

Retreat mode activated. "It was late before you came out here," he reminded her.

Their eyes met, and lust sizzled along his spine. It was still there. The connection between them that he'd thought was lost. Or at least that's what he'd been telling himself since the day she'd hopped a plane to Yale. But he couldn't deny it anymore.

Vivienne shook her head, and it was edged with desperation. "The elevator was a mistake. It shouldn't have happened. A memory," she added, her voice trailing off into nothing.

"It was a hell of a memory," Wes countered.

He stalked closer. One careful step, then another.

Her lips parted on a shaky exhalation, and the answering snap of hunger made his body hum.

In the space of a breath, he'd become the tiger. "You felt it, too."

Her tongue darted out, leaving a sheen on her matte-red lips. "And you have evidence to back up that claim, counselor?"

Such a badass, even when she was the antelope. As true now as it had been then.

His eyes dropped to her chest, her nipples hard beads against the soft cotton of his old T-shirt. His hands itched to feel them pressing against his palms.

She glanced down, a frown creasing her forehead. "Don't flatter yourself. A woman's nipples aren't like a pop-up thermometer in a turkey. You can't gauge a heat level from them."

There she was. His tigress.

It was his turn to lick his lips. "And what do you know about cooking a turkey, Viv?"

Pride lifted her chin, her color gloriously high with that potent combo of anger and lust that they both excelled at. "I know you can order delicious, apricot-glazed turkey breast from Whole Foods that's so good, no one cares who cooked it." He saw her struggle to stop herself, saw the moment she lost her inner war and veered off the high road. "You'd probably love it. You always *were* a breast man."

Wes's grin was all male satisfaction. Sparring with her had always been the best aphrodisiac on the planet. "Still am. Which is how I know that, while that might be true for women in general, *your* nipples have always been incredibly accurate at predicting your heat level."

She crossed her arms over her chest to conceal the evidence. "It's not so tough to read your thermometer either." She dropped her gaze to his crotch, but the ploy backfired. Because he wasn't embarrassed. And there was nowhere to hide when all you were wearing was a pair of white boxer briefs. He didn't miss the way her eyes flared at the result of their exchange of innuendos.

"I wouldn't think so," he conceded, and Vivienne swallowed as he drew closer still, so fucking hard for her. "Being around you always gets my temperature up."

"That's close enough," she warned, flattening her palm against his chest, and the burn of skin on skin almost sent him to his knees.

His heart thudded hard on the other side of his ribcage. "Not by half."

"Why?" She breathed the question and it rippled along his skin, raising goose bumps. Her fingers flexed against his skin. "Even after everything we've been through, why is it like this?"

Her elbow relaxed a fraction of an inch and he leaned into the concession.

"Because I still know your body. I know what you like. What you need."

Her laugh held a note of desperation. "God, you're so full of yourself."

"That's not bragging. It's fact. I spent two years learning you. Studying you. Logging every catch of your breath, every clench of your muscles. I know what makes you shiver. I know what makes you wet."

He lowered his voice. "I know you're wet for me right now."

Her exhalation was a familiar breathy sigh that slid down his spine and wrapped around his balls. She'd made that sound before, in bed with him. Wes clenched his fists against the urge to touch her, to take too much too fast. Desire beat thick and heavy in his veins.

"And that's after a six-year hiatus from you. Imagine how it could have been if I wasn't so rusty."

Viv shook her head against his words, against the persuasive heat pulsing between them, but her arm lost all rigidity, and her fingers slid down his sternum in an inadvertent caress that set his skin ablaze.

"This isn't real."

"Fuck real."

His blunt rejoinder widened her eyes.

"You know what's real? Two billion-dollar tech firms are out for my blood." Anger got tangled up in the lust. "I'm out on bail, and one spectacle of a trial is all that stands between me and prison for the rest of my life. In the meantime, I have no money, no clothes, and no job. Not to mention, my reputation is in shreds."

He was desperate for her, even if it couldn't last.

"Maybe I'm not looking for real. And I know you didn't come out here for a drink."

Fuck real.

Vivienne let the sentiment quiet the inner turmoil that was raging in her gut.

She'd let herself be blackmailed and, as a result, an innocent man had gone to prison.

She'd quit her dream job in a desperate attempt to clear his name.

The odds of any of it working out were miniscule at best, and nonexistent at worst.

But right now, he wanted her. And she wanted him.

Tonight, that could be enough.

After everything, they deserved the illusion. Just for a moment, they could forget the rest. Pretend they were who they used to be.

And she might get there, if she disregarded the beard, dismissed the hardened glint in his blue eyes. If she ignored the million things that had gone wrong between them and the years that had intervened since.

She spread her fingers over his heart, his skin hot beneath her palm, his heartbeat strong and steady. His body shuddered when she stepped closer, lifted her chin.

"Viv." He breathed the words against her lips a split second before his fingers slid into her hair, and the edge of pain as he tugged her head back made her gasp even as he claimed her mouth in a scorching kiss that sent pleasure surging through her. She clutched his shoulders, desperate to get closer.

His other hand fisted her T-shirt in the small of her back, lifting the hem and baring her thighs. Wes opened his mouth over hers again, kissing her, consuming her, as he walked her backward until the curve of her ass bumped up against the edge of the tabletop.

The chill of the marble was a shock against the heat of her skin, and her pelvis jerked in surprise. Wes growled as their hips collided, and the sound, combined with the brief, electric contact with his erection, had her all keyed up.

God, she'd forgotten how much she loved sex.

She gave him her prettiest pout, looking up from beneath her lashes. "It's cold."

His tiger smile revved her estrogen, and her belly clenched with a pulse of heat.

"Let's get you warmed up then."

He slid the T-shirt up her torso, and Vivienne bit back a moan. He hadn't been wrong about her breasts. They were tight with need, her nipples hard and sensitive from the drag of the cotton as she lifted her arms so he could pull it over her head.

Her fingers toyed with the elastic waistband of his underwear as she pressed herself against him, flattening her breasts against his chest, burying her face in his shoulder so she could breathe in his skin. The scent of him was so familiar it made her ache, but she ignored the moment of weakness, bit his shoulder as she slid her hands inside his boxer briefs and palmed his ass.

Wes's reaction was instantaneous, and there was a flurry of motion as he slipped her underwear down her thighs before stripping off his own. Then he was kissing her, lifting her onto the table, stepping between her legs.

It took a second for her to realize that she was sitting on his T-shirt, that he'd covered the cool marble surface before lifting her onto the table, and that funny little ache reared up again, trying to make this more than it was.

But Wes saved her from herself, sliding clever fingers through the slick heat of her, making her buck against his hand. She was drenched for him, and the rasp of his breath let her know that he'd noticed. That he was pleased. That he was on the edge.

And just like that, the slow glide of his fingers wasn't enough anymore.

"No more teasing," she ordered, reaching for his cock, taking him in her hand. Vivienne traced her thumb along the prominent vein that ran the length of his shaft and he went completely still. He was all leashed power in that moment. She owned him, owned his pleasure, and it was intoxicating.

She swiped her thumb over him, spreading pre-cum across the sensitive head. Wes's thighs shook as she guided him right where she wanted him, and then, mercifully, he was pushing inside her.

Vivienne's eyes drifted shut, blocking out reality, and she let everything go back to the way it was. When being with him had been full of possibilities. Her world narrowed to the heat of him, and she clung to his body, biting back a moan as he rocked his hips, plunging into her, driving her higher.

She breathed his name, trying to get closer, even now, when they were as close as two people could be. Physically, anyway. And that's all this was about.

The sturdy table shuddered beneath them as Wes picked up his pace, until each of his thrusts was harder and faster than the one before.

Vivienne gave herself over to the wild sensations building inside her as he pushed her back on the marble, half on top of her, so far inside her. The promise of climax was within her grasp, but when she reached between them to take it, he caught her wrist and pinned it above her head and her eyes flew open at the show of dominance.

"Not this time."

His pupils flared, ringed with blue the color of stormy seas, and he thrust into her again, and again, hard and deep and perfect. It was too much sensation, too much everything, and Viv squeezed her eyes shut even as her body clenched in response to his precise invasion. And then she was drowning in the sharp, roiling pleasure that rushed through her with so much force that she was helpless to do anything but cling to him as they crashed together a final time. Light fractured across the backs of her eyelids and she held him close as she cried out, their bodies shuddering with shared release.

She was still panting as he straightened his arms, lifting his chest from hers.

"Shit."

She frowned up at him at the assessment, but his gaze was focused over her left shoulder, and she shoved up onto an elbow to look behind her.

A pool of murky water dripped off the edge of the table, and on the floor, the vase lay splintered in a million glittering shards, dangerous and beautiful and dotted with dying tiger lilies.

Something shivered down her spine as she and Wes remained perfectly still, catching their breath as they stared at the resulting chaos of their mutual orgasms.

Goddamn symbolism.

CHAPTER SEVEN

WES SQUEEZED HIS eyes shut against the intrusion of the morning sun and pulled a hand down his face, though it didn't feel like his. He still wasn't used to the beard. But he was keeping it—a tangible reminder of his time at Terminal Island. Something to aim his focus where it belonged. On figuring out who'd framed him.

Not that the beard had helped much last night, when the only thing he'd been able to think about was how sexy and responsive Vivienne was, and how damn good it felt to be so deep inside her again. The primal satisfaction he got from making her come had been enough to set off his own climax.

Of course, after they'd cleaned up the botanical carnage, Vivienne had disappeared so quickly and completely that he might have thought it had all been a dream…if he'd actually been able to fall asleep. The couch from hell had done everything in its power to make sure that didn't happen.

He cracked open an eye at the faintest whisper of sound to find Vivienne trying to sneak past him.

Not that he'd been listening for her.

"Pretty sure it's not a walk of shame if your name's on the mortgage."

Bare feet aside, she looked far more untouchable in her charcoal power suit with a pair of high heels in her hand than she had last night in his T-shirt.

She sent him a distracted smile. The kind you gave a stranger.

"You're up early." Viv stopped at the end of the couch, resting a hand on it for balance as she tugged one shoe on, then the other, now that the click of her heels wouldn't wake him.

He pushed himself into a sitting position. "I could say the same."

"I have some research to do on your case. It will probably take all day."

He could read her stubborn determination to make sure that it did in the set of her shoulders. Wes tugged the blanket, baring his left calf so that his ankle monitor was visible. "I'll just stay here."

She ignored the jibe. "Help yourself to whatever's in the fridge. I'll order some Thai for dinner."

His favorite.

"If that's okay with you."

It was a purposeful hedge, an attempt to distance herself from him. The pretense rankled.

"Sure, sounds good," he assured her, playing his role in this pantomime of pleasantries she seemed determined to enact. Not that he gave a shit. He had enough problems to worry about without his cock in the mix. She wanted to pretend they were polite strangers? He could do that.

In fact, that was better for his plan. If they were nothing but compulsory roommates, then he had no reason to feel guilty about his intention to loot her home office for whatever device he could jury-rig into internet access as soon as she left.

He listened to her go through her morning kitchen routine, which judging by the delicious smell wafting from the kitchen, still consisted solely of coffee. Like old times, he thought, and instantly regretted it when his mind used that moment of nostalgia to segue into a series of unwelcome flashes of morning seductions past. Steamy showers where they got dirty before they got clean, quickies where they raced the snooze button timer to climax, the dozens of debauched ways he'd tempted her into being late for class and the dozen more variations she'd used in retaliation to make him late for work.

And today she couldn't get away from him fast enough.

He did his best not to look annoyed by that platonic turn of events as Vivienne appeared just long enough to bid him an awkward goodbye.

He was on his feet the second the door closed behind her.

Her home office was as colorless as the rest of the place, and just as precisely organized. *Everything in its place* was a religion to Vivienne.

Wes's eyes went straight to the wooden rolltop desk that had been converted into a twenty-first century workstation, and the empty laptop dock that sat atop it.

Viv had left with nothing but a small purse and a travel mug's worth of caffeine this morning. Which meant that her computer was somewhere. He just needed to find it.

He went through the room with a meticulous hand—who said you couldn't learn anything from a father who spent most of his time in jail?—careful not to disrupt Vivienne's things in his search for the key to the online kingdom.

There was nothing, he realized, after he'd been through every filing cabinet and carefully stacked box in the joint. He'd even lowered himself to tugging open the desk drawer, in hopes she'd left an older model cell or abandoned battery that he could use to boot up his currently useless phone. Unfortunately, the only thing it contained was an impressive collection of Post-its, a box of paper clips, a stapler, a couple of pilfered pens and a USB drive emblazoned with the Whitfield Industries logo.

Wes shut the drawer with more force than he'd intended.

Shit.

The room was clean. And that could mean only one thing, he realized, stepping out of the office. His gaze snagged on the door at the end of the hallway.

The woman he'd known was a sentimental creature of habit, and he hoped, somewhere beneath her slick haircut and structured dresses, some of that woman still existed. Because *that* woman would have something hidden away that could help him.

Wes's conscience reared up before he'd even put his hand on the knob.

If there was any other way, he promised himself. And then he opened the door and walked into Vivienne's bedroom.

Her king-size bed dominated the room, and it took a good amount of effort not to let visions of her in it dominate his thoughts, as well.

Statistically, people were most likely to keep items that were of value to them in relatively obvious places. Under the mattress, for instance, or—he swung his gaze toward her antique dresser—in the sock drawer. But Vivienne wasn't a statistic. At least not to him.

He turned his head again.

She'd always hidden his presents in the back of her closet. Even after she knew he'd cracked the location.

When he stepped inside, his hands balled into fists. *Jesus.* She had all her pretty underwear on display like a lingerie shop, and Wes swallowed against the surge of lust that swamped him. He remembered her, wrapped around him in the elevator, their bodies rocking in unison, the feel of her beneath him on the kitchen table as she took him to paradise, the way that only Vivienne could—with a naughty smile and total abandon. There'd always been something electric between them.

Wes shook off the memory.

With renewed determination, he forced himself

to take in the scene before him. Everything was perfectly in place, color coordinated to within an inch
of its life, folded, stacked and hung with precision...
except...

His eyes lit on one of her purses, a pale pink one
that was slightly askew. He reached past it, shoved
a black shoebox to the side and hit pay dirt. Vivienne's laptop.

The faster he figured out who'd gotten him into
this mess, the sooner he could get himself out of it,
and out of Vivienne's orbit.

Wes pulled her bedroom door shut behind him
and headed back to the living room, pausing to assess his options.

Tiger lily–less marble sex table? No.

The devil's sofa? Hell no.

He settled for pulling an ottoman up to the coffee table and booted up Viv's computer. Bypassing
the fingerprint lock was easy. Setting up a bit of a
smoke screen in case any eager-to-please FBI agents
were monitoring her internet usage took a little longer. But in truth, the mindless task made him feel
like himself again. He'd missed the work. The work
cleared his head.

Even so, when he'd set up a secure connection for
himself so he could make contact with the world's
foremost expert on his case, he hesitated for a moment before connecting the video call.

There was a lot riding on this, not the least of
which was his freedom itself. He couldn't think of
anyone who hated his guts more than the hacker on

the other end of the secret number that she didn't know he knew. Except maybe Vivienne.

Unfortunately, he didn't have the luxury of being discerning right now. Because if he'd had that luxury, he certainly wouldn't be calling the woman who'd put him in jail out of blind loyalty to Max Whitfield, a man determined that Wes spend the rest of his days rotting behind bars.

With a deep breath, Wes connected the call. It only rang twice before she answered.

"Max, what are you…" The woman's voice trailed off as she recognized him and she rolled her eyes. "Oh, you have *got* to be kidding. How the hell did you get this number? Max is gonna be so pissed when he—"

"Are you alone?" AJ was a rambler…a rare trait for an elite hacker, and he didn't have time for it right now.

"What the hell does that mat—"

"Are you alone?" Wes repeated.

"Geez. Yes. I'm alone." She scowled at him when he stayed silent, shoving her raven curls back from her forehead. "If you think I'm picking up this phone and showing you my place like some virtual real estate agent, you can go to hell. You're the one wasting my time right now."

Oh well. Worth a try. "Is this line clean?"

She crossed her arms over her black T-shirt. "That's why you picked it, isn't it?"

Fair point.

"I need your help."

AJ laughed. "You're joking, right? Why would I help the evil mastermind who fucked over my former boss *and* my current sexual obsession?"

Wes let his surprise show. Last he'd heard, the boss was up close and personal with Emma Mathison, a former Whitfield Industries employee and the original suspect for the hack that had landed Wes in prison. "You and Max, huh? How's his girlfriend taking that?"

"Ew. No. I worked for Max, you perv. It was never like that between us. Liam is my boyfrie—my sex toy," she corrected, but not fast enough.

The fact that she'd quit working for Max intrigued him, but the Cybercore connection was a total blindside. Her screwing the CEO would have been…less than ideal on its own, but the fact she obviously considered Liam Kearney more than a fling did not bode well for his mission.

"Not to mention, I'm the one who caught your ass."

Oh. And there was that.

Wes forced himself to maintain a casual tone. "Yeah. You really fucked that one up. Consider this your chance to atone."

She leaned toward the screen, a Cheshire cat smile curving her lips. "For a man who's not supposed to be anywhere near the internet, I'd think you'd want to watch how you talk to me right now. One press of a button, and I can have you back on Terminal Island so fast your head would spin."

"Really, AJ?" His voice was laced with irritation.

"Isn't all this behind us? You tried to hack Whitfield Industries, and I caught you fair and square. I know that pisses you off, and that putting me away for this breach feels like revenge, but do me a solid and put the bloodlust aside for a second. Think it through. How'd you find me? Was it just a little too easy to connect the dots? And did the path lead straight to me?"

She glared at him, and he knew he had her.

"You know I'm better than that," he said simply. "I wouldn't have caught you if I wasn't."

AJ crossed her arms. "You called me sloppy."

His words rushed back to him, the ones he'd said to Max Whitfield five years ago.

She's got skills, but she's impulsive. Lets her ego get in the way of her work. That's how I caught her. She's talented, yeah, but she's fucking sloppy, and sloppy gets you caught. If you're not careful, you're going to end up bailing her out instead of the other way around. You need a hacker, not a hack.

Not the most flattering assessment, he had to admit. Wes scratched his bearded jaw. "I didn't know you were with him when he called me."

Her frown deepened. "Try again."

"It was a bad day."

"Thanks for the oversimplified recap, dickwad."

"It was a bad day for *me*," he clarified, figuring he owed her at least that. "Jesse had sunk everything we had into scoring Whitfield Industries as a client."

One big client, Jesse had insisted. *Once one*

mega-corp takes us seriously, the others will have no choice but to follow suit. You'll see.

He'd been right, too. But AJ had almost fucked it all up.

"Our contract was one week old when you burrowed through our defenses." Wes shook his head. "You were almost all the way in before I even noticed you. The first real test of my tech, and you were this damn close to breaching it."

Because Wes hadn't been watching. Not like he should have been. No, he'd been too preoccupied with revenge. With showing Vivienne what a colossal mistake she'd made, leaving him before he'd had a chance to prove his worth.

But if Soteria Security was successful? That would be hard evidence he was destined for more than landscaping and manual labor. Proof that unlike his father, he could take care of a family. Proof that unlike his mother, Viv's money had nothing to do with why he wanted to be with her.

And AJ's elegant hack had almost cost him the contract. Which would have cost him his company. And his company was all he'd had left. It had never been AJ he'd been angry at. She'd just been convenient. A stand-in for the woman who'd breached his heart and taken everything.

"I was mad at Vi—" He bit back her name just in time. "—at someone else, and I took it out on you." His jaw tightened. "And the truth is, the only person I should have been mad at was myself. I'm the one who didn't do my job, and I didn't want Whitfield to know it. I shouldn't have said what I did."

It was as close to sorry as he was willing to get, considering she'd landed him in the pen.

AJ stared at him, and he could see her seeing too much. Reading between the lines. It felt like shit to let her, but what choice did he have? And he might not *know* her, but he'd *studied* her—and her hacking style—in the years since well enough to know that the driving need to prove himself against all comers was a motivation this woman understood.

AJ lifted her brows and leaned back in her chair. "Well, this just got uncomfortably honest."

Her version of *apology accepted.*

Wes exhaled with relief. "Yeah, well. I'm on kind of a tight schedule here. I need to know exactly what led you to me. Someone laid that trap you found, and you're going to help me take the bastard down."

"Remind me again why I'm going to do that?"

"Because besides me, you're the best, AJ. And I need the best."

She gave him a hard look, the kind that said she was trying to figure out if he was bullshitting her or not.

"Look, clock's ticking here. What do you want? A show of good faith?"

His fingers flew over the keys, preparing an offering that no hacker worth her keyboard could refuse.

It was the biggest gamble of his life, putting his fate in enemy hands, but there was no alternative. He wasn't going back to jail.

Desperate times, he assured himself as he hit the enter key on Viv's laptop, deploying the nuclear option.

A moment later, AJ's eyes widened. "No way."

He could hear the quick staccato of keystrokes as she verified the gift he'd just given her. "Did you just…was I just granted carte blanche access to Soteria Security? Why the hell would you do this?"

"Because I was framed. And considering you're the one who followed the evidence that led to me in the first place, I figure you're my quickest route to freedom. Thanks to you, I don't have a lot of equipment at my disposal to get to the bottom of this, which means I'm in the market for a contractor."

Her gaze was shrewd as she stared into the camera. "This is a paying gig?"

"You clear my name, I'll meet your going rate. You don't, you get nothing." Mostly because if she didn't, his assets would remain frozen indefinitely.

"Okay, hold up. Let me see if I've got this right. Not only are you going to pay me, you've given me a free pass into the inner workings of the best cybersecurity firm in the business *and* you're telling me that someone framed you?"

"Yes."

"Cash, computers and conspiracy theories." She leaned forward and her face took up the entire screen. "You know those are like, three of my favorite things in the world, right?"

He did. Because Wes made it a point to know everything about people who had the ability to destroy him. "So you're in?"

"Oh, I'm in. I'm all the way in."

Wes took his first easy breath since AJ had answered his call. One good thing about hackers, they were always jonesing for a bigger target, a better takedown, which meant their loyalty could be malleable, if the price was right. "Have a look around. Check Soteria's original assessment of the hack on Whitfield Industries against your own. Let me know if anything rings any bells. I'll be in touch."

"Sure. Whatever." Her attention was already back on her computer screen, and the rhythmic click of the keyboard let him know she was digging into her present with the gusto that made her such an ace hacker in the first place.

"Before you go, I need a secure connection that will keep any heat off me and my current location." He could have done it himself, but why waste the time?

"God. If I'd known you were so needy, I wouldn't have agreed to take your money." A couple more clicks of her keyboard and he had what he needed. "If this is for porn, I'm going to be so grossed out. And next time you call me, put on a shirt."

Wes lifted his head at the rebuke, wondering why the idea that had just struck hadn't occurred to him earlier. "Yeah, about my current wardrobe situation…"

With a few curt instructions for AJ, Wes disconnected the video chat, and used his shiny new untraceable internet access to pull up the latest about Soteria Security. According to several news sites, there was a press conference starting in about an hour, and everyone was all atwitter at the prospect of watching Jesse Hastings announce the future of the company now that his scummy ex-partner was out of the picture.

Which gave said scummy ex-partner just the right amount of time to try to convince the building's concierge to loan the stranger squatting in Vivienne Grant's apartment some tools. Wes glanced at his ankle monitor, then over at Vivienne's Roomba docking station.

He needed a screwdriver.

CHAPTER EIGHT

IT WAS LATE afternoon when Vivienne stepped tentatively into the men's department at Neiman Marcus in Beverly Hills.

She'd filed everything that needed filing before noon and spent the rest of the time looking for reasons not to go back to her place. And then she'd remembered that Wes had nothing but the suit he'd walked out of prison in. And he really needed to start wearing more than boxer briefs to bed if this roommate situation was going to continue. That was how she'd ended up in the T-shirt section, wondering if XL was big enough for his shoulders, and debating the merits of crew necks versus V-necks. And the fact she cared at all was so stupid that she—

Something brushed against her purse, and she whirled around at the slight movement of the strap to find Jesse Hastings tucking his phone into the breast pocket of his stylish navy suit.

"Jesse!"

He looked almost angry for a moment, but it gave way to a smile. "Vivienne."

She stepped woodenly toward him, exchanging de rigueur air-kisses with her former classmate and Wes's business partner. Also *former*, she reminded herself, and the familiar churn of guilt turned over in her stomach.

"Fancy meeting you in Neiman's men's department. What are you doing here?"

"Nothing." The lie came out too sharp. "Just, ah, running some errands," she prevaricated, pushing her hair behind her ear. "My dad. His birthday is coming up so, yeah, I thought he could use a new tie."

"That's funny. I thought your dad's birthday was in January."

Vivienne started. Her father's birthday *was* in January, but she couldn't think why Jesse would know that specific piece of trivia. The two men had never even met.

"I like to stay ahead of things," she offered. "If I'm not four months early, I'm late."

It felt like a long time before Jesse nodded. "You've always been very…proactive."

The adjective choice struck her as odd, but she couldn't say why.

"How are you holding up, anyway? You know, with Wes in jail and everything?"

Vivienne didn't let herself flinch at the question. So, he hadn't heard Wes was out yet. And he definitely hadn't heard she was the reason.

"It's been a long time since Wes and I were together," she lied.

"Well sure, but that doesn't change the fact that you'd never do anything to hurt him. Right?"

Vivienne's stomach dropped as her mind cataloged the multitude of her offenses against the man she'd once loved. "Right," she agreed weakly. Shame ate at her. Seeing Jesse was a stark reminder that Wes's life wasn't the only one she'd ruined when she'd chosen blackmail over telling the truth.

"And after what he did…" Jesse trailed off, shook his head. "It's okay to feel betrayed. I'm still in shock myself."

"You think he did it?" Guilt oozed through her chest, black and sticky. Wes had already lost so much. Viv hated to think he'd lost his best friend, too. Because of her. Because of her cowardice.

"I mean, I don't want to, but it all fits. Still, Soteria was his baby."

Viv flinched, ignoring the squeeze in her abdomen at the choice of words.

"I'm as sick about it as you are. But I can't give up without a fight. Especially not after the big press conference this morning. Paperwork's all gone through. I'm officially the bigwig in charge of Soteria Security."

The announcement blindsided her, and her gut ached for Wes.

Jesse's friendly smile dimmed. "You don't look happy for me."

"Just a little taken aback. Congratulations, Jesse. Truly."

"Thanks. That means a lot, coming from you.

As my first official act as CEO, I've got a meeting at Whitfield Industries this afternoon." Jesse straightened his tie. "Hoping I can convince Max to see reason and keep Soteria on his payroll, now that the guilty party is behind bars. You work for him." His eyes narrowed slightly. "How do you like my chances?"

He hadn't heard she'd quit, either. And for reasons she couldn't explain, now didn't feel like the time to volunteer that information. "I've always found Max to be a reasonable man," Viv offered, a little off balance at the whole exchange.

"Well, I hope you're right. If I can keep even a few high-profile clients, then maybe I can stay solvent enough to take the company public. Wes would have wanted that." He shoved his hands in his pockets. "Despite everything, we were friends. Wes dedicated everything he had to Soteria Security. The least I can do is keep it afloat."

Vivienne had shot a hole right through the hull of Wes's dream, and this was the result. Jesse was doing everything he could to right the sinking ship. And now it was up to Vivienne to prove Wes's innocence and put everything back to normal.

"Are you heading back to Whitfield? I can give you a ride back to the office if you want."

"Oh. Thank you. That's really sweet of you, but I actually… I have a doctor's appointment in an hour. So…"

She could have sworn his gaze dropped to her stomach, and a shiver slid through her.

"Nothing serious, I hope."

Viv shook her head. "Just a checkup."

"I see." Jesse's expression cleared and he took a step back. "Then I'll leave you to it. It was good seeing you, Viv." He reached out, gave her shoulder a friendly squeeze. "If you ever need to talk about Wes, about what he did, you know where to find me."

Vivienne forced a smile as he left, trying to shake off the weird vibes of their interaction. She'd known Jesse for years, and he'd never made her uncomfortable before. Obviously, her guilty conscience was tainting everything, from interactions with old friends to Wes's whole life. Still, she watched until Jesse disappeared from view before she turned in the opposite direction and walked directly out of the store. She needed to get out of there before she ran into anyone else she knew.

An hour and a half later, Vivienne walked into her condo, hands laden with take-out bags. The Thai food she'd promised, because she knew it was Wes's favorite. Which felt like the least she could do, under the circumstances. She made a quick stop in the kitchen to set the burden on the counter, before she continued into the living room.

Wes stood up abruptly at her arrival, stepping in front of the coffee table. To her dismay, he was still bare chested. And as if that wasn't enough on its own, his dark hair was shower damp and his lean hips were swathed in nothing but a white towel.

She really should have bought a couple of those

T-shirts before she'd fled the department store. Viv dropped her gaze from the delectable sight under the guise of hunting through her purse for her phone. "I know that they confiscated your razor in the clink, but you could have opened the pack in the bathroom."

"This is what unemployed people do, Vivienne. They grow beards."

She glanced up as her hand closed around her device, and she checked to make sure she hadn't missed any calls about Wes's case. "And clothes? Do unemployed people not wear clothes?" She set her bag on the couch and toed off her shoes.

"My wardrobe has been seized by the US Government." Wes crossed his arms, and she did her best not to notice all his muscles, or the way they flexed beneath his damp skin.

"I bribed your door guy to take the only suit I own to the dry cleaner with my last hundred bucks. And my unmentionables are currently in the dryer."

More guilt, this time over her aborted shopping mission, swirled in her gut, but she tamped it down. She'd gotten him out of jail. And let him stay here. And she was going to make sure that she got the charges dropped so that he—

Her train of thought was disrupted by a soft, familiar whir.

Vivienne watched with astonishment as her Roomba appeared from the direction of the bathroom, chugging its way down the hall and back toward the couch, where it stopped as abruptly as if someone had ordered it to. Wes's ankle monitor sat atop it, its green light flashing rhythmically.

Her gaze cut to Wes. "What have you done?"

He kept his attention on his robotic henchman.

"If you're asking about the monitor, *tamper-proof* is just code for a challenge. You know that. As for the Roomba, the feds get suspicious if you don't move around a little."

"You programmed it to go to the bathroom?"

"And the kitchen." His eyes grew dark with determination. "I told you. I'm going to clear my name."

"What about my name?" The words ripped from her chest, jagged and sharp. "This is my career on the line, do you understand that? You've been remanded into my care. I'm supposed to make sure you're following the rules. I can get disbarred for this."

"They'd have to catch me first."

Anger bubbled up in her chest. She needed to move. Needed to burn off this frantic, anxious electricity crackling in her muscles. "In case you've forgotten, they already caught you! That's the reason that we're in this mess! How did you even…"

Her eyes lit on her laptop, and all the color drained from her face. Her blood turned to liquid nitrogen in her veins, so cold it burned. "Where did you get that?"

But she knew. Knew it had been stashed in her closet, behind vintage Chanel, right next to a shoebox full of secrets that Wes didn't know.

That she didn't want him to know.

"You went snooping in my bedroom?" When she

turned on him, there was still white-hot anger, yes, but it was the kind that was laced with terror. Had he seen the shoebox? Poked inside it? "You had no right!"

Emotions whirled inside her, banging up against each other, with nowhere to go. She made a move to shove him, but the second her hands met his skin, he caught her wrists, and his fury rose up to meet hers.

"Then why the hell did you get me out of jail?"

The question hung between them, both of them breathing hard, her palms pressed against his chest, her wrists manacled by his hands.

When Wes spoke again, he was dangerously close, and his voice was dangerously soft. "You knew I would do this. Tell me you knew I would do this."

Vivienne was helpless to do anything but nod. Because she had. Her attempts to find her black-mailer and deal with the mess she'd made herself had gotten her nowhere. And the idea of him rotting in prison for a second longer than he already had broke her heart.

Her throat burned, and to her mortification, she could feel her eyes welling with tears that she was desperate not to let him see. But it was too late. She couldn't hide them. Not anymore.

CHAPTER NINE

"Don't cry, Viv."

Wes had meant it to sound soothing, but it came out hostile.

Angry.

Because he was.

He was fucking furious, but he shouldn't be taking it out on her. The only person who'd offered him any sort of help when he needed it the most. The last person he wanted to see him like this...at his lowest.

And now he'd dragged her down with him.

Like he always did.

You can't make things better, so stop trying!

His mother's words echoed through his brain. She'd said it to him every time he'd found her crying her eyes out at the news that his father had pulled some new, boneheaded stunt that had landed him back behind bars. Every time he'd discovered her passed out in a pool of vomit after another failed attempt to erase the pain with booze. Every time he'd come upon her rocking in the corner, strung out on whatever cut-rate product one of the many men who wasn't his dad was willing to part with in exchange for whatever she had to do to get it.

He'd promised himself that one day he'd have enough money, enough power, to prove his mother wrong. To make things better for his little sister so that she didn't have to grow up like he had. To make himself worthy of the smart, beautiful, challenging woman he'd fallen half in love with the night he'd met her.

And for a little while, he thought he'd managed to fool Vivienne into loving him back.

But the truth was that she'd seen him for what he really was early. She'd bailed before he'd even gotten Soteria Security up and running.

To punish her for not believing in him, for not giving him a chance, he'd spent the last six years working himself—and Jesse—into the ground, taking the company from nothing to market dominance in record time.

And as the money rolled in, he thought he'd broken the curse. Proved his mother wrong.

But the truth was, Lorraine Brennan had been right all along.

Because despite his best efforts, he'd ended up in jail. Lost his company and his reputation. He was broke. And ostracized. And he'd just managed to alienate his only ally.

But then Vivienne lifted her chin, eyes still glittering with tears that she wouldn't let fall, and all the vulnerability of the moment before had morphed into sheer force of will. A broken angel. She was absolutely magnificent.

"Why didn't you come to see me?"

"What?"

Vivienne met his eyes without flinching. "At Yale. Why didn't you come after me?"

The question collapsed his lungs, like she'd landed a good hard punch to his solar plexus.

"I thought about it." A million times. Maybe more. But there'd always been one more milestone to reach that he'd thought would make him ready to go after her. Make him worthy of her. "God, Viv. I thought about it, about you. All the time. But I couldn't... I needed to make Soteria a success before I saw you again."

Her brows dipped in an offended frown. "You thought I'd care about that?"

"Of course, I thought you'd care about that! Every moment of being with you felt like a test. From that first night of verbal foreplay to the last night, when you shoved that goddamn plane ticket in my face and forced me to choose."

"And you did." She dropped her gaze.

To his surprise, when she lifted her head again, the anger looked a lot more like pain.

"I guess I just hoped, after Jesse showed up that—"

Everything in him went still and sharp. "Jesse visited you? When?"

"Right after—" Viv cut herself off. Shook her head. "It's not important."

"Then why'd you bring it up?"

"Because it should have been you!"

It hurt to fucking breathe. "You're the one who left."

"And you're the one who let me go."

Wes shook his head, weary. "Don't say it like I had a choice. I thought you were going to Stanford. You *said* you were going to Stanford. Jesus, Viv. We were together two years and you didn't even feel the need to mention that Yale was a goddamn option." The ache of old wounds pulsed in his chest. "I watched my mom give up everything to make my dad love her, and it was a losing game. I swore I wasn't going to make the same mistake."

"Is that what we were? A mistake?" Her eyelashes were tear-damp and spiky, but her voice didn't waver.

"I don't know what we were. I just knew I had to make Soteria a success. To finally do something to prove that I could take care of you."

Anger flooded her cheeks. Not broken anymore. Avenging. "I didn't need you to take care of me."

Something cracked and splintered behind his ribs. "You think I didn't know that? Of course, I knew that! Do you know how many sugar momma jokes I endured from your college friends? How it felt to have your dad look down his nose at me because of the calluses on my hands?"

"And that mattered more to you than how I felt?"

"Not more. But it mattered. What they thought was just one part of it—do you get that? It was about what *I* thought. I needed to prove to myself that I was responsible enough to show up for you in all the ways that mattered. That if we ever got married, or had kids, that I could be better than my con man, absentee-dad role model."

Viv blanched at the confession, and Wes cursed himself. *Jesus.* Why were they even talking about this stuff? It was dead and long buried. Resurrection at this point wouldn't revive anything but a slimy, rotting mess.

"Let me go."

Wes looked down. He'd been so caught up in the moment that he was surprised to see he was still holding her hands against his chest. But when he obeyed the order, she didn't call him an asshole and storm away like he deserved.

She took off her blouse.

"Viv…" He wasn't sure if it was a warning or a plea.

And when her skirt hit the floor, he found he didn't much care.

"I don't want to fight anymore." She reached behind her to unhook her bra.

That hum of awareness that had started yesterday in the elevator was back, arcing between them, charging up his cells. So fucking beautiful.

She slid her panties down her thighs, stepping out of them when they hit the floor. "I'm so tired of fighting."

And just when Wes thought he couldn't get any luckier, she reached out and his towel hit the floor. He had a moment to wonder at the power she wielded over him before it surged bright and hot, and she crushed her mouth to his, clutching at his shoulders as he yanked her up his body. Then she moaned into his mouth as she wrapped her legs around his waist and he was lost. The realization rang an alarm bell in his head.

He was too much like his mother, so desperate to escape reality, to trade everything for a moment's pleasure.

Despite the need coursing through his body, and how good she felt pressed up against him, Wes forced himself to break the kiss.

Vivienne's fingers tightened on his shoulders in protest. "Wes," she breathed. "Please don't stop."

But she wasn't looking at him. Her eyes were closed. Just like they'd been in the elevator. And on the dining room table.

Fucking to forget.

And the thought that she might be pretending he was someone else, even some former version of himself, was more than he could handle.

"Not like this." The words scraped against his throat as he unhooked her ankles from around his hips and set her down.

"Not like what?" she asked. Her eyes were open now, wide with confusion as he stepped back from her.

"I just got out of jail."

The slightest crease marred her forehead. "I know."

"You know, but do you understand what that

means? I'm not the same guy you used to screw in the bathroom at Señor Taco's for kicks." Wes dragged his hand through his hair. "Everything has changed, and we're way past that. So if you want to fuck me, you're going to have to do it with your eyes wide-open. Because I'm done pretending."

Vivienne stared at him for a long time. So long that when she finally spoke, her words didn't make sense in his brain. "Challenge accepted."

"What?"

"Sit down, Wes."

He obeyed, dropping his big frame onto the couch, watching in awe as she crawled on him, planting a knee on either side of his hips. When she'd settled, her breasts were at eye level, pretty pink nipples drawn tight, begging for his mouth. But before he could decide where to start, she curled a finger under his chin and angled his head higher.

"My eyes are up here," she teased. "We haven't even started yet, and you're already breaking the rules. You sure you can handle this?" she asked.

A moment ago, he'd been positive he could. But then she reached between them, and his hips canted the second her hand made contact with his cock, and suddenly, he wasn't so sure.

No one touched him like Viv. Literally. Figuratively.

God, she was beautiful.

He loved the way her eyes widened and her breath caught as she took him inside. The slow, sweet slide of her down the length of him was the most exquisite torture. No better feeling in the world.

And then she sucked her bottom lip between her teeth and started to move and made a liar of him.

Wes ran his hands up her torso, palming her breasts, watching the pleasure ripple across her face as he flicked his thumb across her nipple.

Her mouth parted, and she ran her palms up the sides of his neck until she held his bearded jaw between her hands as she increased her pace.

The pressure was mind-blowing, and when he dropped his hands to her waist, he tried to remind himself that he was the one who'd wanted to slow things down, even as he flexed his thighs, driving his hips higher, burying his cock deeper every time she was on the down stroke.

Her legs trembled with effort as she rode him, staring deep into his eyes, and then she broke with the sweetest cry, melting all over him as her body pulsed around his shaft, squeezing him until he couldn't help but follow her over the edge.

She was breathing hard as she leaned forward, pressing her forehead against his, and he ran his hand up her back, until he reached that constellation of beauty marks. He didn't need to see them to trace them into a star pattern with his finger. He knew them by heart.

"You were right." She breathed, before catching his lips in a long, slow kiss.

"About the benefits of fucking me with your eyes open?" he asked when she finally pulled back.

"No."

Her Cheshire cat smile hit him in the gut.

"About how much this couch sucks." She nipped his bottom lip, and he groaned in protest as she pulled away, getting to her feet in front of him. "Maybe it would be best if you slept in my room tonight."

She held out her hand, and after a long, charged moment, Wes took it, letting her tug him to his feet before he followed her to her bedroom.

CHAPTER TEN

SOMEONE WAS IN the apartment.

Wes's heart rate jacked up, and he was instantly alert at the sound of the front door unlatching. He looked down at the sleeping woman beside him and his fear doubled. Vivienne gave a sleepy moan as he slid her carefully off his chest.

Grabbing his underwear, Wes yanked it on, searching the room for some kind of weapon, considering the merits of stabbing someone with a high-heeled shoe, but then the burglar shut the door with a complete lack of finesse, and he rolled his eyes.

Wes pulled the bedroom door shut behind him as quietly as possible, crossing his arms as he came around the corner. "The reports of your stealthiness are greatly exaggerated."

AJ turned away from the dull wall art to face him. "Hey, I was just giving you a heads-up so you could make yourself presentable." Her gaze slid dismissively over him, from head to foot. "But obviously you suffer from a raging case of chronic shirtlessness."

"That's why you're here. Did you get the stuff?"

"Of course, I got the stuff."

AJ tossed the bag in her right hand at him, and he caught it against his chest. "Your clothes, sir. Because apparently, I'm a fucking personal shopper now. I just brought you a bunch of black stuff."

Wes side-eyed her black Doc Martens, black jeans, black T-shirt and black leather jacket. "We'll match. How exciting."

She held up the duffel in her other hand. "Also, one air-gapped laptop, one burner phone and a bunch of other gadgets you should have asked me for but didn't."

Wes dug a pair of sweatpants out of the tangle of clothes before he gestured vaguely at the couch, and AJ set the tech equipment on it.

"The suits didn't take it easy when they searched your place. They tossed it. And you've still got a few reporters snooping around."

Wes's jaw tightened at the news. "I assume you took adequate precautions. Liam Kearney's current girlfriend showing up at Max Whitfield's ex-lawyer's place isn't quite the low-profile operation I'm trying to run right now."

"You're the one who dragged me into this. You don't like how I operate, then find someone else." AJ joined the duffel bag on the couch, flopping onto the nearest cushion. "What the hell, man? Is this thing stuffed with broken glass and lace thongs or something? It's like they corporealized *uncomfortable* and made a couch out of it."

Wes pulled the sweatpants on before reaching back into the bag for a shirt. "I've never worn a lace thong, but your hypothesis seems plausible. And as I already explained, I chose you because you're the best."

She shot him a saccharine smile as he dragged a T-shirt over his head. "I know. I just like hearing you say it."

Vivienne walked into the living room just then, looking sex mussed and gorgeous in his landscaping T-shirt. She paused as she took in the woman sprawled on her inhospitable furniture. "Oh, hello. I didn't realize Wes had company."

AJ tipped her chin up in greeting, but her shrewd gaze moved from Vivienne's state of undress back to Wes. He ignored her knowing look.

"Nice place you got here. You should change your security code. Mom's birthday isn't even going to keep the amateurs out, let alone the pros."

Vivienne's gaze snapped toward him, but he was already shaking his head. "I did *not* tell her to say that."

Viv turned the unimpressed look away from him and back onto their visitor. "So are you an amateur, or a pro?"

"I'm not really into labels. And I go where I want."

Vivienne frowned slightly, pointed at AJ. "I know you. You were in Max's office."

"When you quit, yeah."

Viv's eyes found his, and Wes nodded, setting

her mind at ease that that connection wasn't news to him. Her shoulders relaxed.

"I apologize if I was rude. I wasn't myself that day."

"No big." AJ waved off the apology.

"Coffee?"

The Roomba zipped back into the room, and AJ's eyes widened with tech envy as she took in the blinking ankle monitor riding atop it. It was the look of eager hacker geeks everywhere. She wanted to play. "I could be talked into staying for a bit."

"Latte okay with you?"

AJ nodded, already reaching for the ankle bracelet.

"Wes?"

"Sure. Please."

Vivienne disappeared into the kitchen, her bare feet quiet on the hardwood floor.

"I didn't know it was like that between the two of you."

Wes didn't acknowledge his visitor with a look, though he kept tabs on her in his peripheral vision. AJ's many talents included an almost preternatural ability to size up situations in an instant, and Wes didn't like the smug set of her body language. "Like what?"

AJ rolled her eyes. "I mean, I probably should have. She was pissed the day she quit. Ripped into Max for ruining you, going on about how you would never betray him."

Something clenched in his chest, and his head

came up with enough speed that AJ's expression turned to one of vindication. He didn't care anymore. "She quit because of me?"

"Uh, yeah, dude. She went *off.* Said her loyalties were with you, chucked her keys on the boss's desk, and stormed out. It was pretty magnificent, if I'm being honest."

He glanced toward the kitchen, where he could hear the faint whir of the espresso machine. *Magnificent.* An apt description of Vivienne Amelie Grant if ever he'd heard one.

"AJ?"

"Yeah."

"Get out."

She grinned at him. "You know, it's kind of sad I wasted so much time hating you. You're all right, Brennan. I'll be in touch when I have news. But you owe me a crack at this ankle bracelet." She set the monitor back on top of the Roomba and headed for the front door.

The second it closed behind her, Wes stalked straight into the kitchen.

"Is your little techie playdate over already?" Vivienne turned away from her fancy espresso machine and held a steaming cup in his direction.

"You quit to take my case?"

She didn't have to answer. He could read the truth of it in the rigidness in her spine and the way the latte sloshed dangerously close to the lip of the mug. Wes took it from her and set it on the counter.

"Why the hell would you do that? You loved that goddamn job!"

She looked startled for a moment, like she didn't think he'd noticed. Granted, their paths didn't cross at work all that often—until the hack, they'd probably only been in the same boardroom three or four times, since Whitfield had an army of lawyers, and Wes tended to bow out of the site visits anytime he could get away with sending Jesse by himself. Wes had always preferred being behind the scenes, focused on the tech. He left the parties and the wooing to his more personable partner.

But he'd seen Vivienne enough, paid attention enough, to know that she was killing it as Whitfield's chief legal counsel. That she excelled at what she did. That she was confident and kick-ass in equal measure. That Whitfield had been lucky to have her on his side.

Which was why it haunted him, the way she was looking at him right now.

Unsure. Uncomfortable.

"Max is the one who sent the FBI after you. He was hardly going to keep me on while I was trying to get the charges dropped," she said simply. But her matter-of-factness was not reassuring in the least. Something dark lit in Wes's belly.

"Is that why you left? Because that son of a bitch was going to fire you? Was he trying to push you out?"

"No. Wes, just…drop it okay?"

"Not until you tell me why the hell you'd give

up your career for me after everything that's gone
down between us."

"I know you're innocent!"

Her voice echoed in his ears. The vehemence. The
way she believed in him. He'd be lying if he said it
wasn't exactly what he wanted to hear. Wished he
could take it at face value and use it to block out the
shitstorm that was swirling around them.

But this situation was way too complicated for
such a simple happy ending.

And the fact that she wasn't looking at him right
now, wasn't standing her ground, told him everything he needed to know.

"How? How do you know that?"

She wrapped her arms around herself in a way
that struck Wes as self-protection, like an animal trying to shield its soft underbelly. Still, he pressed on.

"How can you be so sure that I didn't do exactly
what they say?"

"Because!"

"Not good enough, Viv."

When she raised her brown eyes to his, what he
saw there almost sent him to his knees.

"I'm the one who hacked Max's company, okay?
I know you didn't do it, because it was me."

CHAPTER ELEVEN

THE CONFESSION WOULDN'T compute in his brain.

"I installed the malware on Emma Mathison's computer. She'd put in her notice. She was supposed to be gone. No one was supposed to notice anything before you—"

"Before I what?" he demanded.

"Before you stopped it. I knew you'd stop it." There was a faraway look in her eyes, like she was somewhere else in that moment. "I never meant for this to happen."

And just like that, everything slid into place. Wes shook his head at his own stupidity. "I should have known." He scraped a hand down his face.

"I should have known that first day, when Max called us all into his office to tell us Whitfield Industries had been hacked. You gave yourself away."

She looked so vulnerable then. So small in his old shirt, her long legs bare. He watched as her toes curled against the dark floor tiles, before she crossed her right foot over her left, her heel bouncing in time with her nerves.

"First, you jumped to Emma's defense, even though she was the obvious suspect. Then you uncrossed and recrossed your legs. Which is your tell when you're uncomfortable." He stepped closer, and despite the two feet of distance between them, she pushed back against the counter.

She'd already uncrossed her legs, out of habit, and he saw the second she caught herself, the way her muscles tightened against the instinctual need to cross them again.

Wes cocked an eyebrow and took another step in her direction.

Vivienne's breath picked up, as he placed his hands on the counter on either side of her and leaned close, so close that he could smell that alluring French perfume of hers, the embodiment of wine and tangled sheets and desire. Distinctly, deliciously Vivienne. Her tongue darted out to moisten her lips. "That doesn't prove anything." The protest was barely more than a whisper.

"And then you tucked your hair behind your left ear," he told her, reaching up and doing it for her. The feel of her beneath his fingers, even a touch as innocuous as this, sent heat through him. "Which is your tell when you're lying."

She flinched at the word, but he didn't stop.

"At the time, I didn't know why, but now I get it."

She curled away from him, hands still protecting her stomach, and it hurt him to see her like this, it did. But he had to know.

"What do they have on you?"

Her eyes snapped to his, wide with shock. "What?"

"You're a lot of things, Vivienne. Brilliant, beautiful and ballsy as hell. But you do not have the computer skills to have done this to me on your own."

Anger flared in her eyes and tightened her jaw. "You don't know that. You have no idea what I'm capable of. You still think I'm that naive, wide-eyed girl who threw herself at you at a frat party. But I'm not, Wes. I'm not her. I haven't been for a long time."

Naive. Not a word he'd ever associated with her. She'd been optimistic, and determined and sexually explosive, but she'd never been naive.

She just hadn't been this jaded. This brittle. The change was startling, and now that he'd seen it, he couldn't believe he hadn't noticed it before. "You're not like I remember you."

The idle observation startled a bitter laugh from her. "I guess it shouldn't surprise me it took you this long to notice. I mean, that was always our problem, wasn't it? Good at sex, bad at communication? Sorry to shatter your illusions, but we all have to grow up sometime."

She brushed past him, and he let her, but he followed her out of the kitchen, through the living room, around the corner to the hallway that led to her bedroom.

He didn't speak until her hand was on the doorknob. "And what made you grow up, Vivienne?"

She stopped dead at the question, but she didn't answer.

She just shut down, wilted right in front of his eyes.

* * *

Vivienne's hand trembled on the doorknob.

She wanted him to scream at her. To feel the anger he didn't know was his right. To be furious at her for all her secrets and how they'd ruined his life.

Why wouldn't he scream at her?

She could feel Wes at the other end of the short hallway, feel the burn of his gaze on the back of her neck as he started to approach.

Vivienne squeezed her eyes shut until colors danced behind her eyelids. She needed him to blame her so she could repent. But there was nothing, no punishment to absolve her guilt. Wes was angry, yes, but not at her. On her behalf. And that was more than she could take.

Forcing herself to turn around, Vivienne channeled the frosty demeanor that had held her together for the last six years and faced the man she'd ruined.

The concern in his blue eyes almost sent her to her knees, confusing the situation, melting her resolve. Wanting him. Missing him. It all got jumbled up as they stood there, and she grabbed hold of defensiveness, because angry seemed like a safer option than sad. Especially in the face of his pity.

"Don't look at me like that. Like I'm innocent."

She planted her hand on his chest, and Wes looked down at the point of contact before meeting her gaze, his eyes full of questions.

Angry sex had always been a forte of theirs. He knew she was provoking him, but he couldn't figure out why. And that was good. She wanted him a little off balance. Not so in control.

With a raise of her brow, she gave him a hard shove. Hard enough that he took a step back, but still there was no anger in his voice. Just resignation. "What are you doing, Viv?"

"I did this to you."

She moved to push him again, but he grabbed her by the upper arms, and just for a second, his fingers bit into her flesh before he loosened them. She was getting to him, the flash of pain proved it. A glimpse of the loss of composure that she craved.

"But not by yourself."

She couldn't atone without his censure. Couldn't banish the black tendrils of guilt that snaked through her chest, wound around her lungs, squeezed her heart. There was no catharsis in his kindness.

"Why not? You don't think I can hurt you? You don't think I have the power?"

His hands tightened on her arms again.

Yes. This was what she needed. What she deserved for keeping the truth from him. His rage. She could feel it now, pulsing just beneath the surface.

"Who else knows you like I do?" she goaded. "Who else knows your worst fear is ending up like your father?"

She could feel the leashed emotion rushing through him, and the darkness of it called to her, made her blood run hot.

"I ruined your company. I put you in jail."

The lash of her words had the intended effect.

She could read it in the darkening of his eyes, the way his breathing picked up. His chest heaved as he stared at her. His fingers dug into her skin as he jerked her closer.

Vindication surged through her blood at the lapse of his control.

There was barely any space between them, but it was still too much.

"Stop it," he warned, his voice low and dangerous.

"Make me." Vivienne lifted her head a fraction of an inch, and when he didn't move, she leaned forward and bit his bottom lip.

He sucked in his breath and went still, and then everything happened at once. Wes hauled her close, crushing her to him, first with his arms, and then she was pinned against the wall so tightly that it knocked the breath from her lungs. Rough. Perfect.

Vivienne clutched at his shoulders as he ground his hips against her, and when he grunted into her mouth, she was enraptured.

Elemental. Animalistic. She wanted him to use her. Wanted to use him right back.

Fucking to drown out the emotion that threatened to consume her if she let it.

Straightforward, and simple, and so damn good.

And if he wouldn't give her what she needed, she'd take it from him. She'd push him until he begged her to take what she needed.

She rubbed against him, glorying in the rough sounds her sensuous movements dragged from his throat. "Take off your shirt."

Something wicked and powerful suffused her body when he obeyed, pulling the black T-shirt over his head and revealing his gorgeous muscles.

"Good boy." Vivienne leaned forward, pressing a soft, openmouthed kiss against his pec even as she raked her nails down his abs, and he swore at the dueling sensations.

Vivienne bared her teeth, not quite a smile. "I've been very bad, Wesley. I've done things that I need to be punished for."

Emotion crowded her heart, seeped through her chest like an ink stain, but she held it down, strangling it until it loosened its hold. Nothing mattered right now but the dark heat in Wes's eyes. The rush of fire in her blood.

"Viv." Just her name, but she heard everything in his voice. The question. The anger. The confusion. The desire.

He was so close to giving in.

She needed him to give in.

"What is this?"

"You don't like it?" she countered, running a hand across his chest, tracing the flat disc of his nipple before pinching the sensitive skin. He inhaled sharply, pulling her close, his hips instinctively grinding against hers for a few blissful seconds before he got himself under control again. "I like it," he conceded, his voice husky. "I just don't understand it."

"I thought you liked things a little rough." Vivienne took a step back, pulled her T-shirt off and dropped it on the floor beside his. His gaze dropped instinctively to her chest, now that she was bared to his gaze, and Vivienne egged him on, biting her lip as she ran her hands up her torso.

He swore softly as she squeezed her sensitive flesh, before pushing her breasts together to exaggerate the swell of her cleavage.

The rasp of his breath, the complete focus of his attention, was heady. Vivienne pinched her nipple, not bothering to hide her gasp of pleasure, and she was rewarded as Wes shoved his hand down his sweatpants to readjust himself.

"So what do you say, Wes?" She stepped backward, reaching behind her to push her door open without breaking eye contact with him. "Wanna play?"

CHAPTER TWELVE

"FUCK YES."

Viv's lips curved with satisfaction at his answer, and she hooked her finger into the elastic at his waist, tugging him along as she walked backward to her bed.

Once she'd gotten him where she needed him, she dropped to her knees and stripped off the rest of his clothes with one swift tug.

His cock was so hard it slapped against his abs when she released it from its confines, and the proof that he wanted this almost as much as she did made her bold. She dug her fingernails into his muscled thighs as she leaned forward and licked up the length of his shaft before lifting her gaze to his.

His eyes were dark, more pupil than iris, and she could feel the quiver in his thighs as he stared down at her. She exhaled against his skin, damp from her tongue, and his cock twitched.

"Please."

She shook her head. "Don't ask. Take it from me. I want you to."

He shoved his hand into her hair, and she could feel the effort it took him to hold back. His body knew what she craved right now. She just needed his brain to give in to baser urges.

Vivienne leaned forward, running her tongue along the flared head of his penis without giving him the pressure she knew he craved.

Then his hand fisted in her hair, guiding her, demanding more from her, and her victory pulsed between her thighs.

She took him in her mouth, reveling in the taste of him, seducing him with her tongue until he couldn't help the rock of his hips. But when she would have swallowed him deeper still, he pulled free.

"Get up."

A frisson of desire slid down her spine at the hoarseness of the order. Wes was losing control, and it was exactly what she wanted.

She stopped him when he bent his head to kiss her, tried to pull her into his arms.

Wes straightened to his full height, but his gaze never left her as she moved closer to the bed.

She turned from him, crawling on her hands and knees onto the mattress. She sent him a coy look over her shoulder, enjoying the stark hunger in his expression.

Wes stepped closer, and she shuddered as he reached out and ran his hand along her spine, tracing it from her nape to the lacy band of her panties.

Too gentle. He was being too gentle.

Vivienne pressed back against his cock, until his

hand tightened on her hip and he ground his hips against her ass.

"God, Viv. I need to be inside you."

She wasn't sure if it was the fact that the words sounded like they'd been tortured out of him, or the haste with which he was dragging her black lace undies down her thighs, but whatever the reason, everything was working for her in a big way.

"Do it."

Her inner muscles clenched with need at his answering growl as he positioned himself at her entrance.

"Fuck me, Wes."

His hands gripped her hips and she reveled in the strength of him as he drove into her with more force and less finesse than his usual style. Still, she knew he was holding back.

"Don't be careful." Vivienne pushed the heels of her hands deeper into the mattress, anchoring herself to increase the force of his thrusts. "I want you to punish me."

His hips stuttered at the plea, and Vivienne looked over her shoulder again. "Spank me."

His fingers loosened on her hip, and after a moment of hesitation, he gave her a light swat.

It wasn't enough. Not even close.

"Don't tease. Make me feel it."

The vehemence in her voice surprised her, but not as much as the sudden, sharp smack of his palm against her flesh. The resulting sting made her muscles clench, igniting a ripple of pleasure deep in her core.

"Is this what you want?" Wes's voice was rough. Hoarse.

Jesus. "Yes."

She'd never felt anything like it.

She stole another look at him as their bodies slammed together. God, he was gorgeous. Intense. There was something so erotic about having all that focus on her. Wes always made her feel like the one, the only, and it was a potent sensation, to feel like someone's whole world.

Too soft. Now she was being too soft.

"Harder."

The command made Wes groan. His hand came down again with more force.

The sting spread, like a crackle of electricity across her skin, and the burn of it focused her back in her body. No regrets. No past mistakes. Just Wes. Just her.

"Yes." The cry came from somewhere deep inside her, a place she'd sealed over long ago.

She could feel the way her blood raced to the surface to meet his hand, knew that he was marking her, turning her skin pink.

"Again," she begged.

This time, the smack landed on the other cheek, and she bit her lip as something dark and hot throbbed to life within her.

"Tell me you're with me. Tell me you want this."

Her voice was almost a sob. "I need this. I need you."

Wes's large hand landed between her shoulder

blades, pushing her upper body into the mattress before tangling in her hair and pinning her there. The sting brought a smile to her face. She turned her head to draw in a shuddering breath. The comforter pressed into her cheek as he held her in place and drove deep inside her. She reveled in the way he dug his fingers into her hip as he sped the cadence of his thrusts.

Vivienne pushed back against him, chasing the rush that was building so quickly, afraid to lose the promise of benediction that was coursing through her.

The sound of them, the slap of flesh against flesh filled her ears, set her blood on fire. She was drowning in sybaritic delight as Wes took her to the brink of pain-edged pleasure.

And then his cock hit her G-spot and his palm came down on her ass, and Viv was consumed as her body erupted in a sensation so intense, she wasn't entirely sure she hadn't blacked out.

For a split second, everything was perfect. But perfect never lasted.

As the pleasure receded, it left a gaping emptiness behind, and in the resulting void, there was nothing holding her together anymore. It hurt. It hurt so goddamn bad, like her heart had burst.

She tried to get it back. To concentrate on Wes's rhythmic thrusts. To stay grounded in the physical.

There was nothing titillating about the anguish burrowing in her chest. It wasn't muddled with pleasure, like before.

This was a dark chasm that threatened to swallow her whole from the inside.

"I need you."

It wasn't what she'd meant to say. It had been far too romantic for the moment.

But in the middle of the most darkly desperate fuck of her life, those were the words that had spilled out of her.

Brutal in their honesty, leaving her flayed to her emotional core.

The physical marks he'd left would disappear, she knew that, but the emotional marks were forever. Not even the six years between then and now had faded them. She'd just buried them deep enough to fool herself for a little while.

And now everything she'd pushed down, refused to feel, came rushing out to fill the empty space in her.

The tears caught her by surprise, dripping onto the comforter before she'd realized she was crying. It was impossible to breathe through the violent sobs that racked her body.

She cried for the lost pieces of her heart.

The piece she'd surgically carved out so her mother's death and her father's disinterest had no hold on her.

The piece she'd salted and burned so that her time with Wes would stop haunting her.

The piece that had been ripped from her when the promise of life inside her was extinguished without her permission.

What was left of her heart ached.

Behind her, Wes went dead still.

"Viv?"

His voice sounded distorted and far away, as if she were submerged in her tears, as if they were trying to drown her and steal what was left of her tenuous physical connection to Wes.

"Jesus, Vivienne." He pulled out of her, leaving her empty on every possible level.

Viv shook her head, lamenting the loss of his body. Trying to reassure him through her sobs, but she couldn't stop.

Suddenly, Wes was beside her, his arms tight around her, pulling her close. "What's wrong, baby? Did I hurt you?"

She hated him for comforting her even as she buried her face against his chest and let him rock her.

"I'm sorry. I'm so goddamn sorry. Please don't cry. Tell me what you need."

She didn't want solace. That wasn't why she'd gone after him, pushed him to the brink. Why couldn't he understand that?

He wasn't the one who should be apologizing. She had to tell him that. He had to know.

"I've done such awful things." The words burst from her, desperate and soaked in self-recrimination. "Things you should hate me for."

He didn't push her away though. He just kept soothing her, whispering her name against her hair, and it hurt so badly because she didn't deserve any of it.

"Why don't you hate me?" The question was phys-ically painful, like it had been ripped from her throat.

In answer, he pulled her closer still, and she couldn't fight him anymore. Because in that instant, his arms, the strength of him, were the only things holding her together.

CHAPTER THIRTEEN

Wes woke up alone in Viv's bed. He wasn't sure if it had been minutes or hours since the most intense sexual experience of his life, and its emotional fallout.

All he knew was that when Viv had finally cried herself out, she'd fallen asleep in his arms as he stroked her hair. And it had changed something monumental between them.

He shoved himself up on his elbows, wondering where she was. The faint sound of the shower flipping on in the en suite answered his question.

Wes rolled out of bed, padding to the end of the mattress to grab his discarded sweatpants, but he paused with them in his hand, and his gaze wandered back toward the bathroom door. He spent a pleasurable minute indulging in visions of joining her in the shower, of having Vivienne, slick and soapy, beneath his hands. Despite the pleasant throb in his groin at the prospect, he decided against it, stepping into his sweatpants instead.

She'd been through the wringer earlier, and the

fact that she'd snuck out of bed without waking him was probably a sign that she could use a little time alone to sort through all the same stuff that was swirling in his own head.

His stomach rumbled, and he decided he'd see what she had in the fridge that wasn't takeout. He could whip them up a little something and they could talk over food. Figure out what came next, now that... well, now that things had changed between them.

Wes headed into the living room, following along in the Roomba's wake until it veered right and whirred back to its spot by the couch, while he continued on to the kitchen.

One o'clock in the afternoon, according to the digital screen on the convection oven. The perfect time for the culinary masterpiece that was the grilled cheese sandwich. Wes rooted around the kitchen for the ingredients, relieved and strangely touched that she'd set it up almost exactly the way he'd stored things in their old place.

He'd just flipped the first sandwich when the sound of her heels on the hardwood brought his head up.

She was fastening an earring in her left lobe as she came around the corner all buttoned-up in another of the tailored dresses she favored for the office...and stopped dead.

"What's all this?"

"Lunch." He thumbed toward the pan. "Fair warning, you only have one kind of cheese, so if it's not as good as you remember, that's probably why."

There was a moment of awkward silence. And then: "I'm actually not that hungry. But thank you. That was…"

Shit. Wes's shoulders tightened, bracing for impact. Whatever she was about to say, he didn't want to hear it.

"Nice."

Nice. Wes set the spatula on the counter with a lot less force than he would have liked to use. *She thought he was being nice.*

"My fault," he said, as she placed her purse on the edge of the counter. "I should have asked if you had plans." He didn't bother to mask the sarcasm in his voice. "You going somewhere specific? Or will anywhere do?"

The verbal swipe got her attention.

"What's that supposed to mean?"

"You tell me. I'm the one making you lunch so we can talk about whatever the hell just happened between us. You're the one bailing."

"I'm not bailing." Her attempt at blasé failed miserably as her entire body went rigid. "There's nothing to talk about."

"Really? Because I've got a list going. Screwing. Spanking. Sobbing." He held up a finger for each verb. "And that's just the *S*'s."

"I knew this would happen," she muttered, digging through her purse for something that never materialized.

Now it was his turn to play defense. "And exactly what do you think is happening here?"

"You're turning this into something it never was. Assuming too much." She gestured at the kitchen in general. "Trying to make things better by staging this trite, Dickensian tableau!"

You can't make things better, so stop trying!

The paraphrase of his mother's favorite refrain caught him where he lived, but he took the hit without staggering. Much.

"I can never remember, is the doggy-style spanking scene in *A Tale of Two Cities* or *Great Expectations*?"

Her eyes told him to fuck right off, and there was poison in her voice. "You're the one out here making grilled cheese sandwiches. Because that's what we used to do. But this isn't a Ghost of Christmas Future kind of situation."

She inflicted the cut with surgical precision.

"I'm not your girlfriend. I'm your lawyer. I'm trying to keep you from going to jail. You are here because the court ordered it. This is *not* some magical glimpse into the future we could have had if we'd stayed together." That desperate little laugh of hers made his fists clench, even before she added, "I knew you'd read too much into this."

"Okay. Right. That's all this is. Me, reading too much into things. I guess I missed the memo on which rule book you're using today."

She crossed her arms, like she was above the fray, but he wasn't the only one with white knuckles right now.

"So to recap, when you shove me up against the

wall and fuck my brains out in the elevator, that doesn't mean anything. But when you seek comfort in my arms while you cry your heart out, and then beg me to forgive you before you fall asleep on my chest, that also doesn't mean anything. Got it." His nod was curt as he shoved the pan off the burner and killed the flame with a turn of the dial. "I don't know how I could have screwed that up when it's so obvious to me now."

"Wes."

There was a softness in the way she said his name, a note of pleading, that caught him off guard after their heated exchange. It took him a second to realize her hand was on his bicep. When had she moved so close?

"Please. Don't be mad. We're—"

Her phone buzzed in her purse, and he used the interruption to steel himself against her touch.

"You should get that."

The phone vibrated again, and her hand dropped away as she turned to retrieve it, bringing it to her ear.

"This is Vivienne Grant. Yes. That's correct." Her forehead creased slightly with concentration. "So what does this mean for my client?"

Her client.

That's what he'd been relegated to. All he was to her.

"Okay. That's great news. We can definitely make it there in an hour." Vivienne nodded. "I'll tell him. Thank you so much."

"Tell me what?" he asked as she disconnected the call.

Vivienne dropped the phone back in her purse. "You're free."

"What?"

"The charges have been dropped."

Wes frowned at the sudden reversal. "Max changed his mind?"

"Not Max. New evidence exonerating you has come to their attention, and they are *pursuing other leads*," she told him, obviously quoting whoever had been on the other end of the call.

Wes's brain scrambled to keep up with what she was saying. "But how…that's not… It doesn't make any sense."

"It doesn't have to make sense. When the result you want comes up, you take it."

A soft whirring drew both of their attentions down to the floor, as the Roomba made its scheduled appearance in the kitchen, just like he'd programmed it to.

"Guess you'd better put that ankle monitor back on so you can get rid of it for good, huh?"

He leveled his gaze at her, felt the jolt of connection when her eyes met his. "So that's it?"

He wasn't talking about his case.

Her shrug was barely discernible, even with all his attention focused on her. "That was the plan from the start, right?"

Wes didn't have an answer for that. Right now,

"the start" felt like a million years ago, and he couldn't remember it with any clarity.

Vivienne glanced at the clock on the microwave and cleared her throat. "You'd better eat fast, so you have time to change. This judge is a stickler for punctuality."

Wes grabbed the pan and tipped the contents into the trash, before dumping the Le Creuset in the sink with a loud clatter.

"I'm actually not that hungry either," he mocked, before heading off to don his freshly dry-cleaned suit.

CHAPTER FOURTEEN

It HAD BEEN a week since his ankle monitor had been removed. Well, in an official capacity and not just as a Roomba attachment, anyway. A week of being haunted by memories of Vivienne, of having her in his arms again, of feeling her beneath him.

He'd tried to drive all that shit from his mind by going through every bit of the evidence AJ had used to bring him down in the first place.

He pored through his own notes and analysis of the hack on Whitfield Industries that had set the entire chain of events in motion. Compared them to AJ's take on how the hack had derailed SecurePay, Max Whitfield's digital crypto-currency app.

He wasn't surprised to find they both thought it reeked of an inside job.

Then he dug into AJ's discovery that the phone that Wes had given to Whitfield's little sister and PR guru, Kaylee Whitfield, after she'd broken hers had been bugged. Wes hadn't done it, obviously, but sifting through AJ's timeline of events, he understood that if he *had* orchestrated the whole thing, a prebugged phone would have been the way to go.

The flaw in the plan, of course, being that there would have been no way for him to ensure Kaylee had shown up that day with a broken phone, eager to make an exchange for the one that had been doctored.

Wes filed that discrepancy away in the back of his brain and kept going.

Next up was the knock-off version of The Shield, Liam Kearney's competing entry in the digital crypto-currency market. Instead of an app, Kearney's company, Cybercore, had opted to create a status symbol, embedding his payment system in a wearable piece of hardware that doubled as a fashion accessory. The specs for which, inconveniently, had been leaked shortly after Cybercore had started testing Soteria's commercial antivirus product for installation on some of their products.

AJ had found a version of the program on Kearney's laptop with a back door installed, which would have made accessing the top-secret plans the digital equivalent of taking proverbial candy from proverbial babies.

All together, it looked bad. Really bad.

And most damning of all, every piece of infected tech had the exact same code in it, a garbage string of eight digits that marked them all as related. And every single one of them could be traced back to him and Soteria Security.

AJ's notes suggested she'd started off thinking it was a date, but like her, he couldn't find any significance. May 10, six years earlier yielded nothing of consequence when plugged into a search engine.

The fact that the code had infected every avenue of her investigation had led her to the working theory it must be some kind of signature. The hypothesis remained theoretical though, since it didn't match the calling cards of any of the well-known, or less well-known, hackers that either he or AJ were familiar with.

By the end of the analysis, Wes was half-convinced he'd done it.

He pushed back from his desk and scrubbed his hands over his face. The only piece of the puzzle he could bring to the case was the knowledge that Vivienne had been blackmailed into installing that original program. And that was just one more link that pointed directly at him.

What he couldn't figure out was who had the talent, and the motive, to have set this up. What he needed was to unleash the full force of Soteria Security on this case, but in order to do that, he needed his impossible-to-get-ahold-of partner to push his reinstatement papers through.

He grabbed his cell and connected the call.

He couldn't say he was surprised when he got shunted to voice mail.

"Jesse, man. It's me. Again. We need to talk. Call me back, okay? Or text me. Or answer one of the million emails I've sent."

Wes disconnected and tossed his phone beside his computer. AJ hadn't figured out the meaning of that garbage code that appeared on all the affected devices. That was the key, he knew it. If he could figure out the significance of that, it would tell him—

"Do you not own a shirt? Is that the problem?"

"Jesus!" He banged his knee on the underside of his desk as he spun around in surprise, frowning as he caught sight of his black-clad interloper. "Don't you knock?"

AJ's grin was smug. "Guess the reports of my stealthiness aren't so greatly exaggerated after all, huh?"

"You shut down a wall of infrared and broke into my place in the middle of the day just so you could throw my comment back in my face?" Now that his heart rate had slowed some, the ballsiness of that struck him. He gave a philosophical shrug at his own summation. "That's a level of petty that I can respect."

He also respected the fact that she'd bypassed his system. He'd have to shore up whatever loophole she'd found to get into his place. Maybe Max had been on to something when he'd hired her after all. Once he exacted revenge on whoever had ruined his life, he might have to see if AJ wanted a job at Soteria.

Wes got to his feet. In deference to his visitor, he dragged an abandoned black T-shirt over his head before joining her in the kitchen area of his swanky loft. "You want a victory beer?"

Her smile faded. "Sure. But you might want to change your order to a beer of the 'drown your sorrows' variety. You're not going to like the reason I'm here."

Unease prickled along his spine as she followed him at a distance. "What am I not going to like?"

"The reason you're off the hook."

Well, shit.

Grabbing two longnecks from the fridge, he twisted off each of the caps with a satisfying hiss and lobbed them into the sink. Then he slid one of the beers across the butcher-block island to her, and his own personal harbinger of doom caught it with ease.

The brown-glass bottle in his hand had already begun to sweat when he tipped it against his lips and indulged in a long swallow. A little fortification couldn't hurt. "Talk."

AJ picked at the edge of the label, as she erased a drop of beer from her cupid's bow with her tongue.

The fact that she was stalling made his shoulder blades itch.

"You know how when Whitfield Industries got hacked, the surveillance footage was missing?"

Wes nodded. While he'd been hauled into Whitfield's office to give a preliminary damage report, Jesse had worked tirelessly to try to unscramble the feed. To no avail. And thank the gods for that, because otherwise Vivienne would be rotting in jail.

"Well, when I was looking into it on the down low for Max, I found that it had been clipped."

Wes set his beer on the counter with a loud *thunk*. "What?"

"The section that would have revealed our perp wasn't scrambled. It was missing. *Poof.*"

A litany of swear words rolled through his brain, even as a hit of adrenaline jacked up his senses.

"I haven't poked too deeply, but chatter is that the G-men have gotten their hands on the footage and—"

"Shut up."

AJ's brows dove low over brown eyes glittering with venom. "Listen up, dickwad. In case you've forgotten, you came to me. I didn't ask to help you ou—"

"I'm serious. Stop talking, AJ." Wes stalked over to his desk.

"What the hell is your problem?"

He rooted through the jacket he'd slung on the back of his chair, liberating his wallet and keys. "My problem is that if you say what I think you're going to say, then you're taking away the only possible course of action I have to protect the woman I lo—" He cut himself off. "Someone who matters a lot to me."

He shoved his phone in the pocket of his jeans as he met her eyes. "So don't say what you came here to say. Once I take care of things, then we can finish this conversation." He could almost see the pieces of his plan clicking together in her brain, and AJ's mutinous expression cleared when they did. "Tell Vivienne I said congratulations."

Wes nodded curtly, hoping it conveyed even a fraction of the gratitude coursing through him right then.

No one understood how to work around the law

like a former thief…except maybe a kick-ass lawyer.
He hoped the future Mrs. Brennan would accept the
necessity of his plan as easily as AJ just had. But Wes
would worry about that hurdle when he came to it.
First, he had to get her to open the door.

Vivienne was at loose ends, dressed casually in
jeans, a white T-shirt and bare feet. In her kitchen.
In the middle of the afternoon. On a weekday.

Unemployment didn't suit her, and now that she
didn't have Wes's case to distract her…

And she could definitely use some distraction, because as soon as her brain was left to its own devices,
it kept turning doggedly back to the same subject.

He'd been gone a week, but the sexual specter of
him lingered.

In her bed. On the couch. On her dining room
table. But worst of all, in her head.

Vivienne took a deep breath, staring at the sink
where the Le Creuset pan still sat at the same awkward angle that he'd left it in.

She should have cleaned it up, but something kept
stopping her. Vestiges of the sentimentality he used
to tease her about.

Maybe today was the day she'd be able to erase
the last evidence of their time together.

A loud rap at the door saved her from having to
follow through.

She hurried over to answer the summons, though
she wasn't expecting anyone. But even with no expectations, her visitor shocked her.

"Wes?"

Her synapses stuttered at the sight of him, and for a moment, she couldn't be sure if he was really there, or she'd just conjured him with her single-minded preoccupation.

Then he pushed past her, barging into her place and sanity returned like a punch in the face. As did her snark.

"No, please. Come in." Vivienne shut the door behind him.

"Put this on."

She caught the small box he'd lobbed in her direction against her chest. Tiffany blue with an iconic white ribbon.

Unease slithered between her vertebrae.

"What is this?"

"*Absolute perfection.* At least according to the sales associate who assured me she had 'just the thing' before putting a sizable dent in my credit limit."

Her hands shook at that announcement. She wasn't sure what felt worse—the way her heart kept throwing itself against her ribcage or the fact that her lungs refused to fully inflate. Her gaze ping-ponged between Wes and the box as she undid the ribbon, lifted the lid, opened the hinged jewelry case inside.

Twinkling up at her was a huge, flawless princess-cut diamond set in platinum with a fleet of smaller diamonds flanking it.

It was, indeed, absolute perfection.

She hated everything about it.

"What is this?"

"Exactly what you think it is." Wes sounded grim.

Vivienne had wasted enough youthful dreams pondering this moment, and to have them acted out in this macabre pantomime felt cruel.

"You can*not* be serious. If you think I'm going to marry you because of a couple of glorious orgasms then—"

"Eight." Her would-be fiancé glared at her. "You had eight glorious orgasms, but we don't have time to go over our highlight reel right now. City Hall closes at five."

"This is ridiculous." Vivienne snapped the box shut on the sham of a ring and held it in his direction. "I'm not marrying you."

Wes remained completely still. "Yes, Viv. You are."

The deadly seriousness of him finally penetrated her shock, centered her. Something was very, very wrong. "What's going on?"

"I can't tell you that."

"Why the hell not?"

"Because the less you know the better!" His words were harsh, but there was something tortured about them, as well. Like he no more wanted to be saying them than she wanted to hear them. "Hell, the less I know the better. Something bad is coming, and after what you did to help me, what you gave up…" Wes raked a frustrated hand through his hair.

"A week ago, it wouldn't have mattered. But we don't have attorney-client privilege going forward. And now I know things that can hurt you."

I'm the one who hacked Max's company, okay? I know you didn't do it, because it was me.

Her foolish confession pulsed hot in her brain. Shame burned through as she came to grips with what an untenable situation she'd put them both in.

"But you know things that might be able to help me figure this out. And now that they've let me go, the investigation is…pursuing new leads."

Oh, God. Her knees shook as she read between the lines. At the realization she was in the crosshairs.

"Now we need to improvise. The faster the better. Get your purse."

She couldn't drag him any further into this than she already had. Not when spousal privilege was black-and-white, and his plan was soaked in so much gray. Vivienne shook her head, trying to make him understand. "This will never hold up in court if it comes down to it. There are a million ways to poke holes in what each of us knew and when we knew it. It won't keep either of us safe for long."

She could see she wasn't getting through to him. That his mind was set.

"We were together for two years," he countered. "We lived together, and we broke up when you got accepted to Yale. Now work has thrown us back in each other's lives, and old feelings have resurfaced. Just stick to the salient facts. Let people assume the rest."

Hearing her inner feelings laid bare made Vivienne tremble. She tried to make him see the truth wasn't enough.

"If they have the kind of evidence that would send you to Tiffany's before knocking on my door, then things are too far gone to fix. I'm guilty of what they think I am, Wes. Best-case scenario is that this buys a little extra time while they figure out how to prove our marriage is a sham designed to keep us from testifying against each other."

"Time is exactly what I need to figure out who did this to you. Why the blackmailer targeted you to get to me. How it all fits together. And I will do whatever it takes. I swear it. I will get us both out of this, but I need your help to make it work."

Her breath shuddered from her lungs, as though it was filled with razor-sharp ice crystals. Not exactly the "I need you," she used to dream of when she'd been sure Wes's proposal was inevitable. The fun house–mirror version of it sat like a rock in her gut.

"You've got two choices here."

Vivienne dropped her gaze to the ring box.

"It's me, or prison. And orange isn't your color."

He stepped close, and his finger was warm against her chin as he tipped her head up, blue eyes boring into hers. "Let me protect you this time, Viv."

The shift of it prickled through her veins, mixing past memories with present in a way that warmed her blood, that made her want impossible things.

Wes's fingers brushed hers as he gently tugged the forgotten ring box from her grasp. He opened it and held it between them, a silent offer, not of love, but of momentary safety.

It wasn't nearly enough, and yet it was so much more than she deserved.

With a trembling breath, she pulled the ostentatious solitaire out of the ring box and slid it on her finger, ignoring the way his shoulders loosened when she did. Because this was going to be painful enough without letting emotions and foolish what-ifs into the mix.

Vivienne dumped the Tiffany packaging on the table beside the door before grabbing her purse. "We should get going."

Wes nodded, pulling the door open for her.

"And for the record," she rallied, squaring her shoulders as she stepped into the hallway, "I look great in orange."

CHAPTER FIFTEEN

THE PROCESS OF procuring a marriage license seemed absurdly easy, Vivienne thought, strangling her purse with sweaty palms as they sat on a bench outside the room where she would become Vivienne Brennan. Just as soon as the ceremony scheduled before theirs was finished.

A couple of signatures and a few dollars was all it took to change your life irreparably. That and the possibility of a prison sentence.

"We should have a contingency plan."

Wes looked up from his phone at the sound of her voice. Calm and cool as ever.

How he could be so blasé about this was beyond her.

"What are you talking about?"

"Divorce papers, in case I end up going to jail." Her voice wavered, and she hated the show of weakness. It took more effort than she'd have liked to swallow it down. "I could presign them so you can just file them if they have enough evidence to lock me up even without your testimony. Or maybe an annulment would go faster for you. We could say I coerced you into marrying me…"

She didn't realize her knee was vibrating with nerves until the heat from Wes's palm seeped through her jeans, stilling her leg. But not her brain.

"Fraud might be better, actually. You could tell them that I—"

"Hey. Take a breath."

He squeezed her thigh in silent acknowledgment as she took his advice.

"How about we get married before we worry about the divorce?"

She nodded jerkily. The bleakness of the situation stained her heart.

Then the doors beside them burst open, and a grinning band of revelers appeared. The bride was radiantly happy, and very pregnant, garbed in a silky white dress and birdcage veil, one hand full of fuchsia peonies, the other hand laced with her groom's. He wore a vintage blue tux and a mega-watt smile.

Viv's stomach twisted at the happy scene, and she reflexively clenched the cotton of her T-shirt, her nails digging into her abdomen and the cold, empty feeling there.

What could have been was a knife to her heart.

Still, she couldn't look away from them, her throat tight as the newlyweds kissed and giggled and oozed optimism all the way down the hall, surrounded by their merry entourage of friends and family.

"Wes and Vivienne? We're ready for you now."

They stood in unison, and the gray-haired justice of the peace introduced herself and the hired witness Wes had paid extra for, before warmly inviting them into the room where they would become man and wife.

But when Wes would have followed, Vivienne grabbed his forearm, stalling him on the threshold.

"I can't do this. I can't do this to you."

"And I can't do this without you." Wes stepped close, lifted his hand to cradle her jaw. She leaned into the warmth of his palm, trying to steal just a little bit of his strength. "But we're out of options here. So we're going to have to do it together, okay?"

His lips brushed her hairline. "All you have to do is close your eyes and pretend with me, just a little longer."

Pretend. Yes. Viv nodded. She could do that for him.

With a deep breath and her cold hand engulfed in Wes's warm one, she followed him inside.

You may now kiss your bride.

He could still taste her on his mouth. The fake sweetness of whatever she'd used to make her lips glossy. Their kiss had been brief, little more than a chaste peck, punctuated by an unrelenting awkwardness that had caused the justice of the peace to clear her throat before hurrying them through the document signing and sending them on their way to register the union so that Los Angeles County could do their part in making everything legal and official. So he could keep her safe.

His bride.

His wife.

How surreal was that?

Not the title so much as the way it had all gone down. Nothing like either of them had thought when they were young and in love. When he'd thought marrying her was kind of a foregone conclusion— not an *if*, but a *when*.

Looked like he hadn't been wrong on that front.

Vivienne was quiet in the passenger seat of his tricked-out Range Rover, staring contemplatively out the window as he navigated the start-and-stop traffic, toying with the gaudy ring on her finger. But he knew it was a temporary lull. That her brain was churning, looking for dots to connect, ways to fix things.

He wanted to kiss her again. A deep kiss that would make her forget, for just a second, that they were no closer to finding their puppet master. A slow kiss that would stop her brain from spinning in circles and remind her that she wasn't in this alone.

She'd gotten him out of prison, and he intended to keep her out in return. To finish his quest for revenge on whoever had blackmailed her into this debacle in the first place. Because if he'd doubted for even a second that he was being framed for this, the fact that she'd been dragged into the fray let him know that this had been an intensely personal attack.

"Can I ask you something?"

She straightened in the black leather bucket seat at the sound of his voice, but it took another second before she tore her gaze from the window and shifted it to him.

"Why didn't you come to me? When you got blackmailed?"

She stiffened like he'd hit her with a cattle prod and looked away from him, staring straight ahead.

He pushed again, even though her body language screamed at him to leave her alone. But he needed to understand. "I founded a cybersecurity firm. I could have helped."

"It was my problem." Her voice was as stiff as her spine.

The answer was so Vivienne that he almost smiled, despite the minor traffic jam that was messing with his attempt to get in the other lane. "You always were the most stubbornly independent woman I ever met."

"We were broken up! And I wanted to take care of it on my own because I don't need to run to a man every time something in my life goes wrong."

"I meant it as a compliment."

Vivienne twisted her new accessory around her finger. "Oh."

Since he'd penetrated her bravado, Wes kept talking. Viv always took a little while to open up.

"My mom used to fade into nothing when my dad was serving time. I thought that's what love was for most of my life…staggering codependence. And then

I met you, and it was, I don't know, kind of refreshing that you didn't need me like she needed my dad."

He felt her gaze on him as they inched their way past the fender bender that had been holding things up, and Wes maneuvered the vehicle into the right lane.

"You were smart, and vivacious, and you had your whole future planned out. And for some reason, you wanted to be with me. That made me want to be better. *You* made me want to be better."

His words had been meant to soothe her fears, but her anguished response let him know they'd had the opposite effect.

"God, Wes. If I'd known what I did would end up with you in jail…"

The threat of tears was there, wavering on the edge of her voice. He knew how much she hated that. Wes blew out a breath. It had been a long day, and she'd earned a break. They both had. They could get into the details tomorrow.

"It was nude photos, wasn't it?"

Her gaze whipped to his profile. "What?"

"You shouldn't have been embarrassed to ask me for help. If you think about it, I'm basically the most qualified person on the planet to help you deal with that kind of thing. Not only am I great with computers, I've seen you naked a *lot*. I'm sure I could have gotten them back for you. After an in-depth verification process to make sure all the photos were legit, of course."

She gave him a shove, but laughter lurked at the

corner of her lips, and relief poured through him that she'd smiled at least once.

It was their wedding day, after all.

"You hungry?"

Her eyes lit up, but she tried to mask it with a stoic shrug. "I could eat."

Wes shoulder checked as he flipped on his signal light and snaked through traffic. "I know just the place."

CHAPTER SIXTEEN

STEPPING INTO SEÑOR TACO'S was like stepping back in time.

"Man. This place hasn't changed a bit."

Vivienne nodded at Wes's assessment as they walked into their old haunt.

The gray brick walls, scarred wood floor and dim ambient lighting gave the place a cozy feel. Washes of color came from the fluorescent signs that dotted the walls, advertising a multitude of Mexican alcohol, from Montelobos to Don Julio, and there was a cluster of intricate iron-work chandeliers hanging from the industrial ceiling over the small open area where people sometimes danced when they had live bands on Saturday nights.

They approached the dark wood bar that was inset with tile mosaics and lined with bottles of booze, backlit by blue spotlights.

"Hey. I'll take a Corona and two shots of house tequila. And two orders of the street tacos," Wes glanced over at her. "*Al pastor* and *carne asada*?"

She nodded at their standard order, feeling stupid

that menu items seemed poignant to her. As did the
offhand way he'd confirmed before ordering, even
though they'd never had anything else off the menu.
She fiddled with the ring on her left hand as Wes
turned back to the guy at the cash register.

"You can add a side of guacamole and *pico de
gallo* to that."

After Wes paid, the guy rimmed two shot glasses
with coarse salt, filled them with tequila, and laid a
lime wedge across each of them. Then he added the
Corona and a metal stand with a laminated number
six clipped to it.

"Someone will bring out your tacos when they're
ready."

Wes passed her his beer before he grabbed the
shots in one hand and their table number in the other
and they turned to face their old stomping grounds.
Vivienne's gaze migrated directly to the back corner, the table she thought of as "theirs."

There were a couple of big guys with long, wiry
beards sitting at it. Internally, she rolled her eyes at
the pang of disappointment. She'd accused Wes of
trying to summon the Ghost of Christmas Future,
and here she was channeling the spirit of Christmas Past.

"Hold these for a second, would you?"

Vivienne accepted the shots in her empty right
hand, even as she shook her head. "You don't have
to…there's a table right over there. It's fine."

"I got this."

She chewed on her bottom lip, watching as he

walked over to the two burly, trucker types. No way were they just going to concede the spot when there was an empty table right in front of them. Vivienne turned to scope out anywhere else they could sit. There seemed to be a vacancy on the other side of the dance floor, as well. But much to her surprise, by the time she looked back, the truckers were on their feet, nodding chivalrously at her as they moved their giant burritos to the neighboring table.

Wes's grin was smug as she approached, and he planted their number on the table like he was Neil Armstrong raising the flag on the moon.

"How'd you manage that?"

"I told them we're on our honeymoon."

Vivienne's hand tightened around the beer bottle at the reminder, and the ring cut into her skin.

"And I gave them five hundred bucks," Wes confessed, relieving her of the shots and setting them on the scarred wooden tabletop.

"Expensive tacos."

"Yeah, well. I figure we saved a lot of cash on our wedding garb," he motioned at her T-shirt and jeans, then his own, "so why not splurge?"

Wes's attempt to keep things light was appreciated, but even so, her stomach gave a weird little bump as he tugged the stools to the same side of the table. The best formation for people watching, taco sharing and intimate conversation. She wondered if it was only habit, or if he'd made the conscious decision to set the table up like they had the night they'd met…and every other night they'd eaten at Señor Taco's since.

She set the Corona on the table and they settled onto their seats.

Wes grabbed his tequila. *"Salud."*

Vivienne followed suit, lime wedge in one hand, drink in the other. With a quick clink, they downed the pungent liquor. Then the sharp, sour tang of citrus made her scrunch up her nose. She and Wes dropped the rinds into their empty glasses in unison.

Wes. Her husband.

She was suddenly struck by the fact that she barely knew anything about him anymore. That little business venture he'd gotten so obsessed with toward the end of their relationship, the one he'd poured all that time and effort into, had grown into something incredible.

Not that she was surprised. Wes might not have gone to college, but he'd always been the smartest guy she'd ever met. She'd known he was destined for big things, even back then.

"So how long have you wanted to take Soteria public?"

Wes frowned slightly, shook his head as he ran a thumb along the condensation on his beer. "I don't. I like not having to answer to anyone. The freedom of being able to try things without the pressure of it having to turn massive profits."

"Oh, sorry. For some reason I thought Jesse said…" Vivienne flicked her hand, dismissing the thought. "I was pretty distracted that day. Must've misunderstood."

Wes stilled. "You saw Jesse?"

"I ran into him the other day in the men's department at Neiman's. He came over to say hi."

There was something about the sudden tautness in his body as Wes crushed the lime wedge against the neck of his beer bottle before pushing it inside.

"It was a quick conversation," she assured him, though she wasn't quite sure why she felt the need to do so. "He was on his way to Whitfield Industries to try to woo Max into sticking with Soteria."

"I've been trying to get in touch with him since the charges were dropped."

"I'm sure he's just really busy. He knows how much the company means to you."

Wes nodded. Took a sip of beer. She was relieved that he looked more relaxed.

"So what were *you* doing at the men's department at Neiman's anyway?"

Vivienne cast around for a reason not to admit that she'd considered buying him clothes because his constant shirtlessness had been wearing down her attempts to keep her hands off him. Since she'd failed so spectacularly at the clothes buying and at keeping her hands to herself, the point was moot. In the end, she went with a classic subject change.

"The real question is, what was Jesse doing there? When was the last time that guy bought anything off the rack?"

Wes chuckled, relinquishing his beer when she

reached for it—a habit so old and engrained that she hadn't even realized she'd done it until the bottle was in her hand. "He does love to blow money on pretentiously expensive custom-made suits."

"And country club memberships," Vivienne added. "Vintage Corvettes. Rolexes." Jesse had always loved a good status symbol. Or eight.

"And a luxury schooner."

Vivienne's eyes widened at the addition, Wes's beer arrested halfway to her mouth. "He did not." She took a long swallow. "Does he even sail?"

"No. He was at some auction and just wanted to outbid that douchey frat brother of his. The one who stole his girlfriend during spring break. Trina What's-her-name. The heiress to the bagged salad fortune."

Vivienne laughed as she handed back the Corona. "I remember that guy! He wore so much cologne." She shook her head. "Jesse really bought a vengeance boat? That is a level of retribution I didn't even know existed."

A pretty raven-haired server with a high ponytail and the most perfectly winged eyeliner arrived with their tacos, and they both dug in with gusto.

Vivienne closed her eyes and hummed at the gustatory pleasure that was Señor Taco's. "Oh, God. How have I stayed away from this place for so long?" she mumbled through the bite of heaven. "Still the best thing I've ever had in my mouth."

Her heart clenched hard at his lazy white smile. "I'll try not to take offense at that."

The sexual innuendo slipped under her skin.

He turned back to his taco, giving her leg a teasing bump under the table, but her body misinterpreted the casual contact as something far more charged. Her muscles clenched at the jolt of heat that Wes so easily unleashed in her.

They people watched as they ate. It was a good crowd. Lots of college students, judging by the number of T-shirts with school logos on them.

Vivienne watched in fascination as a couple of UCLA students stole past them hand in hand, all flushed cheeks and furtive giggles. The fact that they thought they were being sneaky in their quest for a quickie had her rolling her eyes.

"Nice to know Señor Taco's restrooms are still seeing their fair share of action."

"Is that censure in your voice?" Wes shoved their empty plates to the middle of the table. "Because if I remember correctly, you and I were responsible for a good portion of that action."

"That was a long time ago."

Wes stared at her for a little too long, and she wondered exactly what he saw in the dim light. His voice was low when he spoke again. "Not that long ago. And action has its charm. Sometimes talking's overrated."

He shifted on his stool, and their shoulders touched. "Those two agree with me."

Vivienne followed the tip of his chin to find that, at some point during their conversation, a few couples had migrated to the dance floor to take advantage of the sensuous Latin beat. She didn't need to ask who he was talking about.

They were mesmerizing—practically glowing with sexual energy as they used dancing as a thinly veiled metaphor for foreplay. Their bodies moving in unison, brushing against one another, only to retreat before coming together again. It was absorbing, the illicit heat of them.

This time, Wes's leg didn't bump hers so much as slide along it, and Viv sucked in a breath at the unexpected contact that turned watching into something more visceral.

"You remember what that was like?"

His voice was husky, seductive, and it prickled along her spine like a touch.

"Being so into someone that you can't think straight. That undeniable pulse of desire that makes you want to push the limits."

Wes pushed his stool back a little, angling his big body toward her. "That overwhelming rush of lust that makes your skin come alive."

She shivered when his thumb traced the length of her arm. Vivienne was definitely alive in that moment. It was like someone had plugged her into a power source. Her cells vibrated with it. With him.

The scrape of wood on wood echoed in her ears as he grabbed the leg of her stool and tugged it in front of his. And just like that, she was between Wes's legs, his chest at her back, his voice in her ear.

"That's the kind of heat that makes you forget where you are. Who's around."

His hand came to rest on her hip, and her eyelids drifted shut as he traced his thumb along the waistband of her jeans, stopping just beneath her belly button.

"His world is just her right now."

The reminder of the dancing couple made her open her eyes in time to watch the guy's hands as they migrated up from the girl's waist. His fingers were dangerously close to her breasts, flirting with that intoxicating line between PDA and public indecency charges.

"All he can think about is touching her."

With the flick of Wes's thumb, the button on Viv's jeans went slack. She swallowed against the rush of warmth between her thighs.

"About getting his hands on her."

She couldn't hear her zipper over the music, over the beat of her own heart, but she felt the denim grow even looser.

Wes's mouth was so close that his breath tickled her ear. Her lips parted on a silent sigh.

"That buzz is everything. The build of anticipation. The throb of it in their veins."

The thrall of lust wound through her, consumed her.

"He's so hard it hurts, and do you know why?"

"Why?" she breathed the word so softly, she wasn't sure if Wes heard it over the bar din, or if he was just so deep in his story that her answer was irrelevant.

"Because he knows she's wet for him."

She sank her teeth into her bottom lip. So, so wet for him.

"He can smell her arousal. Feel the way she trembles beneath his touch."

Her whole world had narrowed to the burn of his fingers on her abdomen.

"Until they're so turned on, so wild with need, that they can't handle the tease for another second."

Vivienne squeezed her eyes shut as Wes slipped his hand in her panties. The stroke of his finger, precise and unerring, as he circled her clit with just the right amount of pressure.

An involuntary moan escaped her lips at the contact, half relief, half desperation.

"God, you feel so fucking good, Viv."

She bit her lip as he pushed his hand deeper, so he could slip a finger inside her. *Yes*. It was too much, and not nearly enough. She mewled in frustration.

"You want more?"

Thankfully, he didn't wait for an answer before pressing a second finger inside her. Her body stretched to accommodate the slow, slick slide of his hand, and she leaned back against his chest, something solid as the promise of pleasure began to make the rest of the world go a little wavy.

She could feel the heat of his chest seeping into her back, the jut of his erection pressing against her ass.

Before long, she was rocking her hips in time with the steady drive of his fingers in her mindless quest for climax.

"Jesus. You make me so hard. I wish I was inside you."

Wes finally gave her what she wanted, and with the twist of his wrist, the pad of his finger brushed her G-spot with every thrust.

Vivienne bit her lip, working herself against his hand, desperate for release. She was close. So damn close.

The rasp of his breath in her ear let her know he knew it, too. "That's right. Come apart for me."

Her body tightened at the sexy order, squeezing around his fingers, and then Wes pressed the heel of his hand against her clit and caught her earlobe between his teeth. The weightless free fall of orgasm rushed through her with unstoppable intensity.

CHAPTER SEVENTEEN

"LET ME TAKE you home."

That's what he'd said when she could finally breathe again. When her heart rate had returned to normal operating parameters and she'd settled back into her body to find they were still at Señor Taco's and that she hadn't transcended into another plane of existence all together.

Which was why she shouldn't have been surprised when Wes pulled up at his place, not hers. And as much as she wanted to look around the ritzy loft, with its big windows and manly, brown leather furniture and surprising sense of hominess, that was going to have to wait.

Right now, she needed to get Wes's pants off.

She would have, too, but he impeded her progress by shoving her up against the door the second it closed and pinning her arms over her head so he could capture her mouth with his. The flavor of beer and tacos on his tongue might not do it for some women, but Viv figured their youthful antics had classically conditioned her to drop her panties faster for that taste than any response Pavlov had managed to get with his stupid bell.

With a groan, Wes pulled his mouth from hers, let go of her wrists.

"Not here."

Since she disagreed with that assessment, Vivienne slid her hand between his legs, and did her best to change his mind. "Not exciting enough without the taco crowd? We could move this in front of the window and hope a bunch of people walk by."

His answering chuckle loosened something in her chest. "Tempting, but this time I want you all to myself."

Before she'd realized his intentions, Wes ducked down and hoisted her over his shoulder in a fireman's carry. Her stomach hurt from laughing by the time he'd marched her across the floor and dumped her on his mattress.

He dragged his T-shirt over his head. "I mean to have you in my bed, wife."

Vivienne froze at the pronouncement. Wife. She was his wife.

He was her husband.

She watched as he shucked his jeans and underwear, revealing the perfection of his body. Strong. Sexy. For two years of her life, he was all she'd ever wanted. And tonight, he was really hers. Boyish and eager, with mussed-up hair and sex on his mind.

Despite everything that had brought them to this point, all the guilt and wasted time, she didn't want to miss the moment. She could worry about the rest tomorrow.

"You're falling behind there, Mrs. Brennan." He grabbed the hem of her shirt and pulled it up over her head. "Let's get you naked," he said, giving her a playful shove to make her lie down so he could do the same with her jeans and underwear.

When he was done, Vivienne sat up and scooted to the middle of the bed so there was room for Wes to join her. He positioned himself on his back, with his head on the pillow, watching as she reached behind her back to unhook her bra.

There was something about the look in Wes's eyes when he watched her undress that did it for her every time. With a coy smile, she crawled toward him, leaning down to catch his mouth in the kind of kiss that let him know exactly what she was thinking.

When she lifted up, his eyes were that dark, swirling blue that let her know he was on the same page. Or at least she thought he was, but when she made a move to slide down his body to take him in her mouth, he stopped her.

"Grab the headboard."

"Wes…"

"Do it." There was a little bit of darkness in his voice as he issued the order, and she was helpless to disobey. He grabbed her by the hips, once she'd complied, and she had to admit, it was kind of sexy the way he manhandled her, positioning her with a knee on either side of his head.

"I'm calling the shots this time."

She should hate it. At least that's what she told herself.

She was independent. She'd built herself a life and career without him. Without anyone. And that's how she liked it. Because if there was one thing she knew, people never failed to let you down. To leave. Wes had done both already.

Then his breath trailed along her inner thigh. And it made her want what she shouldn't.

Him.

But it felt good to let go of the control, just for a second. To rely on someone else with no worry that it might end in heartbreak or disappointment. Because the truth was, though she might struggle to trust him with her heart, he'd always been the master of her orgasms.

When his tongue touched her, the shock of pleasure sizzled through her. He was the one who growled, though. "It's been way too long since I've tasted you."

She tipped her head back in ecstasy as he licked straight up the center of her. Her fingers tightened on the headboard as Wes alternated between slow, open-mouthed kisses and then switched it up with surprising moments of suction that had her on the precipice in no time. Vivienne tightened her thighs, and the novelty of the rasp of his beard against her sensitive skin drove her even higher. The heat built fast, almost too fast considering she'd come so recently. This time was different though. In the bar, the steady drive of his fingers against her G-spot had unleashed something deep and pulsing in her belly. But this, the swirl of his tongue against her clit, was a shallower kind of pleasure. Not worse, just different, like static electricity crackling across her skin. And then Wes did that thing she liked where he pressed his tongue hard against her and moved his head just so—oh God, it felt even better than she'd remembered—and the myriad sensations coursing through her culminated in a flash of heat and light as her pelvis jerked and she came apart with Wes between her thighs.

She was boneless as he helped her slide down his body, until she was lying on top of him. With a satisfied sigh, she pressed a kiss to his talented mouth as he traced the length of her spine with his knuckles.

His cock was hot and hard between them, and she teasingly wiggled her hips. "You didn't want to come, did you? Because I'm all tired out."

"No problem," he assured her. But before she could tell him she was only joking, he'd rolled her onto her back with a swift, hard kiss.

"You just lie back and let me do all the work." The offer was made with a cocky grin that convinced her libido that she could probably muster the energy for round three. The slide of his body as he eased himself inside her dispelled any doubt, and Vivienne wrapped her arms around him, sure she would never get enough of the way he made her feel.

He was gorgeous when he fucked. Predatory. She'd forgotten the intensity of him. The focus. How he turned straight-up missionary into the most consuming, intimate kind of pleasure.

She drank in the familiar sight of him as he thrust into her, the feel of his muscles bunching and releasing beneath her questing fingers. She'd missed the feel of him, exciting and familiar, all at once. Vivienne bent her knees, sliding her heels closer to her thighs, because she knew what he liked, too, and she wanted to thank him for the thing he'd done with his tongue.

Digging her heels into the mattress, she countered his thrusts, circling her hips and wringing a curse from him. Yeah. He loved that. And she loved giving it to him. Wes's muscles drew tight and his hips started to speed up as he hit the point of no return. Then he was groaning her name as his body convulsed with the force of his release. Vivienne wrapped her arms around him, pressing her lips against his neck and holding him close as he shuddered with the aftershocks of their desire, hoping that he'd felt even an echo of what he'd made her feel.

When his breathing returned to normal, he pushed off her, rolling onto his back, and they lay side by side in his giant bed, staring up at the ceiling.

After a moment, Wes grabbed her left hand with his right and began idly stroking his thumb across her knuckles. It was hypnotic, and surprisingly electric considering how tame it was compared to all the ways, all the places, he'd just touched her. The memories distracted her, and it took her a second to realize that he was twisting the ring off her finger.

Something like panic fisted her heart, squeezing to the point of pain.

"Done with me already?" It was supposed to be a joke, but it held no levity. The symbolism of it was a fissure in her heart, growing wider by the second.

He turned his head toward her on the pillow. "I know you don't like it. I saw your face when you opened it."

Shame washed through her. She'd been a total bitch to him after the intensity of what had happened between them that last day at her place. Being spanked had pushed her to the physical brink, made her more vulnerable than she'd ever been, and she hadn't been able to process the emotional fallout. Or the inescapable connection that had sprung up between them. From the second Wes had pulled her into his arms and held her while she cried, she'd known something monumental had shifted between them. Something she couldn't undo. And so after she'd used him, slaked her need for punishment, she'd discarded him without explanation. Pushed him away with brutal efficiency, intentionally hurt him in an attempt to avoid dealing with the shift in their relationship.

And still he'd shown up at her door to help her.

"I was just…surprised." Terrified. Desperately happy.

"Uh-huh." To her amazement, he sounded amused, not offended. "I've got something for you."

Her shriek of shock turned to a laugh as he rolled his big body on top of her, before bringing her along for another half turn. When they were done, he'd usurped her side of the bed, and she was on top of him.

Planting her knees in the mattress on either side of his torso, she pushed herself up so she was straddling his stomach. The expensive ring clattered against the end table as he dropped it there before lowering his hand to the drawer pull and tugging it open. "Can you grab that red box for me?"

Vivienne leaned slightly to the side, her gaze snagging on a red velvet ring box tucked against the back corner of the drawer. Her fingers shook as she reached for it, turning it over in her hands, avoiding the next step.

"Open it."

Swallowing back her fear, Vivienne complied. The hinges were tight, and the box snapped open. For a moment, she thought her heart had stopped.

"Wes…"

A small diamond was set in matte white gold that reminded her of vines. It was like nothing she'd ever seen before. Too modest for a man of Wes Brennan's current means, too thoughtful for a stand-in ring for this sham of a wedding, too perfect for any of that to be a mistake.

"It's yours."

The wording struck her as odd, ringing an alarm bell deep in her bones.

And she knew. Without question. That this ring was hers. It had been intended for her all along.

Her chest felt tight, crowded with emotion, as her gaze found his.

"You were going to propose?"

His embarrassed grin sent her heart careening into a free fall. "I mean, one day. Once I'd made something of myself."

"I told you I didn't care about that."

"Because you grew up with a father who was a named partner of a corporate law firm. My mom was trying to support two kids and a raging drug habit as a grocery store cashier. When she bothered to show up for work, that is. And I didn't know how to make you understand that I needed to be able to provide for you, not because you couldn't, but because not being able to would make me too much like him."

His dad. Wes had described him as a low-budget con man who only showed up when he needed money, who only called when he needed bail.

Wes's self-recriminating laugh broke her heart as he took the little box from her numb fingers. "When I bought this, I didn't think this moment would be so far in the future."

Then, before Vivienne could even fathom what he was doing, he lifted her hand and slid the ring onto her finger.

I, Wesley James Brennan, take you, Vivienne Amelie Grant...

She replayed the vow he'd made her at City Hall in her head, his voice solemn and deep, as she stared down at her hand and the unique, perfect ring that completely eclipsed the generic princess-cut diamond she'd worn earlier.

Vivienne leaned forward, bracing her forearms on his chest so she could catch his mouth in the kind of kiss they hadn't shared in a very long time. One that lacked the crackling heat and promise of deep, drugging pleasure. One that, instead, promised something far more profound and lasting than physical pleasure.

As if he'd sensed the difference, there was a question in Wes's blue eyes when he opened them, and the difference in the way he was looking at her gave her chills.

Wes lifted his hand, his fingers tracing the curve of her cheek. "Viv?"

"Yeah?"

"The last time we were together, when you wanted to be spanked?" His fingers stilled against her face. "Was I…was I not giving you what you needed before? Would you have stayed if the sex had been dirtier? More adventurous?"

The sheer vulnerability of the question was enough to rip her heart out of her chest, to break through the wall of bravado and ice she'd constructed to keep it safe after she'd driven him away six years ago. The layer of shame that kept her from admitting how desperately she wanted this fake marriage to be real. The bone-deep knowledge that she still loved him. Dirty, sweet and every which way in between.

"You're enough for me, Wes. Just this. Just us."

He always had been. Always would be.

And to prove it to him, she leaned forward, pressing a kiss to his chest, right above his heart as she slid her other hand down his body, taking him inside her so they could rock together until the heat between them raged out of control again.

CHAPTER EIGHTEEN

"WHERE DO YOU think you're going? I'm not done with you yet."

Vivienne laughed as she slipped out of his grip and made a break for it, crawling toward the edge of the bed. "I need to hydrate or I won't last the night."

"I'll allow it," Wes decreed. "But be quick," he advised, with a smack on the ass that made her giggle, but also made her want to hurry back and explore the pulse of heat that flared in her belly. Grabbing his T-shirt from the floor, she pulled the black cotton over her head.

His lips twisted with wry humor. "Yes. Modesty is key after how we've spent the last four hours."

In response, she pulled the pillow from beneath his head and smushed it on his face.

"There's some bottled water in the fridge," he advised, his voice muffled by her feather-filled retribution.

Vivienne padded her way across his loft, eyes roving over the decor, his possessions. It was a classy place, for sure, but it didn't scream tech billionaire. It

was more understated than that. Cozier. It took her a
second to realize the reason for that was all the little
personal touches that he used to tease her about. The
ones, she suddenly realized, that she'd phased out of
her own life in the intervening years.

Picture frames on the table, a shelf full of books,
things he used to be far more utilitarian about.

"Oh my God. Are these throw pillows on your
couch?" she teased with faux horror. When they'd
lived together, he'd been adamantly anti–throw pillow since beading and tassels and fringe made them
uncomfortable, which, he'd argued, robbed them of
their pillow destiny. Granted, his were plain, but it
was still a big step for Wes.

"What can I say? I guess you rubbed off on me."

The idea of that pleased her more than it should,
but her grin faded as she approached the kitchen and
her eyes lit on his stainless steel fridge.

Or more accurately, on the crayon drawing that
was proudly displayed on it.

To Uncle Wes, it said. *From Jeremy.*

The sudden buzzing in her brain was disorienting, and she braced a hand against his butcher-block
island as she tried to catch her breath.

Reality was not to be denied though. It seeped
through all the cracks in her heart, reminding her
that there was no happy ending for her and Wes.
They'd tried this once, and it had all gone to shit.

They were only here now because she'd lied to
him.

The vilest of lies.

She looked down at her finger. At the perfect ring. Perfect because he'd chosen it for the old her. The one who hadn't known yet what a coward she would become.

"Viv?"

His voice was too loud, and the realization that he was behind her snapped her head up.

She swiped a hand across her cheek to erase the tear that had escaped against her will, wondering just how long she'd been standing there.

"You okay?" There was concern on his handsome face as he stepped up to the fridge, pulling open the door and grabbing each of them a plastic bottle from the door rack.

He'd pulled on his jeans, but he hadn't done them up. Her throat ached at the sight of him as he set the water on the counter beside her.

"I was just looking at your picture." Her voice sounded small, but it echoed in the empty feeling in her chest.

He glanced over his shoulder as he cracked open the lid on his own bottle. "Nice, right?" He was grinning with pride when he turned back to her, but there was something else there. Something that sliced at her heart. Love. "You might not recognize me, but that is actually a very accurate depiction of my backyard soccer skills."

"Erin had a baby." A little boy that Wes obviously adored. He was an uncle.

"Yeah. She found herself a good guy. Peter's a high school chemistry teacher." Wes took a long swallow before putting the cap back on the bottle and setting it next to the one she hadn't touched. "But Jeremy, that kid's the best. You're gonna love him."

It was the worst possible thing he could have said. Including her like that, like part of the family, brought everything roiling to the surface, past and present clashing in such a painful, disorienting way.

"We didn't use a condom."

He frowned at her abrupt announcement, and she braced for his fury before she realized it was just confusion. And concern.

"I know. We haven't used one since we established we were both clean after the elevator, remember? Do you want to sit down? You look a little pale."

Wes lifted her onto the counter before she had a chance to protest. Not that she could have even if she'd wanted to, because other words started spilling out of her mouth instead. Words she should have said to him a long time ago.

"Not now. Then. That night in your car." About a month and a half before everything had gone oh so wrong. "Our second anniversary."

They'd been driving to dinner to celebrate when Wes's hand had wandered far enough up her thigh to ruin his anniversary present—a black lace garter belt and thigh-highs that Viv hadn't been able to resist. Wes had felt the same way. They'd pulled into an alley so he could unwrap his gift right away, which had resulted in them missing the window of their fancy reservation. They'd ended up improvising their anniversary dinner with fast-food burgers and milkshakes in bed, followed by a couple more rounds of dessert.

She could see the memory solidify behind his eyes. Then he went deathly still.

"So?"

But as nonchalantly as he might have meant for it to sound, the syllable was cocked and loaded. Viv could actually feel him processing the news, the way his body braced against the unwelcome realization.

Her tears stung, salt on a wound that had never healed quite right. That she knew now never would. But she made herself say the words she'd never said aloud before.

"I was pregnant." The words hollowed out her chest, like someone had dug her heart out with a spoon, leaving her raw and scraped up.

Wes shook his head, like his body couldn't process what his mind had already pieced together. "When you shoved that goddamn ticket to Connecticut in my face and told me that if I really loved you, I'd drop everything to go with you? You were pregnant?"

"Yes."

He staggered, like the word was a blow.

"You didn't tell me." He shoved his hands in his hair, looking helpless for a second, before anger flashed in his eyes. "How could you not tell me?"

"Because I was terrified!" The words came out with more force than she'd intended. "More scared than I'd ever been in my whole life. You'd been so distant, so focused on Soteria."

She couldn't hold back all the old feelings. "I needed you, Wes! I needed you to want me. To want to be with me. Not because I was pregnant, but because I was important to you. More important than all those investor dinners Jesse kept dragging you to. More important than your business plan and your goddamn computer."

"Are you fucking kidding me right now? You think that's a good enough reason?" He stepped back from her.

It wasn't. She knew it. She'd known it then. While they'd fought. While they'd had sex. While she'd boarded the goddamn plane.

"I meant to tell you. After I left, I spent weeks trying to figure out the best way to tell you."

Wes sneered at the flimsiness of her defense. He stepped back again. "Oh, you meant to tell me. You meant to fucking tell me that we had a baby."

She shook her head, and her throat constricted at the prospect of telling him now. "There was no baby."

The anger had been a good distraction, but now the overwhelming sadness was back. Tears dripped down her face.

"I'd made an appointment for a ten-week ultrasound to find out the sex."

An appointment she'd had to cancel. For a baby that would never be.

"I thought that's how I'd tell you, because you'd want to know. I practiced it so many times. 'Wes, I'm pregnant. It's a girl,' or, 'It's a boy.' But three days before, I woke up and everything hurt so badly. I remember calling 911. Then I passed out."

Vivienne stared at the ring on her left hand as she twisted her fingers in her lap.

"When I woke up from surgery, I asked about our baby. I swear to you, it was the first thing I asked. But the doctor explained that I was in the hospital because I'd had an ectopic pregnancy and my fallopian tube had burst."

She forced herself to meet Wes's eyes, even though he was blurry through her tears.

"It was all for nothing." The words clawed at her throat. "Our whole lives changed and there wasn't even a baby." *Breathe*, she reminded herself. "There wasn't even the chance of a baby. And so I told myself it was better if you didn't know, because when I asked you to come with me, you turned me down."

The stricken look on Wes's face hurt her all the way to her bones, and she hopped down from the counter at the sudden need to go to him. To erase the distance that had sprung up between them. But when she would have reached for him, he stepped back from her, did up his jeans.

"I need to get out of here." He stalked toward the door, grabbing the hooded sweatshirt from the coat rack and shoving bare feet into his sneakers.

Vivienne watched as the man she loved walked out the door, flinched as it banged shut behind him.

Her greatest fear made manifest. Again.

Everyone who'd ever mattered to her left her when she needed them most. Her mother. Her father. Wes.

She'd known they were destined for this. It was why she'd fought her feelings so desperately. Because if she and Wes were meant to be, it would have worked out the first time.

CHAPTER NINETEEN

PREGNANT.

When she'd first said the word, it was like someone had shoved a spike through his skull. Disori-
entation. Nausea. Agony. He couldn't get his brain
to focus.

Now, after an hour of walking aimlessly down the
street in the middle of the night, he was just numb.

He couldn't feel anything anymore.

Wes jammed his hands deep in the pockets of
his hoodie.

Pregnant. But not pregnant.

Wes walked faster, hoping motion would help dissipate some of the toxic emotional cocktail that was
swirling in his gut. He was trying so goddamn hard
to hold on to the anger, but other stuff kept getting
in the way. Especially after he pulled his phone out
of his pocket and googled *ectopic pregnancy*.

Vivienne had never been totally sold on the idea
of having children. She'd told him that once, a few
weeks into their relationship when she'd asked him
if he wanted kids and he'd said yes. One day.

She hadn't quite been able to squelch the fear in her eyes.

"I'm not sure if I do," she'd confessed. She was worried that she wouldn't be a good mom because no one had taught her. Cancer had stolen her own mother before she'd had a chance to learn anything.

The memory chilled him.

Vivienne had been knocked up and terrified, and instead of turning to Wes, she'd fled across the country alone.

It broke his fucking heart to think he was the greater of two evils for her in that moment. A moment when he should have been there for her.

And that wasn't even the worst of it.

Burst fallopian tubes, according to what he'd read, could be life-threatening.

She'd almost died and he hadn't even known. How could he not have known something like that?

Jesus. No wonder she'd left him.

At the time, her sudden announcement that she was going to Yale instead of Stanford, that stupid ultimatum with the plane ticket, had struck him as incredibly selfish.

But he'd been selfish, too. She wasn't wrong. He'd been caught up in Jesse's plans to schmooze investors and turn Soteria into something big, right out of the gate. Maybe if he'd been paying better attention, he would have realized that something was going on with her.

Because he knew. He knew what losing her mom had done to her. How abandoned she'd felt by her father afterward. She'd told him how she used to dream about her father choosing her over work, how she used to scan the hall during piano concerts and dance recitals in hopes that just once, he'd pick her instead of a meeting, or a business lunch or golf game. She'd trusted him with that knowledge, and then he'd acted just like the son of a bitch who'd raised her. Let her fly across the country without him. Abandoned her when she'd needed him the most.

Just like he was doing right now.

The realization hauled Wes up short. She'd trusted him again, and he was fucking it up. Walking away when what she needed was his understanding. The realization disgusted him, and he cursed himself silently as he turned around and started the long walk home.

He knew she wasn't there the second that he opened the door. Not that he blamed her for leaving. God, he was such an asshole.

He considered going to find her right then, had his keys in his hand, but he stopped himself. Set them back down. Dismissed the idea as he pulled off his hoodie and draped it over the back of his desk chair. If she'd wanted to discuss things further tonight, she wouldn't have left. They could both use some time to let what had just happened settle and get a couple hours of sleep.

Tomorrow, he'd go and get his wife.

"Viv? C'mon. Open up."

Wes knocked again, ignoring the tingle at the base

of his spine that was turning into a bad feeling about the fact that she hadn't answered the door yet.

He punched the eight digits of her mom's birthday into the security panel and burst inside. "Viv?"

He strode past the kitchen, through the living room, into the bedroom.

Empty.

Memories of the last time he'd come home to find her gone assailed him, twining the past and the present together in a way that constricted his breathing.

His heart started to thud against his ribcage with more force, but he swallowed the panic. He wasn't going to lose her again. This was just a problem in need of a solution. He was good at finding solutions. She was somewhere, even if she wasn't here, so all he had to do was—

The vibration of his phone in his pocket interrupted his train of thought, but any hope that it was her was dashed as he glanced at the screen.

"What the hell, man? I've been trying to get in touch since the charges were dropped."

"I know." Jesse's voice was calm. Eerily so. "My lawyers advised I shouldn't speak with you."

Wes's fingers tightened on his phone. He didn't like the sound of that. "Your lawyers," he repeated, matching Jesse's composure. "Don't you mean our lawyers? Because I'm pretty sure the esteemed law firm of Denisof Price Goldberg represents Soteria Security. Or at least that's the way they made it sound when they told me to fuck off after I was put in handcuffs and hauled off to jail. But now that my legal woes are behind me, we've got some reinstatement paperwork to sign. Isn't that right?"

The long silence on the other end of the line told Wes everything he needed to know, even before Jesse spoke again.

"This isn't how I wanted this to go down. We've been partners, friends, for a long time. But Soteria is hemorrhaging clients since you went to prison. And I've been doing everything I can to keep us afloat!"

Not so calm anymore.

"You're a goddamn liability."

"The charges were dropped," Wes countered.

"And then you turned around and married the goddamn enemy! How do you think that's going to play in the media? That the second you're cleared of wrongdoing, you hitch yourself to the FBI's next target!"

"She didn't do this." Wes's voice was flat and hard with conviction.

"Tell that to the video surveillance footage. I've got to go. I have a joint meeting with Max and Liam in a couple of hours, and I need to prepare. If I can keep them on board, then this media storm will stabilize, and I can finally implement my plan to take Soteria Security public by the end of the year."

The announcement blindsided Wes.

"What the hell are you talking about? I thought we agreed no IPO. We always said Soteria could be more innovative, and do better work, without having to answer to shareholders!"

"We didn't agree. You used your fifty-one percent share to cock-block me, and what I've wanted, for years. I'm the one who sacrificed for your genius. I'm the one who parceled out my shares to get new investors, to take Soteria to the money-making behemoth it's become. Now that I have controlling interest, you honestly think I'm giving it back to you?"

Wes realized in that moment that his plan to preserve the business by signing his shares over to Jesse before he went to jail had turned out to be Soteria's death knell instead.

"You're freezing me out of my own goddamn company?"

"Don't act all hurt. You brought this on yourself. For once in your life, you're going to see what it's like when everything doesn't go your way. And Wes? Don't call me again. From now on, any communication between us needs to go through my lawyers."

Wes was still reeling from the precision of Jesse's vindictive attack, the intensely personal nature of it, after he'd hung up the phone. Between the two of them, Jesse Hastings was the gregarious one, the figurehead who was out front, drumming up business and dealing with clients, while Wes preferred to stay behind the scenes, creating.

Jesse was always the guy scouting for new opportunities, trying to grow their coffers, and with every big monetary milestone they'd reached, he'd broached the subject of taking the company public one day. But Wes had always managed to talk him down, to convince Jesse that it was the work that mattered most, not the money, but the innovation. At least he thought he had.

Apparently, he'd been wrong.

Wes ran a hand down his face and shoved his phone back in his pocket.

He'd worry about the professional blow later. Right now, he needed to find Vivienne.

As he stalked back through her condo, something bright and orange on the kitchen table caught his eye, drawing him over.

A tiger lily in a vase.

Along with the flower, there was a black shoebox, a nondescript envelope, some official-looking papers, her wedding ring, and a handwritten note from Vivienne. His hand shook as he reached for the sheet of blue stationery.

Wes,
If I'm going to jail, there's somewhere I have to say goodbye to before that happens. In the meantime, I hope that, whatever you came here for, you'll find it on this table.
Viv

Wes glanced at the legal documents—a set of presigned annulment papers and a set of presigned divorce papers. Viv always was an overachiever.

The envelope contained the blackmail letter, which ended up a little crumpled when anger made his hand clench, and a thumb drive with the Whitfield Industries logo on it.

Despite the note's strict instructions to dispose of the thumb drive once the program was installed on Whitfield's system, Vivienne had found a way to preserve this key piece of evidence.

That's my girl, he thought, turning it over in his fingers before dropping it back in the envelope with the now-mangled note. *So fucking smart.*

He lifted the lid off the shoebox, and the contents were like a gut punch of sentimentality. A bunch of photos of the two of them, looking young and fresh faced and in love. The frame with the pressed tiger lily that used to sit by their bed—she'd made it with one of the flowers in the bouquet he'd given her the night of their first date.

There was a notebook, too, and Wes had to leaf through only a couple of pages to realize it was a diary of sorts. The dates on the tops of the pages told him these entries spanned her nonviable pregnancy, from terrified start to tragic end.

He snapped the book shut at the realization. Because as desperate as he was to know, to understand what she'd gone through, he wanted to hear it from her. Face-to-face. But when Wes slipped her diary back in the shoebox, something else caught his eye.

Not the hospital bracelet itself, but the number sequence printed beneath her name. The date she'd been admitted for emergency, lifesaving surgery.

May 10. Six years ago.

The exact eight numbers in the string of garbage code that had popped up repeatedly throughout AJ's investigation. She'd been right on both counts. It was a date and a signature.

What had Viv said? Something about *"...after Jesse showed up...right after..."*

The realization of what she'd left unspoken hit him like a lightning bolt. Jesus Christ.

Precise. Vindictive. Intensely personal.

Wes glanced over his shoulder, through the kitchen to the foyer where Vivienne's security camera was logging the comings and goings of all her visitors and transmitting them to her phone...and anyone who might have bugged her phone.

His partner's out-of-the-blue phone call suddenly made a lot more sense. The bastard had watched him walk into Viv's apartment.

A cold rage flooded Wes's veins at the betrayal.

Poaching Soteria Security was one thing, and if Jesse wanted to punch below the belt in some desperate attempt to hurt him for whatever slights and transgressions he'd already found Wes guilty of, well, Wes could take care of himself. But exploiting Vivienne's trauma in some sociopathic attempt to twist the knife in Wes's back a little deeper? Monitoring her phone and her security feed? Hurting the woman he loved?

Jesse would pay dearly for that.

Wes pulled his own phone out and waited for his call to connect.

"AJ? Never mind how I got this number. I need you to get me into that meeting with Whitfield and

Kearney that's happening later. I know who fucked me over, and I'm going to bury the bastard."

Grabbing Vivienne's ring from the table, Wes shoved it in his pocket.

Then he gathered up the rest of the evidence she'd left him.

He needed to pay a little visit to the FBI before his meeting.

CHAPTER TWENTY

WES STRODE INTO the lobby of Whitfield Industries at precisely 2:00 p.m. and headed straight for the elevator. A familiar black-clad figure hit the button as he approached.

"They're expecting me?"

AJ slid him a look drenched in annoyance. "You know, you really need to stop second-guessing my methods. It makes me not like you."

"You never liked me," he pointed out reasonably, straightening his tie. There was a certain poetic symmetry to ending things as they'd begun. Which was why he'd changed back into the gray suit he'd been wearing when he was arrested before arriving at Whitfield Industries to deliver the coup de grâce.

The silver doors dinged open, and once the herd of office drones disembarked, AJ and Wes stepped inside. A harried, balding guy tried to join them, but AJ stopped him.

"Sorry, this one's full."

The doors slid shut on the man as he gaped at

the two of them, alone in the twenty-eight-person-capacity elevator.

Wes lifted a brow as he hit the button that would take them to the top floor.

"What? These elevators are the worst when people are hopping on and off at every floor. Especially when you're trying to get to the penthouse." AJ reached into her leather jacket and retrieved her phone. Her thumbs flew over the screen, and then she looked up at the elevator control panel.

Wes followed her line of sight in time to see a small light in the upper right-hand corner switch from green to red. Override complete.

"There. Isn't this better with no one bugging us?"

Since he couldn't disagree, he changed the subject entirely. "For the record, I wasn't second-guessing you. I actually thought we worked pretty well together."

AJ frowned at the commendation. "Why does that sound so leading? It's like you're *this* close to offering me a *fabulous opportunity* that's going to end with me hawking shady pyramid scheme products and drinking a lot of Kool-Aid."

"Because you're very jaded and don't know how to take a compliment. How do you feel about IPOs?"

"Are you kidding?" She scoffed. "The whole reason I'm starting my own thing is because I don't even want *one* boss, let alone a team of rabid shareholders pestering me about dividends and shit."

"We should talk after I've got this situation under control."

Her whole body grew wary. "Are you gonna try to convince me to work for you?"

"Not exactly. I'd like to work with you."

AJ's eyes widened at the prospect. "Like partners?"

He shrugged, letting the possibility hang out there. He didn't want to spook her.

It took three more floors before her posture switched from cagey to contemplative. The second it did, Wes pounced. "We'll talk after?"

"It's under consideration," she hedged, just as the elevator drew to a stop.

The doors slid open to reveal a gleaming modern lobby that offered spectacular views of Los Angeles thanks to its floor-to-ceiling windows, but neither of them spared a moment's thought for the scenery. Heedless of the executive assistant's protests, they strode across the white-tiled floor, directly to their destination.

The office was brimming with hostility. Whitfield was on his feet the instant they breached the door, which caused the two men who sat in the visitor chairs facing him to whirl around to see who dared intrude on their meeting.

Max's voice was as cold and harsh as the arctic tundra. "What the fuck is he doing in my building, AJ?"

Goddammit.

Wes slanted her a glare. "Oh, good. They were definitely expecting us."

Her shrug was unrepentant. "They were expecting me," she said, walking straight to Kearney. Wes didn't miss the moment of silent communication between them, the way the man dialed it back from wanting to rip Wes's throat out to casually speculative with nothing more than her slow nod.

Jesse, on the other hand, had molten rage bubbling inside him. It glowed in his eyes.

Wes unbuttoned his suit jacket. "You guys should really see your faces. You'd think I just got released from prison for betraying you all or something."

Slowly, purposefully, Jesse rose to his feet. With his gregarious facade ripped and torn, Wes could see the anger pulsing just below the surface. He barely recognized his partner. The man he'd considered his friend.

And for the first time, Wes realized that what was in front of him now was the truth, and it was the rest of it that had been lies.

In that moment, betrayal cut both ways.

"Give me one reason I shouldn't hit this button, Brennan."

Max's voice startled him, snapped his attention back to the now.

"It will have security here in under a minute."

Wes nodded, pointed at him. "Keep your finger on the trigger. I just wanted to talk to my buddy Jesse here in person, because it's been hell trying to get a hold of him lately."

"I have nothing to say to you."

Wes's chuckle held no mirth. "Great. Fewer interruptions. Since the charges were dropped, I've spent the last week poring over the evidence AJ used to put me away. Pretty damning stuff. I mean, think about it."

He shoved his left hand in his pocket, dragging the right one contemplatively down his beard. Max settled back into his chair, wary but intrigued, too.

"First, Whitfield Industries gets hacked and thanks to some modifications I made, we catch the breach and ring the alarm. But when we get here, *I'm* the one who delivers the bad news to the client, and my outgoing, personable second-in-command goes to investigate the surveillance footage."

Jesse's skin was mottled, his anger manifesting as red splotches against his tanned skin. "It was a massive security breach. I'm a stakeholder in the company. Of course I wanted to help figure out what went wrong. Whitfield Industries is our flagship client, and I'm the one who landed the account," he added smugly.

"Next up, the phone that I gave to Kaylee Whitfield after she broke hers starts misfiring. And when they crack it open, it turns out it was bugged— monitoring her location, logging her calls and transmitting her conversations."

"I'm sorry. Are we all supposed to stand here while you list off all the reasons you should be back in jail?" Jesse raked an agitated hand through his blond hair.

"Hey, I get it, man. You're the CEO of Soteria Security now. Shopping at Neiman's to do, private medical records to hack."

Precise. Vindictive. Intensely personal.

The attack straightened Jesse's spine. "I don't know what the fuck you—"

"I thought we agreed, no interruptions. I don't want you to miss anything. Especially since I think you're really going to like the twist ending. And I don't want Kearney here to feel left out."

The CEO of Cybercore stiffened up at the sound of his name, and AJ set a comforting hand on Liam's shoulder.

"He tests out Soteria's commercial antivirus software. Coincidentally, counterfeit versions of his latest product start flooding the market not long after you show up to install some updates, on my behest."

Jesse slow-clapped, four loud cracks of sound in the otherwise silent office. "You're really nailing this performance, Wes. You sure you don't want me to get the FBI in here so they don't miss the drama of this confession?"

"Sounds like one, right? But that's when I realized that I'm not the only one who looks bad here. Because you're the one who volunteered to check the surveillance footage after Max got hacked, which gave you the opportunity to make it disappear. And Kaylee's bugged phone? That was the new business phone that you configured for me. It was never meant for her. I screwed up your plan when I gave it away. And let's just be honest, since we're among friends here—I never sent you to update Liam's test software like you told him I did."

"I'd like to see you prove any of it."

Wes's smile was feral. "I already have. You got

sloppy, and AJ found your fingerprints all over this case. She couldn't figure out what that string of garbage code that linked all the attacks meant. But I did."

For the first time since he'd walked into the office, Wes saw fear in Jesse's eyes. An involuntary confession.

"I'm not going to stand here and listen to bullshit accusations." Jesse turned to stalk from the office, but the second he drew even, Wes pounced, shoved him up against the frosted glass of Max's office wall by the lapels.

"I know what you did, you son of a bitch." He angled his forearm across Jesse's chest, his elbow dangerously close to the bastard's windpipe. "I'll bet if I look at her phone, I'll find the same goddamn bug that was on Kaylee's phone. That's how you found Viv at Neiman's. That's how you knew we got married. And that's why you phoned me this morning, to threaten me. Because you have control of her phone, which means you can watch the feed whenever the mood strikes. And when you saw me on it, you were worried your little plot might unravel, since it only works if Viv and I aren't sharing secrets."

Wes applied a little more pressure against Jesse's trachea, and the bastard clawed at his arm.

"You want to take me down, fine. But you should have left her out of it, because you might have gotten away with it if you hadn't blackmailed her."

There was a dawning horror in Jesse's eyes, and it was all the confirmation Wes needed.

"Yeah, that's right. She told me what happened

after we broke up. In fact, she's the reason you're going to spend the rest of your life in prison. She kept a diary, one that proves she never told me about the pregnancy. Which absolves me from being the blackmailer. There's also an entry in there about the day she was rushed into lifesaving surgery. A date that I think the feds are going find very interesting when they compare it to that garbage code AJ found. And then there's my favorite—the story of how you went to visit her at Yale, shortly after she'd been released from the hospital. Did you already know what had happened before you went? Or was it the visit that made you curious enough to do some digging?"

Jesse opened his mouth to reply, but Wes cut him off. "You know what? Don't tell me. It'll make the trial so much more compelling if I have some surprises to look forward to. But I'll bet the FBI agents I gave it to this morning will get a kick out of it.

"Viv kept it all in a box, with a pressed tiger lily and some framed photos from back in the day. You're even in a couple of them. You know how sentimental she is."

Wes couldn't help his mocking grin. "You poured the time and effort and the resources of an elite cybersecurity firm into screwing the two of us over, and she took you down with a diary entry and a hospital bracelet, you dumb fuck."

And courage, Wes added silently. So much damn courage that she'd quit her job to get him out of jail. Sparred with him. Driven him to unparalleled heights of frustration and desire. And despite their complicated history, she'd never given up on him.

Jesse's forced laugh was all bravado. "Tell me it hurt. Tell me it killed you when you found out what she'd done. The secrets she kept from you."

The dig had no power, and Wes's muscles relaxed slightly at the realization.

Because it had hurt. It had hurt them both. But it hadn't killed them. In that moment, Wes recognized that they were stronger for it. *Bad at communication, good at sex.* That's why they'd broken up the first time. But not this time. This time was different.

Because it wasn't his computer prowess that had solved this case. It was the fact that he and Vivienne had actually talked to each other. Laid the ghosts of their pasts to rest.

He refocused on Jesse. "How the hell did I not know what a malicious son of a bitch you were?"

"You're like a goddamn cat, you know that? Always landing on your feet. You get all the credit for Soteria, even though you'd still be working out of your junkie mother's basement if it wasn't for me! For my connections and all the investors I brought in. But you're the one the magazines write about! You're the one they praise. Like I'm nothing. I just stand by and watch you get everything I want. More of the money. More of the fame. The only reason you even met Viv is because I took you to that party, and then you got her, too!"

Jesse's chest heaved with fury.

"I knew the only thing that would hurt you more

than losing your precious company would be to know that the love of your life betrayed you. Got to admit, I didn't think Vivienne would crack. She's usually such a cold hard bitch."

Wes increased the pressure of his arm. "You're going to want to watch what you say to me right now."

Jesse's smile was a little manic. "Keep it up, tough guy. You want to strangle me? Punch me? Put my head through the glass? Go for it! I'll press charges so fast you'll be back in the slammer faster than Vivienne dropped her panties for you the night of the frat party."

Wes's muscles shook with the control it took not to take him up on the offer. He shoved Jesse back against the glass one last time, with enough force to make him feel it. But he'd made the wrong decision six years ago, when he'd chosen Soteria over her, and again the night before, when he'd walked out on Vivienne after she'd confessed her deepest, darkest secret to him. He wouldn't do it a third time.

"I thought I wanted revenge on the person who framed me more than anything in the world. You took my company from me, and I planned to savor every second of watching you get frog-marched out of here in cuffs as they hauled your ass to jail. But thanks to you, I've got more important things to do."

Because Jesse, and Soteria, were his past, but Vivienne? She was his future. She always had been.

Somewhere behind him, Whitfield's voice penetrated Wes's consciousness.

"Sherri, can you please send security to my office immediately. And then get Special Agent Behnsen on the phone. Tell her there's been a break in the case."

"Guess he wasn't kidding about that button, huh?" Wes pried his hands from Jesse's suit and adjusted his own jacket, just as two burly security guards entered the office.

"Looks like you'll be in good hands after I leave. And Jesse?" He waited until the prick met his gaze with a seething glare. "When Max and Liam are done with you, you'll be hearing from my lawyer."

He just had to find her first.

CHAPTER TWENTY-ONE

VIVIENNE SAT ON THE porch swing, one foot tucked beneath her, the other skimming along the painted wooden deck planks as she swayed back and forth. The rhythm of the movement was slow and soothing for her frayed nerves. She stared contemplatively through the railing at a bed of tiger lilies on the edge of the gorgeously landscaped property.

The first time she'd fled to the Phoenix Inn, she'd been young, and terrified, nursing a broken heart as she recovered from the emergency surgery that had both saved her life and changed it irreparably. Like a desperate philosopher, she'd spent hours on this very porch swing, convincing herself that a nonviable pregnancy was basically the same as not being pregnant at all. Which meant there was no real reason to tell Wes. Because there was nothing to tell.

The irony that the decision she'd made then was the reason she was here now, and that she was on the precipice of jail time because of it, was not lost on her. She'd chosen to keep a secret, which had turned septic so quickly that she couldn't remember what it was like before it had seeped into her bones and become part of her. One more experience in a long line of experiences she'd used to justify to herself that she was better off alone. That loving people hurt too much.

But then she'd reconnected with Wes.

And she'd finally accepted that, no matter how much it hurt, she couldn't stop loving him.

The burn of tears threatened, but through sheer force of will, she held them back. She'd given in to tears the last time, and they hadn't helped. This time, she'd be stronger.

The back door creaked open, and Vivienne kept her eyes stubbornly forward, not quite ready to give up her solitude, no matter how well-intentioned the innkeeper was.

"I'm not really in the mood for company right now, Sally."

"She said you'd say that."

The sound of Wes's voice brought Vivienne to her feet. But even though she recognized that he was standing with her on the porch where she'd spent so much time thinking about him, it still took everything she had to turn and face him. To make it real.

He was gorgeous in a light gray suit, pristine white shirt and dark gray tie. His thick brown hair was the perfect amount of mussed, and he'd trimmed his beard back from "verge of unkempt" to "dangerous bad boy."

It was too much, having him here with her, and she turned toward the yard, grabbing the railing and focusing on the tiger lilies instead of the nerves that jittered in her stomach.

"What is this place?"

She closed her eyes, letting his deep voice wash over her. "It's where I came after…everything." Lost pregnancy. Lost love. Lost self. "To heal. And clear my head."

"Serendipitous choice of flowers."

"Not really."

Wes joined her beside the railing, and she made herself look at him.

"I planted them. When I came here the first time." She turned back to the profusion of orange blooms. "Part of the healing I was talking about."

He was quiet for a long time. When he spoke again, his voice was solemn. "Thank you."

She looked up in surprise. "For what?"

"For letting me be part of that piece of your life."

A poignant smile tipped the corner of her mouth up. She'd never thought of it like that. That planting tiger lilies had been a connection to Wes. That in some small way, he'd been here with her even as she'd been so desperately trying to push him away.

He shoved his hands in his pockets and rocked back on his heels. "So why are you here now?"

"The threat of jail made me contemplative, I guess. And I can breathe when I come here. No matter how bad it gets."

"Well, it might not get as bad as you think."

She frowned at the riddle.

"As of this morning, you're no longer suspect

number one. I'm sure Whitfield won't press charges against you, and even if he does, you can dust off those kick-ass lawyer skills of yours, turn state's evidence, and testify against Jesse."

The announcement blindsided her, dropping her heart into her stomach. "What?"

"It was Jesse." Wes's voice was laced with a hint of rancor.

Of course, it was. All of the evidence, so inextricably tied to Soteria…everything pointing just a little bit more toward Wes and letting Jesse off scot-free. Because Jesse had his finger on the scale of justice.

The realization that someone she'd considered a friend had betrayed them both like that quaked through her. But to her surprise, the bitterness that usually rushed in when someone she cared about let her down didn't overwhelm her. Instead, her heart was full of concern for the man standing in front of her.

"Are you okay?" She almost reached for him then, but she stopped herself just in time. "What's going to happen to Soteria?"

For a man who might have just lost his life's work, his shrug was more laissez-faire than she'd expected. "It doesn't matter. I've got other options in the works, and I'll land on my feet. I didn't stick around to sort through the details. I had something more important to do."

Vivienne's heart melted at the look in his steely blue eyes. The meaning behind his words, as evidenced by the fact he was here now. With her.

"How'd you find me?" The words scraped her throat.

"I hacked your phone."

His self-effacing smile nearly sent her to her knees. God, she'd missed him so much.

"Since not tracking you was the only promise I ever made you that I kept, I thought maybe if I blew that one up too, we could start over. Try this again without all the baggage."

Something inside her cracked open, and all the hope she'd buried so deeply when she'd fled here at twenty-two bloomed in her chest, riotous and color-ful, like the bed of tiger lilies she'd planted all those years ago.

"You remember how you said we're good at sex and bad at communication?"

Viv bit her lip, nodded.

"I didn't catch Jesse because I outwitted him or because of my coding skills. I figured it out because of you. Because we finally talked to each other. And I am so fucking sorry I walked out after you told me what happened."

Wes's forehead creased slightly, as if he was searching for the right words to say. As if he didn't understand that he'd already found them.

"If you hadn't shared what you went through with me, he might have gotten away with it. But he didn't. And that got me thinking about us. About what we've been through. I know things didn't work out between us last time…"

He trailed off, and the silence was overwhelming.

She took a step forward because she needed to be closer to him. "Last time isn't this time."

Wes nodded at the assessment. "Well, in that case, I've got a question to ask you."

The air got thick and hard to breathe as Wes reached into his pocket and pulled out the ring. He took her left hand in his, and it was like plugging into an electrical socket. Her skin came alive. Her heart thudded against her ribs.

But that was nothing compared to the jolt of unfiltered emotion that buzzed through her when he lowered himself onto one knee in front of her.

The tears she'd held back earlier spilled freely down her cheeks now.

"Vivienne Amelie Brennan, I am desperately in love with you. Even when I'm trying really hard not to be. And if you're up for it, I thought we could give this another try, because I want to spend the rest of my life being good at sex *and* good at communication with you."

Her heart squeezed as she watched him slide the ring, *her ring*, back onto her finger. She looked into the eyes of the man who had seen all of her—the good and the bad—and yet he'd flown across the country anyway. Because he loved her.

"So, what do you say? Want to stay married to me?"

Viv was nodding before he'd finished the question, and he surged to his feet, catching her around the waist and lifting her up as she wrapped her arms around his shoulders and whispered her answer against the soft, warm skin of his neck. "I do."

When he finally set her back on her feet, Vivienne stared up at her husband. Having him with her, here at the Phoenix Inn, where she'd endured so much sadness, went a long way to making her heart feel whole again. "I love you so much," she confessed through the emotion clogging her throat.

Tenderly, Wes pulled her closer and pressed a kiss to her forehead.

Vivienne stood there in his embrace, letting it all sink in. But as was often the case in Wes's presence, it didn't take long before the heat of him worked its way into her blood, morphing the sweet relief of having him here into the sultry desire to have him naked.

"I don't want to alarm you," she teased, even as she pressed closer, stoking the fire between them, "but we may have officially crossed into old married couple status."

Wes looked down at her with sham horror. His fingers dug into her hips, and she could feel his body start to harden. "I'm not taking the blame for that. You're the reason we're at a bed-and-breakfast right now, instead of somewhere sexy."

He backed her up against the railing, and the press of his growing erection against her stomach gave the porch some triple-X street cred in her books.

She slipped her hands beneath his jacket and ran her hands up his chest. "Sure, but you're the one who sealed our true love vow with a forehead kiss."

He pressed his lips to the edge of her jaw, and her head fell back, granting him better access. "You're right," he conceded, wringing a low moan from her as he worked his way down her neck with soft, open-mouthed kisses.

"We'd better do something dirty, stat." He rocked his hips against hers and her knees went weak. "Breathe a little life back into this dying relationship. Do they have an elevator?"

She shook her head with faux solemnity as she loosened his tie. "Afraid not."

"How about a sturdy kitchen table?" he asked, as the button on her jeans went slack.

"They do, but it's in a communal area."

His naughty grin made her heart stutter. "Since when has that ever stopped us?"

"This is a respectable bed-and-breakfast, sir. Not some sexy West Coast taqueria where people get freaky in public."

"Then I guess we'd better get to your room before I can't control myself anymore."

Vivienne shrieked with surprised laughter as he swept her off her feet and into his arms. "What are you doing?"

"Carrying you over the threshold so I can have my way with you."

She snuggled against his chest, the ring on her finger glinting as she started unbuttoning his shirt. "Because you're so desperately in love with me?"

Wes shoved the door out of their way in his quest for her bedroom.

"Guilty as charged."

EPILOGUE

One Year Later...

"Come here, baby."

Vivienne smiled to herself as Wes stepped close behind her and dropped a kiss to her exposed shoulder.

"You know I don't know which one of us you're talking to when you say that, right?"

His arms came around her to cradle the six months' worth of baby bump she'd crammed into a red floor-length gown to celebrate the official launch of Wes and AJ's new joint venture, DBS Security.

"I was talking to the kid. But since you're here, too, what do you say we get out of here?"

"This is *your* party," she reminded him, motioning toward the glittering crowd schmoozing in Liam Kearney's palatial Beverly Hills mansion. "The who's who of the wealthy business elite are here to celebrate, and be wooed by, you. Look. There's Aidan Beckett, right over there. I thought it was your mission in life to land him as a client."

Wes tightened his arms around her, pulling her closer so her back was laminated to the front of him. "I mean, I probably shouldn't show AJ up at our launch party by scoring a bigger client than her. Especially not in her own house." He nuzzled her ear, and her knees went a little woozy. "I'll get Kaylee to introduce me to him next week, at Max and Emma's engagement party."

"Prioritizing getting laid over getting clients?" Vivienne's head lolled back against his shoulder as he worked his lips down her neck. "That can't be good for business."

"True, but if we stay and I have to explain DBS stands for 'don't be sloppy' to one more person, I might lose it, and that won't be good for business either. I never should have let AJ name the company." Wes's hand slipped up her torso, skating dangerously close to her breast, making her crave more pressure there.

"So how about you save me from myself and we go check out how swanky Kearney's bathroom is?"

Vivienne feigned shock, even as the promise of sex slid along her spine and pooled low in her gut. "You want to have your way with me while my boss is right over there?"

Wes followed her gaze toward Max Whitfield. His dark head was bent close to his fiancée's blond one. An intimate smile dawned on Emma's face in response to whatever he'd said, and she reached up and wrapped her fingers around the man's tie, tugging him even closer.

"Yeah, he definitely gives a shit that I'm dying to ravage you. Those two are going to beat us to the upstairs bathroom if we don't get a move on." His voice rumbled through her, and she couldn't quite hold back her moan as he caught the edge of her earlobe between his teeth and gave it a slight tug.

"Like you're going to be able to lift me onto the counter," she teased, turning to face him and looping her arms around his neck. "Though I suppose the slit in this dress is immodest enough that we could make doggy-style work."

His eyes darkened at the suggestion. "And I thought you were horny before you got pregnant." His large palm landed with a muted smack on the curve of her ass.

Her smile was decadent. "I could say the same about you."

Wes stepped back from her, cocking an eyebrow in invitation. "Come with me? I promise to make it worth getting fired for."

God. All he had to do was look at her, and her body turned hot with longing. Would she ever not want this man?

With a furtive glance, Vivienne slipped her hand into his, letting him tug her along in his wake, through the glittering crowd and up the stairs. The bright chatter and pulsing music muted instantly when Wes pushed the bathroom door shut behind them.

The click of the lock sent a ripple of anticipation across Vivienne's skin.

"Not bad." Wes pulled out his phone, sending a

cursory look around the exquisite fixtures and high-end finishings as he thumbed the screen. He glanced over at Vivienne and stowed the device back in his pocket.

"I mean, it's no Señor Taco's—" he stripped off his suit jacket and laid it on the countertop "—but I think we can make it work. C'mere, you."

He pulled her close, seducing her with a deep, drugging kiss as he worked her dress up her thighs.

"Mmmm." She smiled when he finally let her up for air. The hem of her gown had migrated all the way to her waist. "You're in a hurry tonight."

"Because it drives me crazy when you wear red," he confessed, voice rough with arousal.

"And I can't wait to be inside you," he added, turning so that she was flanked by his big body and the bathroom vanity.

Without warning, her feet left the ground, and she gave a startled gasp as Wes lifted her onto the bathroom vanity, her hands grasping at his shoulders to steady herself at the sudden movement. His jacket was warm beneath her bare thighs.

"Also, we've got about six minutes, tops, before AJ figures out what I just did to the security camera in the hallway, so we need to get this show on the road."

Vivienne was still laughing as she wound her arms around her husband's neck and pulled him close.

* * * * *

COMING SOON!

We really hope you enjoyed reading this book.
If you're looking for more romance, be sure to
head to the shops when new books are
available on

Thursday 23rd July

To see which titles are coming soon, please visit

millsandboon.co.uk/nextmonth

LET'S TALK
Romance

For exclusive extracts, competitions and special offers, find us online:

f facebook.com/millsandboon

🐦 @MillsandBoon

📷 @MillsandBoonUK

Get in touch on 01413 063232

For all the latest titles coming soon, visit
millsandboon.co.uk/nextmonth

MILLS & BOON
A ROMANCE FOR EVERY READER

- **FREE** delivery direct to your door

- **EXCLUSIVE** offers every month

- **SAVE** up to 25% on pre-paid subscriptions

SUBSCRIBE AND SAVE

millsandboon.co.uk/Subscribe